Perfect Timing

Catherine Anderson

A Harrigan Family Novel

Perfect Timing

A SIGNET BOOK

SIGNET
Published by New American Library, a division of
Penguin Group (USA) Inc., 375 Hudson Street,
New York, New York 10014, USA
Penguin Group (Canada), 90 Eglinton Avenue East, Suite 700, Toronto,
Ontario M4P 2Y3, Canada (a division of Pearson Penguin Canada Inc.)
Penguin Books Ltd., 80 Strand, London WC2R 0RL, England
Penguin Ireland, 25 St. Stephen's Green, Dublin 2,
Ireland (a division of Penguin Books Ltd.)
Penguin Group (Australia), 707 Collins Street, Melbourne, Victoria 3008,
Australia (a division of Pearson Australia Group Pty. Ltd.)
Penguin Books India Pvt. Ltd., 11 Community Centre, Panchsheel Park,
New Delhi–110 017, India
Penguin Group (NZ), 67 Apollo Drive, Rosedale, Auckland 0632,
New Zealand (a division of Pearson New Zealand Ltd.)
Penguin Books, Rosebank Office Park, 181 Jan Smuts Avenue,
Parktown North 2193, South Africa
Penguin China, B7 Jiaming Center, 27 East Third Ring Road North,
Chaoyang District, Beijing 100020, China

Penguin Books Ltd., Registered Offices:
80 Strand, London WC2R 0RL, England

First published by Signet, an imprint of New American Library,
a division of Penguin Group (USA) Inc.

ISBN 978-1-62090-983-6

PUBLISHER'S NOTE
This is a work of fiction. Names, characters, places, and incidents either are the
product of the author's imagination or are used fictitiously, and any resemblance
to actual persons, living or dead, business establishments, events, or locales is
entirely coincidental.
    The publisher does not have any control over and does not assume any respon-
sibility for author or third-party Web sites or their content.

To my husband, Sid,

who appeared in my life with "perfect timing."

Chapter One

Quincy Harrigan's riding boots offered poor traction on the patches of ice-encrusted snow, which in the faint light of predawn looked bluish white on his scraggly front lawn. Carefully holding a mug of coffee in one hand, he picked his way between two muddy ranch vehicles, wondering when his dooryard had become a parking lot for pickups, the tractor, and two dented ATVs. Walking with his head bent, he realized his hair had gotten so long that it dangled in a dark brown hank over his left eye. *Damn.* He'd been out of town and missed his appointment with the barber. Rescheduling was out of the question. From one day to the next, he didn't know when he'd have to leave again, and while he was here, he was far too busy to drive clear into town for a walk-in visit. It was a wonder he even managed to grab a few hours of sleep. This morning, he felt the exhaustion in every muscle of his body, and he seriously doubted the freshly brewed French roast would give him the jolt of energy he needed.

No matter. Compared to his sister-in-law Loni, he had little reason to complain. At least he wasn't fighting for his life. The thought made his heart twist, and the lump that seemed to have taken up permanent residence at the base of his throat throbbed like a toothache. He stopped to gaze across his ranch, taking in the huge taupe-colored arena that loomed over all the smaller buildings. Twenty years ago, this had been an empty piece of land, signed over to him by his father. Now, just having turned forty, Quincy saw the story of his adult life in every structure, fence post, and nail. This ranch had been his dream since childhood, but now that he'd accomplished everything he'd planned, all he felt was empty.

Why Loni? The question had haunted his every waking moment for the past month—ever since the doctor here in Crystal Falls, Oregon, had first uttered the word *leukemia* and referred Loni to specialists at the Knight Cancer Institute in Portland. How was it fair that Loni had been the one stricken with such a serious illness? Quincy's brother Clint worshiped the ground she walked on. She had two children who needed her. By comparison, no one really depended on him.

Quincy blinked away tears and forced his feet to move again. Loni wasn't going to die, damn it. She was young, and up until two months ago, when she'd sickened with what everyone thought was the flu, she'd been the picture of health. There were surely treatments available for whatever kind of leukemia she had. Nearly every day, people were either cured or put into remission. It was silly of him to be thinking such gloomy thoughts. And he sure as hell didn't have time for them. Everyone else in the family except his sister Sam, who had volunteered to care for Clint and Loni's kids, was in Portland to lend their support, and while it was Quincy's turn to stay here, looking after all six ranches, he had to make sure everything ran smoothly. It was a hell of a job for one man, but both Parker and Zach had been trading off with him, and he hadn't yet heard either of them complain. He wouldn't, either.

Halfway to the arena, Quincy stopped to take a swig of coffee, hoping the hot slide of liquid would lessen the ache in his chest. Fat chance. He couldn't think of Loni without struggling to breathe. When had he come to love her like a sister? At first, just being around her had given him the willies. A bona fide clairvoyant who worked closely with the FBI to locate missing children, Loni could get flashes of a person's past, present, or future by a mere touch of hands. Like most men, Quincy had a private life, and there were certain aspects of it that he preferred not to share with anyone. It had bothered him to think that Loni might see him with a woman in an X-rated moment.

Now, after coming to know Loni, Quincy realized that whatever she saw when they made physical contact was immediately buried deep within her. She had no desire to inflict harm or embarrassment with her gift of second sight. Over time, Quincy had stopped worrying about that. If Loni had ever seen him during an intensely private moment, she'd never let on, and he'd finally come to trust that she would never breathe a word of it to anyone, not even to Clint. After that, growing to love her hadn't been a big jump for him.

Now it was a done deal. He could almost see her, big blue eyes dominating a heart-shaped face framed by a wealth of dark, glossy hair. *Pretty*. But, more important, she was every bit as sweet and dear as she appeared to be. No wonder Clint suddenly looked as if he'd been run over by a semitruck, his burnished face tinted with undertones of gray, his brown eyes, so like Quincy's own, filled with inexpressible worry and pain. Clint adored his children, but it was Loni who was the true center of his life. Without her, how would he go on? Just thinking about it made Quincy's stomach roil.

Though March had finally arrived, the air was so cold it burned Quincy's lungs when he drew a deep breath. He wished he'd thought to grab his lined Levi's jacket before leaving the house. Icy fingers curled over his shirt collar and sent a chill crawling down his spine. From the holding sheds, he heard equines neighing and grunting, their way of calling for breakfast. The sound helped to center him and clear his head. He had animals counting on him, and he'd best kick it into high gear.

Just as Quincy reached the berm of snow that had collected over the winter under the eaves of the arena, his cell phone emitted the sound of a horse whinnying, a tone reserved only for members of his family. As he jerked the device from his belt, he half expected to see his dad's name on the screen. Frank had rented a hotel suite near the cancer institute, and he and his wife had been at Clint's side ever since Loni had been admitted there. Always an early riser, Frank often buzzed Quincy to give him an update before the sun came up.

Quincy's pulse stuttered when he saw that the caller was Clint. "Hey, Clint," he said. "How is she?"

Silence. Then Clint's voice came over the air, wobbly and hoarse. "It's bad, Quincy. Real bad. I just talked with the team of specialists taking care of Loni."

Quincy had never heard Clint sound so shaken. "At this hour?" It was all Quincy could think to say—a futile attempt to sound normal when his brother's world might be tipping off its axis. "I thought only ranchers were crazy enough to start work this early."

"They're busy men, and a lot of lives are in their hands." Clint swallowed. The sound came through to

Quincy, a hollow plunk that painted a picture he didn't want to see. "Loni has acute myelogenous leukemia, a very aggressive strain that's often unresponsive to treatment. The doctors say they told me the name of it a while back, but apparently it went in one ear and out the other."

Quincy wanted to ask Clint more questions, but he sensed that his brother needed to get this said without interruption.

"Now they've finally determined her AML subtype. I guess they had a devil of a time doing that—something about the AML morphology under a microscope not matching up quite right with any other cancers they've seen."

"What're you saying, Clint—that she's got one-of-a-kind leukemia?"

"Something like that. By now the doctors would be willing to settle for a close match just to begin treatment. Problem is, she's so far gone it's way too late for remission induction therapy. Her platelet counts are too low for her to undergo chemo or a bone marrow transplant."

"Whoa." Quincy stepped over the pile of snow to lean a shoulder against the eastern exterior wall of the arena. Quelling rising panic, he managed, "If she's too sick for either of those, what kind of treatment can they give her?"

Quincy's blood ran as cold as the crystallized air when he heard Clint sob. He could not recall ever having seen or heard his oldest brother cry as an adult. "Nothing," Clint said brokenly. "There's . . . nothing . . . they . . . can do. At best, they give her . . . a week or two . . . but it'll be a miracle if she holds on that long."

The mug of coffee slipped from Quincy's hand. He flinched as hot liquid slopped onto his pant leg. His brain told him to pull the drenched denim away from his skin, but he couldn't get the message to his hands. He stared stupidly at the spray of brown on the snow. None of this was happening. It couldn't be. Fury at what he was unable to control shot through him in a painful rush. Words blasted out of him.

"Then we need to get her to another center! The Mayo Clinic, maybe. Samantha's brother-in-law, Rafe Kendrick, is standing by to fly her anyplace you name. In his jet, she'll have all the comforts of home. We can't just let her—" Quincy couldn't finish the sentence. "There are all kinds of treatments. Somebody, somewhere, can do something! A really good team of doctors can put her into remission. I know it."

"She already has a really good team of doctors, some of the best." For several seconds, Clint rasped for breath. The sound reminded Quincy of the story he'd once read to his little sister, Sam, about a tiny train that huffed and puffed to get up a steep grade. "It's not their fault she has some weird subtype they've never seen! And it's . . . too . . . late to take her somewhere else. She . . . could . . . die during a long flight. This is my . . . fault, Quincy, all mine. I screwed around, thinking she had a bad case of flu. Jesus, help me. I . . . should . . . have realized! If I'd gotten her up here sooner, they might have been . . . able . . . to . . . save her. Now all they can do is give her transfusions . . . and . . . IV fluids. That helps, but it's a short-term fix, and now she's getting so dehydrated, they have to poke her and poke her to . . . even . . . find . . . a vein."

Quincy hauled in a ragged breath and squeezed his eyes shut. *Focus,* he ordered himself. His brother needed him to say all the right things, and his mind had gone as blank as a crashed computer screen. "Clint, no matter what happens, this isn't your fault. You took her in to see competent doctors here. They just didn't realize what they were dealing with at first, and we lost precious time. If you're sure she's in the best hands available, then we just have to trust in the team up there and pray like crazy that she takes a sudden turn for the good."

"I'm fresh out of prayers." Clint sniffed, and Quincy heard a muffled sound like cloth brushing the cell phone. He could almost see his brother wiping his nose with his shirtsleeve. "The worst part is that she's begging to go home."

To die, was Quincy's first thought.

Clint blew that theory all to hell by saying, "She's convinced she isn't dying. She says she had a vision and saw our third child, a little boy we'll name Francis Wayne after Dad. I can tell she believes it, clear to the bottom of her heart. She thinks she's going to get well and have another child." A brief moment of quiet came over the air. Then Clint added, "You know how, when I first met Loni, I discounted her visions as a bunch of hocus-pocus crap, but she made a believer out of me. I've never doubted her visions since—until now."

Quincy felt tears trickling down his cheeks and turning to ice where they gathered at the corners of his mouth. "What she sees in her visions is never wrong. Hell, even the FBI acts as if everything she tells them comes straight from the Holy Grail."

"Exactly," Clint said, his voice pitched barely above a whisper, "and now I'm doubting what she tells me. Five specialists out in the hall, telling me she's dying. Her looking like a corpse already and spinning dreams I know can't happen—" He broke off. "She's dying, Quincy. I see the signs. No matter what she saw in her vision, I'm going . . . to . . . lose her. And God help me, I don't know how I'll survive it."

Quincy tried to gather his wits. This was new ground for him. As the oldest, Clint had always been the one who held everything together, the one who spoke while everyone else listened. Quincy knew Loni's divinations hadn't been wrong yet, but there could always be a first time. Loni had never been able to see her own future, only those of others. Wasn't it possible that she had indeed seen a third child, named after their father, Frank, but the little boy wouldn't be born to Loni? Maybe in the future, Clint would start over with a second wife, and she would be the one to present him with another son.

The very thought of Clint with some other woman made Quincy want to puke. *No.* It just couldn't happen. Clint was loyal to the bone. He'd never love anyone but Loni.

"You wanna hear the worst part?" Clint asked. "She's clinging to life by a thread, and that vision of a third child is her only hope. What if she looks into my eyes and sees I'm not convinced, that I believe the doctors and not her?"

Quincy had no clue how to respond. His mind kicked into autopilot. *Get there.* He had to help his brother. "I'll book a charter flight. I can be there with you in three hours."

"No. As great as it'd be to see you, I'm honoring Loni's wishes and taking her home this morning. We'll be there by late afternoon. Dad and Dee Dee flew out last night and are at their place now, probably sleeping off the red-eye flight. Parker and Rainie just left for the airport. Zach and Mandy are staying with me to provide moral support, and they'll fly back with me and Loni on the charter jet."

"But, Clint, you need me right now."

"What I need is for you to be *there* looking after my

place. If I come home to a disaster in my stable, I'll lose it, I swear to God. I'm counting on you."

Quincy nodded. "You got it, bro. Everything at your ranch is running like clockwork, and I'll see that it stays that way. If need be, I'll call Dad for help."

"Good. I'll see you tonight?"

"Yeah, I'll mosey over when I wrap it up for the day."

Quincy ended the call and stared blankly at his iPhone, a recent purchase that did everything but tap-dance. Too bad it couldn't also perform a miracle and save the life of his sister-in-law. As he slowly became aware of his surroundings again, he realized that making his feet move took a gargantuan effort. With only deter-mination fueling him, he strode toward the north end of the arena to enter by the personnel door.

If anything on earth soothed Quincy, it was being in the arena-cum-stable at the break of dawn before any of his employees arrived to disturb the quiet. He loved the smells that were synonymous with horses—freshly turned straw, molasses-coated grain, hay waiting to be forked, and manure. The fabulous aroma of frying bacon from his forewoman Pauline's upstairs viewing-room apart-ment added to the bouquet. Though Quincy no longer ate bacon, he still appreciated the scent.

As was his habit, he made his rounds, visiting every mare and stallion to make sure all was well before ending his tour at Beethoven's stall. The stud was Quincy's special baby, and for reasons he'd never clearly defined, he always lingered with him the longest, finding a sense of peace that seemed to elude him everywhere else. Beethoven, a gor-geous black, nickered in greeting and stepped over for his morning ration of petting. The horse was such a love bug that Quincy often joked that Beethoven would morph into a lapdog if he could. The huge beast laid his massive head on Quincy's shoulder, chuffing and rubbing cheeks, a show of affection that always dislodged Quincy's black Stetson. Prepared, Quincy caught the hat before it hit the ground.

"Hey, buddy," he whispered around the logjam in his throat. "I hope your morning is off to a better start than mine."

Beethoven grunted, a contented sound that told Quincy the horse was as happy as a mouse in a cheese factory. He smiled and scanned the stall, checking to make sure all was as it should be. His gaze slid over the far left corner and then jerked back to a lump of green that didn't belong there. He stared for a moment at what appeared to be a woman asleep in the straw. *What the hell?* Surely it was only a trick of the light. His ranch was armed to the teeth with high-tech security, and that was especially true in the arena, with every door, window, skylight, and paddock gate wired to an alarm. If anyone entered without punching in the pass code, which was changed frequently, a siren went off loudly enough to burst eardrums. Quincy had heard nothing.

And yet—well, shit—there *was* a woman curled up in the corner. She wore a getup that reminded Quincy of something he might see at a Renaissance fair. Wrapped around her head was a thick multilayered band of antique linen that was then secured over the crown by a see-through scarf of the same color. The linen band appeared to be of high quality and looked to Quincy like the oil filter on his truck. The transparent scarf shimmered like spun gold and was somehow pleated at the crown and looped loosely beneath the woman's chin. Her hair, a bright, fiery red, followed the slender bend of her back and was surely long enough to reach well below her knees when she was standing. Her silk gown, a deep green and floor-length, judging by the way the skirt billowed around her, sported voluminous sleeves and a plunging, square neckline, which revealed a modest white underdress laced to the waist.

As if she sensed his gaze on her, she jerked awake and, hampered by the long dress, struggled to her feet. To Quincy's amazement, Beethoven merely whickered and circled away. Normally the stallion grew nervous when he was approached by anyone except Quincy.

"God's teeth!" As round as dimes and as clear blue as a Caribbean lagoon on a hot summer day, her eyes flashed with irritation. "Ye scared the bee-Jesus out of me."

Quincy recognized an Irish brogue when he heard one. His dad's mother, Mariah Eileen O'Grady, had been born in the old country. But as Quincy recalled, she'd never said *bejesus* as two separate words or used the expression *God's teeth*. "How did you get in here?" he demanded, doing his best not to notice those expressive eyes or the delicate perfection of her oval face. "The whole place is wired."

Bewilderment creased her brow. She cast a wary glance around the stall. "Where might it be?"

"What?"

"The wire," she expounded. "I see none."

Quincy clenched his teeth. If not for the weird getup, she might have been quite a looker, with that bright red hair, creamy skin, and stunning blue eyes, but Quincy was in no mood to appreciate a woman's feminine attributes. Well, scratch that. Truly beautiful women were difficult for any man to ignore, but he meant to give it his best shot.

"I asked you a question. Answer me." The perimeters of Quincy's ranch could be breached by deer or elk that sailed over the fences, but the warning alarms went off if the cameras detected large body masses that lingered near the property lines, the idea being that any human would take at least a few seconds to scale a five-foot barrier. Voice strained with anger, not to mention worry over his sister-in-law, he repeated the question. "How did you get in my arena?"

"Is that what ye call it, an arena?" Her frown deepened. She swatted at the straw on her wrinkled skirts. As she bent forward, Quincy's gaze shot to the slender nip of her waist and the temptingly round flare of her hips. When he realized where he was staring, he forced himself to look up, only to find his attention riveted to her silk bodice, which showcased small but perfectly shaped breasts. "'Tis so different here."

Losing patience, Quincy raised his voice. "I'll ask you one more time before I call the police. How did you get in here?"

"The police? 'Tis a word I've never heard."

Quincy had an unholy urge to vault over the stall gate and shake her until her teeth rattled. "Listen, lady, you're in serious trouble. Committing a B and E is a felony offense in Oregon, with a sentence of five to twenty. Start talking, and fast, or you'll be cooling your jets in a cell until you have gray hair."

She paled and lifted her chin, which sported a deep cleft that mirrored the dimple that flashed in her right cheek when she spoke. "I do na understand all yer strange words. Me name is Ceara O'Ceallaigh. I seek audience with a man named Quincy O'Hourigan, sir. I shall speak with him, and only him. 'Tis na a tale for the ears of another."

"You have the first name right, but my last name isn't O'Hourigan."

She winced, flapped her wrist, and muttered something

in what sounded like Gaelic. Her quaint mannerisms drove home to Quincy that she was not only beautiful, but also as cute as a button. "Harrigan, I mean. 'Tis forgetful I am. Me whole long life, I've heard naught but the name O'Hourigan and learned of the change to Harrigan only a short while ago. When yer ancestors sailed to this land in the eighteen hundreds, they changed the family sur-name." Her brilliant blue gaze sought his. "So ye are Sir Quincy?"

"No *sir* attached."

Quincy pressed the phone icon on his cell. His favor-ites popped up on the screen, and he was about to tap 911 when she said, "Ye asked how I got in here. Me reply may ring strange to yer ears. 'Tis simply where I landed. I can tell ye no more. I prayed to the Blessed Ones to bring me to a place where I might encounter ye, and here I am."

Quincy froze with his finger poised over the button he'd entered as a speed dial on his phone for 911. "You prayed to . . . Say what?"

She studied him as if he were an incredibly dense five-year-old. Damn, but those big blue eyes did pack a wal-lop. What man could look into them without struggling to break visual contact? "'Struth, sir. No lie has passed me lips. 'Tis where the Blessed Ones dropped me." She trailed her gaze over his face. "I suspected you were Sir Quincy. You bear a striking resemblance to the man I saw in me mum's crystal ball."

Quincy cocked his head, certain that he must have misheard her. "Come again?"

"Please, sir, do not ask that of me. 'Twas a difficult journey, and I've no yearning to endure it twice." She smiled slightly, and with the gentle curve of her lips, her entire face seemed to glow. "Traveling forward in time is taxing. Pray, hear me out. 'Tis good reason I have fer being here."

Quincy stared hard at her clothing. It looked like the real thing, but he knew people created replicas of medieval garments all the time for Renaissance fairs. *Traveling forward in time?* She was a bona fide fruitcake. That was the only plausible explanation. He remembered the phone he held aloft in one hand. "How is your name spelled?" Both her first and last names sounded Greek to him. *Key-air-uh.* He'd never heard it. "Start with your first." He doubted she would tell him the truth, but at least he'd have something to tell the cops.

"By *first*, I'm supposing ye mean me Christian name, Ceara? 'Tis spelled C-E-A-R-A. I am the elder daughter of the O'Ceallaigh, head of our chiefdom in County Clare." She quickly told him how to spell her last name. "I have come forward from the year 1574 to save lives, specifically the lives of the first wives of all O'Hourigan males." She flapped her wrist again. "Begging yer pardon, Harrigan males, I mean."

That cinched it. She really *was* nuts. Even so, he couldn't resist pointing out, "The Tudor era, when Ireland was under English rule, with Queen Elizabeth the First on the throne?"

Her chin shot up, and her cheeks flamed with indignation. "Me home lies in land beyond the Pale, where the *queen* and her edicts are ignored. Me people have our own faith, and our own laws."

Tiring quickly of this game, Quincy directed his gaze to the phone again. Once the cops collected her, they could get her to a facility where she could be evaluated and receive medication for whatever it was that ailed her. He didn't care where they took her as long as it was off his ranch. He had enough on his mind without dealing with a delusional woman, no matter how pretty or entertaining she might be.

She reached up to remove the oil-filter contraption from her head. "I must appear odd to ye. Me mum made me a léine and trews so I would look more like the women of yer time, but I refused to wear such scandalous garments. They were indecent."

Quincy wouldn't have passed up an opportunity to see her in tight jeans and a knit top. He had a feeling all those layers she wore concealed a world-class figure. And why the hell was he thinking about *that*? The woman had forced her way into a high-security area, he had no idea what mischief she'd intended to perpetrate, and he needed to stay focused on getting her removed from the premises.

She swayed slightly, as if she were about to wobble off her feet, giving Quincy an inexplicable urge to scale the gate and catch her from falling. "Me apologies," she said faintly. "The journey has drained me." She sighed and passed a hand over her brow. "Please listen, Sir Quincy. Me energy is quickly flagging." She tossed the headgear onto the straw and straightened her shoulders. "Me O'Ceallaigh ancestress, a woman of druid descent who lived in the fourteenth century, was humiliated beyond bearing when she was left at the altar by an O'Hourigan man, also of druid blood. Her revenge was to cast a curse upon yer entire family. The first wife of every O'Hourigan male will die from a blood sickness, hemorrhaging, or injury that causes her to bleed to death. It has long been a great sadness to me family, and after much deliberation, I volunteered to come forward to this century to end the wickedness fer all time. Me sister, only two and ten, is too young to marry in this era."

She concluded her speech with a curtsy that revealed

she was indeed weak at the knees. As she came erect, she added, " 'Twas the only way to end this horrible curse. A virgin daughter of the O'Ceallaigh must wed an O'Hourigan."

"You really are out of your mind."

She tipped her head, an expression of puzzlement giving way to comprehension. "Am I, now? Do ye deny that yer mum hemorrhaged to death during childbirth? Or that now yer eldest brother's wife is dying of a strange blood sickness?"

Quincy stifled a gasp, recovered, and snapped, "How the hell did you come by that information?" Probably obvious, he realized. Someone good with computers could learn almost anything on the Internet these days, and he couldn't allow her winsome manner and lovely face to distract him from the facts. "Scratch the question. You're clever. I'll give you that." Anger burned through Quincy. How dared she mention his mother's death and then trump it by bringing up Loni's leukemia? "Not clever enough, however. I'm finished with this little performance. I don't know what your aim is, and I really don't give a rat's ass."

"I learned all that I know by looking into me mum's crystal ball." She glanced at his phone. "What is in the wee box?"

Quincy huffed with laughter, but there was no humor in the sound. "It's a phone, not a box, and it's your one-way ticket to the clinker."

"Only *you* can prevent yer brother's wife from dying, sir. So far as me mum could decipher, ye are the last unmarried male in your family line. 'Tis up to *you*."

If Quincy hadn't been so upset, he might have found this incredible situation laughable, but he was in no frame of mind for jokes, no matter how creatively played.

Over the years he had encountered more than a few strange individuals, but never on his ranch. He had no idea how she'd breached security, but in good time he'd find out. He would have a team on it within the hour to watch every second of camera footage. And whoever was responsible for the weakness in his security would answer to him.

Meanwhile, there was only one thing to do. He pressed the screen to call the police and then reported a B and E at his stables.

The woman didn't seem unduly perturbed as he ended the call. Apparently she planned to carry through with this charade until uniformed officers forcibly removed her from Beethoven's stall. Quincy had to admire her nerve.

To his surprise, Beethoven chuffed and walked over to nuzzle her shoulder. She spoke softly to the stallion and reached up to rub between his eyes, one of the horse's favorite places to be scratched. She'd clearly been around equines.

"Ye truly believe I'm mad, do ye not?" She sent Quincy a knowing look. "I venture a guess that I would feel the same if I were not druid and aware that there are things in this world that defy explanation." She turned from the stallion and arched a finely drawn brow. "Surely, being of druid descent yerself, ye're aware of that as well, Sir Quincy."

Now *he* was a druid? Quincy almost laughed. He'd read about druids, but he'd never believed they had magical powers. They'd merely been well-educated individuals who'd found it easy to hoodwink Irish and Scottish peasants into thinking they possessed abilities that normal human beings didn't.

He glanced at his watch. It would take the police

about twenty minutes to show up, yet his burglar re-vealed no inclination to run. In her shoes, he would have been searching for the closest exit. Maybe she was so delusional that she actually believed what she'd told him.

Ceara grew increasingly uneasy as the minutes passed. In her mum's crystal ball, Quincy Harrigan had ap-peared to be handsome, but nothing she'd seen in the glass had prepared her for the reality of him. A man of her time always wore an inar and brat over his léine and trews, which served well to conceal his body. Such was not the case with Quincy. His exposed léine was made of a strange blue cloth that clung to his well-developed shoulders and chest, leaving nothing to her imagination. Through the rungs of the stall gate, she could also see how tightly his trews skimmed his powerfully muscled thighs.

She didn't care for the way he stood there staring at her, as if he were waiting for something to happen. Re-calling his reference to the "police," she decided he'd been referring to his constables, whose job it undoubt-edly was to keep the peace and uphold the law on his lands. But if that were the case, why had the constables not yet arrived? At her father's manor, keepers of the peace were in close residence and didn't take this long to respond when trouble was afoot.

A wave of yearning for home struck her. Though she'd been in this new place for less than a night, she sorely missed her parents, younger sister, brothers, and all the familiar things she'd left behind. Did this man not understand the magnitude of the sacrifice she had made in order to come forward in time? Instead of acting grateful, Quincy Harrigan seemed angry. That made no sense to her. Had she not explained her reasons for being here clearly enough? She was on a mission to save lives.

"Do ye comprehend why I have come here, Sir Quincy?" she ventured.

He pushed at the brim of his black hat, which was far and beyond the oddest headwear she had ever seen. Then he arched a dark brow at her. "I think I have a pretty clear picture," he replied.

"Yet ye are not pleased that I am here?"

He ran his dark gaze down her body, making her skin tingle beneath her garments. His firm mouth tipped up in a humorless grin. "How many months did it take to perfect your Irish brogue? It is part of the role you're playing, right, as vital to the illusion you're creating as the gown you're wearing?" He shrugged a strong shoulder. "What I can't figure is why you've gone to such lengths." Hooking his thumbs over the wide leather belt that encircled his narrow hips, he added, "I suppose that's for the cops to determine and not really my concern." He glanced around the enclosure, his gaze lingering on the other animals' stalls. "Unless, of course, you sneaked in here to harm my horses."

Ceara's indignant denial trailed off as she heard a horrific wailing in the distance. Dogs began barking upstairs somewhere, their cries muffled. Quincy left the area for a moment, then quickly resumed his post at the railing. "Right on time. I opened the gate for the police by remote control."

The awful noise increased, and Ceara heard what put her in mind of thick, heavy doors being slammed closed. A sudden cessation of the wailing preceded a rush of footsteps coming toward the building. Seconds later, voices rang out in the cavernous enclosure.

She jerked with a start when Quincy vaulted over the

stall gate and strode past the stallion to grasp her arm. "This way," he said, pulling her forward. "Beethoven won't react well to a bunch of uniforms."

The relentless pressure of his grip told Ceara that balking would accomplish little. She allowed him to tug her along, stood obediently as he opened the gate, and then exited the stall with him. It wasn't until she saw a blue blur of men running toward them that she grew truly frightened. With a slight shove, Quincy Harrigan forced her forward, and the next thing she knew the men were upon her. They grasped her shoulders with unnecessarily rough hands, spun her around, and wrenched her arms behind her back. Cold metal clamps closed around her wrists.

"You have the right to remain silent," one of the constables barked at her. "Anything you say or do can and will be held against you in a court of law. You have the right to speak to an attorney. If you cannot afford an attorney, one will be appointed for you. Do you understand these rights that have just been read to you?"

Ceara understood the implications, if not the specifics. These men meant to incarcerate her. As two of them flanked her and grabbed her arms to lead her away, she threw a frantic glance over her shoulder. "Me satchel!" she cried. " 'Tis mine! I cannot leave it behind!" The bag held all her keepsakes from home. Without them, she would have no reminders of her family. "Please, will ye not at least let me keep me things?"

The men holding her never broke pace. Ceara continued to look back and plead to fetch her belongings until they tugged her through a doorway to exit the building. Blinding flashes of red and blue created a whirling confusion of light that bathed everything in the semidarkness. Ceara had never seen anything so stunning, not even when her father ignited gunpowder to impress guests at his annual festivals. Surely not even a thousand candles could produce such a lavish display.

Stumbling forward between her two captors, she stared with growing alarm at three shiny, dark blue carriages. While peering into her mum's crystal ball, she'd glimpsed similar horseless conveyances and knew that some mysterious, unseen power propelled them into motion. But none that she'd seen had looked exactly like these. Atop the roof of each one perched a long, boardlike object that emitted the spurts of bright color, and along the sides golden flames had been painted. A third officer hurried forward to open a rear door of the closest equipage. One of Ceara's escorts shoved her toward the opening, clamped a hand over her head, and pushed her down onto an incredibly soft seat.

"Feet inside," he ordered.

Ceara swung her legs up and over the threshold. The man leaned forward to pull a strap over her shoulder and across her torso. With a sharp click of metal, she was imprisoned where she sat, her bound hands forming an uncomfortable lump at the small of her back. Battling tears, she saw that thick wire mesh separated the rear compartment of the conveyance from the front one. She truly was being imprisoned. But what was her crime?

She caught movement from the corner of her eye and turned to see Sir Quincy standing just beyond the window. Booted feet spread, arms akimbo, his face shadowed by the brim of his hat, he looked intense and fearful. In the flashing light, she saw the grim set of his lips and the twitch of a muscle in his lean cheek. What had she done, she wondered, to make him hate her so? Such enmity was born only of a heart filled with malice. He had not troubled himself to bring her the satchel. Indeed, he projected an air of such hostility that she was surprised he had done her no physical harm while they had been alone in that monstrosity he called an arena.

Fear clutched her heart. She knew only one man in this time and place, and clearly she could expect no assistance from him.

Chapter Two

As the officers drove away, Quincy couldn't drag his gaze from Ceara's tear-streaked face, pressed imploringly against the window glass, her eyes filled with urgent appeal. He considered himself to be a good judge of character, and he knew damned well the woman had to be emotionally ill, but something in her expression tugged at his conscience and made him feel like a rotten skunk for having her arrested.

Determined to get on with his day, he shook off the feeling. The world was filled with unbalanced people. Some took drugs. Others were just born messed up in the head and needed treatment to keep them on an even keel. Quincy wished none of them ill, including his intruder, but with his brother's wife at death's door, he already had plenty to deal with, and now, thanks to Ceara O'Ceallaigh, if that was even her real name, he had an extra mountain of work ahead of him.

He reentered the arena shouting for his forewoman. "Pauline! Get down here! We've got a mess on our hands!"

"I'm right here, boss. No need to shout." Pauline, a short, stocky woman of fifty-six, stood near Beethoven's stall. In the dim illumination her salt-and-pepper hair, cut short like a man's, shone like polished silver. A perplexed expression rode the handsome features of her square face and was reflected in her gray-blue eyes. "What the frack happened down here? It sounded like every cop car in the county raced in with sirens blaring."

Quincy nearly smiled. Pauline was a great fan of *Battlestar Galactica* and had watched the series so many times that *frack* had become her favorite curse word. "We had a B and E," he informed her. "Some gal dressed up in Renaissance clothing. Somehow she got in without setting off the alarm."

Pauline muttered the word *frack* with more vehemence. "How'd that happen?"

"Good question," Quincy replied, "but for now, my greater concern is the safety of my horses." A few years ago, several of his sister Sam's horses had been poisoned by her ex, who'd been trying to cash in on equine mortality insurance policies. As a result, everyone in the family, including Quincy, had followed Sam's lead and beefed up security on their ranches to prevent any harm to other equines. "After Sam's experience, it's never far from my mind that it could happen again."

The color drained from Pauline's face, which was, as always, devoid of cosmetics. "You think she laced their grain with something? *Why?*" She shook her head. "I don't get why anybody would do such a thing to innocent animals."

Quincy shared that sentiment, but he didn't intend to overlook the possibility. "We need to empty and wash out every feed bag, toss all opened grain sacks, and discard all loose hay. I doubt she would have tampered with bound bales."

Pauline didn't need to be told twice. She started at the first stall at one end of the arena, pitchfork in hand, and

Quincy began his mission at the other end. He'd barely started working when he was bombarded by his dogs, Bubba and Billy Bob, who had been bunking upstairs with Pauline during Loni's illness to spare them the stress of being bounced back and forth between his home and Pauline's apartment during his absences.

"Hey, guys!" Quincy set aside the pitchfork and crouched to curl an arm around each squirming, red-and-white fur ball. Pauline gave them superb care, but the dogs still couldn't quite grasp why they could no longer be with Quincy all the time. Brothers from the same litter, they'd turned ten on March 7, but neither of them had started to act his age yet. Australian shepherds tended to outlive many other breeds, but Quincy hadn't expected them to still be puppylike after a decade. "So much excitement," he commiserated. "Sirens blaring and people yelling down here—and my boys were locked up in Pauline's apartment, missing out on all the fun." Quincy gave each dog a playful roll on the soft dirt. "Have you been off doing your jobs, sniffing out every nook and cranny to see how that lady got in here?" He briskly ruffled their long fur to rid it of dust. "That's my good boys. Put those sniffers of yours to good use."

When the dogs' excitement had ebbed, Quincy resumed his task, hurrying because the love-in with his mutts had put him behind Pauline, who was working at her usual efficient speed. The shepherds quickly lost interest in stall cleaning and took off, running shoulder-to-shoulder as if physically attached, to sniff up trouble in another corner of the arena.

It wasn't until Quincy reached Beethoven's stall that he remembered the satchel and weird hat that Ceara had unwillingly left behind. He hurried over to jerk open the bag, rifled through the contents, and found nothing to substantiate his suspicion that the woman had entered the compound to poison his stock. *Weird.* Ceara had a myriad of possessions inside the grip, everything from clothing to a sewing thimble. Quincy barely spared the items a glance, his sole focus on finding vials or telltale dustings of powder.

When he met Pauline at the center of the workout area a few minutes later, she lifted her hands. "Nothing. I forked out all the loose hay and straw and rinsed out the feed bags from each stall, but my nose told me there was nothing bad in any of them."

Quincy's nose had told him the same thing. "Well, it doesn't look as if she came here to taint the feed. But just to be on the safe side, when the hands get here, have them toss all opened bags of grain and all the loose bales that are in hay storage. Tell them I want the horses to get nothing that might be contaminated. Grain from only sealed bags and hay from only bound bales. Everything else is out of here."

"You leaving?" Pauline asked.

Quincy glanced at his watch. "I have to call the security company. I want to know how that woman got in here, and then I want to know every move she made afterward." Quincy nearly winced when he remembered that he had all the other ranches to oversee as well. "Damn, Pauline. I can't be in several places at once. I'll need you to check on all the other ranches for me today. When Bingo gets here, turn this place over to him."

Pauline nodded and squared her shoulders. Bingo was an ex–rodeo champ with a bum hip from a bronc-riding accident years ago. Though physically limited, he was still excellent with horses and had it in him to manage the hired hands for a day without firing up any tempers. At thirty-eight, he was still young enough to become

Pauline's replacement, if and when she ever retired, and Quincy had his eye on him, judging his potential for that position on a daily basis. As willing as Pauline was to keep working, she had a bad back, and Quincy knew her days as a horsewoman were probably numbered.

"Gotcha covered, boss." Pauline ran a hand over her short-cropped hair. "Let me know what you find on the security tapes. Once I get the crew lined out and have Bingo on top of everything, I'll spare a few minutes to check things here. If the woman broke in, there must be evidence of it somewhere."

Quincy nodded his approval. Pauline was invaluable to him; she thought for herself and was quick on her feet. His dad had chosen well when he had selected her to become Quincy's foreman at the Lazy H. Quincy had been only twenty-one and as green as grass when he'd started his own ranch. Pauline had advised him at every turn, sharing with him all her wisdom, garnered over a period of years.

"Thanks, Pauline. I always know I can count on you."

She touched her temple in a mock salute. "Appreciate the attagirl, boss, but you're wasting time flapping your lips. We got work to do."

Quincy managed a smile. He'd just pulled his phone from his belt to call the security company when his father entered the building via the personnel door. "Hey, Dad, good to see you."

Wiry and lean, yet well muscled, Frank strode across the sandy arena, his bowed legs bearing testimony that he'd been in a saddle most of his life. Beneath the brim of his brown Stetson, his hair still shone as black as jet, with only touches of silver at the temples. He paused to pet Bubba and Billy Bob, who were excited to see him after so long. Then he sauntered toward Quincy again.

"What the heck happened over here?" His dark brown eyes reflected concern. "I heard the sirens. Woke me up from a sound sleep. Saw the cop lights clear from my place."

"Some woman broke into the arena. I found her sleeping in Beethoven's stall."

"That took gonads. She's lucky he didn't trample her. He don't cotton much to strangers."

Quincy quickly gave his father the rundown. "I swear, Dad, if I was the superstitious sort, I might have bought into her story." With a shake of his head, Quincy laughed humorlessly. "Crystal balls, druids, and traveling forward through time. She has to be a bona fide nutcase."

Frank nodded in agreement. He looked drawn and years older than he had a week ago, when Quincy had last seen him in Portland. Normally when Quincy studied his dad, he took heart that he had inherited good aging genes and would still be fit and strong in his sixties. But this morning the forecast didn't seem quite so positive. With Loni's illness, Clint's pain, and the grim prognosis, Frank was showing his age.

Since his father contributed nothing more to the exchange, Quincy continued his story. "I have to admit she spooked me a couple of times. She probably made up the bit about our name being changed from O'Hourigan to Harrigan way back when, but her knowing about how Mom died and how sick Loni is?" Quincy shrugged. "*That* was downright eerie."

"O'Hourigan," Frank repeated softly. "Why does that ring a bell?" His gaze sharpened on Quincy's face. "I remember now. I think I've seen that name in the old family Bible."

Quincy's nape hair stood on end. "You what?"

"You heard me. When my family came here from Ireland during the potato famine, they changed our surname to something that sounded a little less Irish."

"Are you shitting me?"

Frank swept his brown Stetson from his head and whacked it against his leg. "No, I'm dead serious. You gotta remember that bein' Irish wasn't a plus way back then. Changin' the family name to Harrigan was part of our fresh start in the land of dreams and possibilities."

Quincy couldn't quite believe his ears. "Are you saying our surname was once O'Hourigan?"

"I can't say for certain. I'd have to get the Bible out of the safety deposit box at the bank to check. But O'Hourigan sure as hell sounds familiar."

It was Quincy's turn to give his hat a good dusting on his jeans. "That is too weird for words. How in the hell could that woman have known about the name change when I didn't know about it myself?"

For the first time, Quincy questioned the wisdom of having had the O'Ceallaigh woman arrested. Then he gave himself a hard mental shake and reminded himself that an accomplished researcher could discover almost anything on the Internet nowadays. Ceara O'Ceallaigh was a convincing liar and spinner of tall tales, nothing more. Right about now, the authorities were probably trying to decide which psychiatrist to send her to for evaluation and treatment.

By the time Ceara was delivered to what her captors called the station, she was violently nauseated and shaking like a leaf. The horseless carriage with flames painted on its doors had traveled at such an incredible speed that the landscape had passed by her window in a blur. She'd been terrified every second, her heart fluttering wildly in her throat, especially when the conveyance sped over roads covered with snow and ice. Equally frightening to her had been the voice of a woman that blared repeatedly from out of nowhere inside the vehicle. In these modern times, did not all individuals have bodies? Ceara found that difficult to believe, but she'd definitely heard a female speaking, and she saw no crystal ball from which the voice might have come.

Once she was at the station, Ceara's senses were once again blasted by strange sights and sounds. The earth outside the large brick building was covered with a black, hard substance, the likes of which she'd never seen. At home, dooryards and roadsteads were sometimes cobbled with stones, but mostly they were packed dirt.

Ceara nearly parted company with her skin when a woman's voice shouted from a horn-shaped object attached under a corner eave of the structure. "DV, domicile 1430 Oak Street, ABH in progress. AFA held at gunpoint by AMA. Calling all available cars."

As Ceara was guided forward by her escorts, she stared stupidly at the horn, picturing a woman hovering in the attic to shout at people outside. What kind of world was this? And what was she going to do now that she was stuck here?

Once she was inside the building, Ceara was bombarded by even more noises—loud voices, humming sounds, beeps, and trilling that made her wonder whether maniacal large birds were nesting just out of sight. She was led through a maze of cluttered desks, at which both uniformed males and females sat, talking into black rectangular objects or interviewing people whose wrists were shackled behind their backs, just as hers were. At the far end of the huge room, Ceara was pushed onto a bench already occupied by others.

An older female with missing teeth and frizzy yellow hair sat beside her. She smelled so strongly of flowery perfume that Ceara's eyes stung. The woman's sagging face was coated with a pale substance. Only her eyes, heavily lined with black, her unnaturally pink cheeks, and her bloodred lips lent color to her countenance.

She jostled Ceara with her elbow. "Whatcha in for, sweetheart?"

" 'Tis uncertain to me at this time. I havena committed a crime."

The other woman laughed. Ceara couldn't help but gape at the woman's breasts, which were about to jiggle out over the extremely low neckline of her léine. "That's what we all say, and ain't it the truth. A woman can't make an honest living anymore. Half the money I get from my johns goes to pay fines and post bail."

Ceara didn't understand what this woman meant. How many men named John could one person possibly know? And why did they give this straw-haired female their coin? Before Ceara could ask, a man dressed in dark blue trews and a pale blue léine approached them. "On your feet, Paula. Time to get you processed."

The woman pushed up from the bench to follow the officer. Her tight trews, held up by a gaudy studded belt, rode so low on her hips that the crack between her buttocks showed. Even more shocking to Ceara, someone had drawn or tattooed a dragon on her skin with different colors of ink. Just the thought of allowing another person to see that part of her person made Ceara's cheeks burn, but clearly this woman had done so. It was humanly impossible to draw an image so intricately on one's own rump.

Soon Ceara was fetched by a female officer who led her to a nearby desk. The woman had dark hair pulled back in a bun and brown eyes that seemed flat and hard. Her manner was brisk as she sat across from Ceara and held her hands over an odd rectangular contraption with rows of buttons on it. Instead of looking at Ceara, she stared at a flat, boxlike object that threw out sky blue light from the front side.

"Name?"

Ceara shifted on the chair. "Ceara O'Ceallaigh."

"Spelling?"

Ceara slowly recited the letters.

"Shit, what a mouthful." The woman tapped the buttons. "Address?" When Ceara failed to immediately respond, she glanced up. "Where do you live?"

"Clare, in the chiefdom of the O'Ceallaigh. 'Tis Ireland of which I speak, in case ye do na know of County Clare."

The woman sighed. "What's the *address*, sweet cheeks?"

Ceara frowned. "Address? 'Tis uncertain I am as to yer meaning."

"The street number," the woman elaborated.

"There is only one O'Ceallaigh Road in me sire's chiefdom, so there's no need for a number. The manor where I reside is at the end of it."

"Look, Ms. O'Ceallaigh, I don't have time for games. What's the goddamned house number?"

" 'Struth, there is no house number, nor the need for one. There is only one manor."

The officer rocked back on her chair, startling Ceara so badly that she almost leaped up to keep the other woman from toppling over. "You have to have a house number to get letters and packages."

"Nay, all heralds know full well where the O'Ceallaigh resides."

"Heralds?" The officer laughed, but the sound lacked

any trace of humor. "All right, fine." She rocked forward to tap the buttons again. "Zip code?"

Ceara sent her a bewildered look.

"Your postal code?" the officer tried.

"I do na know of what ye speak."

The other woman shook her head. "Hair down past your ass. Maybe all your gray matter leaked out to provide protein. You a member of some weird cult or something?"

Again, Ceara was mystified.

"What's your DOB?" the woman asked.

"Me what?"

"Your date of birth," the officer said with marked slowness.

Ceara's stomach clenched. If she told the truth, she would never be believed, and yet honesty had been ingrained in her since childhood. "I was born in 1548 on the fourteenth day of March. I just celebrated a name day and am six and twenty years of age."

"And next you'll offer me a great deal on the Brooklyn Bridge. Okay, fine. You talk; I'll enter it, bullshit or not. We're lined up back-to-back, and I don't have time for this."

In Ceara's century, men stood back-to-back only in battle or while practicing with weapons. She glanced around the room, saw no one in a fighting stance, and decided the woman didn't mean it literally.

"You were arrested for breaking and entering. What were you doing in Quincy Harrigan's arena, and how did you get in without setting off the alarm?"

From that point forward, the interrogation passed in a blur for Ceara. She tried to answer each question as honestly as possible, but in the end, her reward was to be escorted into a back chamber, stripped by a female guard, and subjected to all manner of humiliations. After much poking and prodding of her person, she was shoved into a chamber with gray walls and a sloped floor of the same color with a grate at its center. Strange, shiny objects poked out from high on the wall. Below them, cross-shaped handles protruded.

"Take a shower," the guard ordered. "Here's a bar of soap. Toss it in the trash bin when you're finished. With all that hair, you have my permission to use two towels." She pointed to some shelves at the far end of the chamber where white, nubby cloth was folded and neatly stacked. "When you're done, come back out here, and I'll give you some cell scrubs and toiletries."

Ceara had no idea what scrubs or toiletries were, and she definitely didn't know how to take a shower. After the other woman closed the door, she stood at the center of the chamber, staring in befuddlement at the silver protrusions. Then, gathering her courage, she stepped closer to one of the crosses, grasped it in her hand, and gave it a hard turn. Ice-cold water struck her in the face. She gasped and choked. Shuddering, she ran the soap over her body, then turned to rinse off. After dispensing with the blast of icy water, she fetched two towels, wringing the water from her sopping braid before attempting to dry her person. Her teeth were still clacking when she cautiously opened the door to peer out into the other room.

"Hurry it up. I don't have all day." The plump guard held out a bundle of orange cloth atop which lay a small white towel, a comb, a tiny, long-handled brush, and a small, capped container that squished under Ceara's fingertips. "Once in your cell, you can brush your teeth and get the tangles out."

Still shivering, Ceara quickly donned some white underwear and then the orange garments, which consisted of loose-fitting trews and an overlarge léine. She was grateful to at least cover her nakedness. On her feet, she wore blue slippers made of rough, parchmentlike material with stretchy thread stitched around the opening to keep them snug over her instep and heel. As she followed the woman into what was called the women's cell block, she wondered where they had put her gown and undergarments. First she'd lost her hat and satchel, which held all her precious belongings. Now they had taken her clothes.

Enclosures lined either side of a wide passage. As Ceara walked ahead of the guard, she glimpsed several other females peering out at her from behind bars. They all wore the same orange clothes, but that was all that she had time to notice in passing.

The guard pushed a button on the wall to open Ceara's cell door. The slide of the bars gave Ceara a start. How could something so heavy move so easily without anyone pushing on it? Perplexed, she walked obediently inside, her heart catching when she heard the steel barrier slam shut behind her.

"All the comforts of home," the guard said with a laugh. "Sink, toilet, and cot. If you're lucky, you won't have to stay long."

Ceara sank numbly onto the narrow bed. Accustomed to the softness of moss-filled mattresses, she wished fervently to be back at the manor. Coming forward in time to save Harrigan wives had been a fool's mission. She'd been stupid to think she'd be welcomed with open arms, or that Sir Quincy would be grateful that she had sacrificed so much to be here.

"What did they charge you with?"

Ceara turned to see the older woman with yellow hair

standing in the next cell, her wrists hooked limply over a horizontal dividing bar. She looked diminished in the loose orange clothes. Her face was now devoid of false color, her pale blue eyes barely noticeable, and her lips a natural pink. Damp strands of hair the color of old leather dangled limply over her forehead.

"They say I committed a B and E," Ceara replied.

"Breaking and entering? Whoo! You don't look the type. I had you pegged as a working girl."

Weariness lay on Ceara's shoulders like leaden weights. "Pray tell, what is a working girl?"

The woman laughed, the sound raspy. "Ah, come on, honey. It's plain as the nose on your face that burglary is a sideline for you. I saw that getup you had on. Pretty smart of you, actually. I'll bet all those skirts and laces turn men on. The harder they have to work for something, the more they're willing to pay." She cocked her head. "You're a pretty little thing even without makeup. Does the fresh, innocent act work good for you? What's your usual take each night?"

The questions were incomprehensible to Ceara, who was too exhausted, confused, and frightened to puzzle them out. She tossed her towel and jail-issue toiletries on the foot of the cot, then leaned sideways to curl up on the rock-hard mattress. The gray wool blanket was scratchy against her skin. An acrid smell burned her nose. She supposed it was a cleaning agent of some sort, but definitely not lye, which was most often used at home. Tears gathered in her eyes. She blinked, trying her best to get rid of them.

"Not very friendly, are you?" The woman grunted. "No point in wallowing in your sorrows, honey. You'll be out on the streets again before you know it. You got the money to post bail?"

A hard knot formed at the base of Ceara's throat. Her father had given her some money, but she doubted it would be of any use to her in this time. Besides, it was still in the stall at Sir Quincy's arena. "Nay," she said tightly.

"Well, shit, that sucks. Ah, well, maybe you can get a bondsman to take a chance on you. I'd float you a loan, but I'm a little short on cash myself."

Ceara appreciated the woman's desire to help, but she doubted she would ever see the light of day again. She had done naught except land in Quincy Harrigan's precious arena, but that was apparently a serious crime in this century. With no money to bribe her way to freedom, she might grow old in this cell and eventually die. The thought terrified her. At home, it was not uncommon for people to be incarcerated all of their lives for stealing a wee bit of bread.

How would she survive? She was in a strange place, in a time that was not hers, and they hadn't even allowed her to keep her satchel. All her mementos were lost to her.

The journey had drained her of strength. Her limbs felt as limp at wet linen. Her father had warned her that the trip would take a harsh toll on her body. He'd even said that she might arrive stripped of her special powers. She'd had no opportunity to attempt to use her gifts, and now she was too exhausted to try. She closed her eyes, willing herself to sleep, but the woman in the next cell wouldn't stop talking.

"You got an odd way of speaking," she said. "Is that part of your act, or are you from another country?"

"Ireland," Ceara said, injecting no expression into the word. *Ireland*. God's teeth, how she yearned to go back. But that was impossible. Journeying forward was possible for druids, but no one had ever managed to reverse the process. Ceara wasn't certain why that was so, but she had understood the consequences before deciding to come here, and now there was no way to undo the mistake. "'Tis a lovely place, me Ireland." She heard the wistfulness in her voice. "I already miss it sorely, and I havena been gone for a full day."

"I've never stepped foot off American soil," the woman said. "But I've heard Ireland is nice. If I ever get rich, my first trip will be to New Zealand, though—no offense to Ireland. Lord, the pictures of that country are amazing. I'd give my right arm to visit there. Hell, maybe I'd even try to stay."

Ceara had never heard of New Zealand. Feeling dizzy and half-sick, she recalled her amazement when she and her mum had seen the United States in the crystal ball, and she wondered dimly whether explorers had discovered even more new lands over the last few hundred years. "Mayhap ye'll be blessed with riches and go there one day," she said.

"Mayhap? You do talk strange, girlfriend. No matter, I kind of like you anyway."

Ceara thought of the treasures in her satchel—her grandmother's betrothal ring; a lock of her mum's hair; her ivory-backed brush and comb, given to her by her aunt; and the carving of her beloved horse that had died, fashioned for her by the young man she'd once adored. Ah, and she mustn't forget the traveling prayer, which she had committed to parchment, just in case everyone had it wrong and druids *could* travel backward in time. Oh, God in heaven, there were so many little things in that satchel, pieces of home that meant the world to her. Favorite recipes. Notes of family events and history.

Now, because of Quincy O'Hourigan's temper, was

she destined to lose all of it and die behind these bars? She'd never bargained for this. Yes, she'd come forward knowing that she would never see home again. But to lose everything? She curled into a tighter ball and surrendered to her tears.

"Buck up, sweetheart," the woman said. "This is just a pit stop. They don't have room in here to keep all of us for long, and in this miserable economy, the county budget is trimmed to the bone. It costs a lot to keep people in jail."

Ceara barely heard the woman. The pain in her chest grew so intense that she felt as if she might burst from the pressure.

Frank Harrigan accompanied Quincy over to the house to meet with the tech team from Hawkeye Security. Nona Redcliff, a slender and athletic woman of Native American descent with hair as black as Quincy's own, was crew leader and now part owner of the company. Quincy refused to deal with anyone else. Nona was a genius with computers and surveillance equipment. According to Frank, she also had good horse sense, which was Quincy's dad's way of paying the highest compliment.

Today Nona wore her usual faded jeans and lace-up hiking boots, her only concession to company standards being a beige uniform shirt tucked neatly into her belted waistband. When Quincy shook hands with her, he was impressed once again by her neatly trimmed nails and the strength of her grip. She was a lady who always got right down to business, and he liked that about her. She was also attractive in a rugged, no-nonsense sort of way. He'd almost asked her out for dinner once, but then he'd decided to err on the side of caution. Mixing business with pleasure seldom worked out well—at least, not for him.

"So what've we got?" she asked, her dark brown gaze fixed on Quincy's. A thick black braid hung over her right shoulder. "I understand there was a B and E early this morning?"

Quincy nodded. "And it's bewildering as all get-out. My forewoman has gone over the arena with a fine-toothed comb and found no evidence of forced entry. I'm positive every door and window was battened down last night, and that the security system was activated. Both Pauline and I make a tour every night to double-check."

"Did you eyeball the ceiling?" Nona asked. "Sometimes they'll cut through the roof and drop into an enclosure."

"Checked that. Found nothing."

Nona frowned, then shrugged. "Well, we'll figure it out by watching the camera footage. A housefly can't come onto this property without the cameras picking it up."

Without waiting for Quincy to escort her, Nona strode from the kitchen, took a right in the hall, and went straight to Quincy's in-home office, where banks of security monitors flanked one wall. She sat in a caster chair and rolled over to the open laptop, which ran the program for the entire system. Using the mouse, she slumped back to view the five wall-mounted monitors, which housed viewing frames of the immense acreage, the exteriors and interiors of the buildings, and also showed every angle, inside and out, of Quincy's residence.

"What time did you leave the stable last night?" Nona asked.

Quincy thought back. "It was a little after twelve. I've been keeping long hours lately."

Standing behind Nona to watch over her shoulder, Quincy saw that she was backing up the cameras to the stroke of midnight. As she adjusted the speed to a mid-scale fast forward, she asked, "So what's this gal's story?"

Quincy felt silly even repeating it, but he told Nona the whole story. Nona huffed under her breath. "You check with the cops to see if any females fitting her description have slipped away from a psychiatric ward?"

Quincy angled Nona a questioning glance. "Do they still lock people up in wards? I thought most places like that were shut down, and patients are allowed to lead normal lives, taking prescribed medications at home for treatment."

"We no longer have horrific asylums where people are imprisoned and treated worse than animals," the security officer replied. "But nice facilities do still exist, sometimes special wards in regular hospitals for temporary treatment, other times private or publicly funded retreats where people receive individual counseling, medical treatment, and rehab until they're ready to re-enter society. Most of those facilities have high-security wings for patients who are so ill, either temporarily or permanently, that they present a danger to themselves or others." Nona glanced up, meeting his gaze. "Did I just touch on a sore spot?"

A picture of Ceara's face flashed through Quincy's mind. Those blue eyes, that hint of a sweet smile, the dimple in her cheek. He guessed meeting her had made him take a mental step back. "Not a sore spot, exactly. I'm just thinking I'm probably a little nuts myself, and that all of us have our quirks." He waved a hand. "My family is convinced I'm over the edge about my diet and workout regimens. The thought of being locked up because I'm a little weird just gave me pause."

Nona chuckled. "Point taken, and I agree that we're all a little crazy. It's just that some of us need more medical intervention than others, and those who aren't yet ready to follow a regimen of medication at home need to be in a supervised environment for a while. So let me rephrase my question. Have you checked to see if any woman in one of those places who fits your burglar's description has taken an unauthorized outing?"

"No."

"Get on it." Nona adjusted the fast-forward speed of the security tapes. "But first I'd really appreciate a cup of coffee if you've got any."

Quincy got the coffee for Nona while he assigned his father the task of calling Quincy's paternal uncle Hugh, a state trooper fast approaching retirement, to check on patient escapees with red hair who'd flown the coop over the last few days. Frank took only seconds longer to complete his task than Quincy did to brew a fresh pot of coffee. He didn't want to serve Nona the thick black sludge he'd made at four that morning.

"Hugh ran a search," Frank informed them. "No fruitcakes have escaped psychiatric wards in Oregon in the last week."

Quincy winced. "No name-calling, Dad. Let's just refer to these people as confused—or something."

Frank paused while Quincy set a mug of coffee on the built-in desk near Nona's elbow. "Excuse me for breathin'. What put a burr under your saddle?"

Quincy had no idea why he was taking umbrage. "Sorry, Dad. It's just— Oh, never mind. Continue with your report."

"The most recent escape of a *confused* person was eight days ago, a man with tattoos all over his face. No redheaded women, period, Irish or otherwise, in over six months, and all of 'em that escaped earlier than that got picked up and taken back where they belonged. Of course, this Ceara gal could have dyed her hair."

Quincy mentally shook his head. Ceara's hair was a natural red. He would have bet the bank on it. "So where does that leave us?" he mused aloud.

Nona chuckled. "Well, it doesn't leave us with a druid who's nearly five hundred years old. We'll get to the bottom of it. Just relax. Watching camera footage takes patience." She took a sip of coffee, her gaze never leaving the screens. All Quincy saw were frames of the ranch during the dead of night, when nothing stirred except for an occasional horse in its stall. "We'll see where she came onto the property, how she got into the building, and everything she did after she got inside. Trust me on it. And we'll have the weak spots in the system fixed before a lamb can shake its tail."

Quincy had complete faith in Nona Redcliff and in the security system she'd installed. "I'm not worried. It just baffles me how she got in. You come out to check the equipment every six months, and you know immediately at the observation center when a camera goes haywire. It's hard for me to swallow that this happened because of component failure."

Two hours later, Quincy still wasn't worried, even though the camera footage had shown nothing out of the ordinary. He'd given his dad the comfortable leather desk chair while he sat on the less cushioned caster seat reserved for the occasional office visitor. He and Frank sat behind Nona, watching the screens just as closely as she did. The remainder of Nona's team had left the house to test fence perimeter cameras and examine every square inch of the arena. Quincy hoped they'd report back soon that they had found a point of entry.

As for the camera footage, nothing popped up. Absolutely *nothing*. Glancing at the time of the footage being viewed, which was three hundred hours, Quincy was about to lose patience and ask Nona to increase the fast-forward speed. But no, wait. Quincy saw a flash of bright light and knew his dad and Nona had also seen it, because they stiffened.

"What the hell was *that*?" Quincy asked.

Nona clicked on the upper right frame of monitor four to enlarge the view, reversed the footage, and then they all watched that section of film again, this time in the slowest mode possible. Again, there was a blinding flare of light, and the next instant, Ceara stood in Beethoven's stall. Her delicately sculpted face was just as Quincy remembered, too pretty for words, and even on camera, that red hair was extraordinary. She had a dazed look, suggesting that she felt disoriented and confused. She stood on the center of a star-shaped piece of cloth. At each point of the star was affixed a stone that appeared to glow eerily blue. As Ceara stepped off the cloth, the light in the stones vanished. She wobbled on her feet. Then she leaned against the black stallion that normally allowed no one but Quincy to touch him. To Quincy's consternation, Beethoven never even twitched his tail. Instead, he turned his head to nuzzle Ceara's shoulder as if he were reuniting with an old and trusted friend.

After seeming to regain some of her strength, Ceara carefully folded the star, keeping the stones at the center as if to protect them. She then placed the bundle inside the tapestry satchel, which already bulged with other items. Quincy had searched the bag earlier, but he hadn't noticed the star. He guessed that he had mistaken the bundle of cloth for clothing, and wondered what else he might have missed.

There was no time to return to the arena right then to collect the satchel. "Back up," he told Nona. "I want to watch that again. It's a trick of some kind. She used an explosion of light so the cameras couldn't record how she got into the stall."

"That's the only explanation," Nona agreed.

But after several replays, they still could see nothing, because the flare of brightness caused a whiteout. Again and again, it looked as if Ceara had simply appeared in the stall from out of nowhere.

Nona used her cell phone to call one of her subordinates. "I want you to go over the black stallion's stall again," she ordered. "Keep a lookout for anything that could have created a bright flash of light." She listened for a moment. "I know you've examined every square inch of the stall, Matt. But you'll be searching for something else this time." Pause. "Yes, I know, but that's how the cookie crumbles."

She ended the call. "Lunchtime," she said over her shoulder. "It's only eleven, but Matt's already watching the clock for noon break." She backed up the footage again. "Okay, one more time, and then I think we should move on to see what she does and where she goes inside the arena after gaining entry. Agreed?"

"Agreed. If she went near the feed room or hay storage, I swear to God, she'll be an old woman before she gets out of jail."

They resumed watching the footage. After resting against the horse, Ceara wobbled to the stall gate to peer out at the exercise arena. Then, apparently exhausted, she collected her satchel and made herself a bed in the straw in one corner of the stall and lay down to sleep.

"That's exactly where I found her just before dawn," Quincy said. "How the hell does that make sense? Keep watching her. I can't believe she went to the trouble of trespassing onto my land and breaking into my arena, only to take a nap."

"I'm with you on that." Nona let the camera footage continue forward, increasing the speed to save time. After a few minutes, she said, "Good morning, Quincy. There you are, coming in through the personnel door. Our druid is still fast asleep. Maybe she just got tired and planned to do some mischief later, unaware that you always start your day so early."

"This makes no sense." Anger burned at the back of Quincy's throat. "During that bright flash, she somehow got into that stall, and she damned well had a reason."

"Unless she's tellin' the truth, and she just got dropped there," Frank inserted.

Quincy sent his father a querulous glance. "Come on, Dad. Have you lost your mind?"

Frank sat forward on his chair, his gaze fixed on the frame where Ceara was stirring awake. When she struggled to her feet, he rubbed his jaw and frowned. "That outfit she's got on—looks like the real thing to me."

Chill bumps rose on Quincy's arms. "Dad, people create costumes like that all the time. They may *look* authentic, but they aren't."

Frank sighed and stood up. "I reckon you're right." He stepped over to shake hands with Nona. "Good seein' you again." Turning to Quincy, he added, "I'm goin' into town for a bit. Got some errands to run. I'll stop somewhere and grab us some lunch. We'll talk about this some more after my brain has had a break."

Quincy's own brain felt weary, so he couldn't begrudge his father a little time to recharge. "There's a great health food deli on Third."

"Health food?" Frank groaned. "I had my mouth all

set for a big, juicy hamburger loaded with cheese, and an extra-large order of fries."

"You know I don't eat crap like that."

Frank shrugged. "Okay, fine, health food. But I'll order sandwiches, none of the damned green stuff."

"I'll have a kale wrap. The gal knows me. Tell her the usual for me, but to add some bean sprouts this time."

Frank pretended to shudder as he left the room. Nona laughed and shook her head as she resumed watching the camera footage, once again backing up to midnight.

"Isn't that pointless at this stage?" Quincy asked. "With that bright flash, we can't see how she got in."

Nona sighed. "I've learned from experience that I can miss one little detail on a film, and when I finally find it, all the pieces fall together. Sticking tight is my job. There's no need for you to stay."

Quincy had all the ranches covered for the day, and he preferred to keep Nona company until Clint got home with his sick wife. Then, and only then, would his concern for his beloved horses take second seat to his worry for Loni. "Two sets of eyes are better than one. I want this nailed down before the day is over."

Chapter Three

Frank returned an hour and a half later, his arms laden with a cardboard box crowned with two sack lunches from Quincy's favorite deli. As he strode through the kitchen to the formal dining room, he hollered at Quincy to join him. Quincy abandoned Nona to do her job and followed his dad up the hallway.

"I didn't order soft drinks," Frank informed him. "I figured you'd rather have water. And I favor coffee. Nothin' that dissolves a penny overnight is goin' into my stomach unless it's laced with Jack Daniel's."

Quincy was too tired to inform his father that pennies didn't really dissolve in carbonated drinks. "You guessed right on the water. Normally I'm well on my way to downing my daily eighty ounces by now." Quincy grabbed the sack with a Q scribbled on its fold. "What's in the box?"

"Stuff from a safety-deposit box at the bank. Been years since I opened it. Last time was shortly before your mama died, I think." Frank grabbed his own lunch. "The box will keep. After flyin' in from Portland, we didn't get home until four this mornin', and I'd barely grabbed a wink before the sirens woke me up. Didn't eat dinner last night or any breakfast. My belly button is gnawing a hole through my backbone."

Quincy went to the kitchen to grab a glass of water for himself and a cup of black coffee for his father. The two men settled at one end of the long oak table to eat. Before beginning, they crossed themselves and said a blessing. Nona appeared in the archway just as Quincy took a bite of his kale wrap.

"We're breaking for lunch," she said. With a glance at her watch, she added, "Thirty minutes each way and thirty to eat. We'll be back at about two forty-five, give or take."

Quincy managed to swallow. "Enjoy the break. See you in a bit."

Nona left. Quincy turned back to his lunch. Mary, from the deli, had sent him a side of sugar peas and hummus dip. Frank had a bag of greasy potato chips and a fruit tart, one of those assembly-line things full of fat, white flour, and sugar, and with little nutrient value. "How can you eat shit like that?" Quincy asked.

"Just like this." Frank took a huge bite of a double-decker sandwich and grinned with a bulging cheek. After chewing a moment, he swallowed and added, "I'm surprised your eyes ain't green, son. You eat the strangest things. That kale, for instance. Why do you think it's so great?"

"It's a super vegetable." Quincy knew that fell on deaf ears. "Full of iron and calcium. You should read about it, Dad."

"Readin' about it is all I'll ever do. Dee Dee gets some spinach into me every now and then, and I'll even force down asparagus and broccoli on occasion, but that's about as healthy as I'm willin' to eat. I'm a meat-and-potatoes man. I do have a salad every night, but only because she won't serve my main courses until my bowl's clean."

"Meat and potatoes with lots of butter, gravy, and grease tossed in, not to mention heart-attack breakfasts."

Frank chuckled. "I'll die happy. You'll die hungry for some real food."

The argument was one of long standing, so both of them tucked back into their lunches without speaking again. When the sacks and napkins had been dispensed with, Quincy returned to the dining room. "Okay, what's in the carton? I know you didn't open the safety-deposit box at the bank and bring that stuff home just for the exercise."

Frank moved to the end of the table and opened the cardboard flaps. "Old family heirlooms, son. I doubt you've ever clapped eyes on 'em. After your mama passed away, I pretty much couldn't bring myself to look at any of these things. Not because my family history no longer mattered to me, but because your mama got so excited about every little thing. Every couple of months, she'd insist on a trip to the bank, just so she could read this or that. She used to swear that someday, after you boys was grown, she'd track my family clear back to Ireland. I just couldn't face all them sweet memories, you know?"

Quincy's memories of his mother were dim. He'd been young when she died, and when he tried to picture her face, all he saw was the photograph of her that his father had kept on his nightstand until he finally remarried. "I wish I'd known her better."

Frank's eyes grew misty. "Yep, me, too. But it wasn't meant to be, I don't guess, and life goes on. There was a time when I didn't think it would, but now . . ." His voice trailed off as he lowered a hand inside the box. "Well, now I have Dee Dee and a lot of wonderful memories of your mama. In many ways, I'm luckier than most men ever thought of bein'."

Quincy inched closer to the box. "So what have you got there?"

"Harrigan history," Frank said softly. "Some of it to be proud of, and some of it skeletons in our closet."

"Skeletons?"

Frank trailed his fingertips over the leather binding of what looked like an ancient journal about to fall apart with age. "Not all my ancestors was what I'd call normal, let's just say." He motioned Quincy closer. "Come on. Have a look."

Quincy moved to stand beside his dad, acutely conscious as he did that he was only a couple of inches taller than Frank and in almost every other way his duplicate — same build, same square and work-hardened hands, and the same coloring. *Family.* In that moment, as Quincy stared into the carton, the meaning of that word took on a whole new significance. The old Bible and journals were a physical record of Harrigan history.

"Damn, Dad. I'm afraid to touch anything for fear it'll disintegrate."

Frank chuckled. "I kept all this stuff for you kids. Not much point in that if you're afraid to look at it. If one of the bindings falls apart, we can always get it restored."

With cautious reverence, Quincy lifted the Bible from the container. The cover was dark brown leather and fragile with dryness. He could imagine the hands of countless Harrigan ancestors touching the book just as he was now. He turned to the first page, which sported a yellowed and faded family tree. The name O'Hourigan leaped out at him. "Shit, it's true, then. We changed our name from O'Hourigan to Harrigan."

"I thought O'Hourigan sounded familiar," Frank said. "I only needed a quick look inside to know I wasn't rememberin' wrong. Back in the eighteen hundreds, when the Irish immigrated here to escape the famine, name changes were pretty common. Sometimes to make them sound less Irish, other times to make them simpler to say and spell." He flashed Quincy a quick grin. "O'Hourigan, for instance. Here in America, H-O-U-R is pronounced like the hour of the day, with no H sound. Changin' the spellin' was probably a smart move. Everybody probably would've called me Hour-Again."

Quincy smiled and nodded. He'd mispronounced his share of surnames. Behind the original family-tree page, his ancestors had slipped in additional parchment or paper as the years passed to keep track of marriages, births, and deaths. He noted that the record ended with his dad's generation.

"You stopped keeping track?" Quincy asked his father.

"No, of course not. Your mother just felt this Bible was getting too fragile, and she bought a new one. I have it over at my place. She went back a few generations and then recorded our marriage. All you kids is in there." His voice turned thick. "After she died, I had to enter her death and Samantha's birth. It took me a few months to muster the courage, but I finally got it done. Had myself a good cry afterward, feelin' like I'd just lost her all over again. Pain like I can't explain. Nowadays, it's easier for me. I made note of my marriage to Dee Dee, and I've kept track of Clint's babies, and the little one Sam and Tucker lost before it ever got born." Frank's eyes grew moist. "I just hope and pray I won't have to enter the death of another loved one anytime soon."

"Loni." Quincy didn't state it as a question. He knew Clint's wife was never far from Frank's mind. "Any updates since I talked to Clint this morning?"

Frank shook his head. "Not on her condition. Zach

called to tell me Clint is busy tryin' to get ready to transport her home. He's worried about how she'll handle the flight and about them removin' the IV catheters. Once they get a vein, he hates for 'em to lose it. She's so dehydrated that it's the very devil to find a new one. But the nurses at the center refuse to leave 'em in. They say new catheters will have to be used if she's seen here, anyway."

Quincy sighed. For a few hours, the relentless sadness that had formed a lump in his throat had been pushed aside by the events of the morning. Now his concern for Loni came flooding back. All he could do was pray for her. He believed in the great power of prayer, but even so, he was, by nature, a do-it-yourself man. Loni's illness made him feel so damned helpless.

He took a seat at the table to study the family tree. The first entry dated back to the seventeen hundreds, making this Bible nearly three hundred years old. The thought was mind-boggling.

"Dad," he said after a long silence. "Look at this." Frank came around the table to peer over Quincy's shoulder. "Practically all the first wives of your ancestors died at young ages."

"Dyin' young wasn't uncommon back then. Men often lost their wives durin' childbirth or shortly afterward from childbed fever."

Quincy knew that was true, but the theory didn't hold up under closer examination. "Most of the second wives made it. I mean, well, they eventually died, of course, a few of them at fairly young ages, but a good majority of them lived nice, long lives for that day."

Frank fetched his cooling coffee and took a seat beside Quincy to study the tree himself. "I'll be damned. You're right."

A prickly sensation moved over Quincy's skin. He

could only hope he wasn't allowing his imagination to get the better of him. "Mom died at only thirty-one, which was really young by our standards, even then. And now there's Loni. She's what—only thirty-five?" He met his father's gaze. "What about your father and brothers, Dad? Did any of their first wives die?" Quincy knew his uncles and saw them fairly often, but he wasn't familiar with details of their younger years. "Like before I was born, or when I was really little, I mean. Any deaths?"

A thoughtful frown pleated Frank's brow. "My father, your grandpa Zachary, did lose his first wife, now that I think of it. They were both real young when they married. I think she was only eighteen. Then, right here on Harrigan land, she was injured in a farm accident and bled out before Dad could get her to the hospital. It wasn't much of a hospital back then, but he always blamed himself for not gettin' her there in time. Later he made a trip back to Ireland to see some relatives and met my mother, Mariah. They was married over there, and she lived here on this land to a ripe old age." Frank smiled slightly. "You remember Mama, don't you?"

Quincy sank back on his chair. "Of course I do. Not as well as I'd like. I was still pretty young when she passed away, but I'll never forget her Irish brogue and her big laugh. And, oh, man, how I loved her soda bread."

Frank nodded. "No one makes it like Mama did. It was her mother's recipe, straight from the old country."

"So Grandpa lost his first wife when she was really young."

"Yep." Frank took a sip of coffee. "And come to think of it, my brothers all lost their first wives, too. Paul lost his—well, that was truly a tragedy. They'd had three little kids, and after she gave birth to the fourth baby, she got postnatal depression real bad. He came home one evenin' to find her dead in the bathtub. She'd slit her wrists."

"Sweet Jesus," Quincy whispered.

"Back then they didn't have many treatments for postnatal depression," Frank expounded. "Women were expected to buck up and just get on with it. Paul nearly went off the deep end when he found her. For a long time, he blamed himself."

Quincy could understand that. To walk in and find your depressed wife dead by her own hand would be devastating.

"Then there was my brother Marcus. He lost his first wife in a car accident. They was on their way to church, and he had his whole family in the vehicle. A pickup truck came over the center line, and there was a head-on collision. Nobody else was bad hurt, but Marcus's wife came out of it with a severed main artery. She died at the scene. Then there was Hugh, whose first wife was an undiagnosed hemo—" Frank broke off, frowned, and waved a hand. "Hemo-something-or-other."

"Hemophiliac?"

"That's it," Frank said, snapping his fingers. "She died early in the marriage, and Hugh, now with his second wife, has five healthy kids, thank God."

Quincy's mouth had gone dry. "Are you seeing the same pattern I'm seeing, Dad? Your father, you, and all your brothers lost your first wives, and each and every one of them died of things related to the blood. Mama hemorrhaged to death giving birth to Sam. Paul's wife slit her wrists and bled to death. Marcus lost his wife in a car accident due to a severed main artery. Hugh's first wife died of hemophilia." Quincy had to stop and swallow before he could go on. "Now Loni may be dying of leukemia."

"What're you sayin'?" Frank asked. "That this Ceara gal might be tellin' the truth?"

Quincy wasn't sure what he was saying, but this coincidence spooked the hell out of him. "I'm just looking and seeing a pattern, is all. Did you keep up with other branches of the Harrigan family?"

Frank shook his head. "My dad had a fallin'-out with his old man way back when, and he lost touch with all his siblings. If any of them are still alive, I reckon they're in the States somewhere, but Dad never tried to find them, and I never saw much point. To me they're strangers."

"I wonder if there were other Harrigan men who lost their first wives in similar ways." For Quincy, it was a scary thought. He wasn't a superstitious man. He knew that druids had once existed in both Ireland and Scotland, but he'd never for a moment believed that they possessed magical powers. "I wish we could track down some of your other relatives."

"It'd probably be more trouble than it's worth. Me callin' folks out of the blue to ask if any first wives died at young ages? They'd think I was crazy." Frank carefully lifted a journal from the box and opened it. It looked more fragile to Quincy than any of the others. "I never read much of this one," he said. "Far as I'm concerned, it's just a bunch of hocus-pocus. Your mama was fascinated by it, though."

Quincy leaned over to peer at the book. Much of the writing was in archaic English, and some of it was in another weird language.

"Irish Gaelic," Frank explained. "If it looks strange to you, that's because it *is*. At least, to us who never learned the language. As I recall it was based on the Latin alphabet and used fewer letters."

Quincy began studying what appeared to be a recipe,

written in English but still difficult to decipher because of the badly faded ink, odd wording, and elaborate script.

"It's a spell, I think," Frank said. "There was some real weird characters in my family. Apparently they practiced witchcraft of some kind. That's why I've never read much of this journal. Never wanted any part of it."

"And Mama did?"

"Your mama did some research and insisted the *spells* were actually beautiful prayers. My Emily, she was a sweetheart. Never saw the bad in anybody, and especially not in a Harrigan. She couldn't bring herself to believe my ancestors dabbled in anything dark or evil."

Frank carefully closed the book and looked at Quincy. "As much as I prefer to avoid this kinda shit, I can't stop thinkin' about this Ceara woman," he said slowly. "What if she's for real, a druid from centuries ago who traveled forward in time to end a curse on our family?"

Quincy had been mentally circling that possibility ever since he'd seen the old family tree, but it shocked him to hear his father echo his thoughts. Frank always kept both feet firmly rooted in reality. "Dad, you're a devout Catholic clear to your core. You don't believe in stuff like that."

Frank held up a staying hand. "I know it sounds crazy, but there's no denyin' that my Emily bled to death givin' birth to Sam, or that my father's first wife bled to death, or that the first wives of each of my brothers died from things havin' to do with the blood. Now Loni, Clint's wife, is at death's door with a rare form of leukemia. I think you're right; there *is* a pattern. And we'd be fools to ignore it. Loni's life may hang in the balance."

It was Quincy's turn to throw up a hand. "Whoa. That woman says she came here to marry me. Well, she didn't specifically say *me*, but I'm the one she sought out, and

I'm the only single male left in our branch of the family." Quincy cocked his head. "What are you saying, Dad, that I should slap a ring on her finger? That's nuts. Why are we even entertaining the notion that the woman uttered a single word of truth? Traveling forward in time? Ancient curses? Hell, according to her, she's of druid blood, and so are all the Harrigans. What exactly *is* a druid, anyway? In my opinion, they were simply learned people who found it easy to hoodwink the uneducated into believing they had special powers. It was all a bunch of BS then, and it still is now. Stuff like this doesn't happen in the twenty-first century."

Frank drew a can of Copenhagen from his hip pocket. With a flick of his wrist, he tamped down the contents and put a chew in his mouth. "You mind findin' me a spitter? I need to think, and I do my best thinkin' with a wad of tobacco tucked inside my lip."

Quincy left the dining room to hunt up an empty water bottle. He detested his father's tobacco habit and wished Frank would quit, but he'd come to accept over the years that it would never happen. At least Quincy's stepmom, Dee Dee, kept Frank's use of tobacco at a minimum. She pitched a holy fit if she smelled wintergreen on his breath, wouldn't allow Frank to enjoy a chew inside their house, and essentially forced him to sneak behind her back to get his nicotine fixes.

As Quincy passed his in-home office, he saw that Nona Redcliff had returned and was just slipping out of her jacket. He stopped to ask, "Before you took off for lunch, did you happen to find anything odd in the camera footage?"

Nona shook her head. "Nope. If I didn't know it was impossible, I'd swear that woman dropped into Beethoven's stall from out of nowhere."

A cold wave of uneasiness washed over Quincy. "Well, you're right. That *is* impossible, so keep on it, Nona. I'm counting on you to make sense of it."

"You got it." Her brown eyes twinkled with humor. "Being Native American, I was raised hearing tall tales, but even as a child at my grandfather's knee, I never believed any of them. The stars are *not* stepping-stones to the afterworld. The Milky Way wasn't created by snow dropping from the paws of a large bear racing across the sky. It follows that druids cannot travel forward in time. I don't know what the real story is, but I guarantee I'll have an answer soon."

Quincy hoped so. Feeling slightly off balance, he returned to the dining room. Frank gratefully accepted the empty, clear plastic water bottle and removed the cap to spit. "Quincy, don't blow a gasket, okay? I got somethin' to say, and the only way I know is straight-out. I think you should either drop the charges against Ceara O'Ceallaigh or bail her out of jail, one or the other."

Quincy met his father's gaze. "Do *what*? You've got to be kidding. Why the hell would I do either? She broke into my stable. Beethoven is worth two hundred grand, for God's sake! I could probably sell him for two hundred and fifty, just like that." Quincy snapped his fingers. "She must have had a purpose in mind, and it sure as hell wasn't to take a nap in the straw. Give me one good reason why I should get her out of the clinker."

Frank rocked back on his chair. "While you was gone, I took a little journey backward in time, recallin' old stories told to me by my grandfather. He was Irish, straight from the homeland, and I can remember him sayin' that a heap of his ancestors had magical powers. Maybe we *are* druids, Quincy, and over time, we forgot about it." Frank paused for effect. "One of my buyers, who's also a good friend, found out a few months back that his great-great-great-grandmother was a Louisiana slave. He never knew he was part black until he paid someone to trace his family. Ain't that somethin'?"

Quincy shrugged. "There was a time when people preferred to forget if they had certain ancestry. The blacks and Native Americans for sure. Hell, even the Irish and Germans had reason. If a family was trying to bury the secret deep, it wouldn't have been something they'd have talked about at the supper table to make their kids aware of it."

"Maybe the same can be said of druid blood in the Harrigan family, a secret my father or grandfather decided to keep buried." Frank put the mouth of the water bottle to his lips again. As he capped the container, he added, "I don't get why some folks are sensitive about bloodlines, but in some cases, I reckon there's good cause. It wasn't all that long ago that blacks, Irish, Germans, Jews, and Native Americans was discriminated against."

"In a lot of instances, they still are, Dad."

Frank nodded. "Reckon so, shameful as it is." His jet brows drew together in a frown. "And maybe, for similar reasons, my family wanted nobody to know of the druid blood. Think about it. At the next American Quarter Horse Association meetin', how would people react if I announced that I'm part druid? Don't you think a good share of folks might avoid me like I had a nasty virus they might catch? That right there would be reason enough for my family to have buried the truth."

Quincy's knees felt as if they'd turned to water. He took a seat across from his dad. "I wouldn't announce that you're a druid if you want to keep your position on the board of directors. Come on, Dad, this is a time for clear thinking. We can't buy into this woman's story. It makes no sense."

"Nope, not a lick," Frank agreed, "but that don't negate the fact that she appeared, like magic, in Beethoven's stall. Them there cameras don't lie, son." He hooked a thumb over his chest at the box. "And that damned family tree don't, either. You saw the pattern. I saw it. Our first wives die, damn it. And now Loni is dyin'." Frank sat forward on the chair to nail Quincy with a gaze that sparked like flint. "Sweet Christ, think. I know you're concerned about your horses, but bottom line, is that damn stallion as important to you as Loni? What if this Ceara gal can save her life? What if *you* can? Would you hesitate?"

Quincy could no longer feel the seat of the chair under his ass. He groped for words. Was insanity catching? But no, Frank hadn't even seen the woman except on camera. Quincy's brain felt like mush. Finally, his tongue moved. "Of course I wouldn't hesitate, Dad. I love Loni, too. And I love my brother! I know he's going through sheer hell right now. But think about what you're suggesting. I'm supposed to go bail a crazy loon out of jail, and—"

Frank held up a thick, work-roughened forefinger. "A confused lady, you mean?"

"All right, *confused*. Majorly confused, Dad. And in order to save Loni, I'm supposed to marry her? She may have entered my arena to harm my horses. She's sure as hell *confused* by any normal standards. Give me a break! Hand her over to a good psychiatrist and she'll be taking medication for the rest of her natural life."

"Point taken. Maybe she is crazy. But if we get her out of jail, we can put her to the true test, and it's better than any examination by a psychiatrist."

Quincy mentally circled that. "The true test? I'm not following."

Frank spit into the bottle again. "Introduce her to Loni. Let them touch hands." He snapped his fingers. "Loni will know in a heartbeat if this Ceara gal is a fake. A simple touch, and Loni will know. She's more accurate than any damned lie detector."

All the breath rushed from Quincy's lungs. He sank back on his chair. "Damn, Dad, that's brilliant. Loni *will* know, won't she?"

"Of course she will."

Quincy thought about it. "There's a problem. If I drop the charges, and then Loni tells us Ceara is a lunatic, I'll have let her get out of jail, and she'll go scot-free."

"Don't drop the charges then," Frank said softly. "Just post her bail."

Chapter Four

Before Quincy took off for the police station, he needed some time to think. After bidding his father farewell, he felt drawn to Beethoven's stall. If Quincy had a favorite place, he guessed this was it. Some folks liked to sit along a creek, others under a tree or on a hill. For Quincy, tranquillity was found with his stallion.

"Hey, boss," a hired hand called. "How's Clint's wife doing?"

Quincy turned to see Pierce Howlitz, a thin redhead with so many freckles that he appeared to have a perpetual suntan. Soon to be twenty-three, the kid still had the cocky swagger of an untried youth, which had made Quincy worry at first about hiring him, but over time Pierce had proven himself to be a decent sort with a mild manner. Quincy had long since decided that the air of machismo was mostly for show, Pierce's way of trying to compensate for his slight build and lack of musculature. Dumb. When push came to shove, Pierce was deceptively strong and agile, a great fellow with horses.

"Not so good, Pierce, but thanks for asking."

The younger man settled in beside Quincy at the gate to study the stallion. "He's fixing to be a daddy again, you know. I was looking at the breeding records yesterday, and Symphony should foal around the middle of April. I was wondering if you've thought of names for the new baby yet. It's only a few weeks away."

Quincy had been so worried about Loni he hadn't given a thought to the matter. "No, actually, I haven't." He glanced sideways at the youth's freckled countenance. "You got some ideas?"

Pierce grinned sheepishly and dipped his head. "Well, I just been thinking. It's your stable policy to always pick names that have to do with music or singers or famous composers. For a filly, I kind of favor Crescendo. And"— he broke off and widened his grin—"don't laugh, but what about Liberace if it's a colt?"

Quincy considered the names for a moment then finally nodded. "Good choices, Pierce. I'll keep them in mind when the time comes. Just remember that the AQHA can't register two horses under the same name. It'll depend on whether or not those two are already taken."

Pierce's neck had turned a ruddy pink, a telltale sign that Quincy's approval of his ideas had pleased him. He nodded and stepped back. "I hope Loni gets better, sir. I've been praying for her." The blush moved upward to his cheeks. "Some people just *say* that and don't really mean it, but I do. I pray for her every day."

"I appreciate that, and I know Clint will, too, when I tell him."

Pierce hitched up his pants, a habit of his because his belt failed to keep his waistband from riding low. "Well, I better get back to work or Bingo will be calling me a slacker."

Quincy nodded, making a mental note that the kid had grit and was bucking for a future as his foreman. He resumed his study of Beethoven, trying as he did to focus his thoughts once again on Ceara O'Ceallaigh and whether he should bail her out of jail. A dark object in the corner of the stall caught Quincy's attention. *The satchel.* He scaled the gate to collect the crazy-looking hat and small piece of luggage, then hesitated and shot the bundle a suspicious look. This stuff had appeared with a flash of light along with Ceara. Gingerly he fingered it, and then took it directly to his arena office, where he called Frank on his cell.

"Hey, Dad, sorry to bug you, but in all the excitement, I totally forgot that Ceara's satchel was still in Beethoven's stall." He sank onto the leather caster chair at his desk. "I went through it this morning, but I didn't really examine the contents. I was more interested in finding vials or traces of powder in case she'd laced my horses' feed with something poisonous."

"You gonna go through it again now?" Frank asked. "Chances are Nona's boys already did that."

Quincy nodded. "Yeah, it's probably been searched, but I see no harm in doing it again. Thought maybe you'd like to join me."

"Be there in five," Frank told him.

Quincy ended the call and rocked back on the chair to study the satchel he'd set on his desk. The bag was made of tapestry, an attractive variegation of autumn colors that wasn't the least bit faded. His mouth twisted into a smirk. The style of the grip looked antediluvian, but the cloth itself was bright and unworn. *Almost five hundred years old, my ass,* he thought.

A screech of brakes and a slammed door announced Frank's arrival. A moment later he strode into the office, beating his promised time by nearly three minutes. Quincy took off his Stetson and sent it sailing toward the hat tree, where it caught, spun, and then settled in place on a top branch. Quincy grinned at the small accomplishment. He seldom missed, and he sure didn't want to do so in front of his dad. "Damn, Dad, what'd you do, fly to get here so fast?"

Frank chuckled as he sauntered over the Cyprus planks to take a seat across from Quincy. "Maybe I beamed myself down. I hear tell that people of druid blood can do that."

Quincy shot him an irked don't-let's-start-that-again look. "She's not really a druid, Dad. She's a twenty-first-century schizophrenic — or something along those lines."

Frank settled his gaze on the grip. "Mighty pretty lady to be crazy."

Quincy preferred not to think about Ceara's delicate features, big blue eyes, and brilliant red hair. "I don't think insanity is choosy about the appearance of its victims." He stood to open the satchel. "You ready for some snooping?"

Frank pushed to his feet. "Ready as I'll ever be. What's that on top?"

Quincy withdrew the carefully folded cloth. "When I opened the bag early this morning, I thought it was a garment of some kind, but now that I've seen the camera footage, I know it's that weird star of Ceara's with the stones at each tip. Remember, she was standing on it when she was *beamed* down."

A chuckle rumbled up from Frank's throat. "No need for sarcasm." He leaned closer as Quincy unfolded the star. Then he whispered, "Holy *shit*."

For an instant, Quincy didn't know what had startled his father, but then he saw that the stones were glowing an eerie blue again. He was so taken aback that he jerked his hands away from the cloth. The instant he did, the stones turned back to ordinary gray.

"Holy shit is right," Quincy said as he struggled to regain his composure. "There's a simple explanation, Dad. I'm sure there are substances that can be painted on surfaces that react to body heat. When I touched the stones while unfolding the cloth, the warmth of my hands made them glow."

Frank jerked off his Stetson and tossed it on the tall metal file cabinet along a near wall. It skidded across the smooth surface and tumbled to the floor. Quincy opened his mouth to give Frank a hard time when his father announced, "Or the stones react to the touch of a person with druid blood."

"Oh, for God's—" Quincy broke off at Frank's glare. "Okay, okay." A taut silence fell between the two men, broken only by the electronic hum of the office equipment and a sound alert from the computer that an e-mail had just come in. For as long as Quincy could remember, he had admired his father's no-nonsense approach to life. Now all of a sudden Frank seemed all too willing to believe in the impossible. "Dad, can you at least *try* to keep your head on straight about this?"

His features drawn with exhaustion, Frank met Quincy's gaze. "I've got a daughter dyin', son, so maybe I'm wishin' on rainbows and takin' leaps of faith I normally wouldn't. Those doctors are sayin' there's no hope, that she's already as good as dead. Is it so wrong of me to be feelin' just a little desperate right now?"

His father's response struck Quincy like icy ocean spray. He hung his head for a second, staring at the cloth star, ashamed of himself for being so hell-bent on sticking to scientifically proven facts. Miracles *could* happen. Quincy simply wasn't certain that Ceara O'Ceallaigh was heaven-sent. There were other places people could drop in from—or climb up out of.

"I know how you feel, Dad," Quincy replied in a voice gone husky with emotion. "At least, I think I do, because I'm feeling the same. Of course I want to throw common sense to the wind and grab at any possible chance, no matter how crazy. You know how I feel about Loni. We all adore her. We're still reeling. We feel helpless. I'd do anything to save her, but—"

"Then stop bein' so damned *reasonable* for a while and try thinkin' outside the box," Frank cut in. Quincy gaped. His father's tone had changed to one that sounded like an industrial cutting tool. "Just this once, Quincy, let's believe in miracles and magic, even if it turns out we're a couple of fools." Frank raised an arm and banged a fist on the desk. Quincy's hand shot out and rescued the lamp as Frank continued. "I need something to hang on to right now. If Loni tells us this Ceara gal is a fake, then I'll let it go. But, damn it, what if Loni tells us she's for real?"

Quincy had no ready answer, so he began emptying the satchel, carefully placing each item on his desk.

Frank whistled when he saw the ivory-backed brush and hand mirror. "Give me them things. My God, would you look at that? We're talkin' genuine ivory. If it's fake, you can kiss my bare ass in broad daylight on the courthouse steps."

"I'll pass." Quincy fingered the back of the brush, which was intricately carved. It felt and looked like real ivory. "Really examine this, Dad. I agree it's probably genuine ivory, but does it look hundreds of years old to you?"

Frank took the brush and fanned his fingers over the bristles. "Genuine pig bristles," he announced thoughtfully. "You know how long it's been since I seen pig bristles? My mama used to have a pig-bristle toothbrush."

After further examination, Frank sighed, the sound defeated. "You're right, though. Mama's toothbrush wore down to not much more than nubs with years of use. This hairbrush shows little wear as yet."

"Can brushes and mirrors like this still be purchased?" Quincy asked.

"I imagine so," Frank conceded, "if you're willin' to pay the price. You ain't gonna find a set like this at a department store; that's for damned sure. You'd have to special-order it."

"So Ceara O'Ceallaigh may be a wealthy lunatic."

"A wealthy *confused* person," Frank corrected.

Quincy ignored the jibe and dug deeper in the satchel to pull out a thimble that also looked to be made of ivory. "Wow. I think this is the real thing, too."

Frank was still fingering the brush. "Go with me for a minute," he said gruffly. "Say Ceara is really from the fifteen hundreds and she traveled forward in time with these things. In her day, they might have been new, or fairly new, because she's young, and they wouldn't have been showing any wear yet. You followin' me? A woman back then probably had only one brush, mirror, and comb her whole life long, so things were made to last, not like the plastic and nylon crap we buy today. Travelin' forward in time wouldn't make anything instantly old, would it, any more than it made Ceara instantly old?"

A bitch of a headache blossomed behind Quincy's eyes. He wanted a miracle for Loni as much as anyone else did, but was his father actually hearing himself? The entire conversation was moving quickly from strange to totally bizarre. But bizarre or not, his dad's theory made sense. If Ceara hadn't aged on her still-unverified trip, why should her possessions?

Damn. He was losing it, really losing it. He dug deeper

inside the satchel and pulled out a silk gown of burnished gold, similar in design to the one Ceara had been wearing that morning. Upon close inspection, Quincy noted that the cloth looked like genuine silk, but the lace trim resembled—what was that needlework his grandma Mariah had once done, tatting or something like that? As young as he'd been, Quincy could still remember hovering by her rocker to watch her arthritic fingers create lace as delicate as spiderwebs.

Holding the dress up in front of him, Quincy wanted to believe it was a reproduction, but his common sense told him that probably wasn't true. Who in her right mind would go to so much effort to create a replica? And there were other things inside the bag—odds and ends that defied explanation. An intricately hand-carved wooden horse. Prayers and recipes written in elaborate script on paper so different from any Quincy had ever seen that he could no longer tell himself everything he saw was fake. Wordlessly he handed each item to Frank after he'd examined it, and his dad, equally silent, gave it a second looking over.

What if? Quincy was a practical man, but he kept remembering the appeal in Ceara's gaze as the cops took her away. She was either unbalanced or completely convinced she was telling the truth. Of course, that didn't mean she wasn't some kind of a nut. Quincy was still pretty much sure that had to be the case.

But Loni . . . she would know for sure.

"All right," he said hoarsely, "I'll bail her out of jail, Dad. I'm not sure it's smart, but I'll do it."

Frank's shoulders relaxed, angling into a slump beneath his fleece-lined jacket. He nodded. "It's what we gotta do, son. Clint will have Loni home and settled in by early evenin'. The only way we can know for sure if this

Ceara woman is legitimate is to let Loni touch her hand. Then, one way or another, we'll have the truth."

"It may not be the truth you're hoping for," Quincy warned.

Frank's haggard face creased in a weary grin. "I'm aware of that. On the other hand, maybe the truth will be an answer to all our prayers."

Ceara jerked awake from an exhausted sleep to the sound of a female voice shouting, "Oh—kee—alley! On your feet. Somebody posted your bail."

Ceara rolled to a sitting position, nearly falling off the narrow cot in the process. Sleep hazed her vision. Every muscle in her body ached and protested the sudden movement. She blinked and rubbed her face, then slowly brought into focus the round countenance of a female guard with eyes as black as currants and skin as brown as a dried hazelnut. The woman's hair crowned her head like a cap, black curls glistening in the light cast from the ceiling by strange, boxlike objects that somehow produced steady light.

"Do ye mean I'm free to go?" Ceara asked as she wobbled to her feet.

The fleshy woman, dressed in a light blue léine and darker trews, opened the cell door and tossed a shiny red sack into Ceara's arms. "Free as a bird. Get dressed. Leave your scrubs on the cot. I'll wait for you at the end of the corridor."

Ceara didn't need to be told twice. She put the bag on her bed and struggled to loosen the drawstring. In all her days, she'd never seen such a sack. It shimmered like polished satin, but to the touch, it felt insubstantial, slick, and a bit stretchy. It made a faint crackling sound as she pulled it open. Inside were her things—the green gown, her ankle-length léine, her underclothes, and her prized velvet slippers. She hurried to clothe herself, ignoring the curious stares of the other women in nearby cells.

"So, you're getting out in record time," Paula, the woman next door, noted. "What did I tell you, sweetie? We're like cattle in a chute, in for a bit and then booted out."

Ceara had no idea how this turn of events had come to pass, but she thanked God that it had. *Freedom.* She had fully expected to be imprisoned for the remainder of her life. She quickly donned her léine, lacing it tight to her waist, and then tugged on her dress.

"Sweet Christ, you wear enough layers," the older woman said. "Does that really work for you out on the streets? Maybe I need to get me an outfit like that."

Ceara didn't know what Paula was talking about, and she had no desire to tarry for an explanation. "'Twas lovely making yer acquaintance," she said breathlessly as she tested her bodice laces. "'Tis my hope that ye shall be set free soon. 'Tis no place fer a gentlewoman."

"Now, that's a new one," the woman said with a husky laugh. "A gentlewoman, am I? I like the sound of that."

Hopping to get her slippers on, Ceara exited the cell. "Farewell, me friend. May ye be in heaven a full hour before the devil knows ye're dead. 'Twill be me prayer that ye become rich and make the journey to New Zealand well before that becomes a worry."

The woman laughed again. "If I had a beer, I'd toast to that, and same back at you. Maybe you'll return to Ireland soon."

As Ceara raced along the corridor, praying the guard hadn't left her behind, she wanted to shout over her shoulder that she would never again see the Ireland of her birth. But 'twas a wee bit of information best kept to herself.

Once out of the cell block, Ceara was led into a small room appointed with only a chest-high bench. Behind it, a balding man in a uniform stamped forms and made her sign papers, one stating that all her personal belongings had been returned to her. " 'Tis not so," she protested. "Sir Quincy Harrigan kept me hat and me satchel, which contains all me belongings except for the clothing on me back."

The man shrugged. "Take it up with Mr. Harrigan. We are responsible only for what was in your possession when we booked you."

Ceara reluctantly signed the paper with a strange writing implement she wanted to take apart and examine. 'Twas not a quill. There was no need to dip it in an inkwell. How did it work? As she signed her name several times, she kept expecting it to run dry, but it didn't.

The man took the documents and slipped them into a folder. "You're free to go, ma'am. Just don't leave town until your court hearing. Since you have no address here, notification of date and time will be sent to you general delivery. Be sure to stop by the main post office every couple of days to see if it has arrived."

Post office? She would have to find out what that meant, but two words she understood clearly. Her heart squeezed. "Court hearing? So I'm still in trouble?"

"Breaking and entering is a serious offense. Getting out on bail doesn't negate the fact that you've been accused of a crime." He jabbed a thumb at some double swinging doors to her left. "Go out that way, and best of luck to you."

Ceara turned to stare at the exit, and suddenly she felt

like a lost child. Where would she find shelter? What would she have to eat? Though it was mid-March, the weather was still bitterly cold here, even more so than at home. Recalling the yellow-haired woman's words about soon being back on the streets, Ceara almost wished she were in the cell again, where she had at least been warm and would have been fed regular meals, even if only bread and gruel.

Trembling with trepidation, she pushed out through the doors and found herself in a large, well-lighted room lined with wooden benches. Quincy Harrigan stood just inside the glass entrance, which led outside. The breadth of his chest and shoulders was enhanced by a bulky blue inar of sorts, one of the oddest garments she'd ever seen. Instead of flowing loosely over his torso and legs, it hugged his upper body and reached only to his waist. Nevertheless he was breathtakingly handsome, everything about him emanating strength. His hat, broad of brim, sat at a forward tilt on his head, revealing the pitch-black hue of his hair at the sides. She fleetingly wondered if he was a descendant of the Black Irish, for his skin was the color of dried chicory root and his eyes were so dark a brown they reminded her of coal polished to a high sheen.

He didn't immediately speak, and Ceara couldn't think what to say. Had Sir Quincy—what was the term?—posted her bail?

"Well," he finally said, "you look none the worse for wear." With the flat of his hand, he pushed open one of the doors. "After you."

Ceara hurried across the gleaming floor and exited in front of him onto a walkway of inlaid stone. At the end, it spilled into an intersecting path that was gray and made of long, rectangular slabs that felt as hard as rock beneath her slippers. She stopped to gape.

"What is this?" she asked. "Not stone, surely, unless ye've learned how to melt and pour it like iron from a forge."

He paused beside her, his expression wary and yet perplexed. "It's cement." When she still looked at him questioningly, he added, "Concrete."

"Ah." Lifting her skirt, Ceara tapped the surface with her toe. " 'Tis strange to me."

A sudden gust of chill wind set her off balance. With a shiver, she accepted that she was still weak from the journey and wondered how long it would be before she regained her strength.

Quincy shrugged out of his inar and draped it over her shoulders. "Use my jacket. It'll keep the cold at bay."

Jacket. She committed the word to memory as the heat of his body radiated from the lining to surround her with warmth. " 'Tis soft with cáera skin," she said appreciatively as she fingered the wool. " 'Tis good to recognize something. So farmers still raise cáera for meat and wool?"

"We call them sheep." The moment he offered that bit of information, he frowned and muttered something she didn't catch. Grasping her elbow, he led her to the rear of the police station, where countless carriages were parked. In her mum's crystal ball, Ceara had seen Sir Quincy's equipage, a gemstone green monstrosity with an enclosed passenger area at the front and a wagon attached to the back. As they approached the vehicle, Ceara was amazed by its actual size. It sat so high off the ground on big, fat wheels that she almost could have bent at the waist and walked underneath it.

"My truck," he said, thumping the right front door. "Sorry about the dirt. I use it at the ranch. It's not fancy, but it gets me around."

As he opened the door, Ceara stopped and tipped her head back to search his expression. This man planned to take her somewhere, and if she left with him, she would be at his mercy. "I am thinking that ye negotiated me release, sir. Is that correct?"

"Against my better judgment, but yes, guilty as charged."

" 'Twas generous of ye." She drew his jacket close. "But where, may I ask, are ye taking me?"

"Back to my place."

"To yer manor, ye mean?"

A smile tugged at one corner of his mouth but never reached his lips. "It's just a house, not a manor."

A terrible possibility occurred to her. "Are ye taking me there to punish me for me crimes against ye?"

The smile finally won out and slowly tipped his mouth into a disarming grin. Eyes twinkling, he said, "That would be taking the law into my own hands." When Ceara held his gaze, he added, "I have no intention of punishing you. You'll be as safe as a babe in its mother's arms."

Quincy Harrigan stirred several emotions within her, but feeling safe wasn't one of them. She glanced over her shoulder, taking in the world around her. Nothing she saw looked remotely like home. As reluctant as she was to go with him, she couldn't see that she had any choice. With no coin, she couldn't hope to procure shelter or food, and even in her beloved Ireland, 'twas not safe for a lady to wander about a village without a male escort to protect her. Besides, where were all her grand intentions to be brave and self-sacrificing to save the lives of others? All the Harrigan first wives were still fated to die, and despite the hostile reception, Ceara had come here for them.

She gave a startled bleep when Quincy's big, hard hands encircled her waist. With an ease that unnerved her even more, he swung her up onto the seat of his truck. "Buckle up," he said as he closed the thick portal.

Though Ceara's first language was Irish, she prided herself on being fluent in English as well. But what did *buckle up* mean? She perched rigidly on the cushion, which appeared to be dyed leather but was butter soft. Hands folded and clenched on her knees, she watched as he circled the truck and climbed in on the opposite side to sit behind a large thing that looked like a wagon wheel. She jumped when he inserted a key into a slot at the wheel's base and made the truck roar to life.

"God's teeth!"

He glanced over at her. "What?"

"That noise, sir! What is it?"

"Drop the 'sir,' and in answer to your question, it's the engine. Diesels are loud." He leaned across her, groped near the door, and then drew a strap across her chest. The tips of her breasts tingled when the inside of his forearm grazed them. "I thought I said to buckle up."

He jabbed the shiny metal tongue at the end of the strap into a square thing near her hip. Then he straightened and repeated the process with the strap on his side. Ceara deeply disliked feeling trapped. Briefly she wondered whether this was some sort of ritual restraint; then she realized it couldn't be, since he'd imprisoned himself in the same way.

"Whatever shall we do if the carriage topples and we must jump clear to save ourselves?" she asked.

He sent her a sharp, burning look. "Can we dispense with the act for a while? It's a truck, not a carriage, and I think you damned well know it."

He backed up the *truck*, then jerked on a stick poking

out from the wheel column to make the equipage go forward.

"Ye'll not go fast, I pray." She glanced over at him. "'Tis dangerous, surely, at such speeds."

"Don't worry. I never exceed the limit by over five miles an hour." A muscle ticked in his lean cheek. "And I repeat, let's drop the act. As entertaining as it is—and as good as you are at it—my patience with this charade is starting to wear thin."

Quincy tried his best to ignore his passenger as he drove toward home, but he wasn't successful, even by half. When he pulled out onto Main, she squeaked when she saw traffic coming at them in both lanes, grabbed the dash with white-knuckled fingers, and haltingly spurted out a Hail Mary.

Gotcha, Quincy thought, barely managing to squelch a smirk. "That's amazing! People said the Hail Mary way back in the fifteen hundreds?"

She crossed herself. When she looked over at him, Quincy saw that her face had gone as pale as milk. "'Twas mostly taken from the Gospel of Luke, and later on words were added. Have ye not heard of the Council of Trent, where the prayer was sanctified?"

The Council of Trent? Quincy had heard of it, but he couldn't for the life of him recall when it had taken place. In the fifteen hundreds sometime?

When he braked suddenly behind a blue Toyota, she released her hold on the dash long enough to cross herself again. "'Tis a fair new prayer at home, but a lovely one, asking fer the intercession of our Holy Mother."

She resumed her death hold on the dash. Quincy wondered how she managed to make all the color drain from her face. Now, *that* was some fine acting. The lady had missed her calling to Hollywood. "So when are you planning to come clean?" he asked. "You broke into my arena for a reason, and I don't for a second buy that you did it merely to play games with me and my family."

Two bright spots of color flagged her cheeks to chase away her pallor. She spat out some words that he didn't recognize, but it wasn't necessary to understand to know he was being insulted. She was putting on quite a show—he had to give her that—and despite his worry over Loni, a grin tugged at his mouth. That seemed to make her even madder. Then, with an obvious attempt to collect herself, she said in English, "I told ye me reason fer coming. Believe it or not, 'struth!"

Quincy sighed. " *'Struth?* What the hell does that mean?"

"God's truth. 'Tis a common word at home."

Quincy took the highway on-ramp and tromped the fuel pedal as he merged with traffic. He smiled to himself when she loosened one hand from the dash to brace her shoulder against the passenger door. He didn't for a moment believe that she was truly frightened—unless, of course, she was actually crazy and completely delusional.

" 'Tis icy!" Ahead on the asphalt there was a long stretch of packed snow. She gaped at it with eyes that had gone as round as nickels. "God have mercy! Are ye out of yer mind? 'Tis slick. We shall surely—" She broke off, gulped, and closed her eyes. "Hail Mary, full of grace, the Lord—"

"I'm studded up," Quincy said, cutting her prayer short.

She cracked open one eye to peer at him. In all his days, he'd never seen a prettier blue. "Ye're what?"

He felt silly explaining what was patently obvious, but the gentleman in him felt compelled to offer her some reassurance, just in case she really was afraid. Maybe she was so mired in insanity that she actually believed she was nearly five hundred years old. "My tires are studded. Studs, you know?" Keeping his attention on the road, he spared her a brief glance to see if any comprehension showed on her face. *None*. "Studs," he repeated. "They're little nails that poke out from the tires to grab on the ice."

"Ah," she said, the sound tremulous. Then, "Pray tell me—what are *tires*?"

That cinched it for Quincy. Losing what little patience he had left, he flipped on the stereo to end the conversation. At the sudden sound of music and lyrics, Ceara jumped as if he'd stuck her with a hatpin.

"Holy Mother!" She clamped her hands over her mouth, gaping at the dash. Then, apparently getting over the start, she leaned as far forward as the seat belt allowed to finger the electronic screen. "Where are they?" she asked tremulously.

Quincy shot her a wary glance. "Where are *who*?"

"The minstrels," she said, her voice quavering. "Do ye have a crystal ball in there? I can hear them, but I canna see them." She traced the square outline of the display. " 'Tis naught but a box." She fixed wondering, frightened eyes on him. "Do ye have people trapped in there? 'Tis cruel beyond words, sir! And all fer yer pleasure? What manner of life can they have, imprisoned in so small a place?" She twisted on the seat to rest her palm over the speaker in the door panel. When she felt the vibration, she jerked her hand away as if something had burned her. "Lord, have mercy. 'Tis a horrible world I've landed in, fer certain."

Quincy had always prided himself on having a halfway decent imagination, but this gal took fantasy to a whole new level. Even so, for just an instant, Quincy could almost believe she truly was from the fifteen hundreds and seeing things for the first time that she didn't understand. *Bullshit*, his voice of reason told him. If he allowed himself to buy into this poppycock, he was crazier than she was.

"It's a stereo, for God's sake. People aren't trapped in there, and you know it as well as I do. We don't use *crystal balls* to see and hear people. We use airwaves." He'd be damned if he allowed her to play him for a fool. "I've had it with this game of yours, Ceara, if that's even your real name. Don't screw with me. You're way out of your league."

He increased his speed, signaled to change lanes, and studiously ignored her dramatic performance until they reached his ranch.

Nona Redcliff must have heard Quincy and Ceara enter the house, because she appeared in the kitchen before Quincy could divest his guest of the jacket he'd lent her. Nona's dark eyes settled with glittering intensity on Ceara, quickly taking in the details of her appearance and dress.

"So," Nona said, "you are our mysterious Ceara O'Ceallaigh? Just the lady I've been hoping to interview."

Dragging a startled gaze from the many appliances in Quincy's kitchen, Ceara straightened her narrow shoulders and clasped her hands at her slender waist. Until that moment, Quincy hadn't realized how small she was. Compared to Nona, a woman of average height, she looked tiny. Quincy guessed her to top out at no more than five-two, if that. He noted that she'd resumed staring at his stainless-steel Sub-Zero freezer and refrigerator, side-by-side built-ins that had cost him a small fortune. Then she gaped at his double ovens, the two dishwashers, the steamer, and the microwave. It took her a full half minute to return her attention to Nona. "Ye have me at a disadvantage," she replied. "Have ye a name?"

Nona introduced herself but didn't extend Ceara the courtesy of an outstretched hand. Instead she led the way to Quincy's office, where she leaned a hip against his desk, folded her arms, and gave Ceara a long, burning look. Quincy, standing just behind Ceara, studied the flame-red braid that trailed down her back to well below her knees. Convinced it had to be a hairpiece, because he'd never seen a modern-day woman with tresses so long, he searched in vain for a clip or comb that attached the rope of hair to the back of her head, but he saw nothing.

A fax came in, and Ceara jumped at the sound. Her delicate brows pleated in a bewildered frown when paper was ejected by the machine. The next instant, Quincy's desk phone rang, and Ceara jolted yet again. When the answering machine picked up the call and a man's voice came over the air, she weaved on her feet, as if she might faint. Quincy's first instinct was to grab her shoulders, but instead he only moved closer to catch her if she fell.

Meeting Quincy's gaze, Nona asked, "Do I have your authorization to question this woman?"

Quincy waved a hand. "Go for it."

Nona relaxed against the desk and crossed her ankles. A stare-down ensued, with Ceara at the receiving end. "How did you gain entry to Mr. Harrigan's arena, Ms. O'Ceallaigh?"

Quincy saw that Ceara trembled, an almost imperceptible quivering of her whole body. Yet despite her apparent fear, she straightened her spine, lifted her chin, and replied in a steady voice, "I canna say *how* I gained entry. 'Tis beyond me how it came about. I came forward in time to end the curse on the O'Hourigans. Begging yer pardon, the Harrigans. While saying the traveling prayer, I asked the Blessed Ones to guide me to a place where I would be most likely to find Quincy O'Hourigan, and the stallion's stall is where I landed."

A chill coursed the length of Quincy's frame as he recalled his thoughts earlier about Beethoven's stall being his favorite thinking place. And *that* was where he'd found Ceara, asleep in the straw.

Nona's team members appeared in the office. Quincy quickly decided everyone needed to adjourn to the living room, where there was more space. After his guests were settled, all eyes turned to Ceara, who stood at the center of the room as if she were facing a firing squad. In a sense, that wasn't far wrong. Quincy knew countless questions would be aimed at her, each carefully worded to trip her up and trick her into revealing the truth. He felt almost sorry for her but pushed the sentiment aside.

The interrogation proceeded quickly, Nona taking the lead and rephrasing the same question over and over again until Ceara began to pace in a tight circle, chafing her arms as if she were cold. Quincy had laid a fire that morning before leaving for the arena, but he was so focused on the drama playing out in front of him that he didn't bother to get up and strike a match to the paper and kindling.

Spinning on a heel, her long green skirts swirling around her slender ankles, Ceara hugged herself and gave the same answer Quincy had now heard a dozen times. "I stood on the knoll by the stream with me family gathered 'round. Me mum was crying, with her face pressed against Da's inar. He had tears in his eyes as well. 'Twas a very sad moment, ye understand. 'Tis possible fer druids to go forward, but never back, and we all knew we'd never see each other again. Seeing their grief, I almost changed me mind, but I had memorized the traveling prayer and knew deep in me heart that I had to go. I likened it to when me father and brothers went forth into battle, not knowing if they would ever come home to us again. I stayed on the traveling star, closed me eyes, and whispered the words, asking the Blessed Ones to guide me forward on my journey to a place where I would most likely encounter the man I sought, Sir Quincy O'Hourigan. Me mum and I—we had seen in her ball that he was the only unmarried O'Hourigan left. He was the man I needed to meet, no other. And the Blessed Ones granted me request."

"So you didn't enter the arena by a door, window, or skylight?" Nona persisted.

Ceara threw up her hands and widened her pacing circle. With a pronounced shiver, she passed the hearth, then spun back. She gave a flick of her wrist, and the kindling burst into flame with a muted roar, then began to crackle and snap. Nona gasped and recoiled. Quincy started violently and swore. An eerie silence fell, broken only by the pop of burning pitch.

Ceara stared at the flames as they licked higher onto the crisscrossed log rounds. Then, with a laugh, she cried, "Praise God and all the saints, I havena been stripped of all me powers. Weak as I am, I can *still* make fire!"

Chapter Five

Quincy couldn't believe what he had just witnessed. Instant fire with a flick of Ceara's wrist? Frank, who had arrived a few minutes earlier to attend the circus, looked as mystified as Quincy felt. As if Ceara noticed the stunned silence in the living room, she suddenly glanced back over a slender shoulder, her glad smile swiftly fading. " 'Tis sorry I am if I gave ye a start. I forgot meself fer a moment."

His gaze shooting to the fireplace, Quincy pushed to his feet and crossed the room in three swift strides. How in the hell had she done that? He moved closer to the flames, looking for some sort of ignition device hidden in the kindling. He could detect nothing, but he knew there had to be something. He crouched for a better look. Still nothing.

"How did you do that?" he demanded.

Ceara rubbed her palms on her skirt. " 'Tis one of me gifts, the ability to make fire. 'Twas a mistake to use it in the presence of others, and I apologize. I felt chilled, and I dinna stop to think afore I did it."

Nona joined Quincy by the hearth. She clearly shared his suspicion that there was an ignition device under the wood. She grabbed the poker to give the logs a good stir.

Then she sent Quincy a bewildered look before resuming the inquisition. No matter how Nona phrased her questions or how many she asked, Ceara stuck tight to her story and never once got caught up in her lies. If it was true that a person needed a good memory to be a liar, then Ceara's memory was phenomenal.

Eventually Quincy grew weary of the grilling. This was getting them nowhere fast. He politely requested that Nona and her team take off for the day and return tomorrow. Only seconds after the living room cleared, Frank, who had remained behind, got a call on his cell from Clint. He listened to whatever Clint was saying and grunted a couple of times.

When the call ended, he met Quincy's questioning gaze. "Loni is home and settled in. Your brother sounds like he's been dragged through a knothole backward." He glanced at Ceara, who stood near the fire again to absorb some of its heat. "I think it's high time we introduce our little guest here to your sister-in-law."

Quincy nodded in agreement. Damn right it was time. So far as he was concerned, the sooner this fiasco was resolved, the happier he'd be. As convincing as Ceara was, he still doubted her story, and if anyone on earth could tell them for certain whether she was lying, it would be Loni. "I'm all for that. You want to drive over with us, Dad?"

Frank declined the offer. "I wanna swing by and pick up Dee Dee. I think havin' her there to fuss over Loni will make Clint feel a little better. Maybe he'll even see fit to grab a short nap."

Quincy nodded. "We'll see you there then." His dad's place was nearby, and Quincy knew it wouldn't take Frank long to collect his wife. "Don't drive like a bat out of hell. There's no rush. We can wait for you to get there."

Frank was already heading out. Over his shoulder, he said, "I appreciate that."

Silence settled over the living room. Quincy heard the kitchen door click closed, followed by the tap of his father's boots on the plank veranda. He planted his hands on his hips, stared at Ceara for a long moment, and then sighed. She looked as exhausted as he felt. He guessed that this had been a pretty grueling day for her. He tried to tell himself he didn't care, but it was difficult to remain unfeeling when she was so pale and unsteady on her feet. He detested the thought of putting her through anything more—truly he did—but he couldn't postpone her introduction to Loni until tomorrow. His hope was that Loni would touch Ceara, say she was a fraud, and leave Quincy free to wash his hands of the lady before it grew too late to take her back to the station and let the authorities take over.

Still, he had to ask. "Would you like something to eat, Ceara? I can rustle something up."

She shook her head. "Loni, the one I am to meet, she is the sick one, yes? The one who sees what others canna."

"How the hell do you know that?"

She pushed at a stray curl that dangled in front of her ear. In the firelight it glistened like copper. "I saw many things in me mum's crystal ball."

Quincy bit back a curse. So they were back to that, were they? He had to give her credit for being persistent. "Good," he settled for saying. "Then you know I can be one ornery son of a bitch when someone messes with me."

She tipped her head to study him. "And ye believe I am messing with ye? What does that mean, exactly? I've done no harm to yer home or arena."

Quincy rolled his eyes and strode past her. "If you aren't hungry, we'd best get going."

She trailed behind him to the kitchen like a duckling after its mother. He grabbed his jacket off the coat tree and thrust it at her. "It's cold out there. I'm surprised you didn't think to bring a coat when you beamed forward from Ireland. At this time of year, I don't think the weather is much better there than here."

She accepted the jacket. "Snow in me Ireland is like a good houseguest who stays fer only a few days. It seldom gets verra deep or remains to bedevil us overlong. But ye're correct about it being cold. I brought no *coat*—at home, we call it an inar—because it was too bulky to fit in me satchel and much too cumbersome for the journey I was about to undertake." She arched a glimmering brow. "If I wear yer jacket, what will ye have to shield yerself from the chill?"

"Right now," he bit out, "I'm too damned angry to worry about it."

"Angry? Now there is a word I know. So it is angry with me that ye are? And why would that be, Sir Quincy? Yer Loni is dying. I am here at great cost to meself to save her. Do ye not appreciate me efforts?"

Quincy allowed himself a derisive snort as he ushered her out onto the porch. It was getting dark a little later now, with daylight savings time in effect, but it was still colder outside than a well digger's ass. Bubba and Billy Bob, impervious to the weather with their thick coats, bounded up onto the porch, bypassing Quincy to sniff Ceara's skirt and slippers.

"Ach," she said, her tone meltingly sweet. "Ye *do* have dogs in this time!" She crouched and laughed when she received their wet kisses. "I thought I heard them barking this morning right afore ye let the constables take me away." To the canines, she said, " 'Tis so good to make yer acquaintance, me fine friends. Seeing ye lightens me heart!"

Quincy caught himself grinning and forced his lips back into a grim line. He drew Ceara erect. "Shoo!" he said to the dogs. "Back to Pauline. Off with you!"

With happy barks, the shepherds sailed over the steps and hit the frozen ground at a dead run, leaning into each other as they loped toward the arena. Ceara gazed after them as if the sun were blinking out.

"Take care on the steps," Quincy warned. "When the temps plummet at this time of day, the wood can get icy and slick." He grasped her elbow to make sure she didn't fall and felt her tense at his touch. "Purely a gentlemanly gesture, Ceara. I have no designs on you; trust me."

He didn't release his hold on her until they reached the truck. She stepped back as he opened the passenger door. Then she held up a hand to forestall him when he moved to help her inside. "I shall manage by meself."

Quincy left her to it. He dug in his jeans pocket for his keys as he circled the front bumper. With the help of the running board, which Quincy would remove as soon as the spring thaw finally arrived in central Oregon, bringing with it mud axle-deep, Ceara managed to gain the seat by the time he slid in under the steering wheel. When he cranked the engine this time, she didn't act startled. The stereo had been left on, and John Michael Montgomery's mellow voice filled the cab. She didn't peer at the dash or touch the door speaker. Apparently the modern-day wonders of twenty-first-century vehicles were now old hat to her.

As they set out for Clint's place, she said, "Ye still

have me headpiece and satchel. Will ye consider returning them to me? The satchel is filled with all me precious things."

"Both items are over in my arena office. I have no reason to keep them, but I doubt they'll let you have any of your personal effects once you're back in jail."

"So ye'll be taking me back there, will ye?" She seemed to ponder that for a moment. " 'Tis an unpleasant place, the clinker. I've done naught to deserve imprisonment."

Quincy reached the end of his driveway and turned onto the asphalt road. "The jury is still out on that."

Ceara remained silent during the short ride to Clint's ranch. As Quincy pulled up near his brother's house, he tried to see the two-story post-and-beam home, so similar in style to his own, through Ceara's eyes. If she was a gold digger, she'd seen plenty of nuggets today to keep her interested. Quincy and his family members weren't fans of elegant or pretentious living, but they did enjoy fine quality and comfort. A home similar to Clint's would cost more than a million to build, and that wasn't counting any land. If Ceara was familiar with the real estate market, even in this depressed economy, she had to know that she hadn't been dropped into the midst of paupers.

Quincy minded the manners his father had drilled into him since childhood, circling the truck to open Ceara's door and help her out. Then he grasped her elbow as they walked across the yard and ascended the veranda steps. Quincy didn't bother to knock. His father's truck was already here, along with rigs owned by everyone else in his family. Quincy knew that practically everyone would be gathered in the kitchen. He opened the door and pushed it wide.

"Hey, there!" Sam called from where she sat at the table with a goblet of wine near her elbow. "Good to see you, Quincy." Her dark gaze swept over him to land on Ceara. If she was surprised by the younger woman's strange dress, she didn't reveal it. "And you must be Ceara."

Samantha got up to walk across the tile floor with her right hand outstretched. Like all Frank's kids, Sam had the Harrigan pitch-black hair, burnished complexion, and wiry, athletic build. Quincy had never quite determined how his sister had turned out so pretty when she sported their dad's facial features, including the Harrigan nose. But somehow on her, the sharp and mismatched angles looked feminine and dainty. She wore her customary snug blue jeans and T-shirt tucked in at her belted waistband, which showcased her slender yet curvaceous figure, as yet unchanged by pregnancy. She and her husband, Tucker Coulter, had been trying for a baby, had miscarried once, taken a break for a while, and now were thinking about trying again. Quincy figured he'd be a proud uncle again soon.

Tucker, who'd been sitting beside his wife, stood up and set his glass of wine aside on the table. A tall fellow with dark brown hair, massive shoulders, and muscular legs, he stood a good half head above Quincy, but his easy grin and fluid movements made smaller men quickly forget his size. He winked in friendly greeting, then, as his wife had, settled his gaze on Ceara, who was hesitantly shaking hands with Samantha.

Quincy took that moment to do a head count, so accustomed to the marked resemblance between himself and all his male relatives that he could tell who was who at a glance. His father was over by the sink, pouring himself a measure of Coke spiked with Jack Daniel's. Parker and Rainie stood just beyond the kitchen in the hall, heads bent to pore over a document of some kind that they held between them. Zach and his wife, Mandy, were at the stove, stirring something in pots. The contents of one smelled suspiciously like Clint's favored Polish sausage–and-potato soup. The delicious, sweet warmth of baking corn bread emanated from one of the ovens. Quincy's mouth started to water even as his brain clamored warnings that the meal would have "heart blockage" written all over it. Quincy didn't see Clint, Dee Dee, or the kids. He figured they were probably upstairs in the master suite with Loni, who was too damned sick to oversee the mess being made of her kitchen.

And it *was* a mess. Zach had never aspired to be a tidy cook, though he did clean up after he served a meal. A mound of potato peelings graced a countertop. An onion peel fluttered on the tile with every breath of movement. Cream or milk had been spilled on the floor. And in the far right corner, it looked as if a motley kennel had gone into business. Sam's old female rottweiler, Roxie, napped in a tangle with Parker's rot, Mojo; Loni's mastiff, Hannah; and Trevor's St. Bernard, Nana. Standing guard over them, Mandy's brother Luke's mini guide horse, Rosebud, slept as well, her fluffy white mane falling forward to conceal her eyes. If Quincy's shepherds hadn't been temporarily in Pauline's care, they would have been there as well. With the Harrigan ranches all adjoined, the canines could easily follow a master's vehicle to a neighboring house, and consistently did just that. As a result, family gatherings generally included all the critters.

Ceara gaped incredulously when she saw the tiny

horse, which wasn't an uncommon reaction, but before she could exclaim, Tucker stepped forward to greet her. It griped Quincy that his sister and brother-in-law seemed so eager to welcome Ceara into the fold before they knew for certain that she wasn't an impostor. Clearly Frank had been flapping his jaws to convince everyone that Ceara might have the power to perform some kind of miracle and save Loni's life.

Frank turned just then and raised his glass to Quincy. "I'd offer you one to take the edge off, but I know all I'd get for my trouble is a lecture."

Quincy was too exhausted and nerve-worn to smile. "One word would do it, Dad. Triglycerides. Your counts are high, remember?"

Frank took a swig of his drink. "That was more than one word."

Quincy shrugged. He saw that Ceara had been drawn to the table during his exchange with Frank and now sat beside Sam and Tucker, chatting with them as if they were old friends. Parker and Rainie rejoined the family, the document they'd been reading consigned to the telephone nook as they took seats and introduced themselves to Ceara. Typical of Zach, he didn't bother with the getting-acquainted spiel. Instead he descended on Ceara with a cup of the soup, which Quincy knew from experience was loaded with high-fat sausages, potatoes, butter, and cream.

"You gotta try this," Zach said as he placed the cup and spoon in front of her. "It's a Harrigan tradition, my brother Clint's recipe."

Ceara, still wearing Quincy's jacket draped over her shoulders, smiled, her cheek dimpling prettily. "Many thanks to ye. I've eaten nary a morsel since last night."

Quincy felt gazes turn toward him—condemning ones.

"I offered to feed her before we came," he defended himself.

"What was on hand over there, a cold broiled chicken breast wrapped in kale?" Zach asked. "She'll like this better." To Ceara, Zach added, "I can get you more if you like it."

Ceara fiddled with the spoon, lifting it from the cup to turn it this way and that. Quincy half expected her to comment that the spoons in her time were made of shells with sticks attached as handles. Instead, after ending her examination of the implement, she took a taste of the soup, then closed her eyes with an expression of pure bliss. The only time Quincy could recall seeing a female look that pleased was during or after good sex.

He scowled. This was no time to be thinking about sex, not with Loni on the verge of death and an emotionally imbalanced woman conversing with his family as if she'd known them for years. He grabbed the document from the phone counter to see what Parker and Rainie had been studying so solemnly. He saw that it was the results from Loni's blood tests yesterday. And he soon understood why his brother and sister-in-law had been frowning. The numbers meant nothing to a layman unless compared to the normal range, which was off to the right of each line in brackets. With a fast back-and-forth read, Quincy saw that few of Loni's counts were normal and the others were terrifyingly high or low. His sister-in-law was clearly a very sick lady.

He glanced up to find Rainie looking at him, her expression stricken with sadness. As always, she looked beautiful, her brown hair wildly curly and kissed with blond, her gathered print skirt and pink peasant blouse thrift-store chic. Quincy guessed that Rainie would never again dress like the wealthy and sophisticated woman she'd once been. Somehow wearing expensive clothing rekindled memories in her mind of her maniacal ex-husband, who'd nearly succeeded in killing her. Fortunately, the style worked for Quincy's brother, Parker, who worshiped Rainie and always would, no matter how she dressed.

Just then Quincy heard heavy footsteps coming down the stairway, which ended in the hallway just beyond the kitchen. Clint appeared in the archway. Seeing him gave Quincy a jolt. His brother's face was lined with weariness, and his usually bronze skin had become ashen. His broad shoulders, usually held proudly erect, now slumped as if he carried an invisible thousand-pound yoke.

"She's awake and as rested from the trip as she's probably going to get." Clint's dark, pain-filled eyes settled on Ceara. "She's ready for a visit now, but I'll ask all of you before we go up, please keep it short and don't ask how she feels. That requires an answer, and talking tires her very quickly."

The family's climb up the stairs was a solemn one, everyone stepping lightly and whispering. Even the animals joined in the procession, Hannah and Nana, the in-house residents, leading the furry entourage. At any other time, the sight of a horse and so many dogs going up the steps would have amused Quincy, but this evening it seemed right, even necessary. The critters loved Loni every bit as much as the humans did and wanted to bask in her presence, if only for a moment.

Quincy deliberately held Ceara back so they would be last in line. At the landing, Clint opened the door of the master suite, a gigantic chamber adjoined by a mammoth bath and two walk-in closets larger than some people's living rooms. Loni was ensconced on the king-size bed, propped up with pillows, her arms curled around her children: Trevor, her adopted son, who had turned thirteen in January; and Aliza, her and Clint's biological daughter, who had turned five only days ago. Loni was so pale that it was hard for Quincy to tell where her skin ended and the white pillowcases began.

Seeing Loni like that—so very close to death—brought tears to Quincy's eyes. He blinked rapidly to get rid of them. The last thing Loni needed was a bunch of weeping fools gathered around her bed. He was glad to see that the animals stood back at a respectful distance, and then just as quickly it hurt his heart. Normally the critters would be all over Loni, clamoring for a word of affection or a comforting pat. It was as if even the dogs and horse understood that their beloved friend was dying and lacked the strength to fondle them.

It took a moment for Loni and Aliza to notice Quincy and Ceara standing near the still-open door. The child immediately sat erect, her black curls bouncing over the sleeves of her pink top, her dark eyes going wide with delight. "Look, Mama!" she cried. "It's *her*, the lady we've seen!"

The little girl clamped a small hand over her mouth and sent her mother an apologetic glance. Loni smiled faintly and touched her daughter's hand. "It's okay to forget sometimes," she whispered. Then she looked straight at Ceara. Voice tremulous, she said, "It is good to finally meet you, Ceara, an occasion a long time in coming."

Quincy sliced his gaze to Ceara. What the hell was this all about?

Ignoring Quincy's questioning gaze, Ceara drew away from him and wove her way through the crowd to reach the bed. Extending a slender hand to Loni, she replied,

"The pleasure is all mine. 'Tis eager I have been to meet ye."

This wasn't going the way Quincy had expected. He'd hoped to tell Loni nothing about Ceara that might predispose her to imagine that she'd *seen* something she actually hadn't. Only now it appeared that Loni was a step ahead of everyone. Apparently she had already seen Ceara in a vision. The idea gave him the same feeling in his gut that he'd gotten as a kid when the Thriller Killer roller coaster went into its hundred-foot dive.

The two women extended their hands. Loni's fingers closed over Ceara's. Her eyes went oddly blank. Quincy had seen that look and knew Loni was no longer aware of anything around her. She had slipped into what he thought of as her psychic mode. The room went so quiet that you could have heard dust motes floating in the air.

When Loni resurfaced from whatever it was that she'd just *seen*, she weakly asked Clint to take the children from the room. Then she glanced imploringly at Dee Dee, a short, plump redhead of sixty-three. "I must speak with Ceara alone," she said in a quavering voice.

Dee Dee plumped Loni's pillows after the kids evacuated the bed. Then she turned to flutter her hands at everyone in the room, signaling them to leave. Quincy wanted to stand fast, but a warning look from Clint had him hurrying downstairs in the wave of departing bodies. Once in the kitchen, Clint dispatched his children to the family room to challenge each other on the PlayStation 3. Aliza was no sooner out of earshot than Quincy rounded on his brother.

"How long have you known that Aliza has second sight?" he demanded.

Clint passed a hand over his eyes. "Since before she

was born. Loni saw in a vision that Aliza had the strawberry mark on the nape of her neck."

Quincy couldn't quite grasp what he was hearing. "We don't keep secrets in this family! Why the hell didn't you ever say anything to me?"

"Why would I have?" Clint shot back. "So you could avoid swinging her up into your arms or holding her on your lap for fear she'd see something she shouldn't? Loni had a horrible childhood because of her gift. We want Aliza to be treated like any other child. From the moment she started talking, Loni has tried to teach her to be discreet. Today she forgot when she saw Ceara. If not for that, you still wouldn't know—not if I had anything to say about it."

Quincy felt as if his brother had slapped him. "I'd *never* treat that little girl different just because of her gift."

"Bullshit," Clint fired back. "Think about it, Quincy. You have a private life. Do you think Aliza has a filter in her mind to block X-rated visions?"

Standing with her arm encircling Parker's waist, Rainie inserted, "I *thought* something was up. One time when she stayed all night with us and I was holding her on my knee to read her a story, she looked up at me with tears in her eyes and told me she was sorry he'd been so mean to me. I thought it peculiar at the time; then I passed it off as one of those silly things children sometimes say. Now I realize she must have seen a violent incident that occurred during my previous marriage."

Quincy sank onto a chair. *This isn't happening,* he thought. But at the edges of his mind, he knew that it actually was. Like Rainie, he remembered when Aliza had said odd things to him, most notably once during a hello hug when she'd cupped his face in her little hands, looked blankly into his eyes, and whispered, "Oh, Uncle Quincy, she's so pretty."

For a moment, that awful sinking sensation attacked his belly again. Aliza had *recognized* Ceara. What did that mean, exactly? That Quincy was fated to marry the woman, whether he wanted to or not? *No*, he assured himself. Ceara had popped into their lives. The mere fact that Aliza had seen it happen before the fact meant nothing. Some of the tension eased from his shoulders.

Zach stepped over to check the soup. Mandy, her sorrel hair gleaming in the brightly lit kitchen, moved the baked corn bread from the oven into the warmer. Though it was now well past the dinner hour, no one seemed to feel like eating. Dee Dee set herself to the task of helping with kitchen cleanup. Frank nursed his drink. Clint collapsed on a chair and stared grimly at the floor. Parker and Rainie sat across from Quincy, leaning into each other like two saplings being buffeted by a high wind. Sam and Tucker had adjourned to the family room to play electronic Trivial Pursuit with the kids, not, Quincy felt sure, because they wanted to miss out on the adult drama taking place, but because they felt the youngsters needed to be kept away from it.

Each second seemed to last a small eternity. Quincy couldn't bear the waiting and got up to pace. He'd worn a path back and forth from the table to the furry mound of sleeping animals in the corner by the time Ceara appeared in the kitchen archway. She glanced past everyone else to home in on Clint.

"Yer wife is verra spent, but she wishes to see all of ye straightaway."

The procession up the stairs was repeated, without the children or Sam and Tucker this time. Loni looked exhausted and was fighting to keep her eyes open. She became more alert when she saw Quincy and struggled to sit more erect. Dee Dee hurried over to brace her with pillows.

Her voice so faint she could barely be heard, Loni said, "Ceara O'Ceallaigh is precisely what she claims, Quincy, a woman from the fifteen hundreds who has come forward in time to save my life." She paused to collect her strength, looking at each of her sisters-in-law. "Both of you will die too. It's only me in danger right now, but if Ceara doesn't break the curse, your times will come. Only Sam and Dee Dee are safe."

Loni let her head fall back against the pillows and closed her eyes. For a moment, Quincy thought she'd gone to sleep. But no. Her lashes fluttered back up, and with a hand diminished to little more than bone, tendon, and skin, she beckoned Quincy closer.

When he stood at her side, she gave him a ghost of a smile. "I know you're a doubting Thomas, Quincy, but you shouldn't be this time. Ceara truly is of druid descent, and according to her, so am I, though my druid ancestors were from Scotland." When she saw Quincy stiffen, she tried to smile again, but her white lips barely curved. "I think the term *druid* is unsettling for everyone. It might be better to think of Ceara as someone with special gifts bestowed upon her by God." She sighed and closed her eyes again. "It explains so very much. In every generation, one girl in my mother's family receives the 'sight.' We always believed the other children were passed over, but Ceara claims all the women and men in my mother's line have special powers of some kind. They've simply not been aware and have failed to practice their gifts. Some have a special affinity with animals. Others can control the elements. The list is long." Her brown lashes fluttered up to reveal her bloodshot blue eyes. "I look forward to everything Ceara can teach me after I get well." Loni locked gazes with Quincy. "*If* I get well. As Ceara would say, sweet brother-in-law, 'tis up to you, and only you. My life depends upon your decision. Rainie's and Mandy's lives are on your shoulders, too."

Chapter Six

Dee Dee hurried over to the bed. After checking Loni's pulse, she made shooing motions at everyone else. "Out of here. She has to rest. This has pushed her to the limit, I'm afraid."

Clint wasted no time in ushering everyone but his stepmother from the room. Once in the hallway with the door closed behind them, Clint rounded on Quincy. "You can't second-guess this. If Loni says Ceara is for real, then she's for real. You have to do as Ceara says and marry her as soon as possible."

"But—"

"There are no goddamned *buts*, Quincy! My wife is dying! She's out of time. If your marrying Ceara will save Loni, you'll marry her if I have to beat the shit out of you on your way down the aisle!"

Quincy stared at the jam of people in the hall. No one said a word. Obviously they all agreed with Clint. He stared after his family as they slowly descended the stairs. He was left alone on the landing—or so he thought, until he felt a light touch on his sleeve. He glanced down to see Ceara beside him. The overhead lights were off, and in the dimness her eyes shimmered like sapphires. " 'Tis sorry I am, Sir Quincy. I chose to make this sacrifice. Ye are being forced. 'Tis not fair to ye, but then, as me mum always says, there is little in life that is fair."

She moved away, lifted her skirts, and carefully picked her way down the steps, so slight of build that she barely made a riser squeak. Quincy stared after her, trying to sort his thoughts. *Impossible.* This had been the day from hell, and there was no making sense of any of it.

Feeling a hundred years old, he trailed behind Ceara to the kitchen. The moment he stepped into view, everybody except Ceara turned to stare at him with accusing eyes. It didn't take a genius to figure out which way the wind was blowing. If he refused to marry Ceara and then Loni died, all of them would blame him. He felt as if he'd been caught up in a rush of floodwater and was going under fast. A hideous picture of himself explaining his refusal to marry Ceara to Loni's children shot across his mental TV screen, and he barely suppressed a shudder.

Loni was just about out of time, and Quincy was completely out of options. "Okay, okay. Fine. I'll marry the woman. We'll take the first available flight to Reno, do a quickie at one of the chapels, and it'll be a done deal." As Quincy finished speaking, he congratulated himself on his creativity. As a Catholic, only a marriage officiated by an ordained priest or minister counted as the real thing. He could *marry* Ceara in Reno but still be free to walk away later. If there truly was anything to this cockamamie story of hers, Loni would get well, the curse would be forever broken, and no more first wives of Harrigan men would die of blood-related complications. "How's that strike everyone?" Quincy tugged his phone from his belt to find a flight schedule. "No fuss, no muss."

Ceara caught his attention by lifting her hand. "Begging yer pardon, Sir Quincy, but what is a 'quickie'?"

Ignoring a sputter of smothered laughter from Parker,

Quincy explained, "In Reno, they have little chapels on nearly every block with people who are licensed by the State of Nevada to officiate at weddings. They even have two witnesses available. For a fee, a couple can get married in a matter of minutes." At her disapproving frown, Quincy asked, "What? It's all legal and binding."

"But is it binding in the eyes of God?" Ceara asked. "In order fer this to be a *true* marriage that will break the curse, we must say our vows before a priest or some other man of the cloth. 'Tis me preference to be married by a Catholic priest."

Quincy felt as if a noose were tightening around his neck, but, once again thinking quickly, he retorted, "That's impossible, Ceara. To be married in the Church, all couples are now required to take marriage preparation classes, and the banns must be posted for a period of time. Loni won't last that long. And we can't just walk into a Catholic church and demand to be married on the spot."

Frank set his glass on the counter with a sharp click that drew everyone's attention. "Hold on a minute. Father Mike ain't half the priest I think he is if he can't be convinced to bend the rules. It's plain as a freckle on a pig's nose that Loni won't live long enough for the usual steps to be taken."

"That's true," Clint concurred. "Father Mike is a good fellow. If he understands the urgency and the dire consequences if he refuses, I think he'll agree to do it."

Quincy had lost count of how many times that day he'd felt stuck in a waking nightmare, but this turn of the tide definitely took the prize. Almost before he could blink and collect his composure, everyone in the room was grabbing their coats, eager to drive into town to plead their case to Father Mike.

Sam entered the kitchen. "Where's everybody going?"

Frank stepped over to kiss his daughter's forehead. "We're off to get Quincy and Ceara married. You wanna come?"

Sam shot Quincy a sympathetic glance. "I sure do, but I think Tucker and I should stay here with the kids." She walked over to hug him. "I always thought I'd be there if and when you ever got married. I hate to miss it. But this is a really hard time for Aliza and Trevor—Trevor especially, for some reason." She shrugged. "Aliza is worried, of course, but not as much. Maybe she can see something the rest of us can't."

Quincy couldn't argue the point now that he knew Aliza had inherited her mother's gift. And he totally understood his sister's reasons for staying behind. What he *didn't* understand was the eagerness of everyone to see him put a ring on the finger of a woman he barely knew. It was madness. This was a family that believed in the sanctity of marriage. As far back as Quincy could recall, his father had lectured him about never marrying in haste. This was about as hasty as it got. He hadn't even known the woman a full day.

Clint, already in his jacket and Stetson, hesitated before stepping out the door onto the porch. "I'll swing by Fred Meyer to grab a couple of rings." He glanced at his watch. "It's already seven. No other jewelry stores will be open at this hour."

Full darkness had descended by the time Quincy exited the house with Ceara. Since Dee Dee had elected to stay behind to care for Loni, Rainie and Parker decided to ride into town with Frank. Quincy and Ceara followed closely behind Frank's Ford in Quincy's Dodge Ram, with Zach and Mandy practically riding Quincy's back bumper the entire way. What did they think, that Quincy might make a run for it? Well, if he did, he sure as hell wouldn't be dumb enough to take Ceara with him! Okay, so the thought of bolting had crossed his mind. Was that so unusual? He desperately needed some time to think of a rational solution to this mess that wouldn't involve holy matrimony. Talk about a shotgun wedding; if this wasn't a modern-day version, he didn't know what was.

He had nothing against marriage, damn it. Hell, he'd spent most of his adult life searching for the right woman. Only in his late thirties had he finally given up and decided that he would never find that one special person meant only for him. He'd jokingly told his brothers that the only way he'd ever get married now was if God dropped the lady of his dreams directly in his path.

Well, Ceara had *dropped* into his path, all right, but she wasn't the lady of his dreams. No how, no way. Not that she wasn't pretty. Stealing a quick glance at her, he saw that she looked great even with her face bathed in the green glow coming from the dash. *Pretty* didn't say it by half. The lady was beautiful. But gorgeous women were a dime a dozen. That didn't mean he wanted to marry any of them.

Panic nipped at his nerve endings and snapped his abdominal muscles into hard knots. *Calm down*, he ordered himself. There was still a way out of this. Even if he married Ceara in the Church, he could walk away and never look back if he didn't consummate the union. The realization eased the tension from his body. To save Loni and please his family, he would go through with this, if Father Mike could be convinced to officiate. Then, if Loni miraculously got well, he'd rejoice right along with everyone else, wait awhile, and then petition the Vatican for an annulment.

*　　*　　*

Ceara felt as if she'd eaten handfuls of live bugs. There was a horrible, wiggly sensation in her stomach that kept crawling up her throat. She'd come forward to marry Quincy Harrigan, but now that the reality of it was upon her, she wondered what she had been thinking. Because her intended husband had been killed in a riding accident and her kindly father had never pressed her to form an alliance with another to help secure his lands or add coin to his coffers, she was six and twenty and had never yet lain with a man. Just before her departure from home, she'd been closeted with her mum to learn what to expect on her wedding night. Ceara had thought it all sounded simple enough. She was to undress, wash herself, and then wait in the marriage bed for her husband to attend her. No matter what, she should utter no objection. 'Twas her job as a wife to pleasure her mate, and her mum had made it clear that some men had strange fancies. She'd also warned Ceara that 'twould hurt the first time, but a wise bride didna cry out, and the ordeal would be over with quickly. Afterward, Ceara should not be frightened by the blood. 'Twas the way of it the first time fer every woman.

Blood? Ceara wished now that she had asked her mum more questions. How badly did it hurt the first time? What caused all women to bleed? How much blood was normal? And, almost as alarming, what were the strange fancies of some husbands? Ceara had no clear idea what was coming. Did Quincy Harrigan have deviant desires? What exactly might he expect of her in the marriage bed? Would it be painful? Humiliating?

Now that it was too late to ask her mum for more details, Ceara's mind swam with concerns. She clenched her hands on her knees, shrank against the seat, and wished she'd never been so stupid as to leave home in the first place.

But no. Thinking that way was selfish. She remembered Loni's white face and the feeble clasp of her hand. The poor woman was dying, and only Ceara and Quincy could lift the curse that was killing her.

Lights shone from the rectory windows, which meant Father Mike was home. He taught Bible studies on Wednesday nights and Thursday mornings, so he usually took Thursday evenings off. Sometimes he dined at the homes of parishioners or took in a movie, but more often he just enjoyed quiet time at his residence. When he answered the ring of the bell, the warning chime of his alarm system pealed through the rooms behind him to indicate that a door had been opened. A plump, balding man, he was everyone's picture of an aging Irish priest, with graying dark hair, merry blue eyes, and a noticeable brogue. His round face creased in a worried frown when he saw so many Harrigans standing on his porch.

"Ach, no! Has our Loni taken a turn for the worse?" He stepped back and pushed the door wide, treating everyone outside to a rush of warm air and the smell of fresh popcorn. "Ye could've called. Let me grab me satchel, and I'll be right with ye."

"No, no," said Frank, who stood front and center on the welcome mat. "It's not an Anointing of the Sick that we're needin', Father Mike. Loni's in a bad way, but that ain't why we're here."

"Well, come in then, come in!" Father gestured them forward. "'Tis cold enough out there to make the wee folk sneak in through every crook and cranny. Hurry, hurry. Me heating bill is already so high, the church council is giving me the very devil about lowering the thermostat." He chafed the sleeves of his black shirt. "Me old bones can't bear the cold anymore, and I've outgrown all me sweaters. If they want me to live in a frigid house, they can increase me monthly allowance so I can afford new jumpers! Until they do, me thermostat stays at seventy."

Quincy grasped Ceara's arm as the press of bodies moved into the spacious foyer, which sported a painting of the Sacred Heart, and gilded cherub plaques. The rectory had been built to provide residence for two priests, but at present, Father Mike had no associate to assist him, so the second private living area was unoccupied, and he was free to use the house as he wished.

Father led the way to the main front room, where a flat-screen television cast flickering light. Quincy noted that the priest had been watching a tennis match, now on mute. Ceara froze when she saw the television, and Quincy gave her a nudge to get her feet moving again.

"Please find a seat," the priest said cordially as he flipped on more lamps. Rubbing his hands together, he asked, "Can I get ye anything? I made too much popcorn. I'm more than willing to share. And the good ladies of the parish make sure me fridge is always stocked with a nice selection of soft drinks."

By turn, everyone declined, including Ceara, who said very sweetly, " 'Tis fine I am, Father, but thank ye for yer kindness."

Father Mike's eyebrows shot toward his receding hairline. "Sweet Mother, are ye Irish, lass?"

"I am," Ceara replied. "I left there only last night and miss me family sorely already."

Father Mike clasped his hands and leaned slightly forward. "Ye poor thing, ye must be exhausted. 'Tis such a grueling journey! I used to go see me mum every year.

Now that she has passed on, I go only now and again to see me brothers and sisters. The older I get, the more draining the flight is for me."

Ceara gaped at him. "Ye mean ye can fly?"

Quincy put a hand on Ceara's arm. "Wires are getting crossed, Father. Ceara says she didn't come here from Ireland on a plane, and that's why we're here, to explain how she supposedly got here and her reason for coming."

A mystified expression settled on Father Mike's face. Frank asked the priest to sit down. "It's a long story, Father, and a hard one to swallow."

Father Mike took a seat on one of the sofas, and all eyes turned to Quincy where he sat in an easy chair adjacent to Ceara. He cleared his throat, not entirely sure how to begin. But once he started talking, the words came more easily, and in a matter of minutes, he had related the entire story.

Quincy finished with, "According to Ceara, the only way to lift this curse and save Loni's life is for her and me to marry. And with Loni hovering at death's door, we don't have much time."

Just then the doorbell rang again. Parker got up. "That'll be Clint, I'm thinking. He went to Fred Meyer to pick up the wedding rings."

"Hold on," Father Mike said. "I haven't yet agreed to officiate at a wedding."

Frank nodded. "We know that, Father, but we're hopin' to convince you that it's the only thing to do."

Parker led Clint into the rectory. When Father Mike saw the eldest Harrigan son, his kindly blue eyes went sparkly with tears. He stood up and extended a hand. "Ah, me poor boy, ye look like ye've seen a ghost."

Clint stepped forward to shake the priest's hand. "Not

yet, Father Mike, but Loni's as close to being a ghost as anyone can get without crossing over. Time is running out for her." Glancing at his family, Clint asked, "Have you told him everything yet?"

Father answered the question. "Yes, and 'tis a difficult story to believe."

Clint nodded and found a seat on the other sofa, where Zach and Mandy sat huddled together. "Not so difficult after it grows on you," Clint said. He had removed his hat and left it in the foyer, as had all the other men, and in the lamp glow, his black hair glistened as he inclined his head at Ceara. "Listen to her version of the tale, Father Mike. You've counseled a lot of people. I'm sure your instincts are honed far better than ours to detect a lie when you hear one. I, for one, am completely convinced that this young lady is telling the truth. Loni touched her hand, and she swears everything Ceara says is absolute fact." He held the priest's gaze. "You know Loni well. You not only believe in her gift of second sight but have seen proof of it for yourself. Even the FBI accepts her abilities. Before she got sick, she was working nearly every day with agents from different states, and more times than I can count, she's helped law officers in other countries find missing kids. She's the real thing. You know it, I know it, and so does everyone else in this room. So if Loni says Ceara is telling the truth, then she is, no ifs, ands, or buts."

Father rocked back on his heels, his hands clasped loosely at his waist. "Ceara, will ye join me in me office, where we can chat privately?"

Ceara followed the priest to the front office just off the large foyer. Quincy sat forward on the edge of his chair. Part of him wanted Father Mike to call a halt to this insanity, but another part of him prayed that Ceara would pass the test. If there was any chance for Loni to live—any chance at all—Quincy would do whatever was necessary to make it happen. Even marry a woman he'd known less than twenty-four hours, who had appeared in a flash of light in a box stall.

Even through the closed door, Quincy could hear the priest and Ceara talking. At first, their voices were heavy with solemnity, but then he heard Father Mike laugh, a warm, rumbling sound peculiar to the priest. The next instant, Quincy heard the two of them engaging in a conversation he couldn't understand. Gaelic? Yes, Quincy, decided. They'd slipped into speaking Irish. Occasionally Father Mike would interject in English, "Ah, lass, ye're losing me. Ye use the old Irish, and me ears are tuned for the new." Then, "Slow down." And, "Can ye repeat that for me?"

Before long, Ceara was laughing, too. Quincy had never heard her cut loose and laugh. The sound had a musical ring, almost like wind chimes tinkling in a fresh spring breeze. Clearly the aging priest was forming an instant bond with her. They were chatting like old friends.

Quincy heard Father Mike say, " 'Tis such a blessing, lass, to hear the first language of me homeland again. I haven't visited Ireland in almost four years, ye know. Me brothers and sisters call as often as they can, but 'tis a costly way to keep in touch. We mostly share e-mails."

"E-mails?" Ceara repeated. "What might those be, Father?"

Father Mike gave a hearty laugh. "Ah, lass, ye have so much to learn! This age is filled with many wondrous inventions."

"Like the wee box Sir Quincy calls a phone?"

Again Father chuckled. His mirth increased when Ceara told him about the traveling minstrels that she'd initially believed Quincy kept trapped in a box inside his truck.

Eventually the pair returned to the living room. Ceara's cheeks were pink, and her blue eyes glistened with an almost feverish brightness. She resumed her seat in the chair beside Quincy's, and Father Mike sat back down on the sofa.

"Well, Father?" Frank Harrigan said. "Will you marry the kids, or will I have to find a Lutheran minister to do the honors?"

All trace of humor vanished from Father Mike's expression. "Ye're asking me to disregard the rules of this diocese, many of which are edicts straight from the Vatican. Fortunately, being from the old country, I am a priest who believes there are many mysteries in this world. For instance, I'm not entirely convinced that the wee folk of Irish lore don't exist. And it's a strong believer in the forces of good and evil I am. Perhaps there are people who can put curses on others. It isn't a proven fact and certainly isna a teaching of the Church, so far as I know, but then, I can cite several instances in this country's history of people being possessed by demons and purged by an exorcist. Were those individuals victims of a curse? Normally I would seek the advice of the bishop before making this judgment call, but 'tis away he is at a retreat and can't be reached except in cases of extreme emergency." Father lifted his hands and shrugged. "Besides, if Loni is as close to death as ye say, there's no time for a decision by committee."

"Are you saying you'll do it, Father Mike?" Clint asked.

The priest sighed. "I do a great deal of reading, and I've always been fascinated by the concept of time travel. I honestly believe it will one day be possible, so it isn't a far stretch for me to think someone with special gifts might manage such a feat now. Ceara has assured me that she has never used her special powers for financial gain, personal recognition, or to cause harm to others, and it is documented by the Church that there were saints somehow capable of bilocation." He glanced from one face to another, and elaborated, "Bilocation is the ability of a person to appear in two places at once. There is no scientific explanation for this phenomenon, but unbiased witnesses have attested to the truth of it. I, for one, believe in their accounts. Thousands, if not millions, of learned people are also convinced." He shrugged. "I don't know how bilocation can occur. I only know it has. I suppose it is a leap of faith that I've taken. That being the case, it is not difficult for me to take another leap of faith and believe Ceara's story."

"So?" Frank pressed. "That sounds like a yes to me, Father."

The priest held up a hand. "Not just yet. Before I reach a final decision, we have one very large wrinkle to iron out." He gestured at Ceara. "The lass has no papers."

Clint swore under his breath. "I never thought of that." He glanced at Ceara. "Without papers, she doesn't exist legally. She needs a birth certificate, a Social Security number, and some sort of life history. Otherwise, the marriage can't be recorded."

Frank spoke up. "I know a fellow with a few . . . well, I guess you'd say *seedy* contacts, and I think I can get her set up with the whole works." He rubbed his thumb and fingertips together. "Money talks, but it'll take a little time."

"We don't have any time!" Clint almost shouted.

"Calm yerself, Clint," Father Mike said softly. "It's

merely a wrinkle, not insurmountable." His brow pleated in a thoughtful frown. "In the early days of the Church, people didn't have identification records like we do now, but marriages took place just the same, some without the presence of clergy and according to local custom. The Church has evolved, as have the requirements for marriage. I can officiate tonight, but everyone must understand that the union will be spiritual only—a marriage in the eyes of God but unrecognized by the state." Father Mike held up a hand. " 'Twill have to be rectified as soon as possible, understand." He inclined his head at Frank. "Once you get her an ironclad identity, she and Quincy must take marriage preparation classes, we'll post the banns, and then I will make record of the marriage as if it takes place at a later date."

"You'd do that?" Frank raised his brows at the priest.

"It's the only option. A couple cannot receive the Sacrament twice." Father smiled at Ceara and Quincy. "We can, however, have a ceremony so ye can reaffirm yer vows, and sometimes at celebrations like that, couples dress as a bride and groom. It boils down to a personal choice. You can also invite friends to witness the exchange. Perhaps, by doing that, ye'll feel it's more of an actual marriage the second time around. Rest assured, it won't be, though. Tonight will be the *real* marriage."

"Sounds to me like you'll be stickin' your neck out, just askin' to get your head whacked off," Frank observed. "We need your help, Father Mike, but it ain't our aim to get you in bad trouble."

The priest smiled. "Nothing so severe as beheading will result, Frank, but if the bishop gets wind of a shenanigan like this, there will be serious repercussions. That said, sometimes a priest must follow his heart." He sighed and directed his gaze at Quincy and Ceara. "Before I agree to take that step, I must ask both of ye a very serious question. Yer answers will be the deciding factor for me."

Before the priest could voice his question, the doorbell rang again. Father Mike got up to answer the summons, but before he made it halfway there, Quincy heard the front door open. The security system chimed a warning, and then Loni's mother, father, grandmother, and sister spilled into the room, still bundled up in winter outerwear. Quincy nearly groaned. He wasn't surprised to see them. At the cancer institute in Portland, they'd been in constant attendance. Naturally now that Loni had been brought home, they'd quickly followed her south. Quincy liked Clint's in-laws, but Loni's grandmother and mom were spirited women, Scottish to the marrow of their bones, and bold as brass.

The grandmother stepped forward first, her arm extended. "Hello, Father Mike." The pair shook hands. "You may not remember me. I'm Aislinn MacDuff, Loni's grandmother." She turned to refresh the priest's memory about her companions. "My daughter, Annabel. Her husband, Matthew. And Loni's sister, Deirdre Lavena."

Father Mike clasped hands with everyone and then motioned for the Harrigans to squeeze over to create more seating. He needn't have bothered, because Aislinn and Annabel were on a mission. Standing side by side, they were clearly mother and daughter, of similar slight builds with delicate features and deep blue eyes. Aislinn's once dark hair had gone nearly white, but her face looked nearly as unlined as Annabel's.

"No need for polite folderol," Aislinn said. "We've been on the phone with Dee Dee and aren't here for chitchat. My granddaughter is dying, and without your cooperation, Father, we'll lose her." Aislinn straightened her frail shoulders. Though eighty-four, she was still a power to be reckoned with, and Quincy could tell she didn't plan to accept no as an answer. "I'll tell you right up front, we are all devout Catholics, Father. I probably say my rosary more often than you do."

Annabel chimed in. "And I do as well. We realize that you will be breaking all the rules to perform this marriage, and that you may be severely chastised, but rest assured, my mother and I will go to bat for you with the bishop. If necessary, we'll even seek audience with the pope to defend your decision."

Father Mike sighed. "I appreciate yer sense of urgency and yer loyalty to Loni. But this is a decision I must make without interference."

Aislinn spotted Ceara in her antiquated gown and walked with amazing spryness across the carpet. A waft of stale cigarette stench trailed in her wake, a sure sign that she still chain-smoked. Quincy expected Aislinn to introduce herself to Ceara, but instead, much to his dismay, the old lady bent over to gather the folds of Ceara's skirt in her hands, closed her eyes, and went absolutely still. After a moment, she let go of the silk and straightened. "Loni has it right. This girl is telling the truth." Aislinn turned to the priest. "Like my granddaughter, I have the *sicht veesions*, Father. My gift isn't as strong as Loni's. I must always touch items belonging to a person to divine information about them. Touching Ceara's clothing let me see into her past. Let me just say that where she came from sure as hell ain't Kansas."

Father Mike laughed and held up his hands in surrender. "Ye're preaching to the choir, Aislinn MacDuff. I've talked with Ceara, and I'm already convinced the lass is telling the truth. Now, if ye'll *please* take a seat, I will talk with this couple and reach a decision, hopefully without yer input."

Aislinn huffed but found a seat at the end of one sofa. Loni's father, Matthew, led his wife and daughter to sit at the table in the dining room, which was open to the living area and near enough for an easy exchange of conversation.

The priest rested his gaze on Quincy and then searched Ceara's eyes. "Do ye both comprehend the sanctity of marriage and understand that it is a spiritual bond that lasts a lifetime? Ye can't use this marriage as a 'get well' ticket for Loni and then separate. If I bend the rules and sanction this marriage, I must feel confident that ye both have every intention of honoring yer vows and remaining married. Otherwise, 'twould be making a mockery of the Sacrament, and I cannot officiate."

Quincy felt the noose around his throat growing tighter. He ran a finger around his collar, caught himself, and lowered his hand at once. When he glanced at Clint's haggard face, he knew he couldn't run from this obligation.

"I completely understand the sanctity of the Sacrament, Father. I also understand that even though it won't be a marriage recognized immediately by the state or the Church, it will be recognized by God." In order to protect Father Mike from any repercussions, Quincy was willing to jump through all the hoops necessary to make this a legal union, recorded by both Church and state. After that was accomplished, all bets would be off, though. He had no intention of remaining married to a woman he didn't love. To *him*, that *would* make a mockery of the Sacrament. Maybe it was wrong of him to lie by omission, but desperate situations called for desperate measures. He soothed his conscience by thinking of all the people who'd been married in the Church and later sought annulments for one very good reason or another. Surely never consummating a marriage would be considered by the Vatican a viable reason for dissolution. "You can count me in."

Ceara's cheeks lost their color. She glanced at Quincy, her eyes mirroring so many emotions that he couldn't pinpoint them all. He did know she looked frightened. " 'Tis why I came, Father, to end this terrible curse. Now that I am here, I must follow through. I will honor me vows to Sir Quincy and be a faithful wife. 'Tis not a game I came here to play."

Father Mike rubbed his hands together. "Me vestments are over at the church." He sighed and shook his head. "I could be defrocked for doing this." He emitted another, lengthier sigh. "Ah, well, I'm fast approaching retirement, anyway. There are worse things than living out me final days with a fishing pole in me hand."

Aislinn MacDuff sprang to her feet. "And hopefully with a nice, cold beer in the other, Father. Let's get this done."

Quincy stood with everyone else and followed the priest from the rectory.

All his life, Quincy had envisioned being married during a beautiful nuptial Mass. The reality fell far short. Father Mike emerged from the sacristy wearing his white collar and the appropriate vestments, but he smelled strongly of popcorn. Quincy, his bride to be, and all the family members present had gathered at one side of the altar.

Without any preamble, Father herded everyone into their appropriate positions, opened a book, and cleared his throat to begin. Every intonation of the priest's voice bounced around inside Quincy's head, sounding like gibberish. Even so, Quincy retained the presence of mind to say his vows when prompted, and so did Ceara. He knew she had to be just as drained as he was, if not more so. What a fine pair they were, parroting promises neither of them felt in their hearts.

Clint had done well picking Quincy's wedding band, but Ceara's was way too big. As Quincy slipped it on her tiny finger, he wondered if humans had doubled in size over the last five hundred years. He wasn't a large man, but he dwarfed his bride. In that moment, Quincy knew that he had finally come to believe Ceara's crazy story. In her large blue eyes, he saw nothing to indicate deception. What he did see was a bride with nervous jitters. How old was she, anyway? He'd been looking at her practically all day, noting the delicacy of her features and the glorious glint of her hair, but he'd been so busy trying to disprove everything she said that he hadn't taken time to judge her age. *Shit.* She looked young, really young, early twenties, maybe. Maybe even younger. Hell. Quincy hadn't dated a woman under thirty-five in more than three years.

He couldn't do this. He wasn't a cradle robber. Only even as the objection sprang to his lips, he heard Father Mike pronounce them man and wife. It was done. He was asked to kiss his bride. When he grasped Ceara's shoulders, he felt the tremors that racked her slight frame. He bent his head and quickly grazed her quivering mouth with his. *Double shit.* Thank God he'd figured a way out of this sham of a marriage, and there would be no consummation. He wasn't into deflowering virgins, willing or otherwise, and Ceara, for all her determination to carry through with this ceremony, was definitely *otherwise*.

Everything after that passed in a blur for Quincy. The handshakes and hugs. The whispered congratulations, which rang hollow. He and Ceara had to stay behind to sign documents, which Father Mike would date later. Everyone else dashed back home to be near Loni, elated because she would now supposedly be past the crisis and on the road to recovery.

Quincy had driven halfway home before he realized he was completely on autopilot, so lost to his troubled thoughts and physical exhaustion that he could barely make out the road signs. Ceara said nothing. She just huddled on her side of the seat, staring straight ahead, her face pale in the glow of the dash lights. Quincy couldn't think of a single thing to say that might reassure her. Hell, he needed some reassurance himself. He'd married a stranger. And, hello, if he found that alarming, how in the hell was she feeling? She'd told him early this morning that she was a virgin—*a virgin daughter of the O'Ceallaigh*. She was probably expecting him to jump her bones the second they stepped into his house. He wouldn't do that. He'd *never* do that to any woman. But how could he tell her that? If he brought it up, she'd be bound to think he was hoping to do that very thing.

When they reached his ranch, Quincy pulled the truck up in front of the house and turned off the ignition. The vehicle's interior and exterior lights remained on for a few seconds, but the sudden silence after the diesel engine sputtered out was absolute, broken only by the pop of cooling metal under the truck hood.

"Well, we're home." It was all Quincy could think to say.

"Perhaps ye are home, Sir Quincy, but I am na and never shall be again."

Quincy didn't want to seem unfeeling, but the bottom line was, he had played no part in her departure from Ireland, and he couldn't help but wish she hadn't come.

Thinking that way made him feel like a bastard. If he was coming to believe that Ceara was actually from another century, then he needed to wrap his mind around the fact that this marriage might be Loni's only salvation, not to mention that of his other sisters-in-law.

"I know this must be—" Quincy broke off. He detested it when anyone patronized him. "Well, I don't know how you feel. All I can really say is that somehow we have to make the best of this."

Quincy exited the vehicle, slammed his door, and walked around the front bumper to help Ceara get out. To his surprise, she made no attempt to manage by herself this time, a telltale sign that she was even more exhausted than he was. As he opened her door and grasped her elbow, he made a mental note to get some food and drink into her. So far as he knew, all she'd eaten that day were a few bites of Polish sausage soup.

They ascended the steps. Quincy unlocked the door and opened it, guiding his wife over the threshold in front of him. He reached to the right to flip the wall switch. Light bathed the kitchen. Ceara blinked owlishly.

"'Tis so bright." She looked up at the lights embedded in the ash tongue-and-groove ceiling. "Do ye not worry about the candle flames setting fire to the wood?"

Quincy glanced up. "There aren't any candles up there, Ceara, only bulbs powered by electricity."

"Electricity?"

Quincy helped her out of the jacket and hung it on the coat tree. "Yeah, electricity. It's sort of like lightning during a storm, only with modern technology we've learned how to harness it and feed it through wires for power."

She frowned, clearly in over her head, which Quincy thought was understandable. He didn't fully comprehend how electricity worked himself, and he'd been using it all his life. "We need to get something to eat."

He no sooner spoke than his cell phone whinnied. He drew the apparatus from the case riding his belt and saw his own image on the screen. Clint, wanting to FaceTime. Quincy unlocked the phone and answered. Only it wasn't his brother's face that popped up. Aislinn MacDuff stared back at him. Ceara, still standing at his elbow, gasped when she saw the image.

Leaning close, she asked, "How did she get in there, pray? Is it a modern-day crystal ball, only shaped different?"

"I'll explain later," Quincy whispered. "Hi, Aislinn."

Aislinn clearly meant to waste no time on pleasantries. "It didn't work."

"What didn't work?" Quincy saw the buttons on the old lady's blouse, then the top of Clint and Loni's cooking range. "Aislinn, are you still there?"

"I'm here. And it's the marriage that didn't work! Loni's as cold as death. I'm in the kitchen filling bottles with hot water. We need to get her body temp up." Quincy glimpsed Aislinn's face again and saw tears glistening in her eyes. "We're losing her, Quincy. Clint is about to fall apart. He expected to see an improvement when we got back. Instead she's worse."

Ceara clasped Quincy's wrist. " 'Tis too soon," she said. "The marriage will break the curse. Please tell her Loni *will* get better. 'Tis only that we haven't yet consummated the union."

Quincy felt as if the slate floor under his boots turned to soup. His only ace in the hole—not consummating the marriage—had just flown out the proverbial window. His brain froze. His tongue wouldn't work. All he could do was stare down into Ceara's blue eyes.

"Well, for God's sake, get the hell off the phone and consummate the damned marriage!" Aislinn cried. "Loni's losing ground fast. You do know how, right, Quincy? You're no untried lad."

Quincy wasn't about to honor that question with a response. "Aislinn, we just walked in the door. Ceara hasn't eaten all day. She's so exhausted, she's weaving on her feet."

"Stand her by the bed and let her fall on the mattress. She can eat something after you get this finished."

The screen blinked out. Ceara stared, bewildered, at the bright little icons that popped back up. Then she bent slightly to peer at the back of the phone again. "Where did she go? This works verra different from me mum's crystal ball."

"She was never here. That was only a camera image of her. It comes through the air, transmitted on waves." Quincy realized that sounded insane even to him. He'd never witnessed anyone using a crystal ball and wasn't sure, even now, that he believed that they worked, but because that was Ceara's only point of reference, he added, "It works sort of like a crystal ball, I guess—with images and the sound of voices coming to me through it." Her bewildered expression made him sigh. "I'll explain it better later. What would you like to eat? I have some low-fat cheese and whole-grain crackers. Does that sound good? With maybe a tall glass of skim milk?"

Ceara still gaped at the phone as he shoved it back in the carrying case. Then she jerked and refocused on his face. "There will be time fer eating later. Where is yer sleeping chamber? I shall go prepare meself and wait for ye there."

Wait for him there? Quincy wanted to argue. Ceara was trembling like an aspen leaf in a brisk breeze, clearly scared half out of her wits about what lay ahead. And, *damn* it, he wasn't exactly looking forward to it, either. But instead of objecting, Quincy envisioned Loni's white face and clawlike hands, then directed Ceara to his bedroom.

Chapter Seven

Ceara located the sleeping chamber that was clearly used by her husband. It was a large room done in rich tones of amber and varying shades of brown. A pair of Sir Quincy's boots lay in a corner of the sitting area, and a discarded red léine was draped over one of two dark umber chairs. The huge bed was rumpled, the blankets and spread pushed back to reveal a pillow enveloped in a crinkled tan case. The cool air was lightly perfumed with a rich masculine scent, a pleasant blend of evergreen and musk that Ceara had come to associate with Sir Quincy. She guessed he used some kind of scented water after bathing, much as she did at home.

Shivering with cold, she stared with yearning at the massive stone fireplace on the far wall. Near the hearth, a black metal rack held several log rounds and smaller kindling. She was sorely tempted to use her gift to start a roaring blaze, but after Quincy's last unpleasant reaction, she decided to err on the side of caution and refrain. She had no time to light a fire the conventional way if she meant to be prepared for her husband before he joined her here.

With a quick glance around, she noted that there was no washstand visible. How was she to clean herself in preparation for her wedding night without a pitcher of water and bowl? Then she recalled her experience that morning at the jail when she'd been thrust naked into the shower room. It seemed to have happened a year ago. Perhaps Sir Quincy bathed in a similar fashion, standing under cold water that shot from a wall.

In addition to the entrance door, she saw three others. One stood ajar. She crossed the thick amber carpet to peer into the room. A long slate counter, topped by a horizontal mirror of equal length, sported two recessed porcelain washbowls. Between them, a basket held prettily folded brown towels similar to the white ones at the jail, only these were tiny. She also noticed a squat green bottle with a bright gold cap. Curiosity propelling her toward it, she grasped the strange container and exerted all her strength, which was still much diminished by the trials of her journey, to pull off the lid. By accident, she discovered that the cap had to be twisted off. *God's teeth! No cork?* This new century had countless marvelous things to learn about. She sniffed the opening of the bottle and smiled as the familiar piney-musk smell assailed her nostrils. The men of her time rarely used perfume, yet Sir Quincy apparently did on a regular basis.

To her left, an arm's length above the floor, was a huge porcelain depression enclosed by slate. With a graze of her fingertips over the cream-colored surface of the porcelain, she concluded that it was a bathing tub, though dissimilar from those at home, and so gigantic that it would take three strong men and a boy to carry it. And it appeared to be immovable. *Strange.* How did one dump the water out after bathing? 'Twas yet another mystery akin to electricity that Quincy would no doubt explain later.

She returned her attention to the tiny towels, deciding

one of them would serve well enough to cleanse herself. She needed only to figure out how to get water. She stepped closer to the right-hand washbowl, eyeing the bronze fixture at the back edge. It wasn't in the shape of a cross like those at the jail, but instead had a leverlike handle. She pulled up on it, and water gushed out. She expected it to be cold and was pleasantly surprised by the warmth when she put her fingers in the stream. *Amazing.* At home, they filled buckets at the well and heated water over the fire.

Reluctant to waste a single drop, Ceara turned the fixture off. She had no idea where the warm water came from, but such a miracle surely must be in limited supply. She opened the cupboards underneath, searching for a bucket or vat. *Nothing.* Mayhap, in this modern day, water vessels were hidden in the walls.

Refusing to think about the ordeal ahead of her, Ceara quickly undressed, dampened a tiny towel from the basket, and made fast work of washing herself. Behind her, a large glass door led into a slate enclosure. High on the wall she saw a bronze, bell-shaped object and realized it must be a shower spout, similar to those at the jail. Two gigantic brown towels hung on a hook just outside the bronze-framed door. She confiscated one to cover herself and returned to the sink to scrub her teeth with her finger. Her toothbrush, along with everything else she owned, must still be where she'd left it in the straw of the stable.

Oh, how she wished for her satchel and the small bottle of rose water she'd brought from home. A bride was supposed to smell nice when her husband joined her in the marriage bed. Ceara's mum had stressed the importance of that. Sadly, it was about the only thing Ceara knew for certain. She studied her reflection, finding fault with everything. Her hair needed a good wash, but drying it would take hours, and her brush was in her satchel. She pinched her cheeks, nibbled on her lips to bring some color to them, and, after quickly using the toilet, following the lead of women at the jail to flush it, she forced herself to exit the bathing chamber.

As she approached the bed, her stomach clenched and her heart did a jig. She couldn't help but recall the few times she'd been unfortunate enough to glimpse her father's stock animals mating. The mares had screamed and tried to evade the stallions. The boars had mercilessly accosted the much smaller sows. Even the hens had flapped their clipped wings to get away from an amorous rooster. In Ceara's estimation, procreation seemed to be a base and unpleasant experience for females of all species. She had no idea why men found it so enjoyable.

She drew the covers back on the unused side of the bed, dropped the towel, and slipped between the bedsheets to lie on her back. With the coverlet drawn to her chin, she lay motionless with her arms stiff at her sides, stared at the ceiling, and waited, her ears pricked for the sound of Sir Quincy's boots on the stairs. Aside from being a wee bit gruff, he seemed to be a nice enough man. She tried to tell herself that she needn't dread what was to come, but it didn't work. She closed her eyes and prayed that he would make fast work of his business. A stab of longing for her mother swept over her as she realized she didn't even know how long it would take.

Quincy hadn't dated much over the last few months. He'd grown weary of the getting-acquainted rituals, and he had definitely given up on finding the woman of his dreams. Even so, he wasn't a nervous bridegroom by any stretch of the imagination . . . until he entered the master suite and found Ceara lying naked in his bed with her eyes squeezed shut. He could almost feel her trembling.

Shit. She really *was* a virgin. And a frightened one.

Apparently she heard him enter, because she started and cracked open one peeper as he approached the bed. When she saw that he was still fully clothed, she frowned and said, " 'Tis me understanding that this deed is accomplished without garments, but I am new at this, so perhaps I have it wrong. Shall I fetch me gown?"

Quincy sat on his side of the mattress and cast her a look over his shoulder. Was that how wedding nights went in her time? The husband walked in stark naked, deflowered his bride, and then rolled off of her to fall asleep? It sounded barbaric.

"You don't have to get dressed again," he told her softly. "Unless you'd like to, of course." He let that hang there for a moment. "How old are you, Ceara?"

"Six and twenty. I ken that I'm quite long in the tooth for a bride, but me intended, a young man I adored, was killed in a riding accident when I was young, and afterward, I ne'er met anyone else I could accept, and me sire, being the O'Ceallaigh, dinna press me. His coffers were full, and he had no need of a strong alliance with another clan, so he allowed me to remain a spinster." She drew the covers close under her chin. " 'Twas only over the last year that I began thinking about breaking the curse, and once me father agreed to let me come forward, it took a goodly amount of effort to find ye Harrigans. Me mum was using the name O'Hourigan in her chants."

Quincy recognized nervous chatter when he heard it and decided to go with it. Perhaps an exchange—the longer the better—would help her relax. He couldn't resist asking, "Why did you volunteer to come, Ceara? You must have known it would be dangerous."

She nibbled her soft bottom lip as she considered her answer. " 'Twas mostly fer me father. He nears the end of his life, and the curse, cast upon innocent women by someone in his line, has long been a great burden on his conscience." She shrugged. "It troubled me as well. Those who ride under the O'Ceallaigh colors commit no violence against women and children, and yet a vengeful O'Ceallaigh ancestress cursed countless women of the future, not because she bore them any personal animosity, but because she wanted to punish the O'Hourigan man who humiliated her at the altar. 'Tis not our way to wreak vengeance on the innocent—nor is it a proud and just way to right a wrong. 'Tis a black mark on our name, and only a virgin daughter of the O'Ceallaigh can lift the curse. Me sister, Brigid, is too young to marry in this century."

"So the job of coming fell to you?" For Quincy it really wasn't a question, and he hadn't missed the sadness in Ceara's voice when she'd said her sister's name. "How old is Brigid?"

"Two and ten," she said with a slight smile. " 'Tis glad ye should be that 'twas not she who came. Me father says she will drive him deep into his cups before he can get her married off." Her smile widened. "He jokes, of course. The O'Ceallaigh scorns the practice of forcing daughters into loveless marriages."

"And yet he sent you here, knowing you'd be forced into the same?"

Her blue eyes widened on Quincy's. "Nay! 'Twas na the way of it. At first he forbade me to come. 'Twas only because I kept pestering him that he finally relented, and even then, he worried that something might go wrong."

Quincy had never had children, but he knew he wouldn't hesitate for an instant to put his life on the line to protect his nieces and nephews from harm. "What did your father fear might go wrong?"

" 'Twas uncertain—all of it. Druids have traveled forward, but none have been able to return to report on their journeys. Me father was terrified I might leave Ireland and land in the wrong place. 'Tis a very big land, yer country."

"Weren't you afraid, too?" Quincy asked.

She nodded. "But me life there had no real purpose, so I chose to take the risks. To me, it was the one gift I could give me father to ease his heart before he passes on. Me sire is a fearless warrior, and so are me brothers. I've ne'er done anything brave fer the good of others, so here I am."

According to Quincy's calculations, her father had already passed away more than four hundred years ago, but to Ceara, that time in history was still as real and immediate as this moment. "So you came forward not only to ease your father's conscience but also to save the lives of others." Quincy mulled that over for a moment. "In that case, when you volunteered to come forward, why didn't you choose to come earlier in time, say two or three centuries ago, to save even more Harrigan women from the curse?"

Her expression turned bewildered. " 'Twas impossible," she said with a lift of one slender shoulder. "I canna clearly explain why, but a druid can come forward only to a future that he or she can see in a crystal ball. I've no idea why so many years had to pass and so many other lives had to be lost." A crease formed between her brows. "All I know is that me mum could call up only this time, and no other choices were left to me."

Quincy muddled his way through the tangle of possibilities and finally gave up on making sense of it. Her brow creased again, more deeply this time. " 'Tis all verra confusing. I canna figure out time and how it works. How can me time and yer time exist at the same moment?"

Quincy's temples panged with the effort to decipher what she'd said. "So, in your time, your mother was able to see only *this* time in her ball."

She nodded. Then, after studying his frown, she smiled wanly. "Do na trouble yerself with the how of it, Sir Quincy. Not even the wisest druids of me day can understand it. I wish I knew more, but I do na. I can only say me heart was in the right place and I came forward to save the lives of those I could. The most difficult thing fer me to accept was knowing I could ne'er go home again."

Quincy couldn't fathom how that must have felt. His family, this land—the sense he had of being where he belonged—meant the world to him. Would he willingly board a flight to some faraway place, knowing he could never return?

"Why is that?" he asked. "If you can travel forward, why not back?"

"For one, traveling forward is said to drain a druid of power, so most wouldna have the strength to return. That is why I was so joyous to learn I can still make fire." She twisted the sheet in her small fists. "I am drained—of that I have no doubt—but at least me gift to make fire has been left to me. Also the learned ones claim traveling backward in time is impossible. I do not know the why of it, but I accepted before I came that I will be here fer always."

For the umpteenth time that day, Quincy felt cold chills of shock and recognition. He had two master's degrees, and had studied physics. He was familiar with Einstein's theories on time, velocity, and the possibility that forward time travel might one day be achieved. He also recalled that the famous scientist had postulated that travel backward in time would always be impossible. *Brain overload*. In a vague, intellectually removed way, Quincy could grasp the concepts of time travel, but when he tried to analyze them, his cranial circuit board started to short out.

The fleeting thought that Ceara might have taken physics at some modern hall of learning occurred to him before he brought himself up short. There was no point in searching for flaws in her story now, not after Loni's assertion that it was genuine. He was coming to believe Ceara, as crazy as it all still sounded. Besides, nobody in her right mind would take a hoax this far, especially not a trembling virgin who was clearly terrified to have sex with a stranger.

Quincy could only feel sad. The first time for any woman should be with someone she at least *thought* she loved. Ceara didn't know him well enough to be sure she even *liked* him, and he couldn't afford to give her more time. In short, everything about this whole mess had to be much more difficult for her than it was for him. Though he wasn't proud to admit it, Quincy had engaged in plenty of hand-shake sex over the years, sometimes with women he barely knew. Ceara had never been with anyone, and now she lay there, so small and defenseless, as vulnerable as a flagpole in a lightning storm.

A throbbing ache stabbed behind Quincy's eyes. He couldn't do this. Well, he *could*, but everything gentle-manly within him recoiled at the thought. He'd never been with a virgin, for starters. And he'd never made love to a shy, reluctant woman, either. It came as a bit of a shock to him to realize that maybe he was like that guy who sang the country-western song about liking his women a little on the trashy side.

He pushed to his feet. He seldom drank alcohol, but tonight called for desperate measures. He kept spirits on hand for members of his family when they visited. As he moved to head downstairs, Ceara peered owlishly after him.

"Where are ye going?" she asked.

Quincy almost said he was going nuts and invited her to come along, but he bit back the words. "I'll be right back."

What would a young woman who'd probably never imbibed like to drink? In the kitchen, Quincy rifled through his liquor cupboard. His dad's Jack Daniel's had quite a bite and wouldn't appeal. He pushed bottles this way and that, thinking maybe he could make Ceara a white Russian, but then he remembered he had no half-and-half. God forbid. The stuff was so full of fat, he got twinges in his arteries just looking at a carton. Sam's merlot was too dry. Maybe chilled white zinfandel would do. It was sort of sweet, more the thing for a first-time drinker.

He opened his Sub-Zero fridge and spied an un-opened bottle of champagne in the door. *Just the thing*. Practically all ladies liked the bubbly. He located an ice bucket in one of the lower cupboards, filled it with cubes, and popped the cork from the bottle before nestling it in the ice to stay chilled. Before heading back upstairs, he fixed a plate with snacks and grabbed two flutes, determined to imbibe tonight with his bride. Maybe knocking back a couple of glasses would ease his headache and numb his senses.

Ceara still lay on the bed like a sacrificial virgin, which, damn it, she actually was. Quincy carried the ice bucket, snacks, and glasses over to the small round table in the sitting area and then went to his walk-in closet to find a clean shirt. When he emerged and tossed the garment to Ceara, she blinked in bewilderment.

"One of my shirts. Put it on, honey. It'll cover you to the knees. While you dress, I'll get a fire going."

"Shirt," she repeated softly. "Is that what ye call it? At home, we call it a léine."

Quincy made a great show of turning his back so she wouldn't feel self-conscious as she slipped from the bed in her altogether. She must have spied the champagne and snack plate, because she cried, "What are ye about, Sir Quincy? Haste is necessary, is it not?"

He hated that she addressed him as *sir*, but with so much else on her shoulders, he didn't want to bitch about it. "Not so necessary that we have to go at this like we're killing snakes."

Ceara jumped back on the bed so fast she made the sheets snap. "Snakes?" she repeated shrilly, staring in alarm at the floor.

"It's only a saying, so don't go running for high ground. There aren't any snakes in here, and no poisonous ones on my ranch, either. Well, only rarely. We get an occasional rattlesnake, but they buzz to warn you."

"God's teeth!"

After he crouched before the hearth, the only sound in the room was the crinkle of newspaper sheets in his hands, followed by the chink of kindling and the thump of logs being placed on the grate. He didn't allow his gaze to waver from the task. Maybe he couldn't court Ceara properly, but he could at least make her deflowering as easy for her as possible.

As he struck the extended lighter and touched the flame to a wad of paper, her voice rang from behind him again. "Why must ye use that strange-looking object that shoots sparks to start a fire? Wouldna it be simpler to use yer druid gift to make flame?"

Quincy chuckled dryly. "I have no druid powers, Ceara." From the corner of his eye, he saw that she'd taken a seat on one of the velvety barrel chairs. "When powers were being passed out, I must have been standing at the back of the line."

"Well, 'tis silly beyond measure to labor so, and whether ye grow angry or na, I shall use mine."

She flicked her fingertips toward the fireplace, and the sudden whoosh of flame startled Quincy so badly that he nearly pitched backward onto his ass. He caught his balance, staring with amazement at the now roaring fire—every wad of paper already burning and the pieces of kindling snapping as pitch exploded from the heat. No question about it this time: Quincy knew for a fact that there was no ignition device in that firebox.

"That little trick is one that'll take some time for me to get used to," he said.

" 'Tis possible—even probable—that it is the only gift remaining to me." Sadness laced her voice. "Perhaps God, in all His goodness, shall see fit to let me retain a few others as well. I have not yet put meself to the test. Mayhap that is for the best. It has been a very trying day. 'Tis uncertain I am that I can deal happily with any more disappointments."

Quincy wondered if he was one of her disappointments. Probably. He was forty, for Pete's sake, not exactly ancient by any stretch, but way too old for a beautiful woman of only twenty-six.

"As for yer gifts, or the lack of them," she said, returning to the first subject, "there are two possibilities. Perhaps ye were born with gifts and simply do na know it, or yer blood is so watered down by yer ancestors mating with nondruids that ye're almost a nondruid yerself. In me time, druids marry only druids." She sighed. " 'Twill break me heart if our children are deprived of their birthright. 'Tis a marvelous thing to be druid."

Children? Where was that drink? Within a few hours he'd gone from anticipating sleeping apart and then requesting an annulment, to accepting that he had no choice but to consummate the union, to discussing the traits their children would inherit. His head was spinning, and this marriage was starting to sound damn permanent. Which it would be after he made love to her. Then he truly would be tied to her, no wiggling his way out, and no turning back.

He pushed erect and stepped over to the table to pour them each some sparkly. Between filling flutes, he glanced out the window. "No," he said with a groan. "It *can't* be snowing *again*. It's supposed to be turning spring."

Ceara waved a hand, and just like that, the snow stopped. She laughed with delight. "Did ye see that, Sir Quincy? I am still able to control the elements!" She flattened a slender hand over her chest, looking too adorable for words in his blue work shirt, her red braid falling over her shoulder and curling like a rope on her lap. "Oh, me, that made me feel faint. Coming forward has weakened me powers. I can feel it deep inside. But at least I havena been completely stripped of them."

Quincy gave her a long, sharp look. He couldn't believe, not for one second, that she'd stopped the snow from falling. It had to be a coincidence.

She noticed him studying her with a frown. "Do ye want the snow back?" she asked. "I was only trying to please ye. Ye dinna seem to welcome it."

"Yes," Quincy said, "I want the damned snow back."

She waved her hand again, and the downfall of large flakes resumed. *Not a coincidence.* The realization shook Quincy to his bones, and he almost downed champagne straight from the bottle. For an instant he thought of reruns he'd seen of the TV show *Bewitched* in which a woman could work magic by twitching her nose. He finished pouring the champagne with a shaky hand, handed her a flute, and sat on the other barrel chair to gape at her.

"Ceara," he said carefully, "the way I see it, the weather should be controlled only by Mother Nature. Stopping the snow could interfere with the ecological balance."

She crinkled her shimmering brows in a frown. "Is Mother Nature a powerful female druid?"

Quincy couldn't help laughing. "No, it's just a saying. God, Mother Nature—the two are synonymous when it comes to nature and the elements."

Her frown deepened. " 'Tis strange. Will God na take offense, being referred to as a female?"

Quincy almost replied that some people of his day preferred to think God was a woman, but he decided Ceara had dealt with enough weird stuff to keep her mind racing with questions. "I think God has far weightier matters to worry about," he settled for saying.

Quincy noticed that she kept tugging on the tails of his shirt to hide more of her legs. She had gorgeous ones: trim ankles, shapely calves, and at the sides of the shirt where he could glimpse her thighs, they appeared to be sleek and firm. He especially liked the little dimples on her knees. Nice view, but he wasn't one to enjoy himself at someone else's expense. He flipped up the lid of the small storage ottoman and tossed her a plush brown throw. As he did, he wondered about his choices in color schemes. Everything was brown or gold—with one notable exception: Ceara added plenty of contrast to the room with her flawless ivory skin, big blue eyes, and red braid. As she juggled her flute while covering her legs with the throw, her every movement made her hair spark like fire. Having her around would be good for him. She added brightness.

She finally settled on the chair, her modesty temporarily preserved, and sniffed the champagne. She immediately sneezed and drew back her head, looking surprised. " 'Tis wiggling!" She trailed a fingertip up the side of the glass, marking the progress of a rising bubble. "Would ye look at this?"

Quincy grinned. Lifting his glass to her, he said, "It's safe," and to prove it, he took a swallow. "It's called champagne, or sparkling wine. I believe it existed in your time, but maybe none of it ever drifted your way. It's effervescent, thus the little bubbles. Some people call it bubbly."

She tried a taste. Her eyes widened and then she smiled at the tickle on her tongue. "I quite like champagne," she informed him.

In that moment, Quincy realized just how very beautiful she was. Perfection in miniature, he decided, much smaller than most women of this era, but bigger didn't necessarily mean better. "So, Ceara, in your time, are you on the small side for a woman?" he asked.

"Nay. Me mum is a wee bit of a thing, but I got more height from me da. In his day, he was a strapping man, as tall and stout as a tree." She gave Quincy a quick assessment. "Not nearly so tall and stout as ye are, but a big man fer the time. After being here, me opinion is that mankind has grown much larger over the centuries, just as the earth itself has."

"The earth?" Quincy queried.

"Oh, me, yes. D'y'na know that new and wondrous places have been discovered?" Her eyes sparkled with incredulity. "Why, yer verra own country was found and settled eventually, and I was told today of a faraway land called New Zealand that no one knew about in me time."

Quincy reviewed his history and realized that New Zealand had been colonized long after the sixteenth century, which did make it new to Ceara. He settled back on his chair to watch her enjoy her drink, pleased to see her downing it rather quickly between taking bites of cheese and crackers from the plate. She'd soon feel warm and relaxed, which was precisely his aim. As sick as Loni was, she would applaud Quincy's decision to give Ceara this short time to relax before the marriage was consummated.

Ceara's lips pursed as she chewed. "Yer cheese is . . ." A blush flagged her cheeks. "Well, 'tis na so rich and flavorful as what we make at home."

"It's low-fat, much better for your heart."

Judging by her slight frown, she preferred good taste over healthfulness. Quincy made a mental note to stock the fridge with some whole-fat dairy products. "You actually *make* your own cheese?" he queried.

Her eyes widened on his. "Ye do na?"

He loved the way she spoke, and nearly chuckled. "No, I buy it already made."

"Ach!" Her cheek dimpled in a glowing smile. "Ye need a new cheesemaker, Sir Quincy. This isna as good as what we have at home." As she chewed a bit of cracker, she held up a finger. After swallowing, she said, "And 'twill be *me*! Yer new cheesemaker, I mean. Ye'll think ye've died and gone to heaven. Me mum's recipe is grand!"

He definitely needed to go grocery shopping. Ceara

could afford to lose no weight, and she obviously wasn't going to adapt well to his preferred foods. "I can't wait to try it." He could almost feel his arteries preparing for the onslaught. "Maybe I can help you make a batch."

When she drained her flute, he sat forward to refill it and then his own. She was well into the second glass when his cell whinnied again. He plucked the phone from his belt to see that it was Clint calling. Or so he hoped. He wanted no more barked orders from Aislinn.

"Yo," Quincy said after answering. "How's it—"

"Have you gotten the deed done yet?" Clint demanded.

Quincy was glad he hadn't turned on the speaker. This experience was bad enough for Ceara without his whole damned family calling in rush orders. "No. It's what you might call a delicate situation, Clint. We'll get there. Just give us a reasonable amount of time."

"Loni's worse!" Clint cried, talking so loudly now that Ceara straightened on the chair, giving Quincy the uncomfortable feeling she could hear his brother's every word. "She's bleeding from her gums, and pink shit is coming from her eyes. Her pulse feels weak. I'm afraid she won't make it until morning. I called our hospital here. The ER nurse says they can give her IV fluids and a transfusion if they can find a good vein, but I'd have to take Loni into town for both. She refuses to go. If she's going to die—and she stresses the *if*—she wants to be at home with her family."

"I can't get anything accomplished until you get the hell off my phone!"

Quincy rammed his thumb on the "end" icon, knowing even as his hand shook with anger that he had no business being pissed. Clint was desperate, and he obviously couldn't spare a thought for what this might be like for Ceara.

Quincy saw Ceara set aside her glass of champagne, fold the throw, and lay it on the ottoman, so he knew she'd heard Clint's roaring. She stood and held out her hand to him. He enfolded her fragile fingers in his, rose from the chair, and followed her back to the bed.

At the foot, she wiggled her hand free. "I am prepared to do me duty. Are ye prepared to do yers?"

Quincy had no idea how to commence. He yearned to make this at least nice for her, but how the hell could he do that when she was shaky with nerves and his frantic family members were calling for updates?

Standing before him, she loosened her braid, tossing the leather tie to the floor atop a rumpled towel. In seconds, her glorious red hair flowed around her body like a flaming curtain of rippling heat. As she removed the shirt, Quincy went to turn off the overhead lights, plunging the room into amber-kissed shadows. He couldn't drag his gaze from her as he closed the distance between them. *Maybe*, he thought, *God knows better than I when it comes to what's good for me.* Ceara was the most beautiful thing he'd ever seen, her petite but curvaceous body artfully concealed with long, undulating curtains of hair, the parted strands revealing a glimpse of bare hip as creamy and luminous as ivory satin, the dip of her slender waist, the flatness of her belly, and legs so lovely that most men saw their equal only in dreams.

She scurried to one side of the bed to slip between the sheets. As she lay back, she requested in a tremulous voice, " 'Tis grateful I will be, Sir Quincy, if ye'd make short work of this, please. I shall ne'er ask it of ye again, I promise. Me mum says a man quite enjoys his baser pleasures, and it is a wife's obligation to endure his whims. I will pleasure ye in any fashion ye wish, every other night fer the rest of our lives, but fer tonight, 'tis me wish fer it to be finished quickly."

Quincy believed in using a slow hand when he made love to a woman, and he hated to give Ceara short shrift. But as he sat on the opposite edge of the mattress to kick off his boots and shed his clothes, he thought of Loni's bleeding gums and the pink seepage coming from her eyes. No matter what, he and Ceara needed to get this first time over with as quickly as possible. He glanced down and sent up a quick, silent prayer. His tool was limper than wilted lettuce.

As he stretched out beside Ceara, who awaited his invasion of her body with closed eyes and a resolute expression, he got a strange, twisting sensation in his chest. Beautiful *and* brave. He knew in that moment that he no longer questioned the truth of her crazy tale of time travel, and he greatly feared she was in the process of stealing his heart. He'd never met anyone quite like her.

He was far too old for her. She was far too young for him. Yet when Ceara opened those blue eyes, Quincy saw deep wisdom in their depths. No child, this, but a woman full-grown who was ready to sacrifice herself for the well-being of others—right now Loni, who was little more than a stranger to her. Searching Ceara's gaze, Quincy knew it was important to her to end this curse. And, damn it, he should be just as committed to ending it. He would never forget the day his mother died from hemorrhaging during labor and then childbirth with his baby sister, Sam . . . the kitchen floor covered with pools of her blood before his dad got to the house and could rush her to the hospital. His eldest brother, Clint, had never really gotten over it. Quincy suspected that Clint blamed himself for their mother's death, but if so, it was something Clint never discussed.

This lady wanted to end all that. She was here to save Loni's life, and the lives of all Quincy's brothers' wives, not to mention the wives of future Harrigans. It was a noble intention, which he must keep foremost in his mind. Big problem. In order for him to consummate this marriage, a certain part of his anatomy had to rise to the occasion, and that wasn't happening.

As if she sensed Quincy's dilemma, Ceara turned onto her side and touched her palm to his cheek. "Ye're a kindly man, Sir Quincy. 'Tis sorry I am that ye've been forced into marriage and now must lie with a woman ye do na want."

How could she think he didn't want her? Dear God, she was every man's dream. "Sweetheart, you're beautiful. It's not lack of wanting that bothers me."

She trailed her fingertips over his hair, her touch so light he yearned for more. "Push yer troubles from yer mind."

Quincy lowered his head and kissed her—a feather-soft pressure of lips, a quick exchange of breath. He felt the tip of one of her breasts graze his chest as he drew her into his arms until only her lovely hair formed a partial barrier between them. He felt her stiffen at the intimate contact of their bodies, but then the tension drained from her, she pressed her face to his neck, and he felt her lips curve in a smile.

" 'Tis not like with pigs," she whispered with a shaky laugh.

"*What?*"

"Me father's pigs. 'Tis a terrible sight when one of the gigantic boars corners a first-year sow."

Quincy choked back a startled laugh, and then, following instincts he hadn't known he possessed, he rolled with her in his arms until she lay on top of him. She planted her bony elbows against his armpits and reared back to frown at him. "What is it that ye're about, Sir Quincy?"

"Trying my damnedest not to act like a pig," he replied, barely able to suppress another chuckle. The press of her thatch just above his groin brought Old Glory to attention, and her blue eyes widened when she felt the stiff nudge against her silken thigh. "As I recall, you're absolutely right. The mating rituals of pigs *are* a terrible sight. So how's about you get us lined out here, doing things the way you think will be nice."

Her elbows pressed deeper. She shook her head. "Do ye have rocks betwixt yer ears? The wee bit I know about this . . . this *process* is what me mum told me in private."

Quincy splayed one hand over her back, tracing the prominent little bumps of her spine with his forefinger. She shivered, and goose bumps rose on her skin. He made a mental note to revisit that erogenous zone later.

"Kiss me," he whispered huskily. "That's usually the first step."

She bent to do that, coming at him nose-to-nose with her first try, which was quickly aborted because his prominent schnozzle got in the way. She backed off and tipped her head to try a new approach, and this time, as her lips barely brushed his, Quincy cupped his free hand over the back of her head, applied gentle pressure, and guided her in for a more satisfying landing. She sighed as he deepened the kiss, exploring the recesses of her mouth, tasting how sweet she was. Then, with no prompting, she slipped her arms around his neck, letting her body melt against his, and returned the kiss with a notable lack of experience but plenty of enthusiasm.

Magic. Quincy had always searched for it with other

women, but never had he found this spark of something inexplicably right. Ceara tasted like honey and champagne. She moaned into his mouth. That was the only signal he needed to forget everything else, let nature take over, and make love to the lady properly. He felt as if he were embracing a sunbeam. She responded as if she belonged in his arms, and only his. He kept trying to remind himself that she was bound to be shy, but he was an experienced lover, and soon he let most of his worries drift away.

Ceara couldn't think, and at times the sensations Quincy evoked within her were so intense and wondrous, she could barely breathe. His hard, work-roughened hands touched her everywhere, so gently but masterfully that she felt one rush of pleasure after another. She forgot to be afraid. She no longer worried about the strange fancies of some men. In his arms, she felt safer than she ever had, protected on all sides by the heat and strength of him. When he closed his mouth over the tip of her breast, she cried out at the rush of tingling that zigzagged through her, and later, when his hand slipped between her legs to find her most secret and guarded place, she arched to press her pelvis against the heel of his palm, wanting more—and more. A curious tension mounted within her, and with it came need. His masterful fingertips stroked that need to a fiery urgency. She lifted her hips to accommodate him, and then it felt as if she lost control of her body. Her every shred of consciousness centered on the place he touched. As if from a distance, she heard herself panting and crying out. And then, as if controlled by invisible strings, her muscles started to jerk and quiver as a lovely, molten jag of what felt like lightning coursed from his fingertips up through her body.

Afterward, Ceara went limp, her heart pounding, her skin dewy, her breath coming in uneven gasps. Quincy gathered her close to his chest and feathered soothing kisses over her face, whispering words she couldn't quite catch, but his tone told her all she really needed to know, notably that what had just occurred was the natural way of things.

She felt rather than saw him position himself over her. A crinkling sound brought her eyes open. He'd just opened a small, shiny packet, and as she watched, he withdrew a round object. Her mum had warned her of this.

"Nay," she protested weakly, and plucked it from his hand to toss it aside. "No sheepskin. 'Tis an act of procreation as well as pleasure. In order fer the curse to be broken, naught must separate us when we join as man and wife."

"But, Ceara, I don't want to get you pregnant. It's way too soon. We need some time to get better acquainted and enjoy each other's company."

Ceara no longer felt quite so uneasy about what was yet to come, so she looped her arms around his neck and drew him to her. " 'Tis a worry fer later. Tonight it is our *duty* to break the curse, and naught else matters."

She felt him tense, and then the resistance left his muscular frame. He pushed up on his elbows to gaze down at her. His eyes glistened, looking different from before, and a flush colored his corded neck. Ceara caught his face between her hands.

"What is it?" she asked.

"I don't want to hurt you," he said, his voice oddly ragged. "And I know I will this first time."

Earlier, Ceara had dreaded the virgin's pain, but now, after experiencing the wonders of being in Quincy's arms, she no longer felt so frightened. "Women have endured it for centuries," she assured him. "I'm made no differently than they."

"You're tiny, much smaller than most women today. What if your insides are tiny, too?"

Ceara's mum had given birth to five plump babies. "I think me insides are made to stretch. I doubt yer manly part is larger than a newborn babe." She didn't allow herself a glance down to check. "Forget about hurting me, Sir Quincy, and get on with it."

He laughed weakly. Then he leaned down to kiss her. She felt his manly part growing long and hard again. Mayhap it *was* as big as a newborn babe—or bigger. But before Ceara could collect her thoughts enough to become frightened, he pressed himself partway into her. Her passage was slick and ready for him, but the fit was tight. Ceara knew that he had prepared her well, though. When he nudged gently against the barrier of her virginity and hesitated, she clasped his narrow hips, bumped up with her own, and brought the entire length of him into her. Her body clenched with that first, tearing stab of pain. But it ebbed quickly, and she sighed.

"'Tis good," she told him. "Ye've given me pleasure. Now ye must find yers."

Ceara expected to feel little pleasure herself from this moment on. But when Quincy drew back and then plunged forward again, explosions of delight went off deep within her. Limned by golden firelight, his muscular arms and shoulders glistened as richly as seasoned English elm polished to a high sheen. *Beautiful,* she thought. And then she forgot everything—absolutely *everything*. At some point, Quincy's muscles snapped taut, bunching the full length of his body, and his thrusts deepened with enough force to push her upward on the bed.

The jolts of delight within her became stronger. Her

vision went dark until all she saw were bright sparkles. And for the second time, a burning need built within her, a need so great that she found his rhythm and started pushing up with her hips to meet his thrusts. They reached the pinnacle together, both of them crying out and then going limp in each other's arms, their skin slick, their hearts pounding, his a hard, vibrating slam against her breast, hers quicker and out of time.

Even so, as Ceara drifted over the edge of exhaustion into blissful sleep, she decided that their heartbeats harmonized beautifully, creating a perfect lullaby to carry her off into dreams.

Chapter Eight

Quincy didn't know how long he and Ceara slept, but when he wakened, it was still dark beyond the windows, the fire had burned down to a red glow that barely lit the room, and he was flat on his back with his bride lying on top of him like a soft blanket that was too short to cover his ankles and feet. Her weight was so slight that he felt pretty sure he could endure the burden all night—if it weren't for the fact that the pressure of her body against him had rekindled his desires and nudged him from dreamland into passion.

Not happening, he warned himself. Having sex with a man out of duty was something no woman should have to endure even once, let alone twice in a row. From this moment forward, he would insist that Ceara come to him out of desire, which could happen only with time and the development of deep feelings between them.

As if she sensed his wakefulness, she stirred and lifted her head to peer at him through the gloom. Quincy saw her eyes widen when she realized they lay skin-to-skin, with his thigh riding between her legs. As if poked with a sharp pin, she jerked, scrambled off him, and grappled with the rumpled sheet to cover herself. When her body was concealed, she sent him a wary look through the shadowy gloom. In all his days, Quincy couldn't recall starting his day with the sight of a sweeter or lovelier face.

"Good morningtide," she said.

"And to you, but I don't think it's quite morning yet."

She snuggled down on her side of the bed, finding a cushion for her cheek on the other pillow. Clearly, their earlier intimacy was something she wanted to pretend hadn't happened. Quincy lacked practice when it came to morning-after shyness. In fact, he'd made it his policy never to hang around very long after having sex with a woman. He was more a "that was great, and where's my hat?" kind of guy. The mere thought of his belt buckle wearing a spot on some female's bedpost gave him the jitters, and he was always careful to select partners who sought mutual pleasure and understood that it came with no strings attached.

This time there were definitely strings, and if he guessed right, Ceara might already be regretting that. He wondered if it was because he'd performed poorly as a lover and she dreaded having to endure more of his advances. His mind still foggy with sleep, he couldn't formulate the words needed to assure her that he didn't expect a repeat performance anytime soon.

Settling on his side to face her, he said, "We've done our duty now, Ceara. Nobody can expect more from us than that. Loni will either get well now, or she won't. How you and I move forward from here will be entirely up to us." He rubbed a hand over his eyes, wishing he'd phrased that better. "More precisely, it will be mostly up to you. I won't be forcing my attentions on you merely because we're married. That sort of intimacy should stem only from mutual desire. Don't you agree?"

"Me mum says a wife must be available to her husband at all times."

"Well, your mum isn't here to run our marriage, and in this century, women aren't treated like possessions by their husbands. At least, they shouldn't be. Nothing more will happen between us unless you want it to happen. Sound fair enough?"

"But what of yer needs and wants? Do they na play a large part in when we next do it?" She broke off and licked her lips. "It seems unfair fer only the wife to say when."

As sweet and desirable as Ceara was, Quincy had no intention of making the first night of their marriage the sexual template for the remainder of it. If he couldn't seduce her back into his bed, he'd do without. That wouldn't be his preference, of course. He had healthy sexual appetites, and she was delectable. But he wasn't about to press a female for sex when she didn't share his desire.

"I'm accustomed to living alone," he finally replied. "My needs and wants don't factor heavily into the equation." He reached to pull the covers over her. "Dawn won't show its face for a while yet. Why don't you try to get a little more sleep?"

She peered at him through the amber-washed gloom, her expression troubled. Quincy guessed that she had been raised to take her duties as a wife very seriously, even if it meant subjugating her own wishes to please her husband. Over time, he hoped she'd come to understand that a happy, modern-day marriage was built on a foundation of give and take, with both partners making sacrifices to please the other. He would not be a husband who slaked his passion on a wife who wasn't as delighted to be in his arms as he was to have her there.

"What of ye?" she asked. "Will ye sleep longer as well?"

Quincy nodded, jerked a blanket up over his shoulder, and closed his eyes. Moments later, he heard Ceara's breathing go soft and even. He missed holding her against him—wished that things between them were different. But love didn't happen overnight. It came softly and built slowly between two people. Maybe it would happen that way for him and Ceara. Maybe it wouldn't. Only time would tell.

Ceara blinked and rubbed her eyes. The first faint light of morning came through the windows that flanked the fireplace. All she wanted was to go back to sleep, but she felt Quincy stir awake beside her.

"The journey drained me," she told him, her voice gruff from slumber. "Though I have rested, me bones still ache."

He gently smoothed her hair back from her cheek. "It's your own kind of jet lag, honey. Not much to do but sleep it off. Just close your eyes and get more rest."

Ceara had no idea what jet lag was, and she was too tired to ask, so she did as Quincy said and tried to drift back to sleep. She missed the feel of his strong, warm arms around her, but never had she slept in such a wonderful bed. Her moss-stuffed ticking at home had seemed the height of luxury, but compared to this 'twas like sleeping on sticks. His mattress felt firm and yet gave with their weight, molding around their bodies and holding the warmth. From even across the bed, heat radiated from Quincy's skin, enveloping her, soothing her. She found a comfortable hollow in her pillow to cradle her cheek, and let exhaustion carry her away to blackness once again.

Sometime later Quincy's cell phone whinnied. Ceara had been startled at first by the sound of a horse coming at unexpected moments, but now, even as she jerked to consciousness, she registered that the whinny came from the wee box he called a phone. Quincy rolled, showing her his back, and muttered a word she'd never heard, his tone suggesting that it was a curse, as he groped and fumbled for the strange apparatus. Feeling the chill as the blankets shifted, Ceara drew up her knees to hug them, drowsily fascinated by how the mounds of muscle along his spine rippled as he used his arms.

"Yo, Quincy here." His voice rumbled, and she wished she were cuddled close to feel the vibration. The thought made her shiver. "What's up?"

Quincy pressed a bright spot on the phone screen, bringing Clint's voice in as loud and clear as if he were in the room. "Loni woke up a little while ago and asked for some broth! She's hungry, Quincy! And her gums have stopped bleeding!"

"Wow, that's great news."

"Great?" Clint echoed. "Correction, it's *fabulous*. I swear she's got more color. Her lips aren't as white. Dee Dee is warming some broth right now. I'll get back to you as soon as I know for sure that it'll stay down."

Quincy chuckled as he broke the connection. "You hear that, Ceara? Loni may be a little better."

After yawning sleepily, Ceara murmured, "The broth will settle well on her stomach. The blood sickness is gone now."

"Gone?" he echoed, his tone incredulous.

"Yes, gone. She will be verra weak fer a time, but she shall grow better day by day until she is completely well again. We ha broken the curse."

Quincy rolled to face her so abruptly that Ceara drew back and blinked. In the dim light of dawn, his strong white teeth flashed in a broad grin. "We have, haven't we? It worked. It really worked!"

Ceara nuzzled her cheek against her pillow, pleased to see the joy that lightened his expression. "Of course it worked. Do ye think I came so far to perform those beastly duties as a wife because I have rocks betwixt me ears?"

His smile faded. "Beastly? I thought . . . well, last night, I got the impression—"

Ceara laughed. " 'Tis jesting I am. 'Twas surprisingly pleasant, nothing at all like the goings-on between pigs."

His black brows snapped together in a scowl. "That's it? It was 'surprisingly pleasant'? A lot better than what happens between pigs? That doesn't sound so good."

As shy and embarrassed as she felt when she recalled the intimacies they'd engaged in last night, Ceara wanted him to understand that she'd found the act unexpectedly pleasurable, but the rules of ladylike behavior, drilled into her since early childhood to prepare her for a suitable union with a man of status, made her think twice before speaking. "A lady canna wax poetic about that kind of thing. 'Tis brazen. Me mum wouldna approve. Na at all."

His scowl lessened. "So you're feeling brazen, are you?"

Ceara's stomach clenched, for in her time there were strict social mores for all wellborn women to follow, not to mention that the Catholic faith itself had strict moral codes. Those females foolish enough to ignore them paid a dear price. "I dinna say I'm feeling brazen, only that 'twould be brazen of me to discuss it."

He settled his head on her pillow so their noses nearly touched and they shared each other's breath. Without her toothbrush, Ceara had been unable to give her teeth a good scrub last evening, and she worried that her mouth might smell sour. If it did, he gave no sign.

"In this century, a lady isn't considered to be brazen if she enjoys physical intimacy," he told her huskily. "And that is especially true if the lady in question is married to the man she enjoys such things with." His expression grew intent and solemn. "Just to be sure we aren't getting our wires crossed, can you tell me, honestly, if what we did last night was . . . well, you know, just okay, good, really good, or . . . spectacular?"

Ceara had never heard that last word, but judging by the context of his question, she guessed its meaning. And judging by the anxiety she saw in his eyes, he yearned for her to say their joining had been enjoyable beyond description. Sadly, the training of a lifetime made her guarded. She considered carefully before replying.

"Let me say only that if ye approach me again with such things on yer mind, I willna object."

He studied her for a long moment, and then scooted back to his own side of the bed. "Okay, I'll be sure to bear that in mind."

Ceara couldn't think what she might have said wrong. If a lady told a man she wouldn't object to his future attentions, she was inviting him to make advances whenever he wished. But for reasons beyond her, Quincy didn't seem to comprehend her meaning. "Ye're displeased with me."

"Not at all. It's just that I need a bit more from you than that."

Ceara yearned to ask him why, but then she might appear to be throwing herself at him, and that, too, was unacceptable behavior for a lady. "I wish to be a good, dutiful wife," she offered.

"I'm sure you will be," he replied. "But when it comes to sex, strike the word *dutiful* from your mind, because it doesn't sit well with me. If and when we make love again, there will be no feelings of *duty* involved. You'll either *want* to do it, and let me know that in every conceivable way a woman can, or we'll never go there again. Am I clear on that?"

Ceara wanted to make love with him again, but to tell him that—or show him that—well, 'twas unacceptable for her to do either. 'Twas the man who was supposed to be the aggressor. She tried to think how she might explain, but before she could get a word out, he'd closed his eyes, signaling that he meant to get more sleep.

They definitely had their wires crossed, she decided as she plumped her pillow, using a little more force with her fists than was necessary. *Men.* Her mum said they could be dumber than sheep at times, and that was certainly proving to be true of Quincy Harrigan.

Upon awakening a third time, Quincy discovered that he was holding Ceara in his arms. He didn't know whether she'd gravitated toward him in her sleep, or if he'd been drawn by her gentle warmth and softness. He knew only that he liked having her pressed against him—and so did his dick. He gave himself a silent lecture about not making love to her again. For one thing, he couldn't do that until he was sure she wanted him to, and so far, her responses to his questions on that topic had fallen far short of the enthusiasm he needed to hear. Second, though he was no expert on virgins, common sense told him that overuse of her sensitive female anatomy might make her sore, and, hell, he had the rest of their married life to enjoy her body—if and when she ever gave him a green light. Problem. Old Glory, Quincy's name for his dick since childhood, had no common sense and was ramrod stiff.

Quincy tried to distract himself with thoughts of what

he should accomplish today, and for once, the long list of to-dos wasn't related to ranch work or horses. Grocery shopping was high on his list, a chore he dreaded, because he'd be buying high-fat foods that hadn't graced his kitchen in years. *No matter*. Ceara was already a little too thin, so if she wanted real cheese, she'd have it. She'd no doubt turn her nose up at his plastic version of butter, and she'd surely like whole milk, preferably with a layer of cream on top, just as it came fresh from a cow. There was a dairy up the road. Quincy could stop there to see about buying a couple of gallons. And clothing! His wife couldn't go around looking like a participant in some Renaissance fair. He briefly considered enlisting the help of his sister or sisters-in-law, but Loni was the only one with any flair for fashion. Sam, bless her heart, would have Ceara dressed like a ranch hand, and Rainie would deck her out at a thrift store in love-child skirts and peasant blouses.

Quincy's phone whinnied. Glad for the distraction, he rolled over and sat up to grab the cell. Clint wasted no time on pleasantries. "Loni ate dry toast, Quincy! It's the first food she's kept down in over two weeks!"

Quincy grinned, warmth moving through him because he'd played a part in orchestrating Loni's sudden turnaround. "That's fabulous, Clint. What better news is there to start my day?"

"None!" In the middle of a joyous laugh, Clint yawned loudly into the mouthpiece. "Oh, man, I'm wiped. I mean, totally and completely wiped."

"Is Dee Dee still there?" Quincy asked.

"Oh, yeah."

"Then lie down next to your wife and get some sleep. Dee Dee can handle the house and kids, and your crew can deal with the ranch for the day. You've been burning the candle at both ends for way too long, bro. You need downtime."

Clint stifled another yawn, mumbled agreement, and disconnected. Quincy stared at his phone for a second, belatedly realizing that his brother hadn't even said thank you. Ah, well. Loni was on the road to recovery. That was all the reward Quincy needed.

He felt Ceara come awake behind him. He set aside the phone to turn toward her. Wrapped in the top sheet, she'd scooted over to her side of the bed, her rump hugging the edge. With one look into her blue eyes, Quincy realized she still had a bad case of morning-after shyness. This was another first for Quincy. The women he normally slept with didn't feel uncomfortable afterward.

He grabbed his pants from where they lay crumpled on the carpet. *Hmm.* How did a fellow put on his trousers without mooning the woman behind him? He settled for grabbing a blanket, looping it around his waist, and then twisting himself into pretzel shapes to don his Wranglers, sans boxers. As he worked the zipper with one hand, he clenched his teeth on a curse because a tuft of his pelvic hair got caught. *Ouch, and double ouch.* He'd never in his life understand men who wore no shorts under their jeans. It was downright dangerous.

Decently covered from the waist down, he headed for the bathroom, trying his damnedest not to let on that every step jerked a hair out by the root. When he'd managed to unfasten the pants without bawling like a fresh-branded calf, he carefully pulled the zipper back up.

As he reentered the bedroom, he didn't miss the death hold Ceara still had on the sheet. Since he'd pretty much seen—or at least touched—almost every part of her during the night, he didn't quite get what her deal was. He guessed it had to do with men being from Mars and women from Venus. Or was it the other way around? He'd never bothered to read that book.

"So!" He rubbed his hands together, dismayed when she jumped at the sound of his voice. Okay, so when it came to recently deflowered virgins, he was totally out of his element. "We have a big day ahead of us! Grocery shopping, buying some suitable clothing for you, and since my kitchen isn't stocked to your tastes, I was thinking about hitting a restaurant for breakfast before we do anything else. We should both grab a shower before we head out." No response. "So, what do you say?"

" 'Tis uncertain I am about how to work yer shower. 'Tis different from the one at the clinker."

"Oh." Quincy felt like a dunce. He hadn't even thought to show her how to use the toilet and could only hope she'd figured it out for herself. "Well, there's a quick remedy for that, honey. Stay wrapped in the sheet, and I'll give you a grand tour."

Ceara had seen women at the jail use the toilets in their cells, and she'd sneaked away three times to use Quincy's or Clint's, but this shower worked differently than the one she'd seen. Quincy joined her in the large stall, which in her opinion was big enough for three, but being in there with Quincy gave her a crowded feeling. She was covered only by the sheet, he wore no léine—no, he called it a shirt—and she was acutely aware of the muscles that roped his brown arms, the breadth of his shoulders, and the triangle of black hair that furred his flat lower belly and disappeared under the waist of his trews. He patiently showed her how to set the water temperature for the shower nozzle and how to pull on what he called the faucet handle to make water come out.

"Where does it come from?" she asked.

He gave her a bewildered look. "Where does what come from?"

"The water."

"Oh! It comes from my well."

Ceara had guessed that much. "But how do ye get it from the well into yer walls, pray?"

He explained about an electric pump, a water heater, and pipes, all of which only confused her more. Then, exiting the stall, he led her to what she'd already concluded was a bathing tub. He pointed out a thermostat on one side, quickly explaining that the red numbers on it would tell her how hot the water was.

"Aim for anywhere between ninety-seven and a hundred. Anything over a hundred is too hot for me. Not to say it'll be your preference. I just feel like a slug when I get out."

Then he indicated several round holes covered with knobby glass that he said were mood lights, and some open holes that he called jets.

"It's a Jacuzzi whirlpool tub." He arched a dark brow at her. "Do you like baths, or do you prefer to take a shower?"

"At home, we take baths."

"Well, then, a bath it'll be." He pushed a bronze stopper at the bottom of the rounded enclosure, turned the handles, which she now knew were called faucet handles or levers, and soon steam drifted up from the rising water. From a cupboard under one washbasin, he fetched a bar of soap wrapped in fancy paper, and two large bottles with odd push nozzles on top. "Shampoo," he said, as he set the one with the white nozzle on the slate skirt surrounding the tub. "This one with the black cap is conditioner."

"And what is shampoo?" she asked.

His expression went from bewildered to startled. "Um, it's stuff to wash your hair, sort of like soap, only it's in liquid form and has all kinds of nice stuff in it to . . ." He sighed and pushed on the white nozzle to squirt a creamy blob onto his hand. "Once you're in the water and have wet your hair, you rub this in until it lathers up." He glanced at her tresses. "You'll need a lot of it. Once you've lathered, you rinse, and then you use the conditioner the same way, rinsing thoroughly afterward."

Ceara nodded. " 'Tis a chore to dry me hair. It takes hours."

"Not with a blower, it won't."

"What is a blower?"

"Never mind, I'll help." He left her by the tub to exit what he called the bathroom, then returned moments later with a robe that looked as if it were made of towels. "You can wear this when you get out. It'll cover you better than the sheet." He saw that the water level had risen and leaned over to shut off the faucets. Gesturing over his shoulder, he said, "That towel on the hook is clean." He stepped to another cupboard. "And here's another one for your hair. Oh, and a washcloth. You'll be needing one of those."

Ceara felt the sheet slip slightly, and his gaze followed the descent. 'Twas silly of her, she knew, but memories of the intimacies they'd shared last night had her feeling skittish and more than a little embarrassed. He'd suckled the breast she was now so determined to keep covered, he'd caressed her in places she'd never dreamed a man might, and unless he truly was dumber than a sheep, he must know she'd liked it. That being the case, why had he insisted earlier that he wouldn't consider touching her again until she made it clear that she wanted him to? Surely her moans of pleasure last night had conveyed that to him. She didn't understand why he insisted that she say it with words. 'Twas unseemly for a lady to speak of such things. Mayhap married women were allowed to be more direct with their husbands, but if that was the case, Ceara's mum had failed to tell her so.

"If you want the jets on," he said, indicating the button to push, "the control is right there. Same for the lights. One punch gives you one color; two gives you rotating color. To turn something off, just punch it again."

Ceara nodded even though she didn't completely understand. He moved back to the door. "If you need anything, I've turned on the intercom system, so just yell, and I'll be here lickety-split."

" 'Tis fine I shall be," she assured him, wondering what an intercom system was. She'd been taking baths her whole life long and doubted she would need help. "Thank ye. I'll be about me business, then."

After the door closed, Ceara fiddled with the knob until she figured out how to work the lock. The last thing she wanted was for Quincy to make an unexpected appearance when she was stark naked. Once she felt certain the lock would hold, she sighed, dropped the sheet, and stepped into the lovely warm water. As she sat and slid low, heat enveloped her, and she sighed again. At home, the tub was small, and she could wet only parts of herself at a time, using a dipper. To sink as deeply as she liked into hot water was a luxury she'd never experienced or even imagined.

After a moment, she began staring at the buttons. What were jets? Her long hair floating all around her, she leaned forward to punch the button Quincy had shown her. At first she heard only a gurgling sound, but it was soon followed by a muted roar, and water suddenly surged around her as if it had come alive. She was so startled she nearly shrieked. Then, as the whirling streams began to pummel her body, she groaned in delight, sank low in the tub, and closed her eyes. How wonderful! She liked a whirlpool bath even more than champagne.

Something tugged on her hair. Ceara's eyes snapped open. When she tried to sit erect, the pull on her scalp grew sharper. Following the tautness of the strands with her fingers, she discovered that her hair was being sucked into a hole. She jerked and pulled, to no avail. She imagined being drawn under as the tub slowly gobbled her tresses.

"Holy Mother of God!" she screamed. "Help! Quincy, help me! 'Tis drowning I am!"

Quincy had his head in the refrigerator, looking for anything he might fix as a prebreakfast snack for Ceara, when her screams came over the intercom. Drowning? His heart felt as if it dropped like a rock to bounce off his bare toes. He tore for the hallway, took the stairs three at a time, ran into the bedroom, and reached the closed bathroom door. Locked?

"Jesus H. Christ!" He could hear Ceara shrieking and splashing around in the tub. There was terror in those shrieks. He put his shoulder to the wood. It didn't give. He backed up, wishing he had boots on so he could give the damned thing a solid kick. No such luck. He charged forward to ram the thick panel with his shoulder again. A crack as loud as a rifle shot rang out, and the thick ash portal gave way, rocking off the hinges for a moment before it fell to the stone floor with another explosion of sound.

Quincy ran to the tub. Ceara was down on one hip

and elbow in the whirling water, pulling frantically on her hair, which seemed to be stuck in the outtake valve.

"What the frigging hell?"

Regaining his senses, Quincy jabbed the jet control, the water stopped churning, and Ceara, braced against the current, fell back against the opposite wall of porcelain, her face whiter than the glossy surface behind her. She was sobbing, clearly terrified. Quincy grabbed the discarded sheet, threw it over her, and then, despite the odd angle, lifted her, sopping wet, into his arms. No major feat of strength—she weighed little more than a child.

Shaking uncontrollably, she locked her slender arms around his neck, buried her face against his now soaked shoulder, and jerkily cried, " 'Twas ... eating ... me hair, pulling me down. I couldna ... get away."

Quincy's legs felt as if they'd turned to rubber. He dropped onto the toilet, vaguely glad the lid was down, and angled his wife across his spread thighs. Now that it was too late, he recalled having to tug washcloths loose from the outtake valve. He doubted that Ceara's hair would have been pulled past the grate guard. There was surely a safety feature to prevent that, which he'd check out later. But he knew the experience had frightened her half to death, all the same.

"It's okay, honey; it's okay. It wasn't eating your hair; truly it wasn't. I'm pretty sure it only felt that way."

She jerked and gulped, trying to regain control, but the violent shudders that racked her body told him she still hadn't recovered from her fright. Quincy whispered to her, uncertain what he said, and just held her close. When she finally lay still against him, her sobs dwindling to soft twitches of her shoulders, he shifted his gaze to the destroyed door and added another chore to his to-do list for the day. He'd need to call his contractor and schedule repairs.

When he felt that Ceara had calmed down enough to entertain the thought of another try at bathing, he said, "How about we forget turning on the jets, and I stay to help you get washed up?"

"'Tis naked I am!" she protested thinly.

"Yeah, well, you can keep yourself covered with the sheet so I won't see anything. It won't be so bad; I promise."

Two hours later, Quincy felt as if he'd put in a half day of hard work. Drying Ceara's hair, even with a hair blower, had turned out to be a challenging task, and after getting her all finished up, he'd had to take a shower, wipe up puddles of water, fill the washer with sopping sheets and towels, and then try to think of something to feed his wife before he dragged her off to town. Not much, he decided. Just a bit of nourishment to bolster her strength for the drive, her first visit to a restaurant, and then shopping.

Now, back in her Renaissance gown, with her impossibly long hair braided, she sat at his round kitchen table dutifully eating whole-wheat cereal with skim milk, neither of which seemed to delight her taste buds, judging by the way she wrinkled her nose every time she took a bite.

"At home, me mum serves hot bread, fried pork, and fresh eggs to break our fast," she informed him. "If fer some reason she has no time to cook, we eat cold bread and a hunk of her lovely cheese."

Quincy nodded. "I'll stock up on things more to your liking." Sitting across from her, he leaned forward to pull the bowl away. "Forget the cereal. I'll take you out for breakfast. There's a fairly nice greasy spoon at the north end of town. You can order a platter of artery-clogging delights."

Her cheek dimpled. "What is a greasy spoon, and what are artery-clogging delights?"

Quincy was still trying to explain about coronary artery disease as they drove toward Crystal Falls.

Ceara's nose was bombarded with the heavenly smells of delicious food when they entered the establishment her husband called a greasy spoon. She well knew what grease was, and spoons as well, but what those words meant in connection with this building, she couldn't imagine. The first suspicious glance she'd given it revealed no obvious grease, spoon, or disorder. The front eating area, nearly as large as her father's dining hall, was spotted with small tables covered by red-and-white squares of cloth. People stared at Ceara as Quincy led her to an empty table and drew out a chair for her.

Instead of sitting, Ceara leaned toward him and said, "I've great need of a toilet. Do ye think they have one here?"

He whispered back, "In public places, the toilets are in what we call restrooms." He pointed to an overhead sign not far from them. "They're off that short hall. By each door, you'll see stick figures. Go into the one with a stick figure in a short skirt."

That seemed simple enough, so Ceara ventured across the dining hall into a shorter corridor, chose what she hoped was the correct door, and entered. A line of bowls like those in Quincy's bathroom lined one side of the room, below a shiny flank of mirrors. Across from them were a series of cubicles with doors that came only partway down to the floor. They were half-open and each contained a toilet. Ceara went inside one cubicle and peered into the bowl, which was filled with yellowish water and had a large amount of soggy paper floating in it. She backed out and tried the next cubicle. This one contained only clear water. She shut the door and quickly did her business, marveling over the things she discovered. There was a metal container on the wall filled with squares of see-through stuff that resembled onionskin, and a white can sat beside the toilet with a sign above it that read, DISCARD TAMPONS HERE. She had no idea what a tampon was and decided to ask Quincy later.

When she stood up, she got one of the greatest frights of her life. Unlike the toilets she'd previously used, this one flushed all on its own, without her pressing a handle, gulping down one's offerings with a loud, sucking whoosh that made her fear she might go down the hole, too. Gown still hiked high, she fell against the stall door, nearly screamed, and then slowly collected her wits. She wasn't about to be sucked into a pipe. This was only yet another frightening oddity of her husband's time.

Exiting the stall, she crossed to the row of sinks and looked in bewilderment for what he called faucet handles. There were none, just the faucet itself jutting out over the bowl. Perhaps there was no well here to provide water, but if that was the case, then why have faucets at all? Ceara tentatively tapped the faucet. No water appeared. She curled her fingers into a fist and banged it lightly on the end of the faucet. Still no water.

There had to be a way to get water out of the faucet, she reasoned. She ran her fingers across the faucet, brushing them beneath the open end. A swift gurgle made her jerk her fingers away just before water squirted out. She had no idea how she'd done it, but Ceara quickly washed her hands without soap. There were no towels available to dry them, even though she carefully examined the big metal containers hanging on the walls by the bowls. Wiping her fingers on her skirt, she exited the restroom, eager to experience her first meal at a greasy spoon.

Ceara returned to their table to find Quincy with a platter of food at his elbow. When she sat across from him, he pushed the plate and a large but thin book toward her. "I ordered a sampler and some fruit I thought you might enjoy. While you're nibbling, you can look over the menu. Choose anything you like, and don't worry about price. Whatever it costs, I can afford it."

Ceara's gaze went to a bowl of fruit at the center of the table containing peeled and sectioned oranges, a rare treat in Ireland. She couldn't resist snitching a segment of orange, which was so delicious she closed her eyes to savor it.

"You like fruit?" he asked.

"Oranges, yes," she replied, helping herself to another bite. "What are the other bits?"

"Cantaloupe slices."

Ceara tried some of the melon as well and found the taste equally delightful. When she finally opened the menu, her eyes were immediately assaulted by so many choices with strange names that she had no idea what to choose. The prices were also listed in a form of currency she'd never seen. Quincy didn't seem interested in the sampler, which had somehow appeared on their table as if by magic. She looked around, searching for a kitchen, but though she could see the heads of people moving back and forth through an opening in the far wall, she saw no smoke or chimneys and heard no crackling fire to indicate food preparation.

Hungry to the point of starving, she grabbed one of the flat things on the platter. It was cut in a wedge, and when she bit into it, sheer heaven burst to life in her mouth. She tasted cheese, *real* cheese, perhaps not quite as good as Mum's, but almost. "Mmm," she murmured appreciatively. "What is this?"

"Cholesterol City," he said, frowning as if she were eating dog dung.

Just then a woman in a scandalously tight léine and blue trews came to their table. She had something in her mouth that she chewed, much like a cow did its cud, only whatever it was snapped and popped. She held a tablet in one hand, a writing utensil in the other. "What can I get you, ma'am?" She glanced up. "Wow, cool dress. Is there a Renaissance fair somewhere nearby?"

"In Bend," Quincy interrupted. "They wrapped it up this morning. We were on our way home and got starved out, so we stopped to eat before my wife got a chance to change."

"Awesome reproduction. My mom is into it, but the gowns she has don't look as real." She snapped her cud again. "Special this morning is eggs Benedict smothered in our house Hollandaise with a side of cottage fries and country gravy."

Ceara had no idea what eggs Benedict was. "Your Cholesterol City is delicious. I'll have that."

The woman gave her a bewildered look. Quincy broke in again to explain, "She's having you on. She means she'd like her own order of the breakfast quesadillas. Throw in a side of sausage links, a bowl of orange sections, and biscuits with country gravy."

"And you, sir?" the woman asked. "You don't seem to be eating the quesadillas, and I'm sure they're cold by now."

"I ordered them for my wife while she was in the powder room, and they came from the kitchen faster than I expected."

"I'll be happy to comp them for you then."

"Don't worry about it." Quincy smiled. "I'll have two basted eggs on dry whole-wheat toast. Unless you happen to have a Swiss chard stir-fry with eggs, light on the sesame oil, with a dash of lemon."

The woman shook her head, moved her jaws, and her mouth began emitting popping sounds again. "We got a spinach omelet with sausage and a special cheese sauce."

Quincy shook his head. "I'll stick with the eggs on dry toast, thanks."

As the woman walked away, Ceara jabbed a finger at his abandoned platter. "If this is called . . . what was it? Something about breaking the fast, then why, pray, did ye tell me 'tis called Cholesterol City?"

He flashed her a wry grin. "It was a joke, Ceara. I'll try not to do it again, but in the meanwhile, you shouldn't take everything I say so literally. What if I'd said it was a pile of shit?"

Ceara recalled the delicious taste of the cooling cheese, so unlike the flavorless stuff Quincy had served her last night. "Is that, then, another name for this lovely stuff? Then I would have said I wanted a pile of shit. 'Tis verra good. Now what is the matter?" she asked, as Quincy's face suddenly creased in a deep frown. Shrugging, Ceara leaned back in her chair. "So this is a restaurant? I canna see any smoke from the cooking fires."

He chuckled. Then he winced. "Damn. I should have ordered you some whole milk."

Quincy had no idea where to take a woman shopping for decent clothes. No secondhand or discount stores for his wife. He drove up Main and took a U-turn to park in front of a stylish-looking ladies' boutique. He figured there'd have to be a fashion-conscious saleslady on duty, and Ceara was going to need clothing from the skin out. Ever since college, he'd prided himself on being able to guess a woman's bra size with a passing glance, but beyond that, he was at a complete loss. What kind of bra did Ceara need? He liked thongs—oh, yeah, he really liked thongs—but somehow he didn't think Ceara would be parading around in one anytime soon. In short, he was going to need help dressing her. A classy shop seemed just the thing.

Thirty minutes later, Quincy had a bitch of a headache. Ceara refused to wear tight knit tops, whispering to him in a thin, scandalized voice that she might as well wear naught at all. Quincy wouldn't have minded seeing her in the nude twenty-four/seven. The girl had a gorgeous body. But he sure as hell didn't want her leaving the house in her altogether.

Just thinking about it, he got an uncomfortable, hot feeling that surged up his throat. If one of his hired hands so much as laid a finger on her, Quincy would kill him. The thought jerked him up short. God, was he jealous? He'd *never* had a possessive streak. Now here he was having murderous thoughts over something that hadn't even happened yet and probably never would.

Ceara walked from the dressing area in another outfit just then, shoulders hunched, arms covering her breasts. She fixed a fiery gaze on him. "I canna wear the likes of this! 'Tis shameful."

Quincy thought the pink knit top and boot-cut jeans looked fabulous on her, but when he took a mental step back, he could see the problem. The ensemble revealed every line of Ceara's figure, and in her time was undoubtedly something only a whore would wear. Scotch that. In the sixteenth century, even prostitutes had probably worn less revealing clothing.

Quincy detested lying, but as he took the bewildered clerk aside for a private talk, he decided a huge load of bullshit was in order. The slender blonde looked up at him with unnaturally bright green eyes, compliments, he felt sure, of tinted contacts. "I'm out of ideas," she whispered. "She's tried almost everything."

Quincy geared up, swallowing hard and straightening his shoulders. "Here's the thing. I rescued her from one of those weird cults. You know, where they live in communes on remote ranches and the women have to wear long dresses that have collars up to the chin, long sleeves, and . . ." He glimpsed Ceara in a red top that brought saliva rushing to his mouth. "She even had to wear one of those all-over caps that shaded her face and fell down her back. You get what I'm saying? Now she wants to dress like women on the outside, but the tight knit tops and pants are too immodest."

"Oh, the poor thing," the clerk whispered. "Was she held prisoner there?"

Quincy nodded. "And that's all she's known her whole life. Do you have any trousers with a much looser fit, and maybe some . . . hell, I don't know what you call them . . . shirts, I guess, to wear over the knit tops, maybe something she can button halfway up or tie at the waist? Think *super*modest."

The clerk nodded and marched away, clearly on a mission. Quincy flopped on the chair in the waiting area, wishing Loni could have come along. When another hour passed, with Ceara rejecting everything she tried on, he got desperate enough to call Rainie.

"I need help," he told his sister-in-law.

After Quincy explained the problem, Rainie laughed and told him to meet her in thirty minutes at a place called Twice Over on Fourth Street. At that point, Quincy no longer cared if his wife wore secondhand skirts and tops. He just wanted her wearing *something*.

By late afternoon, Quincy decided he owed Rainie a dinner out with her husband—the whole nine yards: wine, fine food, dancing, and a movie afterward, all on his dime. She had come up with a look especially for Ceara, dressing her in full, calf-length skirts and loose-fitting blouses, always accompanied by a coordinating shawl or short-waist jacket. For footwear, Rainie chose cowgirl boots, not the fancy, tooled kind, but the rugged, clean-cut, practical boots accomplished horsewomen wore for riding.

Quincy wasn't big on the look, but he decided Ceara would look drop-dead beautiful in a burlap bag. After paying the tab, he put his muscle into carrying sacks of clothing to his truck, pleased with the haul simply because Ceara seemed happy. Maybe, Quincy thought, it was because another female member of the family, someone Ceara knew, had helped select the clothing—or maybe it was because Rainie had understood Ceara's need for modesty. Whatever. Eventually, if Quincy had his way, his wife would be in bed wearing nothing, and in the end, a husband couldn't quibble over the ugly little details of her wardrobe the rest of the time.

Grocery shopping proved to be a mind-boggling experience for Ceara, because she'd never seen so much food in one place, and Quincy found himself spending far more time in the fresh produce and frozen-food sections, selecting fruits and tossing frozen dinners into the cart, than he'd ever dreamed he might. After getting home, putting the stuff away, and carrying all Ceara's thrift-store loot upstairs, Quincy told her he'd cook supper as soon as he'd checked on his horses. When he left the house, she was putting her clothes away in the previously empty "hers" walk-in closet, making clucking noises that reminded him of a hen about to nest and lay an egg. He figured settling in would take her at least a half hour, so he had a bit of time to take a deep breath and wander through his stable. Beethoven always soothed his nerves, and after nearly a whole day of shopping for a female, Quincy's nerves were definitely shot.

He spent only a few minutes at his stallion's stall gate, then dutifully collected Ceara's satchel from his arena office before heading back to the house. As he walked, he tried to plan a meal—something high-fat, which felt totally foreign to him, not because he hadn't been raised with grease on his chin, but because he'd switched over to a healthful way of eating years ago and had been faithful to the plan ever since.

When he stepped into the kitchen, he nearly had heart failure. Ceara, smart woman that she was, had figured out which appliances were ovens. But instead of simply turning the damned things on, she'd collected firewood and kindling from the living room basket, removed the lower rack, laid a fire inside, and was about to flap her hand to ignite it into a blaze.

"Stop!" Quincy yelled, tossing aside the satchel. "What the frigging hell are you doing?"

Looking adorable in riding boots, a gathered navy blue skirt, a loose red peasant blouse, and a lightweight black wool shawl she'd knotted over her breasts, she sprang erect, whirled, and fixed him with a startled look. " 'Tis me duty as yer wife to prepare the evening meal."

Quincy knew that in days gone by women had cooked over an open fire, and ovens had been heated by a fire-box. With a glance, he determined that Ceara had meant to do the same, building a fire in one oven so she might bake in the other. He couldn't fault her for thinking she needed flame to create heat. It was just more than a little unsettling to realize how close she'd come to creating a disaster. He envisioned his home burned to cinders, with Ceara's remains in the smoking ashes. "I know, I know," he said in a low, soothing tone, not entirely sure whom he was trying to comfort, her or himself. "But my ovens are different from the ones you're used to, honey. Most people don't use wood to cook anymore."

Her brow pleated in a puzzled frown. "How do ye cook then?"

Quincy tossed his hat toward the coat tree, missed his mark, which he rarely did, and blamed it on emotional strain. "Well, with those particular ovens, we use electricity to create the heat, and since they're Miele Master-Chef ovens, you have to learn how to use the programming functions. There's a huge learning curve for anyone, which means there'll be an especially big curve for you, but I'll show you how." He hoped. When he'd first gotten the high-end appliances, he'd had to read the operation manuals several times before he could use any of them.

She stood back as he removed all the wood and kindling. He thanked God and all the saints that he'd returned to the house before she lit the fire. Wiring might have shorted out, and she could have been shocked. That wasn't to mention the smoke, and he hadn't yet taught her how to turn on the exhaust fans. On the counter, he saw a package of chicken thighs and a large bowl of peeled spuds. At least she'd found something to cook, even if she had no clue how to go about it. Lesson one, coming up.

Quincy dispensed with the wood and returned to find his bride blinking back tears. "Hey," he said softly, grasping her shoulders. "What's this?" He caught a silvery droplet as it slipped down her cheek. "It's no big deal that you don't know how to use the ovens. They're not straightforward like most, and even I was baffled by them at first."

She lifted a swimming blue gaze to his. Quincy felt a punch to his heart, as if a strong man had just buried a fist in his chest. As recently as yesterday, he'd fought and dragged his feet, trying every lowdown trick he could think of to avoid marrying this girl. And yes, in his book she was only a girl, well over the age of being jailbait, but still endearingly naive and innocent by modern-day standards. Now he wanted only to gather her close, dry her tears, and promise that he'd lasso the moon for her on the next clear night.

"I canna be a proper wife if I canna cook yer meals," she squeaked. "Me mum trained me up to lay out a fine spread." Her throat worked, and more tears gathered in her eyes, which somehow had a way of making Quincy ache from his solar plexus to his bootheels. "Now I canna please ye in bed, I canna be trusted with yer ovens, I canna take a bath without near drowning, and—" She broke off and gulped, which made her voice even squeakier. "I canna wash yer clothes."

"You pleased me very much in bed, and maybe, over time, you'll do so again."

She flapped her wrist. "'Tis only one of me duties, that. And if I fail at all else, what manner of wife shall I be?"

Quincy didn't hesitate; he caught her up in his arms and twirled her around the kitchen. When he set her back on her feet, he leaned down to kiss the tip of her small nose and said, "Memorize these three words: *housekeeper*, *takeout*, and *Laundromat*."

She blinked and sent shimmery tears cascading down her cheeks. "I fail to understand. Does takeout mean I go outside? And what in the name of all that's holy is a Laundromat?"

Quincy led her to the informal kitchen table, dropped onto a chair, and tugged her down on his lap. When she stiffened, he gently guided her head to his shoulder. "Let me tell you a little story, okay? It's about a man and woman, and they both work at jobs outside the home. I can be a horse rancher, just as I am, but—hmm, let me see. Well, until you go to college, let's say you're like that gal at the greasy spoon this morning, taking orders at a diner."

She sniffed and wiped her tears away on his shirt. "Will I chew a cud?"

For a moment, Quincy couldn't think what she meant, and then he remembered how the waitress had continuously popped a wad of bubble gum. He resisted the urge to laugh. "No, honey, you'd be far too ladylike to ever do that. But you would work all day at the greasy spoon, and at night, we'd both come home at about the same time, too tired to spit, let alone cook dinner or wash our clothes."

Quincy went on to draw a picture of two tired married people who'd gone by to pick up the laundry, all clean and freshly pressed, grabbed a few items for quick meals at the market, and gotten home so exhausted that instead of cooking, they called out for pizza.

"So, you see," he finished, "in this day and age, a good wife doesn't necessarily need to know how to cook or do laundry, so you can just take your time learning about all these new things, and not worry about it. We can order in Chinese, Italian, or fast food. Eventually you'll learn how to use the appliances and be able to put a fine meal on the table; I promise. Until then, you just need to be patient and let me teach you the ropes."

She relaxed in his arms, and so far as he could tell, no more tears were dampening his shirt. He waited for her to say something. When she finally did, he vowed to clean up his mouth.

"What the frigging hell is pizza?"

Chapter Nine

Quincy's inner alarm clock normally went off shortly before dawn, but when he opened his eyes the next morning, daylight glowed through the windows on either side of the fireplace. For a moment, he was startled into a half-erect position. Then he collapsed back onto the bed, grimacing like a man in pain as he remembered last night. No wonder he'd overslept. After giving Ceara a cooking lesson, which had been more a tour of the kitchen, showing her how to operate all the digitally programmed appliances, they'd fixed dinner together and after eating had retired upstairs, with him staring at the ceiling until the wee hours, wishing he could make love to her.

Now wide-awake, he rolled onto his side to reach for her, not to initiate sex but simply to hug her close. He stiffened when he saw only rumpled covers. Where was she? Ceara, on the loose in his house? *Holy hell.* When he thought of all the ways she might hurt herself, his heart sped to a hammer beat. Technicolor visions of her setting the oven on fire shot across his mental TV screen. Jerking on his jeans—again without putting on boxers first—he ran for the landing, zipping his pants as he went. At the top of the stairs, the awful stench of burned popcorn blasted him in the face. *Shit*. She'd used the microwave, the only piece of equipment that Ceara had learned to make work by the end of her lesson last night.

He bolted down the steps, stubbed his bare toe on the last riser, and raced into the kitchen with a hobble in his gait. To his relief, Ceara sat at the kitchen table looking as happy as a chipmunk in a nut factory, her cheek bulging as she chomped on her cremated snack. The opposite cheek dimpled when she saw him. He noted that in addition to popcorn, she'd peeled and divided an orange to eat as well.

She swallowed and said, "Good morningtide to ye!" Dipping a hand back into the charred bag, she added, "I quite like popcorn. Thank ye fer getting it. I awakened with a snarl in me gut, and this is simple to make."

Toe still throbbing, Quincy leaned a shoulder against the wood-framed archway. "Ceara, burned food is really bad for you."

"Burned, is it?" She glanced at the blackened kernels in her palm. " 'Tis bad for me?"

"Yes, it's full of carcinogens."

She stuffed more popcorn in her mouth, smiling as she chewed. "Then 'tis me opinion that carcinogens are *delicious*."

Quincy sighed and limped over to sit across from her. "Next time, set the microwave for a shorter cooking time."

"God's teeth, nay, I like it this way."

An ache of pressure took up residence in Quincy's temples. He cupped a hand over his yawn, thinking that he needed a long, hot shower to wake himself up. Only how could he leave Ceara alone? He briefly entertained the notion of inviting her to join him, but he doubted she would accept. She wore the flannel nightgown Rainie had chosen for her yesterday, plus the oversize terry robe and a pair of his wool boot socks, which she must have filched from his drawer. The ends dangled past her toes, and the heel cups hit well above her ankles. The only skin showing was that of her face and hands. Not the getup of a woman interested in even the preliminaries. *Blast.*

"If I leave you alone down here to go up and take a shower, will you promise me you'll stay out of trouble?"

Her blue eyes sparkled with mischief. "I'll na be making a fire in yer oven, if that is yer worry. After I eat the orange, I may burn meself some more popcorn, however. Me stomach feels as empty as a beggar's pocket."

Quincy decided he'd better fix her something to eat before taking a shower. Otherwise, God only knew what—or how—she might try to cook. Ceara trailed behind him to the refrigerator, poking her head in under his arm to watch as he pulled a package of bulk sausage from the meat keeper. "I see no ice. What makes it stay cold?" she asked as she took the pork so he could collect some eggs. "The—what is it that ye call it? A fridge, yes? 'Tis amazing."

Still groggy, Quincy tried to prod his memory bank into producing a coherent explanation of how refrigeration systems worked. "There's a network of little tubes filled with a special kind of gas that creates cold air. You want cheese on your toast? I can put it under the broiler and melt it to a turn."

Her eyes lit up. "Mm, cheese is one of me favorite things, and I love toast. But how do ye make it in the oven without any fire?"

Quincy had avoided showing her the more complicated settings of the oven last night, so now he explained about the broiler coils in the top of the oven, and how a current of electricity turned them red-hot to brown foods on the rack. He felt as if he had a curious six-year-old glued to his elbow as he cooked. Ceara asked dozens of questions about the Miele MasterChef oven functions, and he wasn't used to talking to anyone except Beethoven until he'd finished his morning coffee. Ah, well, he'd probably fire off questions, too, if he'd been born and raised in the fifteen hundreds. She found it incredibly curious that the bread came in a sack. She wanted to know where the market got the sausage. And where did coffee beans come from? And the chicken he'd fixed last night—did he raise poultry as her family did in Ireland? Where did the cheesemaker live and what type of cows did she raise? Why did the fridge growl and then grow silent?

Quincy almost spilled the eggs he was whisking for a scramble when she frowned and asked her next question: "What is a tampon?"

He could feel his cheeks getting warm. "It's a . . . well, a *thing* that women use when they have their periods." He angled a worried look at her. "Are you having yours? I can run into town and get you some pads. I mean, uh, I don't think tampons would be comfortable for you to wear just yet."

"Ah." She nodded as if she understood. "What is a period? 'Tis a piece of time, but I think 'tis na what ye're meaning."

Quincy couldn't help it. He started to laugh. When she looked offended, he turned off the gas burner on the Viking cooktop and drew her into his arms for a quick hug. "I'm not laughing at *you*; really I'm not. It's just . . ." He considered for a moment. He wanted to say the whole situation was nuts, but that didn't seem right. It wasn't her fault that the world she'd landed in was all so foreign to her. "A period. Now, there's a question. It's when a woman has her cycle."

"Yesterday ye told me the noisome two-wheeled conveyance that passed us on the road was a cycle."

"Um, no. That was a motorcycle. It's not the same thing. I mean . . . uh . . . well, you know. Women bleed every month? That's your cycle."

By the time Quincy had gotten his wife fed and stationed her on the sofa in the family room to watch *Love Story* on a Netflix DVD, his brains felt as scrambled as the eggs. He smiled and shook his head as he ascended the stairs to grab a shower. Life with Ceara was going to be a challenge.

Nearly an hour later, when he reentered the family room, he found her sobbing as if her heart might break. He hurried across the room to sit beside her. "Honey, what's wrong?"

"Yer box," she said, gesturing at the flat-screen television. " 'Tis a terrible thing." She wiped her cheeks and shook her head. "That poor woman is going to die of a blood sickness just like Loni had, but the man canna save her."

Quincy wished he'd selected a chick flick that wasn't so sad. "It's just a movie, not real life," he tried. "It's not real. Those people are pretending."

Ceara looked at him as if he had marbles rattling between his ears. He was beginning to wonder if she was right.

Over the next few days, Loni continued to rally—to the utter amazement of her physicians, both in Crystal Falls and Portland. As Clint's life inched back toward some semblance of normalcy, Quincy felt as if his were spinning out of control. For as long as he could remember, he'd heard his dad say that a man should never get the cart before the horse, and by marrying Ceara, that was precisely what Quincy had done.

How in the hell did a man handle falling wildly in love with his wife? She adored his dogs, and she'd flatly informed him that they were moving back home, no longer bunking with Pauline. That was fine with Quincy; he'd sorely missed Bubba and Billy Bob, but what was he supposed to tell his wife when he found her test-tasting the commercial dog food and pronouncing it "unfit fer man or beast"? She insisted with a stubborn jut of her chin that her new canine friends would eat regular food—by which she meant people food—even if she had to cook it for them herself. Since she couldn't as yet cook much of anything, Quincy got online to research dog food recipes and soon found himself with the additional duty of being the in-house pet chef.

Ceara also seemed to love his horses and couldn't wait to ride, but she had never seen a Western saddle, and Quincy decided to postpone all equine activities until he could focus entirely on teaching her the techniques of riding astride instead of sidesaddle. Ceara took the disappointment in good form and settled for visiting the arena on a daily basis. At first Quincy balked at allowing her to do any physically taxing work, but Ceara was persistent, and before he knew it, she was helping Pauline feed and groom the animals, plus clean the stalls.

She exhibited an uncanny way with horses, and spent hours each day with them. Even his bitchiest mares and orneriest stallions became big old marshmallows with Ceara. It was as if she had some magical way of communicating with them that other human beings lacked. Same went for Bubba and Billy Bob, who, despite Quincy's sporadic efforts, had always been sorely lacking in social graces. Quincy had considered dog obedience classes, but he'd never had the time for it. Now, with his wife in the house, he had dogs that suddenly sat when told and didn't jump up on him or put their paws on the edge of the table during a meal to beg for food. Quincy had always fondly called his Australian shepherds "Mexican jumping beans on speed," but the description no longer fit. Even more amazing, he'd never seen Ceara use a cross tone with them or discipline them in any way; the animals simply worshiped her and seemed to sense what behaviors would please her and which ones wouldn't.

Too bad he wasn't gifted with the same intuition.

Well, Quincy was a goner, right along with Bubba and Billy Bob. How could any man in his right mind *not* fall in love with Ceara? She was sweet and funny and absolutely dear. That she was gorgeous was frosting on the cake. Being married to her was as easy as slipping his feet into a pair of old boots.

Only what about dating? And candlelight dinners? Or talking so long on the phone that their voices gave out, and they were happy to just hear each other breathe? Quincy felt as if the curse had cheated Ceara out of a proper courtship. He wished he could rectify that, but his days had become so busy, with not only a ranch to run, but also a wife who needed to be taught how to do nearly everything, that he honestly didn't have much time for romance.

Ceara and his relationship was fraught with as much miscommunication as it was with pure fun. She found everything in his world peculiar, bewildering, or downright amazing as she familiarized herself with the twenty-first century: automobiles, ATVs, cell phones, radios, stereos, remote controls, computers, iPads, clothing on other women that she felt was indecent, television, Netflix, the theater, and fine restaurants.

On the following Friday night, a week and one day after their wedding, Quincy took his bride to a new French Creole restaurant that was so high-end there were no prices on the menu. Hello? He needed to court his wife, and she deserved nothing but the best.

It went without saying that Ceara couldn't make sense of the entrée selections, but Quincy didn't expect to be baffled himself. What the hell was Crevettes à la Créole or Langouste Grillée? He found himself regretting that he'd studied Spanish instead of French, but to be fair to himself, he'd dined in French places before and had no trouble deciphering the language. Ordering wine was easy enough, and he was feeling so inadequate by the time the waiter brought it to the table that he decided to drink his fair share of the bottle.

Apparently he was scowling, because Ceara asked, "What is it, Quincy? Ye look as if ye want to murder someone."

He gave up on trying to act sophisticated. "I don't know what the frigging hell to order." *Ouch*. When it came to rough language, Ceara was a sponge. "Forget I said that, and don't *you* say it again. Let me rephrase. I can't read the damned menu."

Her eyes danced with delight. " 'Tis wonderful that ye canna. Nor can I." She picked up her menu and squinted at the offerings. "We shall have an adventure!"

Quincy was afraid he'd accidentally order her snails. Most menus in a foreign language had all the entrées underscored with a translation into English to describe the dish. Not so at this joint. He personally enjoyed escargot, but he was afraid Ceara would gag as she tried to swallow. "Let's try the Filet de Truite Florentine. At least I know what it is."

She frowned. "I do na."

Quincy had once seen the dish on a menu and explained that it was trout fried in a light batter and smothered in a tasty lemon sauce. *Fried*. His normally healthful
diet was going to hell in a handbasket. He could almost
feel his arteries going *glug-glug* in protest. He didn't care.
Being with Ceara was habit-forming, and if he took his
last breath well before turning one hundred, at least he
was finally enjoying the journey.

He poured them each some wine. He'd selected a
white, slightly on the sweet side, even though he hadn't
known for sure what they would eat. Ceara wrinkled her
nose when she took a sip; then she smiled. "Not champagne, but 'tis lovely."

Her oval face glowed in the candlelight. Her eyes
shimmered like sapphires. She was so beautiful, even in
her funny-looking clothes, that his mouth went dry. He
hoped as she gazed back at him that she was thinking
similar thoughts about him. He'd decided to spruce up
for the occasion and taken his Western-cut sports jacket
out of storage. In addition to a dress shirt, he wore a
string tie that boasted a hunk of amber imported from
Japan. He felt downright fancy. Hell, he'd even spit-
shined his boots.

The waiter came to take their order. Ceara surprised
Quincy by holding the menu up and pointing to a selection he couldn't see, saying, "I'll be trying this, if ye
please."

Quincy hoped it wasn't something awful, but what the
hell. She seemed to be delighted to have a culinary adventure with him. Maybe, he decided, his not knowing
how to read the menu made her feel on more equal
ground. His being suave and sophisticated clearly didn't
matter to her. He relaxed and began to enjoy the dinner.

Remembering the films of Ceara that he'd studied after her surprising invasion of his arena, he asked her how she so easily charmed his difficult horses, particularly Beethoven.

"'Tis one of me gifts, understanding animals." She fluttered her fingertips near her temple. "I have lost much of it. Afore coming forward, I could talk to them inside me head. Now that is gone." A sad look settled on her lovely features, but then she brightened. "'Tis no big deal." Her cheeks went pink. "That is how ye say it? When something does na matter, I mean."

Quincy nodded. "I'm sorry you've lost so many of your gifts."

"I've not lost *all* of them. It's only that the ones I still have are weaker." She rested her elbows on the table and fingered her pretty lace shawl, the ends of which she'd looped over her breasts. "'Tis strange. When I use me gifts now, it makes me shaky in the legs and a wee bit ill."

"Then don't use them."

She laughed and tugged her braid forward over her shoulder. "'Tis like asking me to stop breathing. If I said to ye, 'Stop seeing,' could ye do it? Me gifts . . . well, I've always had them. 'Tis like using yer hands to pick up things. Ye do not think before ye do it."

Just then the maître d', followed by a waiter with a small platter balanced on his upturned palm, stopped at Quincy's side and set a copper dish, roiling with heated alcohol, at the center of the table. While the waiter placed coffee mugs near the plates, the maître d' added coffee to the bowl, ignited it, and then, streaming blue fire over the tablecloth from a ladle, filled the cups. Quincy had no time to object—or to inform the gentlemen that he hadn't ordered a flaming coffee, which was traditionally an after-dinner drink.

Ceara shrieked, leaped to her feet, and yelled, "God's teeth!" before emptying both her water and wine goblet on the flames. Snatching Quincy's water glass in case the fire needed further baptizing, she whirled on the astounded waiter. "Are ye mad?" she cried. "Holy Mother of God, we're here to be fed, not burned."

The hum of conversation in the restaurant came to a sudden halt. The maître d, forgetting his fake French accent, said, "I'm sorry, ma'am. It scared the hell out of me the first time I saw it, too." His Adam's apple bobbed. "It's harmless, I swear, all just for show."

Quincy had to swallow hard for fear he'd burst out laughing. Ceara's face had gone as white as chalk. She was a spunky little thing, though, and quickly recovered her composure. " 'Tis sorry I am fer making such a mess," she said shakily, "but in future, afore ye set a woman afire, ye should give her fair warning."

Speaking softly to the servers, Quincy explained that the coffee had been delivered to the wrong diners. After apologizing profusely, the maître d' escorted them to a new table, and soon the appetizer Ceara had ordered, raw oysters on the shell, was served to them, along with a new bottle of wine, compliments of the house. Quincy expected Ceara to turn up her nose and refuse to suck slimy stuff into her mouth. But, as always, she surprised him. She studied him as he swallowed an oyster, then followed his lead like a lady born to the manor.

" 'Tis how we eat raw oysters at home as well," she told him. " 'Tis glad I am to know that not everything has changed. Me sister, Brigid, and I always hoped to discover a pearl in one of ours, but we ne'er did."

Watching her mouth purse around the shell and hearing the slight slurping sounds she made gave Quincy a hard-on. He shifted uncomfortably on his chair, glad for the generous fall of the white linen tablecloth. Being with Ceara and sharing the same bed with her every night had his body screaming for release. Over the last few days, Quincy had been making subtle moves on her, trailing a finger along her throat, caressing her shoulder, or toying with her braid so he could titillate the sensitive nerve endings along her spine. Each time, he could have sworn she'd gotten turned on. On more than one occasion, he'd felt sure she'd even smiled invitingly at him. But never once had the words he needed to hear passed her lips.

Saying she wouldn't object was a hell of a lot different from saying she'd enjoyed his lovemaking and wanted to repeat the experience.

Maybe he'd lost his touch. He hadn't dated for so long, his moves might be rusty. *Nah*. He wasn't *that* out of practice. Ceara was either not getting the message, or she was being deliberately obtuse, or she was getting the message loud and clear and purposely ignoring it. He studied her across the table, noting every expression that crossed her face. She didn't strike him as a woman with a talent for playing games. In fact, just the opposite. She was as easy to read as a freeway billboard. So why, for the first time in his adult life, was he striking out with a woman?

He knew their first encounter had been painful for her. Maybe, in her innocence, she thought it would hurt like that every time. If so, he needed to set her straight. He decided to lead into the conversation slowly.

"I've got a question I've been dying to ask you. How did a beautiful woman like you manage to remain a virgin until the ripe old age of twenty-six?"

She smiled slightly. " 'Twasna a choice, ye ken. From the moment of me birth, me da had high hopes of forming a strong alliance with another chiefdom by arranging a marriage fer me with another leader's son. As it happened, I developed a great fondness for a young man who was suitable, but before we could be married, he was killed in a horse riding accident."

Quincy noted that sadness flickered in her eyes for only an instant, and then her expression brightened. "After his death, I couldna find another man to suit me, and as I told ye on our wedding night, me da wouldna force me into marriage with someone I dinna find appealing."

"And during all the years that followed, you never— well, you know—fooled around? Women of today enjoy intimate relationships with men in and out of marriage."

She arched a burnished brow. "Is that what ye call it now, 'fooling around'? In me time, 'tis called fornication. 'Tis unacceptable fer an unmarried lady to engage in those activities. According to the church, 'tis a grave sin, and I also had to bear in mind that, long in the tooth though I was, marrying might still be a possibility. In her first marriage, a woman must go to her husband unsullied."

To Quincy, that sounded archaic, not to mention sexually stifling for the women, but he'd studied enough history to know that attitudes had changed drastically over the centuries. In his time, few brides married as virgins.

"I see," he said.

She gave him a questioning look. "Would ye have preferred a soiled bride?"

Quincy shook his head. "I wouldn't change a single thing about you," he told her, and meant it. He only wished she were a tad more relaxed about discussing sex. He didn't get it. How could it be brazen of a woman to discuss the physical aspects of a marital relationship with her husband? His imagination stopped well short of such things *never* being discussed in the sixteenth century. That said, maybe Ceara's mother had never gotten around to explaining to Ceara that such conversations were okay between a husband and wife.

As they left the restaurant, Quincy very casually slipped an arm around her shoulders. She shot him a suspicious glance. "The sidewalk may be a little icy," he said, which wasn't really a lie, because the night temperatures in Crystal Falls often dipped below freezing at this time of year. "I don't want you to slip and fall."

Instead of protesting, she relaxed against him, her hip bumping his thigh as they walked toward his truck. Again, very casually, Quincy let his hand dangle forward over her slender shoulder so his fingertips could *accidentally* feather across the upper swell of her breast. He felt goose bumps rise on her skin, but maybe they were from the cold air.

"Are you warm enough?" he asked. "That lace shawl is pretty for dinner out, but it can't offer much protection from the chill."

" 'Tis fine I am." Her lips curved in a sweet smile that dimpled her cheek when she glanced up at him. Her eyes shimmered in the moon glow and light spilling from the windows of businesses they passed. " 'Tis only a short way to your truck."

All Quincy's instincts told him she was giving him the green light. So why wouldn't she just say so, damn it? Call him old-fashioned and too much of a gentleman, but he couldn't take this to another level until he knew with absolute certainty that she wanted him to.

As he assisted his wife into his truck, he glimpsed a flash of bare leg where her skirt rode up. His guts knotted with burning desire. He decided then and there that it would be another cold shower for him tonight. If this kept up, he'd catch pneumonia.

*   *   *

All the way home, Ceara chewed the inside of her cheek, so frustrated with Quincy that she wanted to reach across the truck and whack him on the thigh. She'd leaned against him. She'd smiled at him. She'd tried countless times to issue him an invitation with her eyes. He acted as if he noticed none of it, and yet he continued to assault her senses with soft caresses—toying with her hair, lightly trailing his fingertips down her arm, teasing the sensitive spot just below her ear, and sometimes resting a hand over her shoulder, as he had moments ago, to make her nipples throb with yearning for his touch.

The man was driving her to the brink of madness. When they reached the house, he would leave her alone in their bed to take an impossibly long shower, and when he finally joined her under the blankets, he'd settle as close to his edge of the mattress as possible. It was as if an invisible wall had been erected and he'd issued an unspoken rule that neither of them should climb over it.

Oh, how Ceara wished she could talk with her mum. How did a wife encourage her husband to bed her without speaking and behaving like a tavern wench? Ceara struggled to fall asleep each night, her mind filled with memories of their wedding night—the slow glide of Quincy's hands over her skin, the jolts of pleasure he'd sent coursing through her body, and the feverish need that had come over her when his hard shaft had plunged deep into her core. She wanted—no, *needed*—to experience all those feelings again, only she didn't know how to persuade Quincy to accommodate her.

Tonight would end no differently, Ceara thought drearily as she trudged up the stairs to their bedchamber, and the realization had her clenching her teeth. After cleansing herself, she donned her flannel gown, then climbed into bed to await the sound of her husband's footsteps ascending the stairs. When he finally entered the room, he spoke softly to the dogs, telling them to go to their beds, and then, just as Ceara expected, he went into the bathroom and closed the door. Soon she heard the shower come on and Quincy making gasping, shuddering sounds, which told her the water was cold. *Why* would a sane man stand under a stream of freezing water when warmth was a turn of the faucet handle away?

Mayhap, Ceara mused, Quincy simply didn't desire her. She wasn't plump and well-rounded like the dairymaids that her older brothers had found so attractive before they settled down into marriage. Quincy might have similar tastes, preferring accommodating females with lush, generous curves who were free with their favors prior to wedding. Be that the case, Ceara was stuck. She'd not been born a dairymaid who had been taught little if anything about ladylike behavior, and she could think of no way to make her figure more buxom. She ate goodly amounts of food, but none of it ever seemed to add extra padding. Her da had often said his daughters could eat him out of house and home with nary an ounce of fat on their bones to show for it.

Sighing wistfully, Ceara turned onto her side. She felt the mattress give and smiled when her reaching hand settled on a furry ruff. *Billy Bob*. He'd come to comfort her. She curled her arm around the dog's neck and pressed her face against his forehead. At least one male in the house found her appealing.

The following morning, Quincy's father showed up with a manila envelope clutched in one hand. Ceara opened the door to greet him, because Quincy was upstairs shaving. "A cheery morning to ye, Mr. Harrigan."

He laughed, looking so much like Ceara's husband that

she couldn't help but marvel at the resemblance. "Just call me Dad, honey." As he moved into the kitchen, he hooked an arm around her shoulders and pressed a kiss to her forehead. "You're a member of the family now."

Ceara liked the Harrigans and wanted very much to be accepted, but Frank's mention of family sent a pang of longing through her belly for the perfectly wonderful and much-missed kinsmen she'd left behind. " 'Tis an honor."

As Frank drew back, he thrust the envelope at her. "Your identification papers, darlin.' You're all nice and legal now. My contact had a devil of a time finding a shady enough expert to get the job done, but apparently he chose well, because the fella even managed to use your real name. I ain't sure how he pulled that off. I'm told that most times they have to borrow the identity of somebody deceased, and I don't reckon there's too many women in the States, livin' or dead, with a name similar to yours."

"Oh!" Ceara cried, her voice shrill with delight as she drew out the paperwork. " 'Tis perfect! I wouldna have liked using a different name." She peered at the birth certificate. "Even me age is correct." She thanked Frank with a warm smile. "Now I can get a driver's license!"

Frank's dark brows snapped together. "Ah, well, now. Let's not rush into that. Rome wasn't built in a day."

Just then Quincy's voice rang out from behind her. "A driver's license?"

Ceara turned and flapped the documents at him. " 'Tis a real person I am now, Quincy. Yer da got me identification! Now I can begin learning all the things ye've promised to teach me."

The men exchanged a long, charged look over the top of her head. Quincy said, "That's true, but let's not jump the gun."

Ceara's heart sank. "But ye said ye'd start giving me driving lessons. Did ye not?"

Quincy rubbed a hand over his hair, which was still damp from his shower. "I did, yes, and I'm a man of my word. But let's not rush into it."

Ceara could barely wait to drive his truck. "No rush, but 'twould be lovely to get my first lesson today."

"That's a rush." Quincy sighed, but his frown softened when she assumed the crestfallen expression that had always worked well on her father. "Okay, I guess we can probably fit in a short one."

Ceara didn't think he looked very happy about it. Personally, she couldn't see what the big deal was. She'd watched him drive many times now, and in her opinion, it didn't look that difficult.

"Loni is plannin' a hen party," Frank informed them. "She's still too weak to leave the house, but she's gettin' a bad case of cabin fever and feelin' a little lonesome. Dee Dee is goin' over to fix a nice lunch, topped off with her apple pie for dessert. Maybe after Ceara's drivin' lesson, you can take her over to Clint's so she can get to know the girls better."

Quincy nodded. "If Dee Dee's apple pie is on the menu, I'll make a point of it."

Frank grinned. "Men ain't invited. Maybe you and me can help Clint out in his arena. He's been playin' catch-up all week. Tucker is on duty this weekend at the clinic. Parker and Zach are over at Parker's place, mendin' some fences. It'll only be us three not gettin' fed."

"Why aren't the men invited?" Quincy demanded.

"Hen party," Frank expounded. "You know, cluck, cluck. Maybe, if we're lucky, Dee Dee will send us out some food and save us some pie."

Ceara had never attended a hen party, but it sounded

delightful. She hadn't seen Loni since that awful first night when she had been hovering near death. If the woman was feeling strong enough to have callers now, Ceara desperately wanted to go.

Driving didn't prove to be as simple as Quincy had made it look. Ceara got the truck started without a problem, but managing the gearshift baffled her. Every time she tried to move the conveyance forward, it belched like a fat man who'd gulped too much ale, and then the engine died. Either she forgot to step on the rectangular pedal protruding from the floor that Quincy called a clutch, or she didn't maneuver the shift properly, or both. Quincy told her she was making his truck buck worse than a bronc.

"It's all in the clutch and acceleration," Quincy explained.

"What is acceleration?"

"It's pressing your right foot down on the gas pedal."

Ceara knew where the gas pedal was, but managing to accelerate as she let out the clutch was tricky.

"Timing," Quincy explained. "You need to feel when the gear grabs. You'll know when it happens after you've practiced. It takes a while to get it down."

What Ceara lacked in experience she made up for with determination. Soon, even though the truck continued to belch and jerk, she got it to move forward in fits and starts. Quincy directed her to drive through the ranch proper, warning her to stay well away from other trucks, the tractor, and what he called ATVs, which were squat things with four huge wheels that the hired hands often used to get around out in the fields.

After nearly completing one pass, Ceara decided she quite liked driving. As she had suspected, 'twas simple enough to do. She needed only to work on the belching to have it down pat.

Ahead of them loomed an outdoor holding shed for horses. Ceara eyed it nervously, looking frantically for somewhere else to go, but a white fence blocked her way.

"Brake!" Quincy cried.

Brake? She felt around the seat, groping for the handle that should be there but wasn't.

"Brake!" Quincy yelled the word this time. "Now! Slam on the—"

The truck gave a final belch, hopped forward, and smashed into the corner of the holding shed. A piece of roofing came loose and smacked the windshield. Ceara jerked with a start, her only comforting thought that at least the beast of a vehicle had finally stopped.

"Jesus H. Christ," Quincy said softly. He glanced over at her with a spark of anger in his eyes. "Why the hell didn't you hit the brake?"

Despite being appalled at the harm she'd done, Ceara wasn't about to let Quincy blame her for the missing brake. "If ye'd inspect yer truck before starting it, ye'd know there *is* no brake." She leaned forward, looking all around her legs to check. "If there's a brake, where is it? Me father's wagon has one near the driver's left leg, as does every one I've *ever* ridden in. 'Tis not here."

He snorted. She considered telling him he sounded like an outraged horse, but thought better of it. "This is a truck, not a wagon," he tossed over his shoulder as he climbed out and circled the vehicle. Ceara heard him curse. She had a bad feeling that she'd brought disaster to the front of his truck. "My God, in one fell swoop, you've taken out the corner of a building *and* messed up my Dodge."

Ceara couldn't blame him for being angry, but tears

stung her eyes all the same. She climbed out to assess the damage. The big silver bars at the front of the truck were all bent at the center, and the huge rectangular spool he called a winch sat crooked. "Oh, Quincy, 'tis so sorry I am."

He planted his hands on his hips and released a taut breath. "It's not your fault, honey. I should have thought to show you the brake pedal." His mouth twitched at the corners. "For some reason, it never occurred to me you'd look for a wagon brake, but in retrospect, it makes perfect sense." He shook his head. Waving a hand toward the front of the vehicle, he said, "I spent a small fortune on that cattle guard. What a piece of shit. If it folds from hitting the corner of a building, it'd crumple clear into my radiator if I actually hit a cow."

Ceara studied the thick bars. "Do ye run into cows often? I dinna see any around."

He chuckled. "No, never have, but with you driving, it might become a common occurrence."

Ceara had been so excited to try driving. Now, looking at the poor shed and the truck, she wished she'd never attempted it. " 'Tis me guess that ye willna be letting me drive again anytime soon."

His chuckle became a deep, full-blown bark of laughter. He curled an arm around her shoulders to jostle her close against his chest. "Let's just say I don't think you're road-ready yet. With practice, you'll get there."

Ceara had no idea what to expect at a hen party, except that she felt sure no chickens were involved. Ten minutes into it, she was enjoying herself immensely. Perched on a comfortable chair, she sipped wine from a glass in one hand and nibbled what Dee Dee called a finger sandwich from the other. The finger sandwich was triangular rather than finger-shaped, but 'twas delicious nonetheless, and had ample butter. Loni held court at the head of her kitchen table, her face still pale but notably sporting more color. Her lovely eyes shone with a gentle glow. She had a soft, easy smile that made Ceara feel warm and happy all over.

Dee Dee filled in as lady of the house, serving the simple lunch and getting up often from her seat to refill glasses. Ceara fleetingly wondered whether it might be the wine that was making her feel so nice, but it was berry-sweet, and so delicious that she couldn't resist drinking more.

"Hear, hear!" Rainie said, lifting her goblet high. "To Ceara and Quincy for breaking that horrible curse, and to the good health of everyone at this table."

Sam grinned. "I'll drink to that." She winked at Ceara. "Next week, Tucker and I are going to start trying for a baby again. This will probably be my last hurrah for quite some time. I don't want to drink when I might be pregnant."

Mandy giggled. She'd pulled her whiskey-colored hair up into a knot at the back of her head and secured it with what looked like a stick. She wore a lovely green top that skimmed her figure, and Ceara secretly admired how it looked, wishing she were brave enough to let Quincy buy her something like it.

"As I recall," Mandy said to Sam, "you dearly loved that whole process last time. Watching the calendar, taking your temperature, and then calling Tucker home in the middle of the day to screw his brains out until both of you were so exhausted you couldn't wiggle." She sipped her wine. "Zach and I have decided we shouldn't get pregnant until I finish getting my degree in horticulture, so I'm doing just the opposite right now, practicing the ovulation method as a form of birth control." She wagged a scolding finger at no one in particular. "No more birth control pills for me! I'm a faithful little Catholic girl these days. But I have to say I sure do miss having sex whenever we want."

Dee Dee released a blissful sigh. "Thank God I'm postmenopausal. Frank and I don't have to worry about any of that." Her plump cheeks went pink. "He is something, let me tell you. After we got married, I figured he'd dwindle off to maybe once every couple of weeks, but except when he puts in an extra hard day, he's an every-night man." She giggled. "A few months ago, I even tossed my electronic boyfriend in the trash."

Rainie gasped. "You *threw away* a perfectly good vibrator? What if Frank's gone to a horse auction, and you get to feeling horny?"

Dee Dee smiled dreamily. "I'd rather do without until the real thing gets home, so Mr. Purple had to go."

Ceara was fascinated by the exchange, even though she understood little of what was being said. What was the ovulation method? What were birth control pills? And most curious of all, what was an electronic boyfriend, and did Quincy's father know about Mr. Purple?

Rainie giggled after sipping more wine. "You're missing the boat, Dee Dee. Parker really gets turned on if I fool around with Mr. Purple during foreplay." Ceara's eyes widened at the second mention of Mr. Purple. Rainie shivered her shoulders. "God, he gets so hot he turns into a wild man." She took another sip of wine and directed a glance at Loni. "I am so glad you're starting to feel better. It's been *way* too long since we've done this. I've really missed our girl talks."

"Me, too." Loni was still nursing her first glass of wine, which she'd said earlier would help replenish her iron counts. "Clint and I . . . well, he's still in careful mode." She shrugged. "I suppose that's a good thing. I'm much better, but I'm a long way from completely recovered yet." A wistful look came into her eyes. "We've done it once. Milquetoast all the way. He acted like I might break."

Dee Dee reached over to pat Loni's hand. "He almost lost you, dear heart. Once he starts to feel certain you're well, he'll be less careful, and the sex will be fabulous again."

Loni smiled, but Ceara could tell by the way her lips only faintly curved that she was growing weary. She set aside her wine and relaxed back on her chair, her gentle gaze turning to Ceara. "Correct me if I'm wrong, but we've gotten a sex report from everyone but you, sister, dear. How's married life treating you?"

Ceara would have preferred to tell them about mowing down Quincy's shed during her driving lesson. In her time, women didn't discuss the private things that happened between man and wife. Or did they? Her mum had always shooed her and Brigid from the room when her married lady friends came to call. Ceara wasn't sure how she should respond, even if her tongue hadn't been stuck to the roof of her mouth.

"Come on," Rainie urged. "Quincy's a Harrigan. He's got to be phenomenal in the sack." A flush inched up her neck. "Not that I've ever looked at him that way. Parker is my one and only."

"I must ask ye, then," blurted Ceara. "Who is Mr. Purple, and does Parker know about the man?"

There was an instant of dead silence and then the women exploded with laughter. Rainie choked violently on her finger sandwich and had to be pounded on the back by Dee Dee. As soon as she could speak, Dee Dee put a reassuring hand on Ceara's arm. "Dear, we're not laughing at you. It's just that we never thought about your not understanding. A vibrator is something people use to stimulate themselves sexually. They come in different colors. Rainie and I both happen to have purple ones."

Rainie, still red in the face, cleared her throat. "I'm sorry, Ceara. We should have realized. But getting back on subject, how are you and Quincy doing in that department?"

"I . . . um." Ceara felt like a fly stuck to a strip of cloth slathered with tacky honey. "We are . . . doing well. He's teaching me how to cook." She told them about trying to build a fire in Quincy's oven, and everyone laughed until they got tears in their eyes. They succumbed to mirth again when Ceara shared her trials in learning how to program the MasterChef functions.

"I detest his ovens," Rainie said. "Give me a plain old knob to turn any day."

"I have MasterChef," Loni inserted, "and I love both my ovens." She winked at Ceara. "They aren't straightforward, though. It may take you some time to figure them out."

Ceara hoped to continue the conversation as she'd begun, sticking to impersonal topics, but this handful of women, who were so relaxed about sharing intimate secrets, made her feel as if she should do the same. Thinking carefully before she spoke, she finally added, "As for the marital bed, we've been together that way only once, on our marriage night, to break the curse."

Stunned silence fell.

"Only *once*?" Rainie cried.

"Damn," Mandy interjected.

Dee Dee followed with, "Oh, my, that doesn't sound quite right. Is all well between you?"

Ceara had been feeling really happy from two full

glasses of wine in her tummy, but suddenly she found herself looking at these other women with tears in her eyes. "Nay, na well."

As if she were a bottle that had been uncorked, she blurted out the whole story.

Rainie propped her elbows on the table. "Let me get this straight. You made love to break the curse, and it was really nice for you. But the next morning, Quincy got a wild hair up his butt about needing to know that for sure?"

"Yes," Ceara replied, pitching her voice to a whisper. "He wants words from me, so I gave him words, but me words were na what he wished to hear."

Mandy took two big swallows of wine. "Quincy. Doesn't it figure? The man's so anal. What words did you say to let him know you enjoyed being with him?"

Ceara thought back, wanting to tell them exactly what she'd said. Only she couldn't quite recall. "He wanted to know if 'twas good fer me," she revealed, feeling scorching heat blaze to her cheeks. "And to say it in words isna ladylike. Me mum would have fits if I were so brazen. So I told him I wouldna object if he approached me again with thoughts like that in his mind."

Rainie choked, this time on her wine, and spewed liquid out her nose. She swatted at the tablecloth with her napkin, laughing and murmuring an apology, but she didn't appear to be truly remorseful. "You told him you wouldn't *object*?" She giggled again. "Oh, God, poor Quincy. He's so country, that probably totally flummoxed him."

Dee Dee joined in, mirthful and hugging her ribs. "You wouldn't *object*?" She flapped her hand. "Oh, God, I think I'm having a heart attack." When Mandy looked alarmed, Dee Dee waved her away. "Just a figure of speech. My heart is perfectly fine."

Sam broke in. "You know, ladies, this is my brother we're talking about. I know he's a little weird about what he eats, but he's otherwise a man to set the gold standard. This isn't really funny. Think of it from his viewpoint. He and Ceara were forced into marriage. He had no choice but to consummate that very night. Ceara was a virgin. Cut him some slack. *Of course* he's reluctant to go back for seconds. You can make fun of Quincy all you want, but he is first, last, and always a gentleman. He asked Ceara for a verbal go-ahead, and she didn't really give him one."

"Nay!" Ceara protested. "I gave him a fine one! I told him I wouldna object to future advances. 'Tis the way a proper lady conveys to a man that she will welcome his attention."

More hysterical laughter broke out. Even Loni, weakened by her previous illness, giggled until tears came to her eyes. Finally, she commanded silence with an uplifted hand. "Ceara, did you enjoy sex with Quincy that first night?"

Ceara knotted the edge of the tablecloth in her fists. " 'Twas pleasant."

"Pleasant? *Pleasant?*" Rainie nearly choked on her wine again. "Is that what you told Quincy?"

Ceara let her mind drift back to that moment. "Yes, surprisingly pleasant, much better than the goings-on between pigs."

Rainie chortled. Mandy followed Dee Dee's example and hugged her ribs as fits of mirth overcame her. Loni finally called for order with another lift of her hand. "Okay, ladies, enough. What we have here is clearly simple miscommunication. Ceara speaks of these things as she was taught a proper lady should, and Quincy, being from this time, needs a lot more encouragement from her than that."

Wiping under her eyes, Rainie asked, "So what is the solution?"

Loni met Ceara's gaze. "I completely understand that you were raised with strict rules to govern your every word and action. None of us are faulting you. Please know that. But you must find a way, while remaining true to your own code as a lady, to tell Quincy that you enjoyed being with him and want to be with him again."

Ceara truly *did* want to be with Quincy that way again, but she wasn't at all sure he wanted to be with her. " 'Tis possible that me husband finds me unattractive in that way. I am reluctant to press him fer attention if he isna so inclined."

"That's just plain silly," Rainie inserted. "That day when we were shopping, he could barely take his eyes off you. He doesn't find you unattractive, I promise."

"It's just that he isn't certain you find *him* attractive," Loni pointed out. "In this day and age, men are accustomed to women who have no problem speaking their minds about sex or telling a man what they like or don't like. From Quincy's point of view, he's holding back because he doesn't want to press you into making love with him again unless he's positive you really want to. Do you?"

With a swift mental apology to her mother, Ceara took the plunge. "I *really* want to. But all the ways I have tried to let him know have failed to work." She leaned toward Loni. "What words must I say to him?"

Loni lifted her goblet and drank the rest of her wine in three big swallows. "I think the thing you will feel most comfortable with is to slightly change your ladylike response to Quincy. Instead of telling him you will not object to his advances, can you be so bold as to say that you will welcome them? It's a matter of changing only a couple of words."

Ceara considered that suggestion and finally nodded. " 'Tis not strictly ladylike to tell a man ye will *welcome* his advances, but it isna completely brazen to do so, either. I think I can say that."

"Problem solved," Mandy inserted.

"Not completely," Rainie corrected. She settled a solemn gaze on Ceara. "No more mentioning pigs, okay? Leave all the barnyard animals out of it."

Ceara felt that was unfair. "When I told him I felt it was much nicer than what happens between pigs, I meant it as a grand compliment."

Everyone at the table except Ceara went limp with laughter again.

Rainie suddenly shot up her arm, reminding Ceara of her childhood when she'd been tutored with her older brothers and had waved her hand high to garner the attention of their teacher. Everyone at the table stopped laughing and talking.

Rainie fixed a questioning gaze on Ceara. "When I took you shopping, I didn't think to buy any lingerie. You're not still wearing that flannel granny nightgown to bed, are you?"

Ceara shifted uncomfortably on her chair, sensing that she'd made a huge mistake by wearing the garment. " 'Tis a verra comfortable and warm gown. I quite like it."

At least no one laughed this time. Dee Dee looked solemn and said, "Oh, you sweet dear." Loni shook her head and said, "Well, that won't do." Rainie covered her face with her palms and said, "Well, shit." Mandy was the last to comment, with a question directed to Rainie. "You bought a *bride* a *granny* gown? What on earth were you thinking?"

The next thing Ceara knew she was being ushered upstairs to Loni and Clint's bedchamber, with Dee Dee supporting their weak hostess as they made the climb. Once they were all inside the room with the door closed, Rainie said, "Which is your lingerie drawer, Lonikins?"

Loni, now lying on her bed with her shoulders propped up against fluffed pillows, directed her sister-in-law to the proper drawer of her walk-in closet, and moments later Ceara's eyes were nearly popping out of her head when she saw the skimpy bits of lace that these women expected her to wear in order to entice her husband.

"I canna," was all Ceara could think to say. "There is no *cloth*. I canna possibly."

"Honey, you don't buy lingerie for what there *is*," Dee Dee assured her. "You buy it for what there *isn't*."

Loni silenced the feminine chatter with, "Ceara's right. We have to find something that's sexy but also concealing enough that she'll feel comfortable in it. She won't be very seductive if she's so embarrassed she's trying to hide herself." Loni sat forward on the bed, bracing her elbows on her spread knees. "Dig deeper, Rainie. I have a beautiful black camisole slip in there. It reaches almost to my knees. She won't feel as naked in that, and there's also a black lace peignoir."

The mentioned garments were finally unearthed, and Ceara's heart started to beat double-time. "I canna," she protested, but all the other women in the room said, "Oh, yes, you can."

Loni laughed weakly. "Clint *detested* my Winnie the Pooh pajamas when we first hooked up. The first thing he did after we got married was give me fifteen hundred dollars to buy sexy lingerie. He goes wild over red lace, but that might not work with Ceara's coloring."

Rainie groaned. "Like Quincy will notice a clash with her hair if she's in lace and nothing else?"

Ceara was herded to the bathroom to try on the black ensemble. She was pleased with what they called "the camisole slip." It was loose. 'Twas not see-through. Though it was low-cut with tiny strings for shoulder straps, at least she didn't feel completely exposed in it. And the black lace peignoir was lovely, giving her the sensation that she was wearing layers.

When she stepped from the bathroom, Dee Dee and Sam clapped their hands. Rainie pointed a thumb toward the ceiling and nodded. Loni sank back against the pillows and smiled her approval. Mandy giggled and said, "Poor Quincy, he's a goner and doesn't even know it."

Ceara glanced down at herself. Then she fixed a bewildered gaze on the women, who'd somehow come to feel like her best friends during the "hen party." Throat as dry as parchment, she swallowed hard and said, "So if I wear this, the words Quincy needs to hear from me will be unnecessary?"

Dee Dee's plump face cracked in a huge grin. "Honey, a getup like that speaks its own language. If Quincy doesn't take the bait, you come see me tomorrow. I'll have his father take him to the woodshed for a man-to-man talk."

Chapter Ten

As Quincy walked from Clint's arena back toward the house with his father and brother, he slapped his leather gloves on his jeans to rid them of dust and straw before tucking them over his belt. Clint hit the front veranda steps first, bending to pat Bubba and Billy Bob on their heads as he gained the porch. Frank followed second, and Quincy took the rear, his nostrils already catching the faint but delicious aroma of freshly baked apple pie. His mouth started to water. And wasn't that a hell of a note? He'd been married to Ceara only a little over a week, and already his taste buds were staging a full-blown rebellion for high-fat foods and sweets.

He stopped to give each of his dogs a good scratch behind the ears. "Followed your lady over here, did you?" Bubba lolled his tongue, his long-nosed face flashing what could only be a blissful grin. Sparing a hand for the other Aussie, Quincy asked, "How's it going, Billy Bob? You in love with her, too, or just riding shotgun to keep your brother out of trouble?"

Quincy heard Clint open the door that led into the kitchen, the trudge of boots crossing the threshold. He straightened and caught the screen to slip inside right behind his dad. The Harrigan women—all six of them—

were a glorious sight gathered around the table, each of them beautiful in her own way. They were giggling like schoolgirls, heads angled forward, voices pitched low, so intent on the exchange that it took them a moment to realize that men had entered the room.

When realization struck, instant silence descended. Shoulders snapped straight, and suspiciously innocent-looking smiles replaced the laughter. As Quincy doffed his hat, he noticed two wine bottles on the table, one already a dead soldier, the other only half-full. Apparently the hen party hadn't quite ended. He stepped to the coat tree with his brother and dad to hang his Stetson, hoping Ceara would be willing to leave soon. He was hungry for some lunch.

As Quincy turned back toward the table, he got the uncomfortable sense that he had been the main topic of the women's conversation. A blush rode high on Ceara's cheeks. His sister Sam's eyes danced with mischief, and she avoided meeting his gaze. Mandy looked as happy as a barn cat that had just lapped up a whole bowl of cream.

"There they are, our hungry men!" Dee Dee vacated her chair to descend on the refrigerator. "Squeeze over, ladies. I made a second platter of sandwiches and an extra apple pie."

"Well, butter my ass and call me a biscuit," Frank said with a laugh. "I told the boys we wasn't invited and would be lucky if you even saved us some pie."

Dee Dee rolled her eyes. "You *weren't* invited, but that doesn't mean I intended to let you starve." She jerked her head toward the downstairs bath. "Go wash up. Coffee's fresh. We can crack open another bottle of wine if you're in the mood, or you can swipe one of Clint's beers."

Quincy got first dibs on the washbasin, which Clint

had special-ordered to be extra-wide and nearly deep enough to double as a toddler's wading pool. Quincy had liked it so well that he'd gotten one similar to it for his own downstairs bath. When a rancher came in after a hard day, a simple wash of the hands didn't cut it. He needed to push back his shirtsleeves and scrub to the elbows, plus stick his head under the faucet. Loni kept a large basket of bath towels beside the sink, which not only served a man well for drying off, but were great for wiping water off the counters after a good splash and shake.

Gazing at himself in the mirror, Quincy slipped a comb from his back pocket to restore order to his damp hair. *Sex.* The women had been talking about sex. He felt certain of it. No other topic could incite that much tittering and blushing. Quincy didn't mind that females whispered among themselves about such things, but he had a really bad feeling that today's exchange had been centered on him and what had or hadn't happened between him and his wife since their wedding night. *Shit.* What had Ceara told everyone about their one-and-only time together? That it had been awful, good, spectacular, or somewhere in between? He wished he could have been a fly on the wall to listen in on that conversation. Then again, maybe his dad had it right, and nobody who eavesdropped ever heard anything good about themselves.

After Quincy reentered the kitchen, his dad and brother took their turns washing up, and then the women made room for the three men at the table. Ceara patted the chair to her right and dimpled a cheek at Quincy in invitation. Once he was settled beside her, she rested her hand on his thigh. Quincy angled a thoughtful glance at her. Then Dee Dee distracted him with the platter of itty-bitty sandwiches, and his growling stomach shoved all thoughts but hunger from his mind.

Clint opened the fridge and asked over his shoulder, "Who's up for a beer?"

"Count me in," Quincy said. Everyone at the table settled a startled gaze on him. "Hey," he said. "The rest of the family indulges. Why shouldn't I?"

"Hallelujah!" Mandy laughed and leveled a finger at Ceara. "You're good for him, girlfriend. He's finally coming down off his health-nut pedestal and eating normally, like the rest of us."

Quincy almost shot back that healthful eating was *not* abnormal, but after living with Ceara for more than a week, he was coming to realize that maybe—just maybe— he had carried his strict dietary guidelines a little too far. Out of sheer boredom, possibly. When a man had no wife or family, he had to fill up his life with something. Quincy had chosen to fixate on green smoothies, kale wraps, Swiss chard stir-fries, and grueling nightly workouts at the gym.

Dee Dee's finger sandwiches were melt-in-the-mouth good, rich with butter, mayonnaise, and layered deli-cut meats. "These are wonderful," Quincy told her. "I'd forgotten just how good stuff like this tastes." He accepted the long-neck that Clint handed him. Before taking a slug, Quincy lifted the bottle to Mandy in a mock toast. "To unhealthy eating. It may be a fast track to the cemetery, but at least we'll enjoy the ride."

"Enjoying the ride is very important." Mandy grinned and chinked her nearly empty wineglass against his beer bottle. "I'll drink to that."

"Oh, yes, Quincy. It is," Rainie put in, slanting her eyes at him in a wicked glance.

"Be careful with my crystal," Loni complained at the head of the table. "That's *Waterford*, I'll have you know. Clint bought me eight goblets and a punchbowl set for Christmas."

Sam gasped. "No!" She looked over at Quincy. "Please tell me that isn't the punchbowl you got out for Aliza's birthday party."

"I'll buy her another one if it was damaged," Quincy offered.

Clint sat at the corner of the table beside his wife. After gently kissing her cheek, he said, "Speaking of Aliza, when're your folks and Aislinn bringing the kids back?"

"Five-ish," Loni answered. "They're visiting the High Desert Museum just south of Bend. Apparently there's a special raptor exhibition, and Aliza wanted to see all the outdoor stuff as well. Trev is excited about seeing the saw-mill. On certain days, it's in operation. He'll be thrilled if they hit it lucky."

"Your folks and grandmother will be beat." Clint filled his plate with sandwiches. "It was nice of them to take the kids for the day and give you some quiet time."

"Those outdoor walkways may be icy at this time of year," Sam interjected. "I know they're shoveled, but that doesn't make the slopes safe. I hope Aislinn doesn't slip and break a hip or something."

Quincy pictured Aislinn and chuckled. "It'll take more than a slippery slope to get the better of that old gal."

Just then, Zach and Parker stepped inside, Mojo, Parker's rottweiler, rushing in ahead of them to dance in circles with Bubba and Billy Bob, who'd also darted in from the porch. Nana and Hannah, who'd been snooz-ing in the corner of the kitchen, jumped up to greet their furry friends. The two men grabbed chairs, waited for people to make room, and then sat beside their wives.

Hunger appeased, Quincy relaxed on his chair to en-joy the rest of his beer. Aside from the kids and Loni's parents, only Tucker, Sam's husband, was missing to make this a full-fledged family gathering. Quincy hadn't planned to stay after helping Clint catch up in his stables, but Ceara seemed to be enjoying herself, and when Quincy considered the alternatives, he honestly couldn't think of anyplace he'd rather be.

Unless, of course, it was at home, making passionate love to his wife. Yeah, right. Quincy didn't figure that was going to happen anytime soon, so he got up to get another beer.

Ceara couldn't stop looking at the paper sack on Loni's kitchen counter. It held the black camisole slip and lace peignoir, which Rainie had christened "Ceara's seduction outfit." To Ceara, the bag stood out like a sore thumb, and she fretted that Quincy might notice it and, even worse, ask what was in it. He would definitely be curious when she collected the sack before they left for home. Ceara didn't want to lie to him, but she didn't want the surprise to be ruined, either. Dee Dee and all her sisters-in-law insisted that Ceara needed to set the right mood tonight—candlelight, champagne, romantic music on the iPad-controlled stereo. Ceara still couldn't work the stereo, but she had high hopes of convincing Quincy to turn it on for her—somehow. Maybe she could say she wished to listen to music while they cooked dinner.

Clint glanced at his watch. "Why don't we all have dinner here," he suggested. "Make a family night of it. I can thaw some steaks, crank up the barbecue. It'll be fun."

"I'm in," Frank said.

"Me, too," Zach seconded.

Dee Dee lifted a red eyebrow at her husband. "We have other plans, dear."

Frank frowned. "We do?" When Dee Dee returned his scowl, he quickly added, "That's right. We got plans. You kids go ahead without us."

"Count me and Zach out," Mandy inserted quickly. "We have plans, too." When Zach started to speak, Mandy laid a finger against his lips. "Don't tell me you've forgotten. Remember our special date?"

With a befuddled expression, Zach nipped at his wife's fingernail. "Me, forget a special date? You gotta be kidding."

"Tucker's on call all weekend," Sam said. "We've learned never to make commitments. Sure as the world, an emergency comes up. Maybe next weekend."

Loni smiled. "Next weekend would be much better for me." She settled a smiling blue gaze on Ceara. "It's been a fun day, but I'm fading fast."

Clint switched instantly into concerned husband mode. "Oh, honey, you should have said something. Let me carry you upstairs. You probably need a nap."

"I can walk, Clint. Otherwise I'll never get my strength back."

"To hell with that," he said, sweeping his frail wife up into his arms.

Quincy took that as his cue to start clearing the table, and everyone else jumped up to help. Family members visited one another's homes so often that nobody but Ceara had a problem finding the trash bin, plastic wrap, or dishwasher soap. Soon the machine was humming, and the kitchen was spotless—except for a lone paper sack on the counter. Quincy was just reaching for it when Ceara snatched it from under his hand.

" 'Tis mine."

"Really?" Quincy studied her upturned face. Flags of deep pink slashed her cheeks. Her gaze jerked nervously from his when he tried to look her in the eye. *Red alert.* "What is it?"

"Nothing." The flush of her cheeks deepened to a rosy red. "'Tis a small gift from Loni. As ye say, no big deal."

Quincy guessed that a little secret here and there was probably healthy for a marital relationship. Not that he and Ceara actually had one yet. And he was starting to worry that they never would.

As Quincy started dinner, Ceara sneaked upstairs with her paper bag. Hurrying as fast as she could, she looped her braid around the crown of her head, showered, toweled off, and dabbed rose water on her skin, making sure to get the scent in spots where Quincy might nuzzle or sniff. Then, trembling with trepidation, she slipped into the camisole slip and peignoir. Gazing at herself in the mirror, she felt a lot more exposed in her "seduction outfit" than she had that afternoon.

"I canna," she whispered, but the moment the words crossed her lips, she heard all the hens saying, *Oh, yes, you can.*

Ceara stiffened her spine. She'd stepped onto a traveling star to come forward in time, with no idea what the future might hold for her. She'd bidden her family farewell not just for a period of time, but forever. She'd stood beside a stranger and vowed to honor him until the day she died. She'd even made love to him that very night—long before she'd been able to anticipate his smile by that little quirk of his lips or known that his dark brown eyes had beautiful flecks of gold in them. All of that had taken courage—courage she'd never known she possessed until she put herself to the test.

She wouldn't quail with fear now. She *wouldn't.* Following the carefully outlined plan formulated earlier by the hens, Ceara loosened her hair and brushed it to a high sheen. Then she slipped into the towel robe, cinched it at the waist, and slipped quietly down the stairs to carry on with the seduction of her husband.

He stood with his back to her at the stove, stirring something in a skillet that smelled like onions and garlic in that heavenly stuff he called cubed butter that was supposedly bad for the arteries. Ceara gulped to steady her voice. "Quincy, would ye mind putting on a bit of music?"

He glanced over his shoulder and turned down the gas flame. "Not at all. Anything particular you'd like to listen to?"

Ceara had no clue. Something romantic, but she didn't want to say that for fear of ruining everything. "Mayhap something easy that does na sound like a galloping horse. *Relaxing,*" she emphasized after falling upon the word. "Have ye anything like that?"

He winked. "Mood music." When he saw her frown, he added, "Soft sounds with background music—ocean waves, rain on the roof. It's great stuff for falling asleep."

Ceara wanted the man wide-awake—from the tips of his toes all the way up. "That sounds nice." If he grew sleepy, she'd wake him up straightaway with Loni's camisole slip. The hens had all assured her that once he got an eyeful of that he would grab her faster than she could take a deep breath.

The moment he left the kitchen, Ceara dived for the drawer where he kept round little candles he called tea lights. She plopped a half dozen on the table, decided that was too many, returned three to the drawer, and then lit those remaining with a flick of her wrist. Then, feeling a bit faint from using her power, she raced across the room, bent to search the light switch plate for the little slide buttons the hens had told her would dim the overhead glare. She nearly clapped her hands and did a jig when it actually worked. *Perfect*. The room wasn't completely dark, but it was shadowy enough to lend her courage when the moment came for her to doff the robe. Now the champagne.

She found a chilled bottle in the door of the fridge, located the ice bucket and two flutes in the cupboards, and turned her attention to opening the bottle. After peeling away the gold paper, she squinted at the wires that anchored the cork. *Strange.* In her time, corks weren't normally wired to the bottles. And with the lights so dim, it wasn't easy for her to determine how to loosen them. Pulling and pushing on the wires also hurt her thumbs.

Just as she finally managed to get the wires off, she heard music drift into the room through what she now knew were called built-in speakers. *Hurry, hurry.* Quincy would return any second. She needed to be out of the robe and pouring each of them some bubbly before he walked in. She would smile brightly at him and suggest that they make a toast to *this*, the first night of the rest of their lives. And if Dee Dee was right, the camisole slip and lace would say everything else for her.

She heard the fall of Quincy's boots in the hall. Jerking the robe sash loose, she shrugged one shoulder and arm from a sleeve while simultaneously wrestling with the cork. *God's teeth.* She pushed upward with her thumbs, using all her might. Felt it give. Pushed again. When the cork remained stuck, she turned the bottle this way and that, trying to see how it was supposed to come loose.

With a final shove of her thumbs, she heard a loud *pop*. At the exact same instant, pain exploded between her eyes, and all the lights went out.

*   *   *

Quincy was just swinging left through the archway when he heard a pop, spew, and thump, followed by the shattering sound of glass. His heart shot into his throat when he saw Ceara sprawled backward on the floor, surrounded by foamy liquid and wickedly sharp shards of green. Sweet Christ.

"Ceara?" He ran toward her, slipping and sliding in the slop. The smell of champagne blasted him in the face. "Ceara?"

Heedless of the broken glass, Quincy dropped to his knees. What the hell? She was out cold, and a red spot was blossoming just above the bridge of her pert little nose. *Shit.* She'd tried to open a bottle of bubbly and nailed herself in the face with the cork.

Quincy was grabbing for his cell phone to call an ambulance when her thick auburn lashes fluttered. The next instant, he was staring into dazed, bewildered blue eyes. She blinked, refocused on him.

"Wha hit me?"

Quincy cupped her face between his hands. "The cork. Damn it, Ceara, when you want champagne, just say so. I'll open the bottle for you."

She closed her eyes and groaned, making Quincy grab for his phone again. But before he could dial out, she curled loose fingers over his wrist. " 'Tis fine I am," she said weakly, trying to sit up by planting one lace-covered elbow on the glass-strewn slate.

Quincy grasped her shoulders and lifted her to a sitting position. "There's glass all around you. Let me lift you out of it."

He balanced on the toes of his boots, caught her up in his arms, and stood. With three steps, he was lowering her onto a chair. The robe, barely hooked on her left shoulder, slipped off her arm, which hung limply at her side.

"Ice, we need ice." Quincy's heart pounded as if he'd just run a marathon. He grabbed the ice bucket from the table, opened the freezer side of the Sub-Zero double unit, and scooped out enough cubes to chill half her body. "Are you dizzy?" he barked as he got a gallon Ziploc bag, filled it with ice, and wrapped it in a towel. "How about your vision? Are you seeing double?"

"Me head hurts, but I can see fine." She accepted the ice pack and pressed it between her brows. "Oh, Quincy, 'tis a fine mess I've made of it. 'Twas me intent to seduce ye, and instead all I shall get fer me trouble is two black eyes."

Until that instant, Quincy hadn't noticed what she was wearing. Sexy black silk and lace. His throat went tight. Didn't she know that all she had to do to seduce him was crook her little finger?

"Sweetheart, you don't need props."

"Props?"

He gestured with his hand. "The lingerie, candlelight, and champagne. Props. You didn't have to do all this."

"Yes," she said thinly. "Ye dinna like me words. Ye said ye needed more. And the hens agreed."

"The *who*?"

"The hens." She lowered the pack to glare at him, indignation flashing in her lovely eyes. "They say men of this time expect ladies to speak plain, and since I find that difficult, Loni lent me a seduction outfit to say the words fer me. Dee Dee says this outfit speaks a language all its own, and if ye dinna get the message, she'd have yer da take ye to the woodshed fer a man-to-man talk."

The *outfit* in question definitely spoke Quincy's language—or would have if the inside corners of his wife's eyelids hadn't been swelling and turning bright pink. *Damn*. What if she had a concussion? She'd been knocked out, and her head had probably hit the stone floor pretty hard. He wasn't quite sure how to tell her, but the well-planned seduction of her husband was going to be put on hold.

Quincy called his dad's place. Dee Dee answered. No big surprise. His dad was usually in the kitchen at this time of night, helping his wife cook so he could sneak plenty of bacon grease into the skillet every time she turned her back.

"Dee Dee, it's Quincy."

There was a smile in her voice. "And you are calling me *because* . . . ?"

Quincy couldn't see the humor. "I'm calling because Ceara knocked herself out cold trying to uncork a bottle of champagne."

"Oh, dear."

"Oh, *dear*? Is that all you've got for me? The cork hit her right between the eyes, and they're already starting to swell. Her head struck the floor pretty hard. I mean, I *heard* the hit. What if she's got a concussion? Her eyes aren't dilated, but I'm still worried. Should I take her in? I don't know what to do."

Dee Dee sighed. "Quincy, dear, here's your father."

"No!" yelled Quincy loud enough to be heard clear down to his arena. "Dee Dee? Damn it, I don't want to talk to Dad."

"I heard that. Why not?" Frank asked. "If you haven't got that girl back in the sack yet, I'm the one you *should* be talking to. My wife ain't exactly an expert on gettin' a woman into bed."

Quincy rubbed the bridge of his nose. Did *everyone* in his whole frigging *family* know that he hadn't touched

Ceara since their wedding night? He remembered the looks and the giggles when he'd walked in on the hen party, and cringed inwardly. He'd been the subject of the discussion, all right.

"At the moment, getting my wife into bed is the *last* thing on my mind," he replied.

"Then, son, you've got a serious problem. Maybe it's all that green shit from a blender you've been chuggin'. You need more meat and spuds. A man can't drive a spike with a tack hammer, you know. Get some real food under your belt."

Quincy wondered if Ceara's headache was catching. He was developing a bitch of a migraine directly behind one eye. "Why am I not surprised here, Dad? The next thing I know, all of you will be discussing my love life on the *Dr. Phil* show! Since you apparently know all about the big *seduction* scene that was supposed to take place here tonight, let me just say things went wrong. Ceara sent me off to put music on the stereo, and while I was gone, she tried to open a bottle of champagne. The cork got her smack-dab between the eyes, knocked her out cold, and I think her head hit the floor pretty damned hard. I'm afraid she might have a concussion, so I called to ask *Dee Dee* if I should take her to the hospital."

"Well, shit." Frank fell quiet for a second. "Now you wantin' Dee Dee makes better sense. She seein' double?"

"No."

"Any dizziness or pukin'?"

"No, at least not yet."

"Then I'd do with her like you have a dozen other times after a bar fight with your brothers—keep her awake for a while, make sure you ice the bruised spots, and watch her like a hawk."

"She's not one of my brothers," Quincy shot back. "She's a *lady*, and not a very big one, at that."

"I reckon her brains are pretty much like a man's. If you wanna take her in, do it, but you know how it goes at the ER. It'll be a long wait, and when a doc finally gets around to seein' her, you'll be told pretty much what I just said." Frank sighed. Then he chuckled. "A champagne cork? Son of a bitch. That's one I ain't never heard. A real twist on 'Honey, I got a headache.'"

"You think it's funny?"

"No, son. It's just that if it wasn't for bad luck, you wouldn't have none at all."

Quincy decided the mess in the kitchen could wait. Same went for dinner, so he turned off the flame under the skillet before gathering his wife into his arms and carrying her upstairs. He wasn't sure whether swelling in her nasal passages or pressure from the ice pack was causing it, but she was starting to lisp.

"'Tis thorry I am, Quinthy. I dinna mean to ruin everything."

"Honey, you didn't ruin everything. It was an incredibly sweet plan, and just because the cork hit you doesn't mean we can't follow through tomorrow night." If both her eyes weren't swollen completely shut. "It'll be just as wonderful then, I promise, so stop fretting about it."

"Even if I canna s-thay the wordsth ye need to hear?"

If Quincy could have physically pulled it off, he would have kicked himself in the ass for that bit of nonsense. Of *course* Ceara found it difficult to say the words he'd needed to hear. She came from a long-gone era, and she'd obviously been sheltered by her parents. It was so different today. Hell, he'd even dated one gal who'd told him precisely where her G-spot was located before they did the dirty. *I like it hard and fast*, or *I like lots of fore-play, with special attention to my breasts*. No blushing, no hesitancy. Females of the twenty-first century liked sex, wanted plenty of it, and weren't shy about putting in requests for whatever turned their cranks. They not only felt it was their God-given right to enjoy physical intimacy, but also their privilege to tell a man what they especially liked so they *would* enjoy it.

Quincy knew little about the social mind-sets in sixteenth-century Ireland, but apparently Ceara had been taught to guard her tongue when speaking of sex. He'd been crazy at best and totally inconsiderate at worst to expect frankness from her about her physical wants or needs. Cutting himself some slack, he hadn't asked for much by way of frankness, but to Ceara, his expectations must have seemed unacceptable. And he'd been too damned blockheaded to understand that.

As he gently deposited her on their bed, he smiled to himself. She looked so damned sweet, every man's dream from the neck down, all her attributes temptingly displayed in black silk and lace. The *hens* had selected well, choosing an ensemble that wasn't so revealing that Ceara wouldn't wear it but still sexy as hell. It *definitely* spoke a language all its own.

Quincy sat carefully on the edge of the mattress, wishing with every fiber of his male anatomy that he could make love to his wife tonight. But that would be heartless, not to mention dozens of other adjectives he couldn't think of right then.

"Can I have a look at your nose?" he asked.

She lifted the ice pack from her face and met his gaze. He was pleased to note that her pretty blue eyes looked clear, and also that the cold seemed to be minimizing the swelling. The inside corners of her eyes and the bridge of her nose were a gorgeous rose pink, but the lid puffiness was less pronounced.

"You took a hard hit, but judging by what I see now, I don't think both eyes will be black. Maybe just the bridge of your nose." He smiled at her. "I'll get you some shades for when you leave the house, and I'll call you Hollywood for the next week or two."

"What are shades?"

"Sunglasses." At her blank look, he changed words. "Spectacles, only the lenses are tinted dark so you can still see well but the sun doesn't hurt your eyes."

"Mmm." She gingerly touched the sore spot between her finely shaped brows. "Me mum would kiss the hurt away."

Quincy had only dim memories of his mother, but he could clearly recall her lightly kissing his scrapes and bruises. He bent to press his lips to Ceara's nose and murmured, "Better?"

"Nay." The ice pack clunked him on the back of his head as she brought up her arm to hug his neck. "Kiss me lips, Quincy. 'Twill make all of me feel better."

Quincy had never received a sweeter or more welcome invitation. *Problem.* If he accepted her offer, he might be unable to stop from taking things further. "Not a good idea," he whispered. "If I kiss you, I'll make love to you."

She dimpled a cheek. " 'Tis the *only* idea I have in mind."

Quincy felt himself weakening. "You might have a concussion."

"Whatever a *concussion* is, I dinna get stricken with one from a flying cork."

"You need to keep the ice on your nose to minimize the bruising," he tried.

"I shall ice me nose in betwixt."

"In betwixt what?"

Her smile deepened. The ice pack plopped some-where near her on the bed. She locked both arms around his neck. "In betwixt all the times ye'll be making love to me tonight."

"Ah." Quincy had never loved anyone quite so deeply as he loved this slip of a woman. Just looking at her made his heart pang with yearning. "So it's repeated lovemaking sessions that you're requesting?"

She tried to pleat her forehead in a frown but winced at the discomfort. "If ye make me say the words, Quincy Harrigan, ye'll be off to the woodshed with yer da to-morrow fer a man-to-man talk."

The last thing Quincy wanted or needed was a wood-shed lecture from his father, so he threw caution to the wind and kissed the woman.

Chapter Eleven

Ceara forgot all about her headache as Quincy feathered his lips over hers, sharing with her more a whisper of breath than a true kiss. Even so, her heart started to slog, and her pulse pounded with such force through her body that she felt the thrum even in the tips of her toes. She unfastened his shirt and pushed it off his shoulders, entrapping his arms. He reared back, sent the garment flying, and then straddled her hips, all in one fluid motion. No blaze burned in the fireplace, but a ceiling lamp at the other end of the room provided illumination, and the sight of his bare upper torso pleased Ceara so much that she almost protested when he bent to kiss her again, deeply and possessively.

Quincy. Long ago, Ceara had believed herself to be in love with a young man, but never had his chaste and hesitant kisses made her feel this way—her flesh and bones going as soft as candle wax placed too close to a flame. Her body tingled at every brush of his fingertips over her skin, and her breath snagged at every pass of his hands over her curves. He touched her as he might a fragile seashell: lightly, reverently, setting off sparks of heat in her belly—and lower. He made her want with an aching urgency that encouraged her to forsake all the ladylike rules of behavior that had been drummed into her head all her life. If he thought her brazen, 'twas fine, for she *felt* brazen.

Breathing in short, raspy pants, they tore at each other's garments, yearning to be body-to-body, limb against limb, heart-to-heart. Ceara reveled in the feel of his skin beneath her hands, the texture somehow coarser than hers, reminding her of the underside of silk. She explored the lumpy bones in his shoulders, the fleshy hardness of his biceps, the angular shape of his elbows, and the hard, tendon-roped slope of his forearms. But what truly made her blood run molten was touching his wide, thick wrists and broad, work-hardened hands. Their very maleness made her feel deliciously feminine.

Stripped of the camisole slip, Ceara wondered why she'd fussed so much over what to wear, because now she wore nothing at all. But Quincy didn't give her much time to ponder. His hot mouth covered her nipple, and with one draw, he had her hands fisted in his hair and her spine arching. She heard herself cry out his name, and apparently he heard her, too, for he scraped the sensitive tip with his teeth, shrilling her cry to a soft shriek as ribbons of pure sensation spiraled from her breast into the hot, throbbing core of her.

Ceara became lost in the swirl of fiery sensation, feelings so intense, thoughts so dizzy that she couldn't hold on to reason. She felt as if she were turning to liquid and being absorbed into him through the pores of his skin. No more Ceara, no more Quincy. They became one, so melded in passion that no separation existed between their bodies. His mouth, his hands, his igniting heat became her only reality.

This time when he pushed forward, he held nothing back. As his long, thick shaft entered her wet passage, he bucked hard with his hips, impaling her. She heard a scream but was too lost in the throes of passion to care that it had come from her. His rhythm was forceful and fast, and her hips instinctively found the pace so she could meet him thrust for thrust. Higher. Higher. She felt like a champagne bubble, a tiny, sparkly bit of nothing, spiraling upward toward blinding brightness.

They reached the light together. Beneath the frantic grip of her hands on his upper arms, she felt veins pop up under his skin. She squinted open her eyes to watch his face, loving the grimace that twisted his dark countenance and peeled his firm lips back over his white teeth. And then she was caught up in the taut explosion of pleasure herself, bumping her hips hard against him, craving the slower but deeper invasions that set off bursts of delight low in her belly.

Afterward they lay clutched in each other's arms, legs entangled, her head nestled in the hollow of his shoulder. As their breathing finally slowed to a normal pace, he gently placed the ice pack on her nose again, gasping when the cold touched the feverish skin of his shoulder.

"Nay!" she protested.

"You promised to ice it in betwixt, and I'm holding you to it."

In betwixt? Ceara grinned and carefully settled the pack over the injured place. That meant he planned to make love to her again. 'Twould greatly please her if he did.

Quincy stirred to consciousness with Ceara still curled against him. The room had grown colder than a well digger's ass, and he thought about getting up to start a fire. Thinking about it was as far as he got. As if Ceara sensed his wakefulness, she stirred and lifted her head to peer at him through the gloom, her mouth curved in a satisfied smile. She bent to nip playfully at his bottom lip. He didn't know where the hell the ice pack had gotten off to.

"Me mum has it all wrong," she said with a giggle. "The baser pleasures are na a wifely duty to be endured but to be eagerly awaited."

That was all the encouragement Quincy needed to make love to her again. She responded with complete abandon, no longer a hesitant virgin, but a recently de-flowered one who seemed eager to learn all the wonders of sex. Well, she'd come to a willing teacher. Quincy had been with so many women over the years that he'd nearly lost count, but never had he held anyone dearer in his arms, and he'd definitely never experienced such intense sexual pleasure.

Afterward, drained to absolute limpness, he fell asleep with his face buried in her hair. It smelled of her rose water. He needed to buy her some fancy perfume. He'd have to ask his brothers what their wives liked. His last thought before blackness settled over him again was that he'd become very fond of her rose scent and should probably stick with that. To him, the smell of rose petals was Ceara's trademark.

They awakened the next time simultaneously, their eyes popping open like those of exhausted children who real-ized they'd snoozed too long and missed out on too much playtime. Ceara nuzzled her cheek against their shared pillow, pleased to see his sleepy but satisfied grin.

"Ye look happy," she murmured. "Almost as happy as I am."

"So you liked it, did you?"

Ceara traced the frown lines above the bridge of his nose. "A lady canna wax poetic about how greatly she *likes* that kind of thing. 'Tis brazen."

He laughed. "So we're back to that again, are we?"

" 'Tis who I am."

"I know that now," he said huskily. Then he sighed. "Where the hell is your ice pack?"

" 'Tis lost, and me nose has stopped paining me, so I have no further need of it."

"You promised to use it in betwixt."

"In betwixt what?" She flashed him a deliberate grin that she knew dimpled her cheek and made her look as impish and mischievous as her little sister did after she pulled a prank. " 'Tis thinking I am that ye're falling down in your duties, Sir Quincy, if ye expect me to keep me promise about icing during the *betwixts*. I need a bit more encouragement from ye than what ye've given me so far."

"*Sir* Quincy? Please. Surely we've moved past that now."

"A man who pleases his lady so much deserves to be addressed by his title."

"Aha!" he said with a rich chuckle. "Caught you. You as good as told me that you liked it a lot, you brazen little hussy."

Ceara gave him one of her most demure smiles. "Let me say only that if ye approach me again with such things on yer mind, I willna object."

He studied her for a long moment, and then, with no warning, he growled, caught her in his arms, and playfully nipped her shoulder. "You won't object? I'll take that as a green light." His mouth found her breast, and Ceara gasped, unable to suppress the sound. "Mmm." He suckled her, sending jolts of sensation into her belly. "You taste like honey." He tickled the hard crest with his tongue. "And one of my favorite things is honey. What if I have such things on my mind all day today and never let you out of bed?"

Ceara could barely collect her thoughts to give him a coherent answer. "I willna object," she managed shakily.

He laughed and then turned serious as he began making love to her again. Ceara nearly groaned when he abandoned her breast. She wondered whether it would be considered brazen of her to ask him to go back to it. She quite liked the pull of his mouth on her nipple. Ah, but his kisses along her rib cage were just as delightful, and before she could answer her own question, she'd forgotten what it was.

When Ceara next awoke, it was to the urgent sound of someone's stomach growling. Blinking open her eyes, she couldn't be sure at first whether it was Quincy's or her own, but after drifting upward to full consciousness, she determined that both of their guts were complaining of hunger. As if he felt the pangs, too, Quincy opened his eyes, seeming to come instantly alert.

"You're hungry."

He pushed up on an elbow, looking so good that Ceara considered having another taste of him before they ate, but her belly hunger won the vote. " 'Tis *starving* I am."

He swung off the bed, pulled on his boxers, and shoved his feet into his boots. As Ceara stood to pull on the camisole slip, he said, "The kitchen's a total wreck. I'll carry you down. I don't want you cutting your feet." He pinched the bridge of his nose, blinked, and then focused on her face. "Well, shit. So much for using ice in betwixt. You're well on your way to having two beauts."

"What are beauts?"

"Black eyes, Hollywood. Shades for you, coming up." He made circles with his thumbs and forefingers over his eyes. "Great *big* suckers. And you'll wear them whenever we go to town. Otherwise strangers will think I'm a wife beater."

"Yer family willna?"

Quincy chuckled. "Darlin', in this family, any man who lifts a hand in anger to a woman can expect to see his picture in the obits three days later."

"What are obits?"

He circled the bed, scooped her up in his arms, and said, "I'll explain while I sweep up the glass and mop the kitchen floor so your pretty little feet don't stick to the slate."

Quincy turned up the thermostat so Ceara wouldn't be cold in Loni's camisole slip, and after cleaning the kitchen floor, he set to work cooking breakfast. Ceara sat at the table with a fresh ice pack over her nose, but every time he wasn't looking, she lowered it so she could feast her eyes on her husband. She quite liked the trews that he called boxers, she decided. He had legs as brown and sturdy as tree trunks, and his back, chest, and arms put on a show for her, muscles rippling and bulging under his bronze skin. As hungry as she was for real food, watching him kindled other fiery needs within her. She doubted that she would be in need of the spectacles he called shades to hide her black eyes, because, brazen though it might be, she wanted to spend at least the next week in bed with her husband. She had a delicious feeling that he'd introduced her to only little bits of the whole picture when it came to what he called "sex." She felt like a child who was being taught tiny words etched on slate while whole tomes filled with complicated sentences awaited her.

He was whisking eggs, putting so much force into the swirls of the beater that his boxers danced on his narrow hips, when she collected the courage to ask, "Quincy, what is an electronic boyfriend?"

He nearly toppled the bowl of frothy yellow as he jerked his head around to gape at her. "Say what?"

Ceara restated the question. "Dee Dee tossed hers in the trash, but Rainie still has one. They call him Mr. Purple."

"Son of a bitch." He went back to whisking, but with far more enthusiasm. "That's it. No more hen parties for you. The women in my family are teaching you all kinds of stuff you have no need of knowing."

"Why do I have no need?"

She saw his muscular shoulders tense and then relax. "Okay. You *do* have a need. You're in my world now, and I guess females are going to talk to you about stuff like that." He sighed and his shoulders slumped a bit more. "An electronic boyfriend—well, *hell*." He released the handle of the whisk so abruptly to turn to face her again that the implement rocked out of the bowl and splattered whipped egg all over the counter. "It's a gadget." He threw up a hand. "Don't ask what a gadget is. Just let me get this said. When women get . . ." He dragged in a deep breath that swelled his already impressive chest, and then released it with a *whoosh*. "When women get lonely for *male* companionship, they use what they call electronic boyfriends to satisfy themselves. The correct nomenclature isn't 'electronic boyfriend' or 'Mr. Purple.' Its proper name is a vibrator, and when it's turned on, it vibrates. The sensation is . . . well, when applied to certain parts of a woman's body, the vibration is arousing, and a woman can get off using one."

"Get off? Where do they get off to?"

He shot her another disgruntled look and returned his attention to the eggs. "They feel sort of like . . . well, at the high point, when we made love, sort of like you felt all those times last night." Still holding the whisk, he turned to jab a finger at her, shaking beaten egg all over the recently scrubbed floor. "The thing is, you won't need one, *ever*."

"Mayhap ye will be the one to need a Mr. Purple."

That had him bugging his brown eyes at her. *"Me?"*

"Yes. Rainie says if she fools around with Mr. Purple during . . . what did she call it? Foreplay, 'tis the word she used—that Parker turns into a wild man."

Quincy's dark face turned an odd red color, nearly the same shade as the lovely berry wine she'd enjoyed at Loni's house yesterday. "*That* is more about my brother's sex life than I really want to know." He pivoted back to the stove. "Parker? Holy hell. I never would've guessed him to be even slightly kinky."

"Kinky? 'Tis a word I havena heard."

"And a word you don't need to know the meaning of, either." He released a loud sigh. "Back to you and me. Anytime you get to feeling like you need Mr. Purple in the drawer of your bedside table, you just let me know, and I'll blow him clear out of the hemisphere. Got it?"

Ceara didn't get it, but Quincy seemed so disgruntled that she decided to wait and ask the *hens* for more information. A quick change of subject seemed in order.

"So, Quincy, I canna continue to wear Loni's camisole slip to seduce ye, because I must return it, and I was—"

"You don't need *anything* to seduce me."

Ceara remembered Loni saying that Clint had given her fifteen hundred dollars to buy what she'd called lingerie, and Ceara had a feeling *lingerie* must be very important to husbands. " 'Tis not that I feel I need *props*," she informed him. "I am just thinking that a wee bit of lace might be nice when I *do* wish to seduce you."

Egg went flying again. His gaze found hers, and its hold was as physical as an iron fist. "I like little bits of lace, and I damned sure won't complain about the bill if you want to buy some. I've already sent in to get you a credit card. Sky's the limit. Buy whatever you want."

" 'Tis me wish to ask the hens to help select me lace."

He shot her another look over his shoulder. "I could go with you."

Ceara shook her head. "Nay, 'tis me feeling that I will need the advice of the hens."

He considered for a moment and finally nodded. "Mr. Purple? What the frigging hell?" Then he shrugged. "Go for it. All ladies love shopping together, and no matter how crazy they get, my heart is in prime condition." He paused in the whisking, glanced at the sausage frying in a second skillet, and added, "Well, at least it *was*."

Life with Ceara. As frustrating as it sometimes was for Quincy, if he'd been asked how to describe the ways his world had been changed, he would have said, "In so many fabulous ways, it's impossible to put into words."

After a slightly rocky start, Ceara regained her confidence and approached everything in the twenty-first century with curiosity, daring, and determination. When she wasn't with him at the stable to help with the horses, she spent time at home, creating what she called "household" mixtures for cleaning, even though Quincy had a woman who came in twice weekly to muck out the rooms. Apparently Ceara still managed to find soil or dust, and she felt more comfortable using familiar, homemade concoctions for scrubbing or polishing, which meant several drives to town for weird ingredients he couldn't readily find—pure beeswax and lye, to name only two. She also traipsed in the fields to pick spring flowers, which he helped her dry using the dehydrating setting in his ovens, to make fragrant sachets for their clothing drawers. When she wasn't otherwise busy, he helped her choose a contemporary flick on Netflix to better familiarize her with his century. She especially enjoyed films that featured other countries so she could orient herself in her new world, where new lands had been discovered and occupied since the sixteenth century.

She also needed to learn to cook all over again, so Quincy assumed the role of teacher, fearful that her tendency toward easy, packaged foods would become an unhealthy diet regimen for both of them. She found the gas flame burners on the Viking cooktop similar to preparing food over an open fire, so he started her off there with simple dishes, his aim to give her a sense of accomplishment before he moved on to the more complicated features of the appliances, including the steamer, the warmers, the toaster, the mixer, and even the Traeger smoker-grill in his outdoor kitchen. Some of her culinary attempts were, in a word, inedible, but when she pulled something off that tasted great, she danced around and whooped with delight.

Quincy gave her daily driving lessons on his property. Needless to say, fence repairs became a common necessity, because Ceara continued to miss the brake pedal in his truck. But, oh, well. Though Quincy dreaded the day that he turned Ceara loose on an actual road, he was practical enough to realize that she couldn't exist in his world without learning how to drive.

It took two weeks for Ceara's blackened eyes to return to normal, and because she detested wearing sunglasses, which she said made everything look dark, she and Quincy spent most of that time either on his ranch or visiting the homes of his family members. Ceara continued to refer to the other Harrigan females as the "hens," and somehow the tag stuck. Not even the women themselves objected. Instead, they acted as if they'd formed an exclusive club and were glad to have a name for themselves.

Because all the hens had cell phones, Ceara asked Quincy to please supply her with one, which he promptly did, and even more promptly regretted. Ceara was fascinated by the phone's features, which opened up the electronic world of communication to her—with a bang. At first Quincy feared that the technology would baffle her, but Ceara proved to be a fast learner. She caught on to texting and fell in love. When he worked in the arena without her, his phone went off constantly. He had assigned a special ring tone for Ceara—the sound of a hen clucking—and he heard clucking alerts about every ten minutes, which made it difficult for him to accomplish anything. *Hi,* she'd write. *What u doing?* Quincy would text back about his activity of the moment. *I miss you.* He'd zing back, *Miss you too.* Mostly he didn't mind the intrusions and smiled, wishing he could be with her instead of with his horses. But there were other texts that sent his blood pressure off the chart and had him racing toward the house.

Black smoke coming from microwave. When Quincy burst into the kitchen, the aforementioned black smoke had filled the large room and he saw flames dancing through the sooty viewing window of the Miele Speed Oven. Ceara had come across a jar of his all-natural peanut butter in a cupboard, had trouble stirring the oil at the top into the dry mess at the bottom of the plastic jar, and had decided to soften the whole works by nuking it. Quincy wasn't sure what had combusted, the plastic jar or the oil, but after turning on the exhaust fans, he had to drown the microwave with foam from a fire extinguisher to put out the blaze. His pricey Miele appliance had to be replaced.

Marriage, he decided, could be a costly venture. But even as he paid the tab, he couldn't help but smile. Ceara brought so much joy and contentment into his life that he couldn't complain about a few mishaps, expensive though they might be.

He felt more than a slight jolt of alarm when he came in from work one day to find Ceara pecking away at the keyboard of his business computer. The system held all his ranch records, and though he backed it up onto an exterior drive daily, he didn't trust his wife not to accidentally wipe out everything with a few clicks of the wrong buttons. He ironed out that little wrinkle by taking her into town, where she could select her very own laptop. While she played with systems, wearing the sunglasses to hide her black eyes, Quincy wandered the software aisles, searching for educational games she might enjoy, at the top of his shopping list a typing program for kids that was entertainingly interactive. That night, he set Ceara up in her own little corner of his office, got her wireless Internet connected to his home network, and left her to play while he barbecued steaks, baked a couple of spuds, and made a salad for dinner.

Later, when they sat across from each other at the kitchen table, sipping wine and enjoying the meal, Quincy gazed across the flickering tea lights that Ceara insisted on using for every evening meal and wondered how any woman with two eyes splotched with purple and soot gray could possibly be so beautiful.

"I'm in love with you," Quincy blurted. For a second, he wasn't sure what had prompted him to say the words aloud, but then he realized he'd been thinking them plenty, and it seemed only right to get them out in the open. "I mean, I really, *truly* love you, Ceara. I don't know exactly when it happened—or even how it happened—but it's a done deal for me. I'm head-over-bootheels, crazy in love with you."

Chewing daintily on a bite of steak, she pocketed the meat in her cheek, smiled dreamily at him, and replied, "When you walk in at night, me heart does a dance, and I feel happy and warm in me middle just like when I drink champagne."

That was it? Quincy wanted to hear other words from her, notably that she loved him back, but recalling the aftermath of their wedding night, with him expecting words from her that she couldn't say, he decided to settle for whatever he got. If he made her heart dance, that was good. Right? And making her feel all warm in the middle wasn't half-bad, either. They were happy together. They laughed a lot. The sex was phenomenal. He'd be crazy to nitpick.

Just then Quincy's cell phone whinnied. A text from Clint. He opened it up. *I'm glad to know your wife likes your ass, but I think she meant the pic to go to Loni.* Quincy's stomach clenched. Clint had forwarded Ceara's text back to him, and he half expected to see his bare butt shining. He was relieved to see only the seat of his jeans. He glanced up at Ceara.

" 'Tis bad news?"

Quincy shut down the phone. "No, good news, actually." His wife thought he had a sexy ass. He wasn't sure how he felt about her sending the hens texts about certain parts of his anatomy, but he sure as hell couldn't complain about the sentiment she'd wanted to share. "Clint just sent me a little joke."

Her cheek dimpled in a smile. " 'Tis good he is feeling

happy again. Loni grows stronger every day. She and Aliza walked over to Dee Dee's fer the midday meal today, and after resting, she was strong enough to walk all the way home."

After Quincy and Ceara set the kitchen to rights, he volunteered thirty minutes to show her the different features of her new iPhone and then gave her advanced lessons on texting. "It's easy to send a text to the wrong person on this particular device. So when you begin a text, look at the top of your screen to check to whom your text will be sent."

Her cheeks went rosy. She glanced up with a worried look in her blue eyes. "Have I sent texts to wrong people?" she asked.

Quincy had no desire to humiliate her, but he didn't wish to lie to her, either. He settled on saying, "It's just a big possibility, so from now on, when you're texting, always check to be sure of the recipient."

Ceara hunched her shoulders, scowling down at her phone as she tapped the screen to zip back and forth between message threads. Quincy pretended not to notice as he got a beer from the fridge. As he screwed off the cap, he stared at the bottle for a long moment, wondering when over the last four weeks he'd started drinking again. It was kind of like love, he guessed, one of those things that sneaked up on a guy and hooked into him before he quite knew how it happened.

"Oh, dear," Ceara said, her voice ringing with dismay. "I sent the picture of yer backside to Clint, not Loni." She glanced up. " 'Tis what he texted you about."

Quincy shrugged. "No big." He couldn't stifle a grin. "I'm just glad to know you like my backside."

Ceara sighed. " 'Tis verra careful I must be when I text."

Quincy figured she probably would be from now on,

and distracted her with an introduction to the universal
and iPad remote controls, which operated all the stereo,
television, and Internet entertainment options. At one
point, Ceara had everything on at once, the stereo in
party mode, with different music playing in every room,
and a Netflix movie blasting on the flat screen at an ear-
shattering volume. Though she sent Quincy panicked
visual appeals for help, he stood at her side with his arms
folded, determined to let her punch buttons until she figured it out by herself. Smart young woman that she was,
she eventually mastered the devices, and blessed silence
settled over the house again.

Quincy took that as his cue to carry his wife upstairs
to what she still called their bedchamber to cap off the
evening by making slow, passionate love to her.

The Erotic Parrot. Excitement bubbled in Ceara's chest
as Rainie steered Loni's new Suburban into the parking
lot of the establishment. The building was painted a
gaudy purple with pink trim, but Ceara decided the colors were fitting, because this was the home of Mr. Purple,
not to mention a huge selection of sexy lingerie, according to the hens. Mr. Purple. Ceara couldn't wait to see an
electronic boyfriend.

"I didn't think your black eyes would *ever* go away!"
Loni hooked arms with Ceara after they exited the vehicle. "It's too bad you hate sunglasses. We could have
gone shopping a week ago."

Walking behind them, Dee Dee said, "You weren't up
to it a week ago, Loni, and I'm holding you to your
promise to say something if you start to get tired."

"I promise, I *promise*," Loni said with a laugh. "Do
you know how long it's been since we had a girls' day of
shopping? I was thinking last night. It's been well over

six months. I didn't miss it at the time. I think I was start-ing to get sick long before I realized it. No energy for fun stuff."

"And this *will* be fun," Rainie said over her shoulder as she pushed open the glass door. "Quincy won't know what hit him."

"My poor brother," Sam cried. "You guys don't give him credit for all his fine qualities."

"Yes, we do," Mandy objected. "It's just that he's always been so uptight. It's high time to make him loosen up."

Jostled along by the giggling hens, Ceara entered the shop and was instantly dazzled by the displays. To her right, there was a rack of transparent lingerie with sparkly pat-terns that shone like diamonds in the rays of sunlight com-ing through the front windows. Another rack held more transparent garments trimmed in bright-colored feathers.

"Decadent, huh?" Mandy chirped with a grin. "Boy, I love this place. Every time I come, I make Zach's eyes pop out of his head that night."

Dee Dee chimed in with, "I like that they haven't overlooked us older gals with mature figures." She skimmed a palm over her well-padded hip, which looked delightfully round beneath what she called her go-to-town black slacks. "Even us dinosaurs like to look sexy."

"You're not a dinosaur," protested Rainie who glim-mered like a sun-drenched rainbow in a swirly hued blue skirt and a metallic gold peasant blouse topped by a multicolored shawl threaded with more shimmery yel-low, which she'd chosen to wear that day to celebrate the spurt of warm weather. "You're pretty as a picture, and I know Dad would second that vote."

Dee Dee stopped at a glass box filled with odd-looking things that came in all different colors and were shaped like the corncobs Quincy had barbecued on the grill one night. A young woman, boxed in by other glass cases, moved close to smile at Dee Dee over the counter. "Anything particular in mind today, ladies?"

Rainie bent over to peer in. "Oh, *wow*! Look at this gold-plated one, Ceara. You could name him Mr. Midas."

Ceara realized then that the shiny corncobs were what the hens called electronic boyfriends—proper nomenclature, according to Quincy, *vibrators*. Mildly disappointed because they didn't look very impressive, Ceara joined Rainie at the glass and pretended to be more interested than she actually was.

The clerk smiled and said, "The gold one is top-of-the-line, with five different sensation settings. All my ladies who've bought one absolutely *love* it."

"Test run," Mandy piped in.

"Definitely," Sam agreed.

The saleswoman used a key to open the backside of the case and plucked Mr. Midas from his black velvet perch. She handed the apparatus to Rainie. "Try the highest setting, the French Tickle. I hear that the men like it even more than the women do."

Ceara gaped as Rainie pressed a button to make Mr. Midas come alive and then used a slide control to go through the settings with the gadget resting on her palm. *"Nice."* She glanced over her shoulder at the other hens. "I mean, *ooh-la-la*. This thing rocks and rolls."

She handed Mr. Midas to Ceara, who was so startled by the vibration that she nearly dropped it. " 'Tis wiggling. What makes it wiggle?"

"Batteries," Loni chimed in. "Always make sure you've got plenty of D batts, sister dear. There's nothing more deflating than an electronic boyfriend in dud mode."

"She'll take it," Rainie said. "Ceara, where's your credit card?"

"You did bring it, I hope," Sam said.

"I did! Quincy got me one of me own and says I can spend as much as I wish."

"Well, we'll make him wish he'd given you a limit," Dee Dee said with a laugh.

Quincy had lent Ceara a leather coin pouch to carry the card, because she had no purse. As she reached into the pocket of her skirt, the saleswoman said, "No hurry with that unless you're finished shopping."

Rainie hooked elbows with Ceara. "Oh, she has heaps more shopping to do. Can we just bring all her selections here and leave them on the counter?"

"Absolutely."

Ceara found herself being guided by the hens into the bowels of the shop. She felt like a bit of flotsam being swept along by a wave. An hour later, she and all the hens left the establishment with the handles of pretty purple sacks looped over their arms. Ceara carried three that were filled with sparkly, feathery, and lacy night-wear, several pairs of skimpy panties, three half-cup bras, and her very own gold-plated electronic boyfriend, already christened Mr. Midas.

"Now for some more practical shopping." Rainie's voice rang out in the sun-washed April breeze. "She needs some everyday underthings *and* at least a couple of outfits that will knock Quincy's eyes out. The first time I helped her shop, I focused on modesty and layers. This time, I'm thinking tight-to-the calf black boots with heels, a skinny black skirt that hits just above the knee, and a dynamite top of some kind."

"I'm dying to see her in a green knit top," Sam said. "Jade, I think. With her hair, can you just imagine?"

"Lunch first." Mandy placed a hand over her middle. "I'm starving!"

They ate at a place the hens called a fish house. Once seated at the large round table, Ceara glanced at the dining area, trying to determine *why* it was called a fish house, because she saw no fish anywhere. But she could smell what might be fish cooking somewhere in the building. Dee Dee helped Ceara order—halibut in a light butter-lemon sauce with baby red potatoes, steamed broccoli, a house salad, and a glass of white zinfandel.

Ceara enjoyed the food and wine, but the conversation was even more fun. The hens felt free to talk about anything and everything: sex, new recipes, sex, kids, housekeeping, sex, college courses, husbands, marital spats, and, of course, more about sex. Ceara discovered that people coupled in very strange places—closets, laundry rooms, on top of desks or tables, in the shower, and even in bathtubs. Ceara had only ever been with Quincy in bed, and by comparison, she felt boring. That led to an alarming thought. Did Quincy think she was boring?

Before she could agonize overlong about that, Rainie leveled a finger at her and said, "Hair."

Mandy giggled. "I've been thinking exactly the same thing." She sent Ceara an apologetic look. "Not that your hair isn't beautiful. I mean, that color red is totally choice. Women probably pay a fortune to get anywhere close. But the length?" Mandy shrugged. "Ya got no style, sister."

"Style?" Ceara repeated.

Rainie ran her hands back and forth over her blond-streaked tresses, making them go every which way, and then shook her head to make them fall back into place. "*That* is style. A little bit sexy, sort of bed-head once it's mussed, and easy to keep up. It's all about the cut." She eyed Ceara's face. "I'm betting you have heaps of natural curl with all those little wisps that aren't tamed by your braid."

"Just below the shoulder would look fab," Loni inserted.

"And layered, definitely layered," Mandy added.

"It *would* be lovely," Dee Dee agreed.

"And so much easier to take care of if it were shorter," Loni observed.

In Ceara's time, women cut their hair only if they accidently singed it while cooking over the fire. Then again, women in her time never sank chin-deep in Quincy's lovely whirlpool tub and got their tresses caught in the outtake valve. "Shorter," she mused. " 'Twould be nice, I think."

"Unanimous?" Sam asked. Then she grinned. "If we're going to loosen Quincy up, we may as well give him such a jolt we unseat all his bolts."

Chapter Twelve

Quincy had washed up in the arena restroom, so as he paced off the distance from the arena to the house, the nip of the early evening April breeze sank its teeth through the damp shoulder seams of his work shirt, making him shiver. He'd chosen not to wear a jacket and now regretted it. As sunny as the central Oregon weather had been all day, it was now, with the arrival of twilight, turning colder than a witch's tit after a long ride on her broom in freezing temperatures.

Bubba and Billy Bob weren't snoozing on the porch, which told Quincy that both his mutts were inside with their lady. Ceara had won them over completely, and both dogs now preferred to forgo stable time to stay at the house with her. Quincy didn't mind, not really. He loved his Aussies, but seeing the glow on Ceara's face as she fussed over them pleased him. What made her happy made him happy. That was the long and short of it.

He stomped his boots as he scaled the steps and then wiped them as clean as he could on the hemp welcome mat before he entered the kitchen. After taking one step into the room, he froze. A slender redhead stood before the Viking cooktop. She was a vision, with burnished curls tumbling onto her shoulders and partway down her back. She wore a green knit top, a little black skirt that showed plenty of leg, and calf-hugging black boots with at least three-inch heels.

Quincy forgot to close the door behind him. "Where's Ceara?" *And who the hell are you?* He bit back that question. The gal was cooking. Ceara had spent the day out shopping with the hens. Maybe they had convinced her to hire a full-time housekeeper. "My wife, Ceara, where is she?"

Billy Bob and Bubba, snoozing at her feet, both came awake at the rumble of Quincy's voice. Tongues lolling, they gave him happy grins and lumbered erect before racing toward him, losing traction on the slate in the process and bumping into each other with ferocious play growls, eager for a hello rub and scratch behind the ears.

The woman turned from the stove, and Quincy forgot all about greeting his dogs. *Ceara? Sweet Christ.* What had happened to his precious sixteenth-century lady with that incredibly beautiful face bare of cosmetics, impossibly long hair, and layers of clothes to hide her body? Now—dear God—he felt a little faint. Her hair was a gloriously shorter flame of riotous curls that showcased an absolutely perfect countenance, artfully enhanced with shadow, blush, mascara, and a glimmer of lipstick. And from the neck down? Holy hell, a digital billboard flashing, SCREW ME, couldn't have sent a louder message.

Quincy closed the door by going weak at the knees and collapsing back against it. She wore a dark green top that clung to every curve, enhancing her small but delectable breasts. The black skirt hugged her hips and dived pencil-straight to just above her dimpled knees. Skin-tight calf boots with kick-ass spiked heels completed the outfit. His mouth went dryer than arena sand, and his tongue felt as if it had been glued to the roof of his mouth. The first time he'd ever seen Ceara, he'd known that she was world-class in almost every way, but never had he imagined she could look like this. If he took her into one of his old honky-tonk haunts, he'd end up in a fistfight, because every cowboy in the joint would be drooling over her—literally—with their collective saliva pooling in the cleavage of her breasts.

"Holy hell, what have you *done*?"

She dimpled a cheek at him and shot out a hip to provide a perch for her splayed hand. Quincy's gaze snapped to the spot like metal shavings reeled in by a strong magnet. Something else snapped to attention right along with his gaze. Her slender fingers were tipped with shiny, natural nails. No painted acrylic tips, thank God. He *hated* them.

"The hens got me a done-over." Still wobbly on the toothpick heels, she stepped out from the stove and did a slow, slightly precarious twirl to show herself off. Quincy prayed to God she didn't fall and snap a fragile anklebone, even as he noted that the slight sway accented her legs and hips. "What do ye think, Sir Quincy?"

He thought he'd died and gone to heaven. Well, scratch that. He really, *really* liked what he saw, but what had she done with all her beautiful *hair*? It took a lifetime to grow a braid that long, and as big a pain in the ass as it had been to wash, dry, and braid again, he'd still thought it was beautiful. Not that the new cut wasn't equally pretty. Hell, it was downright stunning.

"I donated me braid," she informed him. "To a charity called Locks of Love that makes hairpieces for children who have no hair because they are ill."

He moved slowly toward her. His tongue still wouldn't come loose from the roof of his mouth. The unmistakable scent of Chanel No. 5 drifted to his nostrils. *Man.* He liked roses a lot, but Chanel totally blasted his olfactory senses. And on Ceara, the expensive perfume had its own allure, different somehow than it smelled on other women.

He finally got his tongue pried loose. "You look drop-dead . . ." He couldn't think of an adjective to do her justice. "Drop-dead . . ." Where was his brain, in his hip pocket? "You look—"

Her blue eyes quickened with tears, and she wobbled on the high heels in a speedy attempt to sweep past him. Quincy snaked out a hand to catch her by the arm. *Language barrier.* She didn't get what *drop-dead*, followed by any adjective, meant. "Gorgeous," he blurted. "You are *gorgeous*—you totally *eclipse* any woman I've ever clapped eyes on. You look so beautiful I can barely think."

She turned a questioning gaze on him, her eyes still shadowed with hurt. "Truly?"

She looked and smelled so fabulous that Quincy wanted to devour her right there on the spot. "Oh, yeah." He released his hold on her arm. "Way too beautiful to eat in. Turn off the stove and give me fifteen to clean up. I'm taking you out to dinner. Someplace *incredible.* We'll go into town by cab, wine and dine, and come home by cab. A lady as beautiful as you are deserves . . ." He honestly couldn't think what she deserved. A charter flight to Paris for dinner, maybe? "The sky is the limit. Just let me get cleaned up."

Her worried expression dissolved into an adorable, pleased smile that made his heart jerk. Smoothing her hands over her top and tight skirt in a way that nearly made his Adam's apple stick to the back of his tongue, she said, "I canna go out in *this.* 'Tis a fer-home outfit. An outfit only fer ye. The hens say that is okay, to dress this way only fer ye."

Quincy had always prided himself on being an open-minded, modern-day guy who applauded and encouraged females to express themselves, verbally or in their dress, so it stymied him that he really, *really* liked hearing that Ceara had dressed up in this man-killer outfit only for him. He wouldn't be doling out knuckle sandwiches to any cowboys tonight, after all.

"*That* is the sexiest thing any woman has ever said to me," he told her, and meant it from the bottom of his jealous heart. He stepped back to skim his gaze over her again, which made his pulse kick. "You dressed like this only for me? It's not something you plan to wear—well, you know, out in public?"

"God's *teeth*, no, only in our home, fer ye, and only fer ye."

Quincy felt his shoulders relax. Maybe it was bad of him, but he didn't want some other man salivating over her, and he knew damned well other men *would*. She was a knockout. How great was it that the only lights she wanted to knock out were his?

"Then just give me five to clean up." He stepped over to the stove, took a gander, and changed his mind. "On second thought, how about I stay down here to help, and then we'll go upstairs together?" What *was* that shit in the skillet? Quincy mentally shuddered. It resembled something the dogs might have puked up. Then he looked back at Ceara, and he honestly didn't care. "Scratch that. With you on my menu, who wants to eat?"

He turned off the burner, grabbed her up in his arms, laughing when she squealed, and carried her upstairs. When he peeled off the jade green top, she stepped back from him, wobbling on the spiked heels, and said, "Wait! I need to get Mr. Midas."

"Who?"

Her cheek dimpled in an impossibly irresistible and

impish grin. Waving a hand at him, she disappeared into the bathroom and returned, holding a shiny gold vibrator. With a click of the button, she had it going and touched the tip to that sensitive spot just below her ear. Quincy's mouth watered for a taste of that place. Her grin grew more mischievous, and she trailed the tip of the vibrator along the top of her lacy, half-cup bra, letting her head fall back and moaning.

Quincy was across the room before he knew he'd moved. Okay, okay. He could see how Parker got turned on when his wife played around with Mr. Purple before they made love. He wondered fleetingly if Parker had been told about Mr. Midas. How many brothers knew the color of the vibrators used by their sisters-in-law?

God help me. I'm kinky, too.

After two rounds and no food, Quincy was deep into an exhausted sleep when Ceara shook his shoulder. He smacked his paper-dry lips, tried to peel his eyes open, got a blurry impression of the most gorgeous naked redhead he'd ever seen, and sank back into his recovery zone with a deep groan.

"Quincy, 'tis important! What is *group* text? If I text back, will I reply to the wrong person?" Another shake. "Quincy? I need ye to help me!"

He got his eyelids to crack open a quarter inch. *Group sex?* Nah, this was Ceara, not some bimbo from a honkytonk. He swallowed, wished for a long, tall glass of water, and forced his eyes open wider. Group *text*. Despite the fact that his bones felt like warm bacon grease and his limbs wouldn't move, he managed to fully open his eyes.

"Group text?" he croaked.

"Yes!" Ceara cried. " 'Tis urgent. A hen is in trouble. It says, 'Distress signal!' "

Quincy yawned broadly. Tried to think. "A group text. Hmm. Just reply. It goes to every damned body in the group."

"But na to Clint?"

That brought his eyes all the way open for sure. He pushed up on an elbow to look at her phone. "What the hell's going on?"

Ceara shoved at his shoulder. He was so exhausted from making love to her that he toppled like an uprooted sapling. "What the hell's going on?" he repeated.

" 'Tis *hen* business. Explain to me about group messages."

Quincy tried. His brain was foggy. His body had turned to the consistency of an overcooked noodle. *Just text back. It goes to everyone in the group.* At least he hoped he said that. He sank into darkness, his body still humming from an overdose of pleasure.

Ceara didn't know what to do. Loni needed help with Clint. He wouldn't make love to her the way she wanted. He was afraid of hurting her. Loni felt well enough for what she called a "wham-bam," and she was in tears because Clint had barely done it with her since her illness, and after she'd dressed sexy for him tonight, all he'd given her was "milquetoast." Now he'd rolled over in bed and gone to sleep. She was tired of the "fragile" treatment.

Before Ceara could start to reply, Rainie texted back to Loni. *He needs a wake-up call.* What was a wake-up call? Surely, Ceara reasoned, Rainie wasn't proposing to telephone Clint herself to wake him up? As Ceara pondered that, Dee Dee texted and said that Loni just needed to be patient. At that point, Rainie broke in again and said, *I take it back. You are a dinosaur after all,*

Dee Dee. She needs a good screw, and God knows, after almost dying, she deserves one. Mandy texted, *Hold on; let's not get weird. Clint's just having a moment.* Sam texted to say, *Clint has always been Mr. Responsible. He's just worried about you, Lonikins. Your blood got really thin. You were bleeding out your eyes. He's probably afraid he'll hurt you inside.* Loni texted back. *I cut my finger today peeling potatoes. That is so much BS. I don't have thin blood now.* Dee Dee chimed in, *Be patient, dear heart. He'll get there.* Loni wrote back, *Hello, I am already there, and he isn't here with me. I almost died. I need a good—well, you know. I want to feel alive again, and he's making me feel like I'm still almost a corpse.*

Ceara glanced over at her unconscious husband. Looking at him, she couldn't resist a little satisfied grin, even if it was brazen. She had wiped all thought of *boring* from his mind. But that was behind her, and now Loni, her dear friend and sister, needed help. She stared down at the phone's bright screen, studying the text line. She knew that in order to write, all she had to do was touch it. So she did.

Pecking at the letters, she wrote, *'Tis clear to me we need a hen party. You helped me seduce my husband. Now Loni needs help to seduce hers.*

The response was gratifying. All the hens were up for a party, and Ceara was elected as hostess. Once that was decided, Ceara stuck the charger thing into her phone, switched off her bedside lamp, and snuggled down against her husband. He smelled good, like sweat, horses, and man. She touched the tip of her tongue to his chest. Hungry, because they hadn't eaten, she decided she could sustain herself by nibbling on him all night.

Once he recovered from the hen seduction, of course. Ceara would always be grateful for all the female advice.

Quincy had *loved* Mr. Midas when she'd teased him with it, just as the hens had told her he would.

Life with Ceara. Over the next few weeks, Quincy learned it was folly to expect the usual. As required by the Church, he and Ceara began meeting with Father Mike two nights a week for marriage preparation classes. Quincy had thought the sessions would be serious, rushed encounters, but instead, because both he and Ceara were cradle Catholics, already secretly married, and were getting along well together as a couple, the priest barely touched on religion, gave them little if any relationship counseling, and spent most of the hour laughing and slapping his knee, delighted by his exchanges with Ceara. They often spoke Gaelic, told Irish jokes, and shared stories of their personal encounters with the "wee folk." Though Quincy felt that meeting with Father Mike was mostly a huge waste of time, he didn't complain, because Ceara so enjoyed chatting with the man.

"So when will we be ready to renew our vows and get our marriage recorded in the Church?" Quincy asked Father one night.

The priest shrugged. "Soon, I'd say. These get-togethers are a mere formality at this point, more fer the records than to educate or counsel ye on how to make the marriage work." Father Mike settled a fond gaze on Ceara. "The banns have been posted in the bulletin three Sundays in a row now, so we can arrange for the ceremony to take place anytime." He patted Ceara's arm. "Ye've come a long way, lass, considering that ye started this relationship more or less in a jail cell."

A horrible thought struck Quincy. With all that had happened since their wedding night, he'd completely forgotten to drop the charges against Ceara. "Oh, shit."

"What?" Father paled a bit. "What is it, me boy?"

Quincy quickly collected his composure. "A small detail I forgot to take care of." What if the cops came pounding on his door to arrest his wife? He hadn't checked at the post office to see if she'd received any court summons at general delivery. "I, um . . . hell. In the morning. I'll take care of it first thing in the morning."

Ceara fixed a solemn gaze on him. " 'Tis something bad. I see it in yer eyes. A burden shared is a burden more easily borne."

Quincy really, *really* didn't want to tell her that she still had criminal charges hanging over her head, but in the spirit of total disclosure, which he felt was vital to a solid relationship, he couldn't very well keep the truth from her. "I forgot to go down to the police station and withdraw the charges against you for breaking and entering."

Long silence. Then Father Mike harrumphed as if to clear his throat. Quincy expected Ceara to give him a tongue-lashing. Instead she started to laugh. Her laughter soon turned to helpless giggles, and then she was hugging her sides with tears streaming down her cheeks. Between gasps for breath, she cried, "The men in blue may come and haul me away in me wedding gown!"

How she found that possibility amusing, Quincy didn't know, but somehow her mirth was contagious, and soon he and Father were laughing as hard as she was. The moment Quincy regained his composure, he put a voice-activated reminder into his phone to go to the station first thing tomorrow. For reasons beyond him, that sent his wife and the priest into gales of laughter again.

The next hen party took place at Quincy's house—well, now his and Ceara's house—and when Quincy inadvertently interrupted by entering the kitchen for some lunch, Ceara handed him a tray, escorted him to the door, and told him to eat in the arena office. Quincy felt like a dog that had just been given the boot because he was suspected of planning to pee on the floor. Later, as he munched on a pastrami sandwich with mustard and whole-fat Swiss cheese, he wondered what had happened to a man's home being his castle. *Hmm*. He guessed that when a king acquired a queen, there were always some adjustments to be made.

Late that night, lying in bed beside his wife after an amazing lovemaking session, Quincy received a text from Clint. *What's this Mr. Midas thing all about? Loni bought one this afternoon because Ceara says you like hers so much.* Quincy felt a flush creep up his neck. He propped himself against the headboard, contemplated his sleeping wife and the phone, then wrote back, *Mr. Who?* Clint didn't take that lying down. *You know damned well who. Mr. Midas, gold, cylindrical, and a la-dy's best friend.* Quincy grinned as he shot back, *Mr. Midas may be your lady's best friend, but he's not my la-dy's best anything. I take care of my husbandly duties, otherwise called doing my homework.* Clint returned fire. *Okay, fine, be a jerk. It was your wife who bought the first one.* Beginning to enjoy himself at his brother's expense, Quincy replied, *Sorry, pal. If you're looking for advice, I'm not into the kinky stuff. Parker's your man if you need any pointers.* Quincy could almost hear Clint cursing and sputtering. He turned off his phone volume, settled in under the covers to draw Ceara into his arms, and made a mental bet with himself that Loni had fallen asleep tonight wearing nothing but a satisfied grin.

A few days later, Ceara wore blue jeans for the very first time in order to get lessons using a Western-style saddle, which required that she ride astride the horse instead of perching sideways in voluminous skirts. As sexy as she looked in the tight blue denim trousers, compliments of Sam, Quincy forced himself to concentrate on her seating and reining techniques. To his surprise, she took to the change with a speed that so amazed him he deemed her trail-ready in less than a half hour.

"You're incredible with horses," he told her. "I mean really incredible."

Her cheek dimpled in a pleased smile. " 'Tis true of ye as well, Quincy." Shifting the reins to one hand, she tapped her temple. "Ye have the same gift that I do with horses, though mine is now greatly weakened. If ye tried, ye could talk to them using only yer mind."

Quincy figured pigs would fly before he ever managed to convey anything to a horse telepathically, but that night as he made his final rounds of the stalls, he stopped at Beethoven's to give it a whirl. Crossing his arms on the top rail of the gate, he focused on the stallion. *Back*, he thought, using a command he knew Beethoven understood well. The horse jerked his head up, still munching grain, and stared suspiciously at Quincy.

Heartened because the animal had clearly picked up on *something*, Quincy tried again. *Back, Beethoven. Back!* The horse only snorted and swished his tail as if to rid himself of a fly.

So much for his telepathic ability with animals, Quincy thought crossly as he closed down the arena for the night. During the brief walk across the ranch proper to the house, he wore a scowl. But when he stepped into the kitchen, his frown lines were quickly replaced by an amazed smile. Ceara wore a see-through sparkly negligee trimmed in bright pink ostrich feathers. *Bye-bye, grumpiness; hello happiness.*

Quincy loved his wife's in-house seduction outfits, but

this one truly took the prize. He barely spared a glance for the skillet meal she'd been monitoring, which smelled fabulous. A man didn't live by bread alone.

Two days later, Quincy told Ceara to put on her borrowed riding jeans and the boots Rainie had bought her at the thrift shop. While she changed clothes, he found her one of his spare jackets, a wool muffler, and a pair of old leather gloves that Sam had left behind at his house after a visit. Then he set himself to the task of preparing a spur-of-the-moment picnic lunch, which he'd tuck into a saddlebag. A blanket! He needed to find a nice wool blanket. No spring-afternoon ride with a beautiful woman could be complete without mindless sex under a pine tree.

"So what are ye thinking, Quincy?" Ceara asked as she reentered the kitchen, freshly washed jeans skimming her legs and rolled at the ankle because they were too long on her.

Making a mental note to take her shopping for some proper riding gear, Quincy grinned and swung an arm toward the windows. "Do ye not see the weather, lass?" he said, mimicking her Irish brogue for effect. " 'Tis a *fine* spring day, warm as a weevil in a fresh-baked biscuit! 'Tis off for a horseback ride we go."

She laughed, rewarding him with a dimple in both cheeks, a sight he glimpsed only when she was very pleased. " 'Tis a stranger pretending to be me husband, surely. Me Quincy is American and canna speak the Irish."

"When I mean to seduce my wife, I can speak any language necessary." Abandoning the assorted food items and blanket on the table, he closed the distance between them, hooked an arm around her waist, and tipped her backward until her spine arched for a movie-screen *Gone with the Wind* kiss. As he came up for air, he searched her slightly unfocused but still puzzled gaze. "Did you understand *that* language, Ceara mine? It's a beautiful day. I've made a picnic lunch. I want to take you riding in the wilderness area across the road and make passionate love to you in the woods."

As he allowed her to stand erect, she swept him from boots to head with an assessing look. "Ye're wearing no seduction outfit."

Seduction outfits had become a popular theme with her. *Problem.* Quincy normally depended on Wranglers, dusty boots, a Stetson, and a swagger to do his seducing for him. He made sure she had her balance, held up a finger, and said, "Hold that thought," before he raced upstairs to change clothes.

He had no boxers on hand that were fringed with ostrich feathers. Instead he took the masculine approach and donned his all-black, rarely used barfly-attractant outfit—skintight black Wranglers, a black silk Western-cut shirt, his dressy black Stetson, and his flashy belt with the huge gold championship buckle, which he'd won years ago in a nationwide cutting competition. When he examined himself in the full-length wardrobe mirror, he winked, cocked his hat just so, and whispered, "Hello, darlin', where you been all my life?" If this didn't make her melt into her secondhand boots, he'd find himself in the men's section of the Erotic Parrot, trying to find something sexy enough to please her.

Recalling the night when Ceara had first introduced him to Mr. Midas, Quincy attempted to make a grand entrance into the kitchen. He swaggered into the archway, struck a pose with one hip shot, the knee of his opposite leg bent, and tipped his hat to her. "Darlin', I don't got no feathers or sparkles. This is the best I can do on short notice."

Ceara, who'd been rifling through the picnic supplies, turned and gave him a solemn study, the indentation in her cheek winking at him as she worried the inside of her lip. "Ye're drop-dead *gorgeous*," she informed him, "but ye'll freeze off yer arse without a jacket."

Quincy relaxed. Going with all black had never failed him. "I'll wear a jacket over my seduction outfit."

She glanced down at herself. "But I am not wearing one."

Oh, yes, she was. Quincy liked see-through negligees trimmed with feathers. What man didn't? But what *really* turned his crank was a woman in tight jeans and riding boots. Or a pair of chaps and nothing else. A matter to address later, he decided. Just the thought of Ceara in chaps got his juices flowing and brought Old Glory to full attention.

"You are perfect," he told her. "Way more prime than this old horseman deserves."

"Ye're *not* old. In me time, a lass who is married off to a man so young and fit feels fortunate."

Quincy figured that was another thought to be explored later. Right now, he had his mind on one thing: a romantic horseback ride into the wilderness with his wife. He'd only ever made love to her in the privacy of their bedroom. Today she would be introduced to a host of new sexual experiences.

Instead of sex under a pine tree, they got a snowstorm. Quincy, who'd grown up in central Oregon, knew that only a fool or a newcomer trusted in a weather forecast, but he was still disgruntled by what he recognized as snow clouds moving in to turn the sky gray in spots.

Ceara, fascinated with the landscape, didn't seem to notice the forthcoming change in weather, and chattered like a magpie.

"'Tis so lovely here, Quincy! Even here in the trees, I can see yer beautiful mountain peaks. What is the name of the mountain range again?" After Quincy told her it was called the Cascades, she beamed a glowing smile. "'Tis so different from me Ireland. I ne'er thought to find anyplace but home so breathtaking. I shall like living here for always, with all the green fields stretching out from your house and these gorgeous forests looming behind them. At home, we have hills all covered with green, but our trees are mostly smaller, and we do na have anything so grand as yer mountain peaks." She laughed and added, "I also quite like yer coffee and tea. At home, Mum made tea from roots and such, but ne'er did it taste so good."

Absentmindedly, Quincy answered her endless questions about the flora and fauna they saw in the forest. Soon Ceara could tell the difference between ponderosa and lodgepole pines by counting the needle clusters, and she was an equally fast study at learning the names of the various bushes.

Quincy was far more focused on the threat of a storm. First, the sunshine blinked out. Then the wind kicked up, cold enough to slice chilled butter. He couldn't believe it when the first snowflakes struck his cheeks.

"We need to turn back." He wheeled Beethoven around. Ceara, who'd been following him, rode Elvis, a nine-year-old sorrel gelding that was so gentle and well-mannered that Quincy would have trusted him with any inexperienced rider. "We'll have to enjoy our picnic at home."

Ceara nodded and hunched her shoulders inside the

oversize, lined denim jacket. Her cheeks had already turned apple red above the folds of the gray wool muffler. " 'Tis so *cold*! I canna believe how quickly it came on." She squinted at the sky, which had gone steel blue and spit a haze of snow. Then she looked at Quincy. "Yer jacket, 'tis too thin. Ye'll catch yer death riding back in this."

Before Quincy realized what she intended, she flapped her hand and the snow stopped falling. An instant later, the sun burst forth.

"Sweetheart, you shouldn't have done that."

"The ecological balance, I ken." She grinned. "As soon as we're to home, I'll turn the snow back on, making it even heavier. Yer ecological balance willna be harmed."

Somehow she looked different suddenly. Quincy studied her face, but for the life of him, he couldn't figure out what had changed. "Okay, but only just this once, and not because I'm going to catch my death. I'm more worried about you catching yours."

" 'Tis fine I am."

Quincy nudged Beethoven around Elvis to take the lead, then stopped the horse and shifted on the saddle to make sure Ceara could rein her mount around on the narrow trail. She managed the turn with an expertise that amazed him.

"You are incredible."

She smiled faintly. "Ye should try sidesaddle in long skirts. This is easy."

Quincy nudged his stallion into a fast pace, wanting to get back to the ranch as quickly as possible. As much as he detested snow after what had seemed an endlessly long winter, it bothered him when Ceara messed with the weather. He knew the ecological balance wouldn't undergo a severe shift simply because she'd turned off the white stuff for a few minutes, but it still wasn't nature's plan, and over time, he hoped that she would come to understand that.

They made record time getting back to the ranch. After they drew their horses to a stop outside the arena, they both dismounted. Ceara cast a yearning glance at the bright blue sky, then swung her hand, making it turn gunmetal gray again. The snowfall resumed instantly, heavier than before, just as she'd promised. Quincy saw Pierce in one of the paddocks. The thin young man stood with his hands on his hips, his freckled face crinkled in a perplexed frown.

"What the Sam Hill?" he shouted. "I've seen crazy weather, but if this don't beat all."

Quincy waved and turned to smile at his wife. His lips froze in a half curve. Ceara's face had gone as white as chalk, and she was leaning against Elvis's shoulder as if her legs wouldn't hold her up. Quincy tossed Beethoven's reins over the pommel and circled the horse to grasp Ceara's shoulders.

"Sweetheart, what is it?"

She swayed on her feet and pressed against him for support. "Weak. 'Tis as if all me blood has drained away. 'Twill pass."

Quincy gathered her close. She felt so tiny in his arms—so very fragile, like a miniature figurine of blown glass. Love for her swept over him in a wave, concern following swiftly in its wake. "What caused it, messing with the weather?"

She nodded, the movement of her chin barely discernible. It seemed to Quincy that she leaned against him for at least a full minute. When she finally drew away, he saw that some color had returned to her cheeks.

"Using me powers now makes me feel weak. 'Tis me guess that restarting the snow and making it come down heavier after may have been too much for me."

"Then stop using your gifts. What's the point if it exhausts you so?"

She smiled and straightened her shoulders. " 'Tis better I am now." She looked deeply into his eyes, snow-flakes frosting her auburn lashes. "I know ye canna understand about me gifts, Quincy. How easily could ye stop using yer eyes to see or yer voice to speak?"

Quincy couldn't argue the point, but that didn't stop him from wishing she would quit using her powers.

Her smile deepened. "I have had me gifts always. Me mum says that directly after me birth, I screeched indignantly at the coldness of the air, and the wind picked up in accordance with me temper until a terrible gale and driving rain pummeled the keep. The instant I was swaddled and felt happier, the storm stopped." She shrugged, conveying with the gesture that the story of her birth said it all. "Using me gifts is natural to me. I canna stop simply because ye ask it of me."

Quincy told Pierce to care for their mounts and took Ceara straight to the house, hoping a hefty portion of the picnic lunch that he had prepared would restore her energy. To his dismay, she opened the kale wraps, peered dubiously at the filling, and then sat back on the chair. He quickly realized that any departure from her omnivore diet didn't appeal to her appetite.

"How about eggs and bacon?" he asked. "Or I can grill us some burgers and make homemade fries."

She arched an eyebrow. "Burgers and fries?"

Quincy couldn't help but chuckle. "Ah, another culinary adventure, coming up."

As he put ground beef into the microwave on defrost,

he tried to tally the number of times over the last weeks that he'd consumed high-fat foods. So many times that he'd lost track. Farewell to healthful eating. His wife wanted no part of green smoothies, organically grown chicken, or weird vegetables.

"You're obliterating my plan to eat right," he said over his shoulder. "At this rate, I'll probably croak before I hit seventy."

Her laughter tinkled behind him like dainty wind chimes in a soft breeze. " 'Tis silly to avoid good food. At home, the bounty is great, but nothing on our table compares to the delights of yer time."

She got a croissant from the bread keeper, slathered it with butter, and took a huge bite, grinning impishly at him as she chewed. An hour later, she smeared at least two heaping tablespoons of mayonnaise on her bun. When she tasted her first French fry, dipped in the Harrigan family goop—half mayo and half ketchup—she moaned and closed her eyes.

"Ach, Quincy, 'tis better even than burned popcorn."

He chuckled, as he enjoyed watching her wolf down fries, and promised himself he'd soon have her upstairs, moaning and closing her eyes over something a whole lot better than fat-saturated potato wedges.

Forty minutes and twenty-five seconds later, Quincy was the one moaning in delight as he kissed jam from his wife's lips. For dessert, she'd eaten it straight from the jar with a spoon. Never had strawberries tasted quite as good.

Chapter Thirteen

Quincy couldn't remember ever having been quite so happy. Ceara had become a favorite of the family. Frank called her his "pretty little fire hydrant," in reference to her dark red hair. The hens included her in every get-together, sometimes to Quincy's dismay, because they gave his wife all kinds of strange ideas, everything from shower sex to phone sex, the latter of which interrupted more than one of Quincy's workdays. How in the hell was he supposed to train a horse when his wife talked dirty to him on her cell? Well, not dirty, really—it *was* Ceara, after all—but all Quincy needed to put his mind in the gutter was a whisper in his ear that she wished he were nibbling on her neck. The woman definitely knew how to jerk his leash. Once she embraced an idea, it was no-holds-barred.

His brothers ribbed him unmercifully about being henpecked. They also razzed him more than once about forgetting to drop the criminal charges against his wife, a slip of the mind that Quincy doubted he would ever live down. He gave back as good as he got, and bore in mind that it was all in good fun. So what if he had fallen madly in love with his wife? There wasn't an adult male in the entire Harrigan clan who wasn't totally devoted to his spouse, and Quincy thought it felt damned good to be in the same boat.

Ceara didn't give up her burning desire to get a driver's license. The very thought of her driving fifteen feet beyond his front gate gave Quincy heart palpitations, but he got her a book from the DMV to study anyway, and showed her how to take mock tests on her new laptop. She was smart as a tack and caught on to practically everything—except cooking with the high-tech appliances—quickly, the only problem being that when it came to a vehicle, she still hadn't quite mastered shifting gears and slamming on the brake fast enough. He had no sooner gotten the holding shed repaired than she smacked it again. He was beginning to accept as semipermanent a bent cattle guard on the front of his truck, and he'd lost track of how many sections of expensive fencing she had mowed down. He teasingly told her she would drive him into bankruptcy, but in truth, he enjoyed the lessons, mostly because she had so darned much fun and he never knew what might happen next. Still, he made sure she never drove near any live animals.

Not knowing what could occur in the next five minutes was enough to drive a man mad, but Quincy found instead that his wife's unpredictability had its charm. He especially enjoyed the evenings when they shared a nice meal with a fine wine.

Ceara soon started losing pieces of her clothing after she had a drink. That worried Quincy, because he knew that sooner or later, the hens would ask her to join them for a girls' night out. He guessed he'd just have to trust in his sister and sisters-in-law to make sure she stayed dressed. There was a country song that always moved through Quincy's mind when Ceara's eyes grew sultry and her cheeks became flushed. Something about some gal who first lost an earring after a sip of tequila, and then a shoe, and then—well, hell, a man could worry himself into a loony farm if he considered the possibilities. The only thing that comforted Quincy was that Ceara still draped herself in layers outside the house, although now they were trendier. She wore jeans, which she still deemed indecently revealing, only when they went riding.

She persisted in trying to teach Quincy how to use what she insisted were his gifts. No matter how many times he told her he had none, she insisted that he must. The Harrigans were of druid descent. Therefore, in her mind, it followed that they had to have special powers. Fortunately, as far as he knew, she'd confined her persuasions to her husband. Quincy humored her, flapping his hand at the fire and countless candles. *Nothing.* And he honestly did *try*. Bottom line, he was a watered-down druid, and the only real gift he had was a way with animals. In the quarter-horse industry, he had frequently been called a horse whisperer, but in truth, nothing magical occurred between him and an equine. He just understood them in a way a lot of people didn't.

With each passing day, Loni grew stronger. One afternoon, Quincy dropped by Clint's place unannounced and found his older brother in his arena office wiping tears from his sun-weathered cheeks. Quincy's stomach clenched. He dropped onto the caster chair at the front side of Clint's desk, stared at his embarrassed brother for a long moment, and then pushed out, "Is Loni getting sick again?"

Elbows propped on the blotter, Clint buried his fists in his eye sockets, sighed, and shook his head. In a choked voice, he replied, "No, that's just it. She's well, Quincy. I mean . . . not just better, but really well. I couldn't trust in it at first. You know what I'm saying? But this morning when I went back to the house for something, I found her in her office doing Pilates. She's really, *really* well, man. She's even working with the FBI again to help find missing people."

Quincy felt his own eyes fill. He blinked furiously. Clint straightened, fiddled with his stapler, pushed at a stack of papers, and then started to laugh as tears streamed from his eyes. He gestured helplessly, as if he couldn't find words. "You and Ceara saved her life. At the time, I know I acted like an ass. I've never told you or her how sorry I am for that." He shrugged. "Those aren't easy words for me to say."

Quincy knew that about his brother. Clint could talk a mile around an apology. He'd been that way for as long as Quincy could remember. "You were frantic. If I didn't understand it before, Clint, I sure as hell do now. And so does Ceara. No words are necessary."

Clint hauled in a deep, ragged breath. Then he shook his head. "No, words *are* necessary. That night—right after you married her—God, she was a virgin, and you were a total stranger to her. It shames me to admit it, but I honestly didn't care if you had to hog-tie her to the bed to get the deed done. That was wrong of me, and I'm ..." He swallowed hard. "I'm sorry."

Quincy couldn't help but chuckle. "I'm not. Ceara is the most wonderful thing that ever happened to me, Clint."

"Really? I mean, you're not just making the best of a bad situation with her?"

That sent Quincy's chuckle into a full-blown guffaw. "Bad situation? Clint, I love her, and I think she loves me."

"You think?" Clint's brows snapped together. "She hasn't ever told you so?"

Quincy sank lower in the chair and propped a boot on his knee. "No, when it comes to speaking of love, she's like you are with apologies, finding a hundred different ways to talk her way around saying the actual words."

"That sucks."

"Yeah, in a way. I'd like to hear her say it. I mean, I'd *really* like to hear her say it. But being your little brother, I learned a long time ago to hear what isn't actually said, knowing you felt sorry but just couldn't put it into words. It's kind of like that with Ceara. She acts like she loves me, and she says sweet things. For now, I'll settle."

Clint sighed. "Good luck with that, bro. Maybe I'm just a big old sap, but if Loni doesn't say she loves me half a dozen times a day, I start to worry."

"Do you tell her the same that often?"

Clint's cheek creased in a grin. "More. She's the center of my world, and I want her to know it."

Quincy mulled that over for a second. "Hmm. Maybe that's where I'm going wrong. Because Ceara never says it back, I only tell her I love her four or five times a day."

"Jack it up, man. Women like to hear those words." Clint glanced at his watch. "Speaking of which, I ordered Loni two dozen roses, and they should be delivered by now. Dee Dee picked Trev up after school, and she's taking him and Aliza to Mountain Plaza to play on the trampolines, drive bumper cars, and rock-climb. Afterward, Dad is meeting them in town for pizza, and then the kids are doing an overnight at their place."

Quincy shot to his feet. "I'm out of here. You should have clued me in sooner."

It was Clint's turn to chuckle. "I've been living almost like a monk since she got sick, so I'm way overdue on my homework." He winked at his use of homework, a word all the Harrigan men used in reference to keeping their ladies happy in bed. "What brought you over? You never said."

Quincy had come to ask Clint's advice about Symphony, who was late to drop her foal and hadn't even waxed up yet. Quincy suspected she hadn't taken with the first cover, as he'd thought, but he'd wanted Clint's perspective on it. Should Tucker be called in? Was it safe to wait another week and watch the mare? It was a conversation that could wait until tomorrow.

"Just wanted to say howdy," he fibbed. "Been a while since we hung out."

As Quincy drove home, the distance only a hop, skip, and jump, his cell phone clucked like a hen. He braked on the gravel road that adjoined all the Harrigan ranches to read the text from his wife. *Hurry. Symphony dropping foal.* Quincy gunned the accelerator and went so fast over that last half mile that his truck sailed over the potholes.

He found his wife in Symphony's stall, an extra-large enclosure designed for birthing. Pauline and Bingo, ex-bronc riding champion and hired-hand extraordinaire, leaned over the gate, as if it were their job to hold the damned thing up. Ceara had tossed aside her little indoor jacket and wore only a peasant blouse, gathered skirt, and boots. Her right arm was smeared with blood and fluid, and she sat cross-legged on the straw, holding the newborn foal on her lap. Symphony stood over her, the afterbirth lying on the floor behind her blood-splattered hocks.

"'Tis a colt!" Ceara cried, her smile so bright that Quincy felt as if the sun had just peeked out from behind a cloud. "He tried to come breech, but I got him turned."

Quincy sent a questioning look at his forewoman, who only shrugged, looking bewildered. "Sorry. Symphony caught us with our pants down. No wax, no drop, no nothing. Didn't even know she'd gone into labor until your wife tore in here." She sent a wondering look at Ceara. "She says the mare called to her, sort of like on a cell phone. I don't get that part, but I'm fracking glad she came over. I was busy holding Elvis while he got his shoe fixed, Bingo was cleaning stalls, and Pierce was seeing to a hay delivery. We could've lost both mama and baby."

Quincy vaulted over the gate and went to crouch beside his wife. He didn't doubt for a second that she'd *heard* Symphony calling to her. Almost everything about Ceara was a mystery to him—or had been in the beginning. Now he just accepted what he couldn't really understand and thanked God that she'd dropped into his world like a pebble out of the sky.

He ran searching hands over the foal, so fresh from its mother's womb that its ears were still stuck to its neck and its hooves were still coated with light green stuff that resembled cottage cheese. People who'd never seen a foal born always asked what that *gooey* junk was on the baby's feet. Quincy's stock answer was that the *goo* padded the foal's hooves, protecting the mother's innards. It fell off shortly after birth.

"Well, now, ain't he a beauty?" Quincy murmured.

Ceara nodded, her face glowing. "That's what I want to name him, Beauty."

Quincy didn't have the heart to tell her the colt was already slotted to be named Liberace, or that all ranch-born horses in his stable had handles with a musical theme. If she wanted to call the foal Beauty, that would be his nickname, and maybe his official name could be Ceara's Beauty. That would depend on the AQHA's registry and whether another horse already bore the title. Quincy doubted that would be the case. Until meeting his wife, he'd never met anyone christened Ceara.

"How the hell did you know how to turn him?" Quincy asked.

Ceara laughed. "Me da has horses, and I sneaked to watch the foals being born. He wouldna have allowed me to be there had he known. 'Twas no place for a proper young lady to be, ye ken. I learned a lot by watching."

The foal wiggled, and Ceara gently helped him gain his feet. He stood spraddle-legged, wobbling and unsteady, his knee and hock joints protruding like oversize apples. One of his ears came loose from his neck and poked up, looking as big as a donkey's. His coat was still so wet that Quincy couldn't tell whether he'd be a sorrel or a black, but he had perfect conformation. Beauty was a fine name for him. Quincy called Tucker, his brother-in-law and the only vet he trusted, to come by to check on the mare and newborn ASAP. Not that Quincy believed an exam was really necessary. Ceara had done a great job of this, delivering the foal without a hitch, but it was Quincy's motto that it was always better to be safe than sorry when it came to his animals. Anyhow, the foal needed some inoculations, and now was as good a time as any.

Quincy and Ceara spent most of the evening in Symphony's stall, imprinting the foal. Afterward they left Pauline to watch over mama and baby while they went home to celebrate the occasion with grilled steaks, a tossed salad, baked potatoes heaped with butter, sour cream, and chives, and a bottle of fine merlot. Quincy's reluctantly seduced taste buds loved every bite.

The next morning brought warm spring sunshine. Quincy was thinking about taking his wife for a ride into the wilderness area again, hopefully this time with better weather, but Loni scotched that idea by knocking at their door. Dark hair framing her face, she smiled from ear to ear when Quincy greeted her.

"Dad and Dee Dee still have my kids. I decided to take advantage of the empty house to walk over and have a mini hen party with Ceara."

Judging by Loni's radiant face, the roses and a whole night alone with her husband had been just what she needed. Quincy found it difficult to believe now when he looked at the woman that she'd been so close to death such a short time ago. She was still a bit too thin, but a few more weeks of good grub would put the meat back on her bones.

"Come in!" Ceara cried. "Let me just run upstairs to change." She wore only one of Quincy's work shirts, which on a woman of larger stature might have been indecent, but on Ceara, the tails reached nearly to her knees. " 'Tis quick I will be. Quincy, will ye pour her some coffee or make her some tea?"

Quincy watched his wife disappear in a flash, then turned to motion Loni inside. She blushed as she met his gaze. "I'm sorry, Quincy. I should have called first. I forget sometimes that you're newlyweds."

"No worries. I've got a full day ahead of me. Ceara could use the company." He told Loni about Beauty's unexpected debut yesterday and used the foal's recent arrival as a reason for him to be tied up all morning. "I'll be spending several hours with him. Imprinting a foal during the first few days after birth is crucial. It makes all the difference in the long run."

Loni's shoulders relaxed. "Are you sure? I didn't mean to barge in."

"You're always welcome." Crossing the kitchen, Quincy asked, "What's your poison, coffee or tea?"

"Coffee is great. Black with two sugars, please."

Ceara scurried back into the kitchen just as Quincy was serving their guest. She still wore his shirt over Sam's rolled-up blue jeans. Her hair, tousled from the pillow, was a riot of burnished curls. Quincy found it amazing that she could look so beautiful without half trying.

He fixed a quick breakfast of bacon and eggs, making enough for Loni as well. His sister-in-law quirked an eyebrow at the fare, but blessedly refrained from comment as she picked up her fork. As soon as he could without being too obvious, Quincy made his excuses after eating and left for the arena, not wishing to horn in on the female chitchat.

Four hours later, when Quincy took a break for lunch, he went home to find his wife and sister-in-law finishing off one bottle of wine and about to pull the cork on another. They were both giggling hysterically when he walked in; then there was sudden silence. Quincy knew damned well they'd been talking about sex—and he had no doubt that his name had come up more than once. He wondered what Ceara said about their lovemaking. He had no complaints on that front. Being with Ceara ... well, he couldn't think of enough adjectives to do the wonder of it justice, and he had every reason to believe that Ceara felt the same. Still, what a woman conveyed to her lover might be totally different from what she confided to a female friend. He wasn't entirely comfortable with their love life getting frequent public airings, but the knowledge that his brothers and brother-in-law were in the same boat made it less embarrassing.

"You girls take it easy with that wine, okay?" he said with a warning note. "Ceara's a lightweight."

The moment Quincy finished eating and left the house, Ceara and Loni burst into fits of laughter again. Feeling delightfully warm from the tips of her toes to the top of her head, Ceara grabbed the new wine bottle to refill each of their goblets.

"So last night, ye got the *wham-bam*, and no more milquetoast."

Loni sighed dreamily. "It was so fabulous, Ceara. I feel so *alive* this morning. I can't explain it, but with that part of our marriage on a back burner, I didn't feel complete." Gentle blue eyes growing misty, Loni searched Ceara's gaze. "Are you happy with Quincy? I mean really, *really* happy?"

Ceara nodded. "I couldna be happier." Even as she said the words, though, Ceara felt a tug on her heart. "Well, 'tis not *precisely* true. One thing could make me happier: seeing me dear family again." She swirled the wine in her glass. "Me sister, Brigid, will be turning three and ten soon. I'll ne'er see her as a woman full grown, ne'er whisper to her of secret things as I can with ye. 'Tis a sad thing fer me. And, ach, how I miss me mum. I'd give a king's ransom in gold to see her just one more time and kiss her soft cheek." Tears stung at the back of Ceara's eyes. "Me da, he is old, at the last of his life. 'Twas always me thought that I would be at his bedside as he passed on. Now that can ne'er be."

Loni blinked and wiped a tear from her cheek. "Are you certain there's no way for you to ever return there?"

Ceara waved her hand, knowing she would surely start to cry if they didn't speak of other things. " 'Tis impossible. I knew that before I decided to come here. And now I couldna leave me Quincy. 'Twould fair break me heart." She forced a smile. "So let us laugh again. 'Tis too fine a day to be sad."

Loni nodded and steered their conversation to another topic — how her serious, conventional husband had gone totally wild last night when she slipped Mr. Midas from under her pillow.

When their mirth finally ebbed, Ceara reached across the table to grasp Loni's hand. " 'Tis so blessed I am. Though I left behind one dear family, God has seen fit to give me another one."

Loni grinned. "Sisters always." Then her eyes went oddly blank for a long moment. "He's still alive, Ceara. Your da, I mean." Her smile widened. "Oh, how cool! He's with your mum in a little room. They're leaning over what looks like a crystal ball and seem very happy." Loni blinked and refocused on Ceara's face. "I think they're watching us."

Ceara turned her hand to clench Loni's fingers. "Truly? Ye mean right now?"

Loni nodded. "Wave hello to them."

Feeling a little silly, Ceara used her free hand to do just that, watching Loni's eyes grow distant again. With a tinkling laugh, Loni returned to the moment. "It's true. They saw you and waved back. Your mum blew kisses, and your da is about to cry. Happy tears, though, not sad ones. He's just so glad to see you and know you're okay."

Ceara's heart panged. "Me mum always blows kisses. 'Tis her way, ye ken? And me da—well, he was a mighty warrior in his day, a man who deserves to be head of his clan, but he's ne'er been ashamed to shed a tear or two when he's happy or sad."

"He's very happy right now. My goodness, what time is it in Ireland? I saw a window—more like a stone arch in the wall, actually, with no glass or anything, and it looked dark outside." Loni pulled her hand free of Ceara's and drew her phone from the case at her waist. "World clock," she murmured. "Ah, here's one, and I'll sort by country. Right now in Dublin, it's nine twenty p.m., eight hours later than it is here."

Ceara closed her eyes on a happy sigh. Feeling a connection with her parents was a grand thing, indeed. "So when we go to Mass tomorrow at noon, 'twill be eight in the evening there."

"That's right." Loni chuckled. "You see? They aren't lost to you, after all."

"Thank ye," Ceara whispered. "I shall be pestering ye from now on to peek in on them and let me know how they're doing."

"Anytime," Loni replied. Then she shivered slightly. "Isn't this too weird? I actually *saw* them, as if they are alive right at this very moment." With a shake of her head, she looked inquiringly at Ceara. "Not possible, right? They existed hundreds of years ago."

'Twas a mystery Ceara couldn't explain. " 'Tis only fer God to understand. Somehow they are, just as we are. Mayhap there are many worlds of different times, and we simply do na ken that they exist. We see only our time, see only this world, and in their time they see only theirs."

Loni frowned, pondering the possibility. "That's true so far as it goes, but obviously it's not entirely right. Your mum can see you here in this world through her crystal ball, and I can see them in their world by touching your hand and homing in on them."

"Ach, but me mum is druid, and so are ye. That makes all the difference, ye ken? We be different from others and have special gifts." Again, Ceara felt a tug on her heart. "Me gifts are near lost to me now, but at one time, they were powerful."

"In this day, having *gifts* can be a curse, so don't mourn the weakening of your powers too greatly. For much of my life, I felt like a pariah. Then I met Clint, and he made me see things differently." With a laugh, Loni rose from her chair. "All my life, I've thought of myself as being a clairvoyant, never suspecting it went any further than that. Perhaps you're right, though, and my family is of druid descent. We can trace our lines directly back to Scotland." She took her empty wineglass to the sink and rinsed it out. "Regardless, clairvoyant or druid, I've got to get home. Dee Dee and Dad will be bringing my kids back soon, and Clint will have his hands full if I'm not there. His work with the horses keeps him pretty busy."

" 'Tis pleased I am that ye came." Ceara meant that with all her heart. "Through yer eyes I saw me mum and da. 'Tis a lovely gift ye've given me."

Loni turned at the door to hug Ceara good-bye. "We'll do it again soon. I'll be happy to check in on them anytime you wish."

"I shall wish for it often."

After Loni left, Ceara stood at the center of the kitchen, hugging her waist. She felt more at peace than she had since her arrival in this strange world of Quincy's. Imagining her mum gazing at her through the crystal ball, Ceara spun in a circle, grinning and waving at empty air.

"Da, cover yer ears. 'Tis a private thing I wish to say to Mum." She waited a moment, imagining her da laughing as he left the tiny tower room where her mum surveyed the land all around the keep and another world through her crystal ball. "Ye ne'er told me how fine 'tis to be married," Ceara said in a scolding tone. "I expected me wifely duties to be a chore I would dread, na something magical or so fabulous and fun." Taking a seat at the table, Ceara poured herself a bit more wine, pretending that her mum sat across from her just as Loni had moments ago. "I tell ye this only to wipe all worry from yer mind, not to make yer ears burn. Me Quincy is so romantic that sometimes I get tears in me eyes as we make love. Other times, he has me giggling. Our times together, they're ne'er the same, and I look forward to them like a child yearning fer a favorite sweet. Mayhap ye ne'er shared how special it can be with a man who possesses yer heart because ye feared 'twould ne'er happen that way fer me. But ye were wrong, Mum. I had only to come forward in time to find meself a man as fine as Da."

Ceara lifted her glass. " 'Tis scandalous of me to talk to ye of such things, I ken, but 'tis different here. The women share secrets. I have an empty place in me heart because I canna do the same with ye. To Sir Quincy, me husband. He has brought joy into me life." Ceara took a sip of wine to make the toast official. "Me heart does a happy jig every time I clap eyes on him. I'm fair happy, Mum; I truly am. Ye need na be troubled or worried fer me. I landed in a place where I am cherished and protected by a verra strong arm." With another lift of her goblet, Ceara added, "Many strong arms. Quincy's da calls me daughter. Quincy's brothers call me sister. I lost me dear family in Ireland, but I have a new one here in this place."

Ceara paused, trying to think what else she needed to say. She sensed that her mum was still watching, listening, smiling, but it was fair late in Ireland, and she would soon seek her bed to rest her weary bones.

"Tell Brigid I will celebrate her name day. 'Tis beyond me ken that she will soon be thirteen. 'Tis how they say it here, instead of saying three and ten. Tell her to stop chewing her nails, will ye? And cuff her ears if she farts and blames it on poor ol' Rascal." Ceara glanced down at the dogs lying about her feet. "As ye can see, I have lovely dogs here in this time, too. This is Billy Bob." She pointed at the sleeping Aussie to her left. Then she indicated the other dog to her right. "And this is Bubba, who truly did fart until I made Quincy start feeding them *real* food. Ach, 'tis another thing I must tell ye. I canna cook here in the ovens yet, Mum. I try, and Quincy eats it, but 'tis fair horrible. They do na cook over a fire here. I tried to make bread in one of his skillets over what he calls a gas flame, but 'tis not the same. I ended up with black lumps that I tossed away."

Ceara went on to tell her mother of other things—water coming out of the walls, lights in the ceiling that weren't candles, about the strange power Quincy called electricity, and the wagons that moved without any horses to pull them.

"I have me very own computer now," she told her mum. "It tells me many things, some of which I dinna ken. New lands with strange names that dinna exist in our time. 'Tis fair miraculous. I'll tell ye about that next time. I ken 'tis growing late where ye are, and ye're weary." She sent best wishes to her brothers, and then, with a catch in her voice, she added, "And tell Brigid fer me that every time I think of her dear face, me heart warms with gladness. Give Da a hearty hug from me, and ask him to kiss yer soft cheek fer me afore ye drift off to sleep."

"Who the hell are you talking to?"

Ceara jumped with a start. She hadn't heard Quincy enter, but there he stood, staring at her with worry in his dark eyes. "Me mum."

"Yer mum? Shit, I'm starting to talk like you do. You're rubbing off on me." He sat across from her in the chair Loni had recently vacated. "How can you be talking to your mum? I don't get it."

Ceara lifted her glass to him. "She is watching me through her crystal ball. Loni saw her and Da, happy as weevils in the flour to be seeing me. 'Tis like television, me mum's ball. Ye can see and hear, just like in yer movies."

"Really?"

"Really, 'struth." Ceara wagged her fingers at the air. "G'night, Mum. 'Tis time to turn off yer television. Me husband is to home, and I've a mind to take him upstairs to our bedchamber."

"You do?" Quincy gave her a long study.

Ceara stood up and wobbled on her feet. "Yep." She giggled and curled her little finger at him. "Come hither, me man. Yer wife has plans fer ye."

He shot up from his chair and circled the table to grab her elbow. "Well, shit. You're drunker than a lord." While he held her arm, he plucked his cell phone from his belt. "Did Loni walk home in this condition?"

"Yep, I am thinking so. I didna drink two bottles of wine all by meself."

Quincy speed-dialed Clint and nearly shouted into his cell, "Go check on your wife. She's got close to a whole bottle of wine under her belt, and she's walking home." Quincy curled a strong arm around Ceara's shoulders. "No, I'm not saying she's drunk for sure, only that my wife can barely stand up, and the two bottles of wine on my kitchen table are definitely dead soldiers."

Ceara leaned against her husband, enjoying his hardness and warmth. He ended his conversation with his brother and encircled her with both his arms. "Sweetheart, you may have the mother of all hangovers in the morning. What possessed you and Loni to start drinking so early in the day and kill two jugs of vino?"

" 'Twas a hen party." Ceara burped. She giggled and tipped her head back to study Quincy's dark, handsome face. "A *mini*, but we made the best of it. Now that ye're done with silly questions, will ye take me upstairs and put on yer seduction outfit?" Another belch rolled up from her belly. Embarrassed, she pressed her fingertips over her lips. "Me apologies, Sir Quincy. 'Tis verra unla-dylike to burp aloud."

"I have a very bad feeling that my seduction outfit had better stay on ice. Before the night is over, I'll be holding your head over the toilet. You'll be a very sorry girl come morning. Drinking can run up and bite you on the ass, sweetheart. You can't guzzle wine like it's soda pop."

"What is soda and why does it pop?"

Ceara felt him sweep her up against his chest. Trusting in the safe cradle of his arms, she let her head rest on his shoulder. *Bump, bump*. Her cheek bounced against his collarbone as he ascended the stairs. Somewhere along the way, she fell asleep, and all remained dark until she woke up with a demon inside her head and her face only inches above the blue water in the toilet bowl.

"Jesus save me," she heard Quincy mutter. Then a cold cloth covered her face. She sputtered, gagged, and then went limp. "I barely got you to the toilet in time. I thought only college kids did this kind of shit."

Ceara moaned. Her lips felt thick, and she couldn't open her eyes all the way. "What," she croaked, "is a college kid, and what's got loose inside me skull?"

"A college kid is a young person going to school away from home who sometimes guzzles booze like it's water because he doesn't realize how sick it might make him. As for what's got loose in your head, I'd say it's too much wine." He sighed and dabbed moisture on her gaping lips. "Ah, sweetheart, I'm so sorry. When I saw you two drinking, I should have stayed to monitor your intake. It's all new to you, isn't it?"

At the moment, it all felt very old to Ceara, and as her body snapped taut to purge her gut of more wine, she only wished for it to be over. *Wine.* 'Twas her vow never to take another sip of the stuff. Poison was its name.

When the gagging spasms ebbed, she was dimly aware of Quincy wrapping her in a blanket and leaving her curled up like a baby on the bathroom floor. Later he returned, scooped her up into his strong arms, and carried her back to bed.

"Here, have a sip of 7UP. Maybe it'll settle your tummy down."

Ceara wrinkled her nose, because the liquid reminded her of Quincy's bubbly. She wanted no part of any more alcohol. "Nay, nay," she protested.

"Just one sip, honey. It's good stuff; I promise."

Ceara trusted in his word, just as she trusted in the safety of his embrace, so she obediently swallowed. Then blackness swept over her. From somewhere far away, she heard Quincy talking to someone. "Yeah, well, buck up, bro. If Loni made it to the toilet on her own, you're a lucky man. I think Ceara finished off one of the bottles while she was talking to her mum. Her mother, I mean. Yeah, well, I don't get it, either. The woman's been dead for nearly five hundred years, but Loni hooked them up somehow." Long pause. "Hello? She's *your* wife, not mine. Don't ask me how she's communicating with ghosts. Like *I* know? That's your bivouac, pal."

Chapter Fourteen

The first break of dawn tinted the windows of the bedroom when Quincy jerked awake the next morning. He blinked and went still, sensing that something other than his inner alarm clock had tugged him from dreamland. He patted the bed beside him, searching the lumpy covers for Ceara, who was so small she could vanish under the fluffy folds. *Gone.* Memory crashed back into his brain. She'd been sicker than a dog last night. He bolted upright just as the unmistakable sound of retching drifted from the bathroom.

Dressed decently enough for head-holding in only his boxers, he leaped from bed and ran in to find his wife on her knees with her arms draped over the rim of the commode, her head dangling over what appeared to be only tinted sanitizing water in the toilet bowl. *Dry heaves.* Quincy had done some time in the same position, what he and his brothers laughingly called "worshiping the porcelain god," but somehow it wasn't nearly so humorous to Quincy when it was Ceara paying the piper. He felt responsible, for one thing. He'd known she was an inexperienced drinker. Except for the hen party at Loni's, which had been interrupted by guys with growling stomachs, he'd always been with Ceara when she imbibed, and he'd never offered her more than two carefully measured glasses of wine, maybe three ounces at a whack, six total. And even then, she'd gotten a little tipsy.

Quincy got a fresh washcloth, soaked it with cold water, gave it a quick wring, and crouched next to his sick wife. Crouching was a more comfortable position for him than kneeling, maybe because he had bony knees. He knew only that he could hunker down for prolonged periods of time, something he did often as a horseman, with his ass resting on his bootheels. During Mass or after confession, he put in plenty of time on a padded kneeler, but knee against floor—nope.

"Hey, sweetheart." He cupped her pointy chin in his right hand to lift her head, prompting her to moan and squinch her eyes even more tightly shut. Her face was beyond pale. "Pretty sick, huh?"

Her only answer was to retch again, and after the spasm passed, she gestured with a limp hand, trying to make him go away. Quincy got that. He didn't like an audience when he puked, either. But no way was he leaving her. People got sick. A man stood by his wife through thick and thin, and in Quincy's book, thick and thin included the dry heaves. Yeah, she was humiliated. But she needed help, he'd seen worse, and before the morning ended, he might see *worst*. Too much vino was notorious for giving the imbiber diarrhea. *Shit*, he thought, and then cringed.

" 'Tis dying I am," she said, her tremulous voice bouncing off the curved walls of the toilet bowl. "Call a priest quick to give me last rites, and then just leave me to cock up me toes and bury me in hallowed ground."

Nowadays, the last rites were called the Anointing of the Sick, and judging from personal experience, Quincy doubted she was in dire need of either. Not to say she didn't feel like she was dying. He'd been there and done that. Never again.

He pressed the cold cloth against her slender throat, hoping it might curb her nausea. "You won't die, darlin'. It just feels that way right now. Give it a couple of hours. Then you'll be nibbling soda crackers and sipping 7UP, well on your way back to normal."

Quincy stayed with her until the retching passed, and then he carried her back to bed. As he'd predicted, she awakened three hours later, still pale but feeling more chipper. He thought about fixing her a Bloody Mary, a surefire hangover cure. A little hair of the dog always helped. But instead he took her up a tray of bland crackers with a glass of 7UP, which, much like ginger ale, usually worked wonders on a sick stomach.

By noon, she was downstairs surfing the fridge like a hungry shark. Quincy gave her dry toast, cut into fingers, so she could dip them into hot tomato soup. Something about the acid in tomatoes always helped when his stomach felt topsy-turvy.

"We missed Mass," she said as she dipped and munched.

"Ah, well." Sitting across from her, Quincy rocked back on his chair, relieved that the worst of it was over. "We'll go next Sunday. In fact, I've been toying with the idea of taking you on Saturday nights to the Latin Mass. It's special. It'll still be a little different from what you're used to, but maybe not as much."

She smiled wanly. "I'd like that. But then we must go again on Sunday. Correct?"

"The Saturday-night Mass is a vigil celebration and counts as your Sunday obligation. But if you want to go twice, I'm game."

*   *   *

Quincy expected Ceara to make a full recovery from her dive into a wine bottle, but on Monday morning as he fixed breakfast, she clamped a hand over her mouth and raced for the downstairs bathroom. Puke detail again. He was thankful he had a strong stomach. Anyone who worked full-time with animals acquired one or found another occupation. He mopped up, held Ceara's head, and decided later as he fed her more soda crackers and 7UP that maybe, in addition to the initial hangover, she'd picked up a stomach virus.

Tuesday morning confirmed his diagnosis. Just as he got the bacon hot in the skillet—and, hello, bacon was one of Ceara's favorite foods—she dropped the spatula she'd been using to stir the spuds, covered her mouth with both hands, and made another emergency dash for the bathroom.

Quincy turned off the burners, went to take care of his sick wife, and told himself it was probably that three-day thing he'd heard was going around. No worries. In another twenty-four hours or so, she'd be fit as a fiddle again.

He was wrong.

Toward the end of the week, when Ceara continued to get sick every morning, Quincy was starting to worry, but a red alert didn't flash inside his brain until he walked in from the arena on Friday morning to find his wife at the kitchen table, eating cold pickled artichoke hearts straight from the can and washing them down with a tall glass of chocolate milk, which she'd made, judging by the squeeze bottle on the counter, with the Hershey's chocolate syrup he'd bought to drizzle over ice cream, another of her new favorite treats.

"What the *hell* are you doing?" he asked, fighting to swallow his gorge. It took a lot to make Quincy's stomach roll, but just the thought of an artichoke-and-chocolate-milk combo did the trick. "That's *disgusting*."

Ceara stopped chewing to give him a surprised look. A chocolate mustache lined her bowed upper lip, and a bit of pickled vegetable dangled from the corner of her mouth. "I ken 'tis strange, but it sounded delicious and tastes even better. Me stomach told me 'tis just the thing."

Ding-dong. Is anyone home? Quincy had a strong urge to smack himself on the head. Young female. One night of unprotected sex in mid-March. Puking every morning when she smelled frying bacon. Holy hell, he'd knocked her up.

Quincy had no practice at this marriage business. He'd sort of gotten pushed over a cliff and fallen into the situation. How was a guy supposed to tell a woman that he thought she might be pregnant? *Damn*, they were still only newlyweds, and he'd been so careful ever since they broke the curse, insisting on wearing protection even when Ceara protested on religious grounds. To his way of thinking, a guy sometimes had to consider the teachings of the Church as guidelines, not hard-and-fast rules never to be broken. He and Ceara hadn't had a courtship. Hello, they hadn't even gone out on a frigging *date* before they got married. On top of that, she'd been tossed into a whole new world where everything was foreign to her. He hadn't wanted to complicate matters for her by throwing a baby into the mix right off the bat.

But apparently he'd done just that. Quincy sank onto a chair across from her, watching with a puckered tongue as she shoveled artichoke bits into her mouth and chased them with a slug of sweetened milk. " 'Tis more cans of this we'll be needing," she told him between bites. "We've only one left, and 'tis thinking I am that this is how I shall break me fast from now on." Quincy pictured himself sitting across the table from this spectacle every morning for months and wondered if men could suffer morning sickness by association—or observation.

How the hell had this happened? Quincy could barely wrap his mind around it. They'd had unprotected sex only one lousy time. That said, he'd been warned enough times by his dad in his younger years that it took only once. It just seemed so completely unfair that it had happened to someone like Ceara. Quincy had always wanted kids, and he hoped that he and Ceara would eventually have a passel. Just not *now*. She was still adjusting to cell phones, digital cameras, electricity, surround-sound stereo music, not wrecking his truck when she got behind the wheel, and programmable ovens. She wasn't ready to take on the responsibilities of motherhood in the modern world.

They'd been married in mid-March, and he felt certain egg had met sperm on their wedding night. He did a mental tally. It was nearly the end of May now. She was probably about two and a half months along, give or take a few days.

Carefully phrasing his words, Quincy said, "Sweetheart, I know this will come as a big surprise to you—maybe even more along the line of a shock—but I think you may be PG."

Holding a blob of artichoke balanced on the tines of a fork, she gave him a long study. "PG? 'Tis something serious, mayhap even deadly?"

"No, no." Quincy waved a hand as if to erase a blackboard. "Let me back up. PG is an acronym, honey." He erased that, too. "Well, not really, more just a slang expression in this time. If a woman is PG, it means she's pregnant."

"Pregnant? Ye mean with a babe?" Her blue eyes went as round as quarters. She dropped the fork into the can and placed her hand over her waist. "Oh, Quincy!" Her face broke into a joyous grin. "'Tis why I have been sick of a morn, because I am with child?"

He nodded. "I think it's a strong possibility. I'll run into town and buy a pregnancy test so we can find out for sure."

Ceara's hands trembled as she went into the downstairs bathroom to take the test. Acutely aware of Quincy standing just outside the closed door, keeping an eye on his watch, she did as he'd instructed, wondering how peeing on a funny-looking stick could tell them if she was pregnant. Midstream, she thought, *Start to pee, but do na wait too long before poking the stick under the flow. Then remove it to start the countdown.*

"Now!" she called out.

From outside, she heard him counting off the seconds, and then, "Okay, that's seven. Put the cap back on."

Ceara struggled with the plastic container, which had to be recapped to proceed with the test. Then she cried, "'Tis done."

When she finished tidying herself, she invited Quincy in, and they stood arm-to-arm, staring at the little window in the tester. "It says it takes from two to five minutes," he said.

"Is it time yet?" she asked.

"No, honey, we're only forty-five seconds in."

It seemed to Ceara that the minutes passed more slowly than a cow slogging through belly-deep mud.

"Look," Quincy whispered. "Two pink lines." He grinned broadly and bent to kiss her. "We're pregnant, Ceara."

"Are ye certain?" Ceara peered at the window, yearning to see something more telling than colored lines, mayhap a baby in the window. It wasn't that she disbelieved Quincy, but she distrusted this peculiar contraption he termed a pregnancy kit. "How can lines tell ye fer sure and certain?"

"I don't know how to answer that. But these tests are ninety-nine percent accurate, and yours showed dark pink before two minutes even passed. It's a strong positive." He curled his arm around her shoulders and gave her a gentle jostle. "We're going to have a baby."

Ceara hugged her middle. "Ach, 'tis scarce able to believe it I am. A *babe*!" She looked up at Quincy through a blur of happy tears. "What do ye think 'twill be, a lad or lass?"

He pressed a kiss to her forehead. "We won't know that until they do an ultrasound. That happens at about four months, I think, but don't quote me on it. Loni can tell you for sure."

"What is an ultrasound?"

Quincy had never been quite so happy and frightened both at once. Now that the reality of it had started to sink in, he embraced fatherhood with a sense of joy that truly astounded him, but at the edges of his delight lurked a dark cloud of fear. It was dangerous to the fetus for a woman to drink alcohol during a pregnancy, and though Ceara had never overindulged until last Saturday, she'd had small amounts of wine or champagne nearly every evening.

Stupid, so stupid. Quincy knew he needed a good, swift kick in the ass. He'd *known* that he and Ceara had engaged in unprotected sex on their wedding night, so why had he never given pregnancy a second thought until he found her wolfing down sour artichokes as if they were provender for a queen? If his wife had been of his century, he might have laid half the responsibility for this at her feet, but under the circumstances, if their baby was born with brain damage or physical defects, the blame would rest solely upon him. Ceara had been out of her element here from the start. She'd also been raised in a strict family where the girls were kept innocent and protected until marriage. Hell, back in her time, people probably didn't even know that alcohol and pregnancy could be a disastrous mix.

My fault. The words whispered in Quincy's mind even as he smiled down at Ceara and told her they needed to get her an appointment with an OB as quickly as possible.

"What is an OB?" she asked.

"A doctor who specializes in taking care of pregnant ladies and their babies."

Quincy could only pray that *their* baby would be born hale and hardy, despite the incredible stupidity of its father.

Loni recommended Dr. Marie Stevenson, saying she was the best OB in town, so soon after seeing the positive results of Ceara's pregnancy test, Quincy was on the horn scheduling his wife's first prenatal checkup. Leaving Ceara in the kitchen to happily devour vanilla ice cream and dill pickles, he went into his office to place the call. The receptionist at first maintained that the doctor was booked clear into July, but after Quincy explained that his wife had been consuming alcohol since conception, the young woman arranged for Ceara to be seen during one of the time slots they kept clear each day for emergencies.

Quincy was inexplicably grateful for her cooperation. "I really appreciate this," he told the lady. "Maybe I'm overreacting, but I know alcohol can have a bad effect on a fetus, and I'm very worried."

"I'm not allowed to give out medical advice," she replied. "But I will say that you shouldn't worry too much. Two of my very good friends drank alcohol before they realized they were pregnant, and they both delivered healthy babies." She paused. "Can you have your wife here on Monday morning at nine thirty?"

"Absolutely, and thank you so much for fitting her into the doctor's schedule."

Dr. Stevenson, a slender dishwater blonde who wore her hair slicked back in a French braid, was a serious woman with a gentle demeanor. She explained to Ceara that a blood draw would be necessary, which was something Quincy had sort of dimly realized but failed to warn Ceara about. His wife looked resigned and rolled up her sleeve. "A woman who helped me mum with house chores had this done a few times fer her evil humors, but I dinna know it could tell us about babes. Are ye going to nick me arm with a knife?"

The doctor laughed. "You have a good sense of humor, I see, Mrs. Harrigan. It's just a simple blood draw. I'll have the technician come right in to take care of it, and then we can do the pelvic."

Ceara shot a puzzled look after the departing doctor. Quincy felt his palms start to get moist. He'd neglected to take into consideration that pregnant woman had pelvic exams. He was also a little vague about just what a pelvic exam involved, but he knew every female in his family loathed them. Well, he'd address that part of the office visit later.

"Sweetheart," he said, "this type of blood draw isn't the same as it was in your time. A small needle is inserted into your vein and it draws out a little blood. It may sting a bit going in, but it doesn't really hurt, I promise. I've had it done dozens of times."

She looked anxiously at the closed door, glanced at her slender arm, and then turned her gaze to his with such trust that he got a lump in his throat. "I dinna ken just what ye mean, husband, but if ye say 'tis all right, I believe ye."

Before he could respond in any way except to wrap an arm around her, a brisk young woman came in carrying a small tray. With swift efficiency she pulled on gloves, wrapped a piece of rubber tubing around Ceara's upper arm, felt with her finger, assured Ceara that she had great veins, and drew the blood. Ceara closed her eyes and leaned her head against Quincy, then sighed with relief when the procedure was over. Quincy was just as relieved, though for a different reason. Not until the needle had actually penetrated his wife's arm did it occur to him to wonder whether druid blood was the same color as a regular human's.

"Nice, bright red," he muttered, which earned him a questioning glance from his wife.

Dr. Stevenson returned and explained to Ceara that the in-house pregnancy test would be run at once. Then she asked Ceara a few questions. The one that stuck like a buzzing hornet in Quincy's brain was, "How long has it been since your last menstrual cycle?"

Ceara looked blankly at the doctor. "Me what?"

He probably looked just as dumbstruck, Quincy thought, because so far as he knew, Ceara hadn't had a period since he'd married her, and he'd been too damned interested in sniffing her skirt to notice the lack of one.

Sounding slightly puzzled, the doctor explained, "Your monthly cycle. You know, when did you last bleed?"

Comprehension flashed in Ceara's eyes. "Ach," she said. "Me curse, ye mean. Since afore I left Ireland."

"And it didn't strike you as abnormal when you were late?" Stevenson asked.

"The journey weakened me, ye ken, and 'tis a long way from normal I am just yet."

"Oh." Stevenson glanced up from the chart on which she jotted notes. "Rough trip?"

Ceara cut her gaze sideways at Quincy, which told him she knew to be careful how she answered that question. "Yes, verra rough." Then, borrowing one of Father Mike's stories about a return flight from his homeland, she said, "I got hold of bad food—tainted, I think ye call it—and I near puked up me toenails for many a day."

"Uh-oh. I hope you went in for care."

Ceara nodded. "Went to the ER, and they pumped me so full of fluids, I gained near ten pounds overnight."

"Our ER?"

"A little urgent-care place," Quincy inserted. "Right after we landed in Philly." He hoped to hell flights from Dublin landed in Philadelphia—or that Stevenson wasn't much of a world traveler. "We had to stay over for several days because Ceara was so weak. I think the food poisoning really got her system out of whack—or, at least, that's what we thought it was. When she was late getting her monthly, I mean." His own glibness disconcerted him. Quincy had a high regard for the truth, but prevarication here was better than telling a strange doctor that his wife was actually a druid who had been born well over four hundred years ago and had traveled forward in time to remove a curse from his family.

The doctor nodded. "I suppose with no other symptoms until this past week to indicate pregnancy, that was a logical enough assumption. From here on out, though, when she's late, get an OTC pregnancy test kit. The earlier a mother realizes she's pregnant, the better for the baby. Now, Mrs. Harrigan, we'll get you into a gown and do a quick pelvic. Mr. Harrigan, perhaps you'd like to step outside."

Quincy would have liked nothing better, but he couldn't in good conscience leave Ceara to face the exam alone.

"If you don't mind I'd prefer to stay," he said. It was the biggest lie he'd ever told.

"Well . . . all right," Stevenson replied doubtfully. "I'll send Lisa in with a gown and then we'll get started."

The same young woman who had drawn the blood bustled back into the room, handed Ceara the ugliest hospital gown Quincy had ever seen, and laid a tray covered with wicked-looking instruments on the counter. "Just take off all your clothing, Mrs. Harrigan, leave the gown open at the front, and crack the door a little when you're ready. I've brought both the regular and smaller-size specula. The doctor will decide which will be better to use."

"What is a specula, and what is it used fer?" Ceara's tone was doubtful, and she was giving careful attention to that tray. Quincy could see she didn't like the look of any of the instruments. He didn't blame her.

"The Pap smear and visual exam," said the young woman as she exited the room. Ceara's gaze slewed to Quincy, her eyes wide with apprehension.

"Quincy," she whispered, and shivered. " 'Tis frightened I am. What will they be doing to me?"

Obviously she was expecting him to explain. The problem was, he didn't have a clue in hell exactly what was going to happen. "Well, uh . . ." he began. "First you need to take your clothes off and get into this gown. This is what women wear when they get examined for pregnancy."

She fingered the dingy patterned material doubtfully. " 'Tis ugly. Rainie would ne'er approve. Do the little tie straps go afore me or behind?"

"In front. She said open in the front."

After Ceara drew on the gown, he helped with the ties. Then she perched on the edge of the examining table and shivered in the chill room.

Dr. Stevenson came through the door. "All set? Good. Now if you'll just lie down, we'll get started."

Ceara complied, never taking her eyes off the doctor. Her face had paled, and Quincy thought it looked a little pinched. She was clearly terrified, and scrunched her eyes tight shut when she was told there would be a brief breast examination.

The doctor palpated Ceara's breasts, then slid her hands down to her stomach. Ceara shook her head no when Stevenson asked if there was any pain, and as Quincy glanced down at Ceara, he realized she was holding her breath. When the doctor removed her hands, Ceara let out a long, unsteady sigh, and her eyes popped open. "Are we done?"

"No, Mrs. Harrigan, we still—" Dr. Stevenson broke off, and Quincy felt that for the first time the doctor was looking at Ceara as a woman rather than a patient. "Mrs. Harrigan, have you ever had a pelvic exam before?"

"Nay, 'twill be me first."

"I see. I didn't realize. What's going to happen is that I will be asking you to scoot down until your bottom is at the end of the table. Your heels will be placed in these stirrups"—she indicated—"and your knees will be spread apart with a sheet draped over them. First we'll do the smear. When the speculum is in place you'll hear a slight click. The instrument will open you enough for me to put this swab stick inside to obtain the smear and take a look with my light to make sure everything is fine. After that part of the exam, I will insert my fingers very gently inside you to feel around. That will help me determine approximately how far along you are in the pregnancy." She smiled reassuringly. "Don't look so nervous. There's really not much to it, and I'll be using the smaller speculum, since you haven't had anything inside of you before."

"I dinna mean I've had nothing up there, Doctor," explained Ceara. "Me Quincy is in there regular, and he'd make two of yer little swab stick fer size."

Quincy coughed and felt his face flush crimson. Ceara flashed him an apologetic glance. "He'd make *ten* of yer swab, I mean. At *least*. He's na at all small."

As greatly as Quincy appreciated Ceara's attempt to stroke his male ego, he wished she'd left well enough alone.

Dr. Stevenson's cheek muscles went into a long, twitching spasm. For a moment her shoulders quivered; then suddenly she turned and began making a note on the chart. It seemed to take her an inordinately long time. When she turned back, she explained to Ceara how to position herself properly, and held up an instrument that looked to Quincy like it had come straight out of the Spanish Inquisition.

Ceara tugged the voluminous folds of the gown tightly around her. "Be ye certain that none of this will harm the babe?"

"I'm absolutely positive," Stevenson assured her.

Quincy half expected Ceara to lunge off the table and

dart behind him for protection, but his brave little Irish rose gave a decisive nod and lay back on the table. Quincy took her right hand, and she clamped down on his fingers with all her strength when Dr. Stevenson gently spread her knees apart.

The humiliation so overwhelmed Ceara that she wasn't sure she could hold the position. Then she felt the light. She hadn't anticipated so much heat.

Dr. Stevenson gently touched her inner thigh and told her she would be inserting the speculum. 'Twas uncomfortable, but not nearly as bad as Ceara had feared. She heard the tiny click she'd been told to listen for. There was pressure, but no real pain, just a horrid feeling of vulnerability. The idea of anyone, even a woman, staring at her private places made her stomach clench.

"You're doing fine, honey," Quincy said. "This won't take long."

She hoped not. Resentment flared for an instant, because he was a man and would never have to do this, but as quickly as it came it was gone. If this was part of the modern world and the way women had their babes, she would adjust. Even climbing into bed with a stranger hadn't been this bad.

In a moment it was over, and the speculum was removed. "You did fine," the doctor told her in a sympathetic tone. "The worst part is over. Now I'll be doing the manual exam . . . but that will be easy."

And it was. Ceara trusted Dr. Stevenson, who had looked after Loni during her pregnancy, but most of all she trusted Quincy. She was so glad that he'd stayed with her. The doctor's request that he leave the room had told her it was unusual for the man to be present.

When the doctor departed so Ceara could get dressed again, she jumped off the table and jerked on her clothes every which way, so anxious was she to be covered. As she settled her shirt into place, she saw that Quincy had sat down on the wheeled stool and held his head in his hands. She went to him and rested a palm on his shoulder.

"Quincy? Are ye all right, then?"

Her husband raised his head and she saw embarrassment in his eyes. "Just felt a little light-headed for a second. You were wonderful, honey. I was so proud of you. You didn't know what to expect, and neither did I, but you were terrific."

His praise warmed her right through. She began to thank him when Dr. Stevenson came back, and one look at her face told Ceara that she was bringing joyful news.

Quincy hadn't been wrong in his estimation. Ceara was about two and a half months along. The doctor asked her to lie on the table again. "I almost forgot to share with you the most wonderful part of this visit, and it's going to be a very special treat."

After Ceara was prone again, Stevenson pushed up her blouse and tugged down the elastic bands of her skirt and panties to bare her midsection. Then Quincy was invited to put the stethoscope to his wife's flat abdomen to listen to his child's heartbeat. He wasn't sure whether he was hearing a tiny heart or the protest of Ceara's stomach to a breakfast of three-bean salad and ice cream.

"I hear diddly-squat," he told the doctor.

She smiled and plucked the stethoscope tips out of his ears and inserted them into her own. "Slowly circle with the chest piece," she told him. "Slowly, and then pause, slowly and then pause." Quincy circled, stopped, circled, stopped. "*There*. Don't move it." Stevenson put the prongs back in his ears. "Now you should hear it. Very faint right now, but that's quite normal."

At first, all Quincy caught was the gurgle and churn of Ceara's stomach, but then, like a glimmer of a miracle, he finally heard a rhythmic beat, so faint, as the doctor said, that it was really hard to pick up on. Quincy wanted to hear a damned *thud-thud-thud*, something to tell him his kid was okay. But this was normal, the doc said. A tiny little heart, pumping in a minuscule body not yet all the way formed.

A huge grin spread over his face, making his cheeks almost hurt with the stretch. He kept the chest piece pressed to that exact spot and glanced up at Stevenson. "Put the prongs in Ceara's ears, please. I want her to hear it."

The doctor chuckled softly and did as Quincy asked. Lying on her back, Ceara squeezed her face into an expression of pained concentration, her eyes closed. And then, with a radiant smile, she lifted her lashes. "I hear it!" she cried. "Me babe's heart. 'Tis so tiny a sound."

"Your baby is still very small," Stevenson said. With a smile she added, "But the perfect size for two and a half months." She glanced at her chart. "My notes say you feared that this might be a high-risk pregnancy. Can you explain why?"

Quincy cleared his throat. "I do have a concern." He avoided meeting his wife's gaze. "Ceara . . . um . . . well, *we* have been drinking of an evening. Not a lot, really. Ceara usually had, oh, say, four to six ounces. Only wine or champagne, never any hard stuff. But Saturday before last—she didn't know she was pregnant, you understand—she drank at least a full bottle of wine, maybe a little more than that." Quincy's throat had gone scratchy. "I know drinking is bad for the fetus. Should we be worried about our baby?"

Ceara gasped and clamped a protective hand over her stomach. "Wine, 'tis bad for me babe?"

Dr. Stevenson smiled. "Countless women drink before they realize they're pregnant." She directed her gaze at Quincy. "And many overindulge before they know. I won't say that's *good* for the baby. Alcohol the mother takes in goes straight to the fetus, and the fetus metabolizes the alcohol much more slowly than the mother does, meaning the alcohol content of its blood remains high for a much longer period of time, with the propensity to cause harm."

Ceara's eyes filled with tears, and she shot a frantic glance at Quincy.

"But!" Stevenson held up a staying hand and smiled. "In my experience, mothers who imbibe prior to realizing they're pregnant and quit drinking all alcohol as soon as they do realize rarely deliver babies with problems. In short, Ceara, if you don't drink any alcohol from now on, plus stay away from caffeine and nicotine, I have every reason to believe your baby will be delivered in perfect health."

On the way home, Quincy stopped at a medical supply store and purchased a good-quality stethoscope so he and Ceara could listen to their baby's heartbeat at home. Before he allowed his wife to dash upstairs to lie on the bed and do just that, he told her they had some phone calls to make.

"Calls?" Standing in the kitchen archway in a ready-to-go stance, she fixed him with a puzzled gaze. "What is so important that we must make calls this verra moment?"

Quincy's heart squeezed just looking at her. "Have I told you today how much I love you?"

"Nay."

"Well, I do, more than I ever thought it'd be possible

to love anyone." Quincy waited a beat. "Do you feel the same about me?"

Her eyes shimmered like blue sapphires. "When ye walk into a room, the sight of ye makes me heart do a happy jig."

Quincy really wanted to hear the words *I love you, too*, but he guessed she wasn't quite ready to say them. "As for the phone calls"—he paused for emphasis—"we are *pregnant*." He jabbed his chest and leveled a finger at her. "You and me, doll face. We're going to have a baby!"

Her countenance lit up as if a candle flame flickered within her. "Yes," she agreed, touching her belly. "A babe! 'Tis a miracle, fer certain."

"And news we should share with family. We need to call my dad and Dee Dee first and then trickle down through the hierarchy until we've shared the fabulous news with everyone we love."

Her smile dimmed. "What of me family? 'Twould be grand if we could tell me mum and da."

Quincy wished with all his heart that were possible. He knew she sorely missed her own family, and he guessed that no amount of love and acceptance from his would ever make up for the loss. A sudden idea occurred to him. "How's about we invite everyone over to celebrate with us, and you can ask Loni if she could . . ." Quincy wasn't precisely sure how to phrase it. "Well, you know, hook you in with your mother?"

Ceara's expression brightened. "What time is it?"

Quincy glanced at his watch. "Twelve thirty. Why?"

" 'Tis eight hours later in Ireland, and me mum is old so she seeks her bed fair early. Do ye think Loni could hurry to get here?"

Quincy rang his sister-in-law on his cell. "Ceara and I are throwing an impromptu celebration today, inviting the whole family, and Ceara would like you to come early, as in right now." Quincy laughed. "Ah, no, I can't tell you what we're celebrating right yet. I have to call Dad and Dee Dee first. You and Clint will hear the news next, and so on down the line."

"You're pregnant!"

Quincy winced and held the phone out from his ear. "Don't tell anyone. Dad deserves to be told first. Go ahead and bring Aliza. I'll take her out to the arena to meet Beauty while you hook Ceara up with her mother and father to tell them the good news."

By the time Quincy finished making his calls, everyone in his family had either guessed or felt certain that a baby was on the way. Both Sam and Mandy thought to bring bottles of sparkling cider for Ceara so she could join in all the family toasts to be made with champagne. Dee Dee showed up with a gigantic jar of dill pickles, which she'd apparently had on hand, and a half gallon of rocky road ice cream, which she insisted all pregnant women loved if they liked chocolate. As Quincy put the tub into his freezer, a vision of Ceara topping rocky road ice cream with artichoke hearts flashed through his head, and his stomach lurched. He'd gone to the market over the weekend and stocked up on anything sour and canned, including sauerkraut, and he had shuddered all the way through checkout.

Clint arrived later than everyone else, because he'd stayed behind to pick Trevor up when he got off the bus. Aliza, who'd been in Quincy's care since one o'clock, when Loni had shown up, bounced across the kitchen in a five-year-old gallop to leap at her father as if she hadn't seen him for a week. Clint swung the dark-haired child high into the air, and on the downward loop growled and made gobbling sounds as he pretended to devour her belly. Aliza shrieked in delight. Watching, Quincy wondered if he'd soon have a beautiful little girl to love. Then his gaze shot to Trev, who'd grown so tall over the last few weeks, his dad was threatening to stack books on his head. *Hmm.* Maybe, Quincy decided, he and Ceara would have a boy. Quincy honestly didn't care, just as long as the child was healthy.

After setting his daughter back on her feet, Clint glanced around the kitchen, nodding in greeting to Frank and all his brothers. "Where are the ladies?"

Quincy hooked a thumb over his shoulder. "In my office, talking to ghosts. I went in to say hi to Ceara's parents. Couldn't see anyone, so it felt a little weird. But according to Loni, they can see us in Ceara's mum's crystal ball."

Frank, lounging at the table with his legs outstretched and crossed at his booted ankles, took a sip of his Jack and Coke. "I went in. Figured I should, since we're gonna share a grandchild. Like Quincy, I couldn't see no parents, but maybe they got a gander at me. Hope it didn't scare 'em to death."

Clint found a chair between Tucker and Zach. He lifted a black brow at Parker, who sat across the table near Frank. "You go in?"

"Too weird for me, pal. I'm staying right here."

Clint shrugged. "Nothing weird about it. If Loni says she's hooking in with them, she's hooking in."

"Then get up off your lazy ass and go in to introduce yourself," Parker replied. "Me, I'm more inclined to avoid conversations with folks who've been dead over four hundred years. Gives me the willies just thinking about it."

Zach laughed and took a long pull from his bottle of

Mirror Pond Pale Ale, a brand produced in nearby Bend. "Big pussy. I went in, and I'm not hearing the theme of *Twilight Zone* playing in my ears."

Clint sighed and set Aliza off his knee. "I reckon it'd please Ceara if we both went in, Parker. It's her family, after all."

"And pregnant ladies rule," Zach inserted.

Parker swore and stood up. "Oh, hell, why not?" He directed a compelling glare at Tucker. "Your ass glued to the chair or something?"

Tucker laughed and pushed erect. "With all the girls already in there, won't we be overwhelming them with too many new faces at once?"

Quincy checked the steaks he had thawing on the counter. Over his shoulder, he said, "Your faces won't be new. Ceara's mother has been watching our whole damned family in her crystal ball for nearly a year, and I'm sure her da has seen all of us, too. That's how the woman finally determined I was the only bachelor left in our branch of the Harrigan line."

"You saying two ghosts have been spying on us for months? Uh . . . *all* the time?" Parker sounded none too pleased by the thought. "This family is getting so weird, I could sell tickets."

Chapter Fifteen

Quincy fell in love with being pregnant. Prenatal vitamins. Decaf coffee and tea. Enough cans of sauerkraut in the pantry to hold a Bavarian Biergarten festival at his ranch and feed everyone in Crystal Falls. Jars of baby dills overtaking the shelves as well. Morning sickness, always morning sickness, only Quincy couldn't quite determine why it was called that, because Ceara grew nauseated at all times of the day or night. Worried consultation with Loni had reassured him that for some women this was quite normal. Privately, he suspected that some of Ceara's sickness was because no human stomach could tolerate some of the combinations she put into hers. She had developed a passion for pizza, particularly one local pizzeria's specialty called a Mount Bailey, which was topped with feta, spinach, and artichoke hearts. One night as they watched *Old Yeller*, she cried, tears sliding into her bowl of chocolate ice cream lined with pickle spears—Quincy's most nightmarish version of chips and dip. He'd learned to will his smeller into inaction, but he hadn't yet learned not to look.

But, oh, man, he cherished the whole experience. At four months along, Ceara's nausea abated, and he seriously considered nicknaming her Hoover, because almost overnight she started sucking up food, any kind, with more efficiency than a name-brand vacuum cleaner. She craved crazy stuff, and more than once he made midnight runs to the country store, a corner joint at a deserted junction between his ranch and town, to get his wife weird foods. Peanut butter, because they'd run out, and bananas. One night it had been oven-ready pepperoni pizza. Another time it had been pickled Polish sausages, which made Quincy nearly gag when he bit into one. He brushed three times to get the coating of cold fat off his teeth. Ceara ate all of what remained of the sausages. Quincy couldn't figure out why she didn't weigh three hundred pounds, but Dr. Stevenson seemed pleased with her weight and told Quincy that cravings were normal. In other words, if Ceara got a hankering for something, her body probably needed it.

At a little over twenty weeks, Ceara received her first ultrasound. Although the hens had all explained the procedure to her, she'd been baffled by the idea that a picture could be taken of her growing babe. She climbed onto the table readily enough, but Quincy could tell she felt she was humoring him. Once the screen activated, though, and the doctor pointed out the baby, both she and Quincy stared at the screen, fascinated by the blurry images.

"Would you like to know the baby's gender?" the tech asked with a smile.

Ceara's eyes widened. "Ye can tell if it be a lad or lass?"

"I can," the tech replied. "Well, I'm ninety-nine percent sure, anyway."

Beaming with happiness, Ceara sent an appealing look at Quincy. He nodded at the young woman. "Sure, we'd love to know."

"You have a little girl."

Quincy's heart leaped. Ceara's smile lit up the darkened room as he pressed his cheek against hers and looked at the screen again. "Look, honey, she's got your little nose," Quincy said. Then with a sigh of relief, he added, "Praise God. A girl with my nose—well, that just wouldn't do at all."

A baby girl. Quincy called everyone in the family to spread the word, and that night he posted the film on Facebook so everyone could see his daughter on their own computers. The next morning, he got Ceara up at the crack of dawn.

"Now that we know it's a girl, we gotta get ready!" he told her.

"Quincy," she said patiently, "ye're daft, me man. We already are ready for ten babes. 'Tis a wonder to me that any other mum can find so much as a shift in the stores, ye've bought so much."

"Yes, but it's all yellow and white and green. I want pink! I want to go shopping for my daughter," Quincy insisted. "And, oh, man, we need to think of a name."

"Ach, na until the birth," Ceara informed him. " 'Tis the way in me family."

Ceara spent a lot of time when she was alone at the house watching the ultrasound video of her and Quincy's little girl. She couldn't grasp the concept of an ultrasound—how a woman had rubbed her belly with warm gel and then had been able to take pictures, moving pictures, of Ceara's baby while it was still inside her. Pictures alone, of which Ceara had taken many with her cell phone, were mystery enough. In her time, 'twould be such a strange and inexplicable thing that the picture taker would be suspected of possessing evil powers. Not even the druids whom Ceara had known in her beloved Ireland had been able to capture images of people or things to display on a screen.

When Ceara wasn't watching her daughter's grainy image, she spent hours in what Quincy called the nursery, which was now almost completely furnished. She loved touching the dainty lace on the hood of the bassinet. Holding to her cheek the wee clothing in the drawers brought tears to her eyes. Quincy was unstoppable in shops, filling a cart faster than Ceara could blink. If she just paused over an outfit, or one of those strange pretties called mobiles, Quincy tossed it in the cart, and when they reached what people in this century called "checkout," he never hesitated to hand over his plastic credit card, which he'd explained to her was coded with special numbers so the charges went against his account. Ceara had used her own credit card while shopping with the hens, but at the time, she hadn't quite understood how it took the place of actual money.

For Ceara, pregnancy was a beautiful experience. She would never forget first feeling her daughter move within her womb. Or that fabulous night when Quincy finally felt his wee girl kick. She'd smile for the rest of her days remembering his stunned expression. He'd laughed and said he was signing her up for soccer. Ceara had nary a clue what soccer might be, but 'twas pleased she felt to see her husband's eyes glow with joy and pride.

Morning sickness hadn't been one of Ceara's favorite things, but she enjoyed all other aspects of pregnancy except one: Quincy's insistence that she never, absolutely *never*, use her gifts. 'Twas difficult to obey her husband's order, but Ceara tried, learning to light candles and evening fires with the long-stemmed starter, and never allowing herself to flap her hand to change the weather. 'Twas fer the good of the babe, she reminded herself. Quincy said that if using her gifts was a physical drain on her, it might also be taxing on their baby's tiny body. Ceara would do *nothing* to endanger her babe, and after growing so weak from stopping and restarting the snowstorm the day of their horseback ride, she knew her husband was right. Ceara had been with child even then, and surely her daughter must have felt the awful weakness that Ceara had experienced.

Watching his wife's belly swell. Seeing her start to develop that glow so common to pregnant women. When Ceara was in the early days of her sixth month, Quincy got on his cell, organized a hen party for the ladies at his house, and then called to arms his father and all his brothers for a good, old-fashioned guy get-together with a pony keg of fine draft in Clint's arena, the keg ready to tap when anybody got the urge.

Frank, who wasn't a beer man, stuck to his usual J and Cs. Sipping from a big red plastic cup, he studied Quincy over the rim. "I know you're pregnant, but what the hell are we celebratin' tonight? Exactly, I mean. A set of twins they didn't see in the first ultrasound, or the end of mornin' barf detail?"

Quincy, on only his first beer, took a long swig. Clint had brought in white plastic lawn chairs and set them in a circle on the arena sand. Occasionally a horse whickered or snorted, which was the perfect live music for any Harrigan man. It was totally a guy party, no fuss, no muss. A few bags of chips were all they needed to make it complete, and if a little dirt got into the mix, nobody gave a damn.

"No twins. I'm celebrating the *waddle*."

"The *what*?" Parker asked.

"Just because you aren't pregnant yet don't mean Quincy can't celebrate the *waddle*," Frank said, lifting his cup in a toast. "Your mama." He closed his eyes, clearly reminiscing, and smiled. "Yep, it was along about six months. Started bowin' her back and plantin' a hand just above her fanny, walkin' like a sailor in rough seas. Never was she more beautiful than when she was carryin' my babies." When Frank lifted his lashes, a tear spilled over onto his weathered cheek. "God, how I adored that woman."

Clint shifted on his chair as if fire ants had invaded his boxers. "You've got Dee Dee now, Dad. I mean, we all *loved* Mama, but it's sort of like you still think of her in the present tense."

"True love, the kind that warms the marrow of your bones, it ain't never over," Frank replied. He narrowed an eye at his eldest son. "You thinkin' I'm bein' disloyal to my sweet Dee Dee or somethin'?"

Clint switched knees to prop up a boot. He cleared his throat. "I'm not saying that, Dad. It just sort of—" He broke off and looked to his brothers for help. Nobody raised his hand. "Well, you've remarried now. Seems to me like you should let the dead rest and live in the present. For Dee Dee's sake, I mean. It can't be easy for her, knowing your heart still belongs to our mother."

Frank chuckled. "Spoken by a young fart still wet behind his ears. Dee Dee knew when we married that I'd never stop lovin' your mama. And I do mean never. The heart is big enough and has plenty of corners to love many people, and Dee Dee understands that. She keeps a picture of your mama—the one I always kept on my nightstand—right up on our mantel, bold as brass, along with pictures of all you kids. She's not threatened by Emily or jealous of my love for her memory. At our age, we've loved and we've lost, but we're smart enough to know that ain't the end of it. Took me a lot of years to understand that. Otherwise I might've married Dee Dee when all of you kids was at home and still such a pain in the ass. Could've saved myself a lot of money, not havin' to pay her wages all them years."

Quincy couldn't imagine ever loving any woman but Ceara, and he knew all his brothers felt the same way about their wives.

Zach, always the one who spoke first and thought later, said, "What're you sayin', Pop, that women are kind of like *dogs*? Shit, no, *really*? You love one, but when it dies, you can go out and find a replacement?" Zach squeezed the bridge of his nose and blinked. "I didn't mean that exactly the way it came out. I mean, I know you loved Mama more than you ever would a dog, and that you love Dee Dee a whole lot more, too. I just—"

"Need to stop talkin' before you dig yourself such a deep hole you can't drag your ass out of it," Frank finished for him. Then he chuckled, his way of letting Zach know he wasn't pissed. "Women and dogs ain't on the same plane."

Parker, already three beers in, interjected. "I don't know about that. Not all of them, for sure. My Rainie is a rare gem, but before I met her, I kissed plenty of dogs. Didn't have a real dog back then—the canine version, I mean—but if I had, I would have liked it a lot better than some of the gals I dated. Mojo is a great bed companion. Only off to the side or at the foot, because I've got my Rainie, but in a pinch, he'd be a fine cuddler on a cold winter night. Before Rainie, I'd gone out with the lady I still think of as Claws." Parker crooked one hand in the air. "I mean, acrylic nails so long and sharp, she could have gutted a steer."

Clint got a swallow of ale down the wrong pipe. When he caught his breath, he said, "I hear you. Right before I met Loni I went out with the Giggler."

"The *what*?" Quincy asked.

"The Giggler." Clint grinned. "She sounded like a sheep baaing. Drove me clear over the edge. Nice enough lady, I guess, but I never could get past that laugh of hers."

Zach chimed in. "That's better than the Silent Farter."

It was Quincy's turn to choke on his beer. "You're kidding."

"Nope," Zach said, waving a hand in the air. "She let out blue smoke that made my eyes tear up; I kid you not."

"I dated a gal once," Tucker inserted, "who blew bubbles in her cheek as I laid one on her." He shook his head and shuddered. "I don't know how she accomplished it, but hearing the pop when I kissed her was a major turnoff for me."

Quincy didn't know how his waddle celebration had ended up as a walk down memory lane for everybody. "Hey, guys, this is *my* party. I bought the pony keg."

Clint laughed. "I can make a few toasts to the waddle, Quincy. Loni was at her most beautiful during the last few months of pregnancy. Carrying my baby, her tummy so swollen she couldn't find a comfortable position to sit, and she got leg and belly cramps at night. I used to massage her all over with olive oil. Best damned preventative for stretch marks you'll ever come across. Dee Dee told me to do it."

Parker held up a hand. "More than I want to know, bro. What happens behind our bedroom doors stays behind our bedroom doors, if it's all the same to you."

"Oh, yeah?" Zach never learned and stuck his foot in

his mouth again by saying, "So how come I know all about how much you like Mr. Purple?"

The following evening, Quincy took Ceara to the Saturday vigil Mass in Latin, which had become his wife's weekend preference for worship. She claimed that hearing the liturgy in Latin made her feel more at home, because it was similar to the Mass she'd grown up attending in Ireland. Over the last month, they'd also started to go to some of the weekday morning celebrations, which Father Mike also offered in Latin especially for his more elderly parishioners, who sorely missed the Masses of their childhood.

Ceara, who loved hearing Father Mike's Irish brogue, sat through the homilies with a beatific smile on her glowing face, asked to stay after simply to sit in the presence of the Eucharist, and told Quincy every time they drove back to the ranch that the old-fashioned Masses made her feel close to home and the *old* ways.

" 'Tis still the same Christ, ne'er mind the language," she'd say, "but the Latin—ah, Quincy, hearing the Latin touches me heart." Then she always dimpled both cheeks at him, a sure sign to Quincy that she was happy beyond words. "In me time, every Mass anywhere in the world was said in Latin. 'Tis a *dead* language, ye ken, so it ne'er changes. At home, ye can travel to a foreign land, attend Mass, and except for the homily, ye can follow along without confusion."

Quincy's father was an old-school Catholic who often lamented the changes in the Mass that had come about after Vatican II. Frank claimed the Church had made a huge mistake in allowing the liturgy to be said in country-specific languages, because now world travelers could no longer follow along if they didn't speak the local tongue.

Quincy could understand Frank's point, but having been raised hearing the Mass in English, he wasn't sure he wanted to revert back.

" 'Tis good fer the babe, do ye na think, to sit all quiet in the church with Mum and Da, so peaceful and close to Jesus?" Ceara said.

Quincy never even tried to argue the point. He felt certain that whatever made Ceara feel at peace would also have a calming effect on their baby. Attending weekday Masses cut into his stable hours, but he had Pauline to oversee things in his absence, and both Pierce and Bingo were bucking to be the future foreman, so they weren't slackers, either. With such dedicated, horse-smart people in charge, Quincy could afford to take extra time off to make his wife happy.

Before driving home that particular Saturday night, Quincy pushed the movable console back so Ceara could sit beside him with a seat belt stretched almost to the max across her swollen belly. She spoke softly of the Mass with her cheek pressed to his shoulder. " 'Tis good worshiping on Saturdays, ye ken. But sometimes I'd still like to go on Sundays."

Quincy was surprised to hear that. "Really? I thought you preferred the Latin liturgy."

"I do," she replied. "But when it is Sunday here, it is also Sunday in Ireland, and it makes me feel close to me loved ones when I know I'm receiving the Eucharist on the same day that they are." She turned her head slightly to smile up at him. " 'Tis lovely knowing that, ye ken?"

The yearning Quincy heard in Ceara's voice made his heart hurt for her. He would have moved heaven and earth to make her happy, but closing the gap between her century and his was impossible. "Tomorrow let's go shopping for a crib, top-of-the-line, the finest made."

She nuzzled his sleeve. " 'Twill be a long while afore our babe is big enough fer a crib, Quincy."

"Point taken, but won't it be fun to shop for one? Picturing her in it?" He searched for something to say about cribs that would make her stop missing her family. "Dad loves to tell about the time he went up to check on me during my nap—hell, how old was I?—almost two, I guess, because I was in a crib by then. His mum and da were visiting . . ." Quincy paused, realizing that he was starting to echo Ceara's speech patterns in many ways, but after he considered for a moment, he decided he also parroted his dad occasionally, using incorrect English simply because he'd grown up hearing it. Maybe it was good for Ceara to hear bits and snatches of her time, little echoes of how her family spoke. "They were Irish, ye ken. Me grandmother, she had a brogue as thick and lovely as yours. And Dad was hoping to cart me downstairs to show me off." Quincy smiled at the memory— well, not *really* a memory, but over the years it had come to seem like one, because he'd been told the story so many times. "Anyhow, us boys all shared the same room way back then. It was before Dad built a bigger house. Mama kept harmless things in my crib for me to play with, but apparently I was far more interested in Clint's finger paint. Da found me having a fine old time with a Tupperware bowl and a plastic baby spoon, stirring up a delightful concoction of paint and *eating* it."

Ceara's head came up from his shoulder, and her beautiful blue eyes fixed on his with curiosity. "Ye ate *paint*?"

"It wasn't poisonous, and I guess it looked good to me."

Ceara looped an arm over her belly and burst into giggles. "What did yer da do?"

Quincy so enjoyed the ring of her laughter. If the

sound could be bottled, he'd be a billionaire. "Dad says I was happy as a clam and grinned up at him with a blob of rainbow colors stuck between my two front teeth."

Her mirth so overcame her that tears slipped down her cheeks. "Ach! Ye must ha been a mess!"

"Such a mess, according to him, that when he picked me up, he got paint all over himself, so we ended up in the shower together, with me da using his own toothbrush to get the stuff out from between my pearly whites because he couldn't find my tiny one." Quincy bent to kiss her forehead. "Back then, he was still struggling to make it as a horseman, so he says he couldn't afford a new toothbrush and poured straight bleach over the old one before he used it again."

Ceara giggled for nearly a full minute, recovering only to shake her head and start laughing again. "I see it. Clear as water in a barrel. Ach, what a moment!"

"And when he had me all dressed up cute, and himself all dressed again, he carried me downstairs to show me off, whispering to Mama that they had a hell of a mess to deal with upstairs. Later, praise God, Mama had an old toothbrush she'd saved for special cleaning chores, so they used that to scrub the ridges in the vertical slats of my crib rails, because I'd smeared the stuff everywhere."

Ceara fixed sparkling blue eyes on him. "I may ne'er kiss you again, Sir Quincy."

That set Quincy to laughing so hard that he nearly drove into the ditch.

The following morning, Quincy took his wife into Crystal Falls to go shopping for a crib. He parallel-parked on Main, because there was a specialty baby shop on the four-hundred block where he felt certain they would find high-quality baby furniture. Once inside, they spent some time at an infant rack, looking at tiny dresses, then moved on to consider the cribs. In the end, they saw no baby bed that interested them, but Quincy was quick to grab a flyer from a stack by the cash register.

"Lamaze classes." He flapped the paper in front of Ceara's nose. "It says most couples start taking them at six months along. We need to sign up."

"What are Lamaze classes?"

Quincy was explaining to his wife as they left the shop and headed up the sidewalk toward his parked truck. Suddenly Ceara stopped dead in her tracks to stare at the display window of a place called Curbside Antiques. "What is it? Do you see something special?" Quincy peered through the glass. "We can go in if you like."

" 'Tis a crystal ball just like me mum's," Ceara whispered.

Quincy released his grasp on her elbow to step closer. Sure enough, there was a gigantic glass ball on display. It sat on a scarred wooden stand. He wasn't much into hocus-pocus stuff, but he'd come to accept that it was serious business to his wife.

"Let's have a look." Quincy caught her hand and led her to the door, relieved to see an Open sign. An overhead bell clanged as they entered the shop, which had poor lighting. Quincy guessed it added to the *old* feeling, but the musty smell alone should have been enough. Ceara stepped around Quincy and went straight to the display.

"Ach," she said softly. " 'Tis me mum's all o'er again, Quincy. Near exact the same."

The clerk, an older fellow in tan Dockers, a bluestriped shirt, and brown loafers, hurried over. "I see you're fascinated by the crystal ball. A lot of people come in just to get a closer look at it."

Ceara had bent forward to peer deeply into the ball, as if answers to all life's mysteries might be found there. " 'Tis real," she said.

"Oh, yes, of course. I'd never have it on display without first getting it appraised. It dates back to the middle seventeen hundreds."

Quincy glanced at the man. "How much?"

"Well, sir, it isn't cheap," the fellow replied. "Not one of those dime-a-dozen new ones that you can find online. This is the genuine article, and the purchaser will, of course, receive a certificate of authenticity to verify its worth."

"How much?" Quincy asked again.

"Twenty-five hundred, and that's rock-bottom."

Quincy almost laughed, but one glance at his wife's yearning expression wiped all humor from his mind. He searched her pleading blue eyes. "Ceara, if I buy it for you, you've gotta *swear* you won't try to use it until after the baby is born."

She nodded. "I give ye me word, Quincy."

Quincy relaxed and smiled. "So you really, *really* want that old thing?"

She placed a hand over her belly, looking so adorable in a blue floral maternity top and a gathered denim skirt that Quincy wanted to kiss her right there in the shop. "I do. 'Tis special to me, ye ken. Verra special."

"Sold," Quincy told the shopkeeper. "Make sure you bubble-wrap the sucker. I don't want it getting broken on the way home."

Ceara wanted her crystal ball in their bedchamber near one of the fireplace windows. " 'Tis important for it to be in a high room. To home, Mum does her scrying in the little tower. She says 'tis easier there to focus."

In one of the extra bedrooms, Quincy found a walnut-base pedestal table with a round marble top wide enough in diameter to accommodate the crystal ball and its stand.

"Out from the wall a bit," Ceara directed, standing back and then circling to make sure he situated the table just right. "Ye need light, ye ken. To see things in the ball, I mean. It must be placed to catch the reflection of the fire at night and sunlight during the day."

"You swore you wouldn't use it," Quincy reminded her.

She flashed a mischievous grin. "I did, yes, but I dinna say I wouldna ask Loni to try using it."

Quincy didn't relish the idea of all the hens gathered in his bedroom to peer into a crystal ball. Hell, before he knew it they'd be chanting and lighting candles on every available surface. On the other hand, when he considered the sacrifice Ceara had made by coming here, how could he deny her the chance to truly *connect* with her mum? He couldn't imagine doing the same himself — leaving this land and his horses, and never being able to see his family again.

" 'Twill be like yer television fer me, Quincy. If Loni can conjure up me mum and da in the ball, I shall see them again." She steepled her fingers as if she were praying. "Please do na spoil this fer me, I beg ye."

Quincy gathered her into his arms. She'd already given up so much to keep the baby safe — no more driving lessons, no more riding his horses or using her gifts. "It's not that I want to spoil it for you, honey. I'm just worried is all. What if you forget and try to do some conjuring of your own? You know how weak you feel after using your gifts. It can't be good for the baby."

"I willna try." She pressed her face against his shirt.

" 'Tis me word I give ye, Quincy. 'Twill be Loni, and only Loni who will try to see in the ball. I shall peer in only if she is successful. Looking willna hurt me or the babe."

Quincy sighed and gently hugged her closer. "If you're sure of that, I'll support this one hundred percent."

" 'Tis verra certain I am. 'Twill be Loni's power used, na mine."

The next morning, Dee Dee volunteered to chauffeur Aliza to preschool and watch the child afterward while Loni spent the day with Ceara in the upstairs master suite, trying to conjure up images in the crystal ball. Ceara was so excited that she hurried Loni straight up-stairs, promising to serve her guest some refreshments later.

"I've never used a crystal ball," Loni warned. "I've never needed one. By touching your hand, I can go back in time to see your parents, but I honestly don't know if I can do anything with this particular medium."

Loni angled her chin forward to peer into the sphere. After a long moment, she smiled apologetically at Ceara. "I'm sorry. I see nothing. I know you'd love it if I could call up images of your family, but I'm afraid it's not going to work."

Ceara closed her eyes. 'Twas too great a temptation to peer into the ball herself and try to call up images. "Me mum speaks softly to the ball, a prayer of sorts, if ye will, asking to see what she wishes to see."

"Did your mum have any one special prayer she used?"

Just then Ceara glimpsed Quincy in the open door-way that led to the hall. He winked at her. "I'm going to leave you ladies and go to the stable." He patted his cell phone. "If you need me, just wing a text my way."

Ceara nodded, blew him a kiss, and returned her attention to Loni. " 'Tis uncertain I am if ye should use me mum's words or if ye should simply speak from yer own heart."

Loni nodded and focused on the ball again. Then she began speaking softly. "Powers that be, allow me to see, in this sphere of glass, the people Ceara loves in a time long past."

Nothing. Ceara's heart sank. She felt like crying, but gave herself a stern mental lecture to battle the tears. If she wept, Loni would feel responsible, and 'twas not her fault if scrying wasn't one of her gifts.

But Loni was determined. "Ceara," she said, straightening away from the ball, "one of the things wrong here is that we have no *mood*."

"Mood?"

Loni laughed, her blue eyes dancing. "Yes, *mood*. I'm a very prayerful psychic. I truly believe my gift comes directly from God. At home when I work with the FBI, I keep religious things around me: a crucifix on the wall above my computer, a Holy Bible on my desk." In a lower voice, she added, "I even bless my work area each morning by sprinkling holy water around it. It centers me, helps me stay focused."

Quincy's bedchamber crucifix was hung on the wall above the bed, clear across the room. Ceara ran to fetch it.

"Be careful," Loni cried. "You can't be standing on the mattress in your condition. Let me climb up there to get it."

While Loni fetched the cross, Ceara hurried downstairs to get Quincy's Bible from the living room. She'd stopped in the kitchen to get some tea lights and a lighter when Loni called down from upstairs, "I have a travel-size bottle of holy water in my purse. It's in the big pocket with a zipper. Get my rosary out of there, too."

Ceara was breathless by the time she gained the top of the stairs. She took a moment to rest and then entered the bedchamber to help Loni create the right mood. "Me mum has her Bible and rosary with her in the little tower room when she sees inside the ball. Mayhap ye're right, and one canna *see* without religious things near at hand."

Loni chuckled. "I don't know about that, but for me, knowing that God is holding my hand makes all the difference. No matter how it's sliced, psychic ventures can very easily become dark. I always surround myself with my faith for protection."

Ceara agreed. "If it comes na from God, I want no part of it, either."

Once everything was arranged to Loni's liking, she and Ceara both knelt near the pedestal table to bless themselves with holy water and say a decade of the rosary, asking the Virgin Mother for intercession. They followed with several recitations of the Lord's Prayer.

Afterward Loni sprinkled holy water all around the pedestal table while Ceara lighted the candles. Then Loni gazed into the crystal again, whispering the prayer she'd said before. As if acting on instinct, she lightly moved her hands over the crystal, whispering, "Let the light that's within me enter this ball. Let all sight that comes through me shine bright in these depths." Then, suddenly, Loni lifted one hand from the glass to reach toward Ceara. "That's what's missing. I'm not touching you."

Ceara stepped closer to grasp Loni's fingers. Loni said, "Don't look deeply into the glass. Let me be the one to do this. Promise? Quincy will have my head if anything happens to you or the baby."

"Ye've me word on it."

With her free hand, Loni stroked the crystal again. "Powers that be, allow me to see, in this sphere of glass, the people Ceara loves in a time long past. Let the light that's within me enter this ball. Let all sight that comes through me shine bright in these depths."

A strange glow surrounded the crystal sphere, creating shimmery sparkles similar to a halo. Ceara's pulse kicked. She felt Loni's hand tighten on hers. The glow surrounded the hand Loni had left resting on the crystal, then suddenly went out. Loni jumped and Ceara heard her gasp faintly.

Then Ceara saw that familiar, distant expression enter her sister-in-law's eyes. Ceara felt a tingling on her skin. It seemed to her that the very air in the room grew charged with some unseen force.

"I see them," Loni whispered. "And, oh, Ceara, so much more clearly now than before. Your mum is so *lovely*!"

Ceara inched closer to the sphere, paying special attention to how she felt and any sudden movement of the babe in her womb as she directed her gaze deep into the murky crystal. The babe didn't move. Ceara experienced no sense of weakness. Something flickered, swirled, formed into her mum's sweet face.

Home. The rock walls of the tower room, the arched opening that looked out on the land around the manor, her mum's chair over near the hearth, where an afternoon fire burned cheerfully in the grate. Ceara took a deep breath and slowly released it, once again taking measure of any physical effect this connection might be having on her. *Nothing*. She felt right as rain. 'Twas Loni's gift at work, not her own. Ceara felt certain there would be no danger to her or her child.

"Mum!" she cried, touching the fingertips of her free hand to the glass. "Oh, me sweet mum!"

Ceara's mother gazed back at her with tears in her eyes. "Ye're growing big with child," she said, her voice faint but clear. "I've been watching ye in me ball and seeing yer middle swell, but I ne'er dreamed ye might find a way to see me as well! Ach, 'tis a miracle that brings tears to me old eyes, Ceara, me darling girl."

Ceara was so happy she felt a little light-headed, not from any physical stress, but simply because she'd thought ne'er to see her mum again. Clinging tightly to her friend's hand, she had the presence of mind to say, "Mum, 'tis me sister-in-law Loni, here with me. Ye've seen her before, if ye recall. She is wife to Clint, me husband's eldest brother. Loni, meet me mum, Daireann Eibhlin O'Ceallaigh."

Daireann inclined her head, smiling warmly. " 'Tis pleased I am to meet ye, Loni."

Loni returned the pleasantry, and then Ceara intervened. "Where's Da, Mum? Is he about?"

Her mum leaned sideways to yell, "Riordan, come quickly! Ceara is in me ball, and she can see me, she can!" She flashed a radiant grin, revealing several missing front teeth. " 'Tis up the stairs he must come. Four flights. 'Twill take him a wee while."

"Mum, how be ye feeling? Yer bones? And is yer heart still bouncing about sometimes?"

Daireann placed a hand over the center of her chest. "Me heart is fair bouncing about now. 'Tis so pleased I am to have this happen, Ceara. Now that we be talking, 'tis brimming with questions I am. Yer hair, me dear child, what went with yer hair? I near fainted the first time I saw ye without yer braid."

Ceara laughed even though tears slipped down her

cheeks. "Ach, the hens—me friends and sisters here in this time—got me a done-over, and one of the things to make me look more of this time was to get rid of me long hair."

"And the babe?" Daireann asked. "All goes well?"

"Yes, very well," Ceara said with a laugh. " 'Tis a lass, Mum, and I be six months and one week in."

Daireann's wrinkled brow drew into a bewildered scowl. "A lass, ye say? Ye ken this afore she comes? Has a midwife dangled a weighted string from your belly?"

"Nay, no weighted string." There were so many strange things in this new place that Ceara couldn't begin to explain them all to her mum. "In this time, they can see through me skin and flesh to look at me babe. 'Tis called ultrasound, though it makes no noise, and 'tis a lass fer certain, Mum. She shall be born afore we know it, only two months and three more weeks to wait." Just then Ceara glimpsed a dear face she'd thought ne'er to see again. "Brigid!" she cried. "Me sweet wee sister!"

When Quincy returned to the house to check on his wife, the first thing he heard was the wonderful chime of Ceara's laughter ringing from upstairs. He hurried to the second floor, and when he entered the bedchamber, he saw Loni and Ceara hovering over the crystal ball, both of them talking a mile a minute, Ceara's cheeks drenched with tears. When she saw Quincy, she beckoned him over.

"Ye must come see me mum and da! And me sister, Brigid, Quincy. Hurry afore Loni loses them!"

Quincy doubted he would be able to see anything. He knew from experience that he had no druid gifts, period. Even so, he stepped up behind Ceara and peered dubiously over her shoulder. Before, the ball had looked murky and dull to him, but now it shimmered, and muted light swirled deep at its center. He nearly lost his balance when he saw the craggy faces of an old man and woman, clear as could be. Behind them, he glimpsed a gigantic stone fireplace. Along another wall, he saw what looked like an arched window of sorts without glass that was flanked by wooden shutters.

"My God," he whispered. The woman must have heard him, because she gave him a wink and a jaunty wave. Quincy felt as if his eyes were going to pop right out of their sockets. The stamp of the woman's features exactly duplicated his wife's.

The couple appeared very old—too old to have a child Ceara's age. Surely they weren't Ceara's parents. "Your mum and da?"

"Yes!" she cried, flashing him a joyous smile. "Mum, Da, 'tis pleased I am to present to ye me husband, Sir Quincy Harrigan. Quincy, meet me da, the O'Ceallaigh, given name Riordan, and his lady, me mum, Daireann Eibhlin." Just then a young girl stepped into view. She so closely resembled Ceara that Quincy did a double take. "And me wee sister, Brigid. Brigid, this is me husband, Quincy."

Quincy greeted each person, hoping he sounded half-way sane. Talking to people who were more than four hundred years dead—well, it was a bit much to take in. And he couldn't get over how ancient Ceara's parents looked. By comparison, Quincy's dad was still young and robust. Though he knew people back then had aged at a faster rate and died much younger, he still would have guessed these people were his wife's great-grandparents if he'd met them under any other circumstances. Meeting them at all had him seriously off balance. He put a hand on Ceara's shoulder. This was beyond weird, yet it was happening.

Brigid was what Frank would call a pistol. She immediately began teasing Quincy, first about his funny hat, then about his léine and trews. And why, she wanted to know, had his hair been shorn? Quincy, reminded of his manners, swept the Stetson from his head.

"Some men in this time still wear their hair long," he told the child, "but most of us prefer a shorter cut."

Just then, three older men entered the room. Quincy could scarcely credit their odd dress or the fact that they wore no shoes. Ceara quickly introduced Quincy to them, one by one, and Quincy was even more startled to learn that these fellows, who looked to be at least a decade older than Clint, were his wife's brothers. The eldest was named Adamnan. Then, in descending order of age, Quincy met Aidan and Caelan. Ceara was ten years younger than Caelan, and Brigid was the baby of the family.

Suddenly the brightness within the crystal began to dim. Loni sent Ceara an apologetic smile. "I'm growing weary, I'm afraid. To do this for so long is taxing. It's time to say good-bye — and quickly, please. I'm not sure how much longer I can hold on."

Ceara squeezed her sister-in-law's hand and leaned close to the ball. " 'Tis time fer farewell, I fear. The sight of yer dear faces has gladdened me heart! Soon, mayhap, 'twill be possible fer us to visit again. Brigid, ye behave yerself, and mind what mum tells ye!"

The good-byes coming through the ball and so many centuries grew faint and then fainter still, and suddenly the glow inside the crystal blinked out completely. Quincy curled his hands over his wife's shoulders. She stood with her head bent for several seconds, still clinging to Loni's hand. Then, after taking a deep breath, she looked up and beamed a smile.

" 'Twas wondrous!" she cried. "Thank ye so much, Loni. Ye'll ne'er know how much it meant to me, seeing them again and hearing their dear voices."

Loni gave Ceara a hard hug. "Oh, I think I know, sweetie, and I'm more than happy to have helped bring it about." As Loni drew away, she winked at Quincy. "We'll do it again very soon, I promise. At least once a week, so you can keep close tabs on all of them."

Moments later, after Quincy had seen Loni out and closed the door behind her, he turned to find Ceara standing near his elbow with a perplexed frown pleating her forehead. "What does it mean, keeping close tabs?"

Quincy laughed and gathered her into his arms. "It means keeping close watch on someone, just another way of saying it. And that, by the way, is why I came back to the house so soon." He splayed his right hand gently over her belly. "I was worried about you and our little girl."

Ceara placed her hand on top of his. " 'Tis fine we are. I ne'er used me gift. Loni used hers. The babe sleeps, happy as a bedbug in the straw because her mum is so verra happy."

"Good, good." Quincy encircled her in his embrace again. "I'm sorry for being a worrywart. Normal, I guess. I just don't want anything to go wrong."

She looked up at him, then stepped away a little, tilting her chin in the manner she had before she put a question to him. "And?"

"And what?"

"Yer expression says ye feel as if ye've been kicked in the head by a horse. 'Twas a bit difficult for you to believe, I ken?"

"Well, uh . . . yeah. I guess it was. I mean, I know it happened and all, but I didn't really think . . . I mean, how did Loni . . . Oh, hell, I don't know what I mean. I still can't believe I've been talking with people who lived over four hundred years ago."

Ceara's laugh rippled out and she flung herself on him. Her stomach pressed against him as she hugged him hard. "Ye will, Quincy; I promise ye that. 'Twill soon seem as natural to ye as electricity now does to me. Do we have any three-bean salad left? I like the tart taste."

Chapter Sixteen

Quincy wasn't surprised that evening when Ceara announced that she wanted to celebrate her reunion with her loved ones. He was all for it, even if he still felt shell-shocked about it. Under Quincy's tutelage, she'd learned to make a mouthwatering chicken curry with a coconut-milk base, which he deemed a healthier choice than half-and-half or dairy cream. After pouring them each a flute of sparkling cider, Quincy set to work at the right of the cooktop to prepare a salad, a task he relished, because he could slip in different varieties of vegetables that Ceara would hesitate to eat otherwise because they seemed strange to her—rainbow chard, green peppers, leaf lettuce, ripe avocado, diced kale, tomatoes, and half of a white onion. His wife loved her onions. Because she was also obsessed with sour stuff, he planned a Mediterranean-style dressing with olive oil, fresh-squeezed lemon juice, and a dash of Herbes de Provence, a blend he'd created himself using a recipe he'd found in a Mediterranean cookbook. It would be a nice, romantic dinner for two, complete with soft music and candlelight.

Ceara worked beside him, stirring the curry, adding spices, and then offering him samples with a tasting spoon. When Bubba and Billy Bob moaned with hunger, Ceara reached into the pot and tossed them bits. They gobbled, gulped, and eyed her worshipfully. Quincy grinned. His two big moochers knew where their next bite of curry was coming from.

"Oh, man, that's delicious," he said each time she fed him a bite, and then he'd dip his head to sample her lips. "But not nearly as delicious as you."

Ceara would laugh and say, "Ach, behave yerself. I am on the menu for dessert."

Quincy truly couldn't remember ever having been so absolutely happy or content with his life. He'd worked hard for nearly twenty years to make a go of his horse ranch, and before Ceara had dropped into his world, he had acquired all the trappings of success—a big, beautiful home, a small fortune in the bank, an impressive investment portfolio, and a group of trusted staff in the arena, which would have allowed him to take all the time off he wanted for family vacations, if he'd only had a family. Now—finally—Quincy had it all: a beautiful, sweet, wonderful wife and a baby on the way.

Having Ceara beside him was the culmination of all his dreams. And as of tonight, compliments of Loni and the crystal ball, she had been able to see her family again. The link hadn't been as clear as, say, speaking to people on Skype, and according to Loni, communication might sometimes be difficult, if not impossible. But at least it was something, and though it wasn't quite as nice for Ceara as a real visit with her loved ones in Ireland, she seemed tickled and peaceful in her heart. He was so thankful for that damned ball and Loni's ability to make an occasional reunion happen in the future that he would light candles after Mass tomorrow morning and spend a good fifteen minutes doing knee time.

After peeling the onion, he leaned down to kiss Ceara lightly on the cheek. "Do you have any idea how very much I love you?" he asked.

She nodded. Quincy waited for a response, still yearning to hear her say the same words back to him. "You've nothing to tell me?" he asked.

She glanced up and grinned. "Ye fill me heart with joy, Quincy. Just seeing ye makes me toes tingle and gladness warm me bones."

He sighed and reached for the big chopping knife, which he'd just sharpened. "That's it?" He cut the onion in half with a frustrated chop and started to position the blade for another downward snap. "I make your toes tingle?" That was something, but he still longed for the words she'd never spoken. Dammit, he *knew* he made her toes tingle. She made him tingle, too, but a little bit higher.

Ceara, monitoring the concoction she stirred, laughed and bumped his left arm with her shoulder. A teasing jostle, Quincy knew, but she was short and caught his elbow at just the correct angle to shove his left hand, which was holding the onion, sharply to the right as he put downward force behind the knife. Quincy felt the razor-edged steel hit his wrist. *No big*, he thought, because he felt no pain. The next instant blood spurted upward, nailing him right in the eyes. He couldn't see, but he could feel the rhythmic streams of thick liquid hitting his chin, then his shirt. He also heard Ceara scream—a horrible, panicky shriek of sheer terror.

An artery, he thought stupidly. *Shit.* He'd slashed his wrist. "I'm all right. I'm all right," he assured her, even though he knew damned well he wasn't. What was worse, he couldn't see to get the bleeding stopped. He tossed the knife and grabbed his wrist, but the clench of his grip didn't stop the spurting. "It's okay. A rag, I need a rag to wipe my eyes. Get me a towel, Ceara, quick! We've got to tie this off!"

"Nay!" Ceara cried.

Quincy felt her slender hands shove his aside and close over his wrist, her fingers pressing in on the wound with a strength he hadn't realized she possessed. A strange heat radiated into his hand and up his arm. Then, from his shoulder to his fingertips, the heat turned electric, as if he'd just grabbed hold of a live two-twenty wire. He weaved on his feet.

"What are you—" Quincy never finished the question, because he *knew* what Ceara was doing—using a gift she'd never told him about: the ability to heal. "No!" *Oh, God, no.* He'd seen what using her powers did to her. He tried to pry her fingers loose from his flesh, but she held on with tenacity, and with one hand and his fingers slick with blood, he couldn't get a good grip. "Ceara, don't! The baby! You can't be—"

Her fingers went suddenly limp under his. Her hand slid away. He heard a thump. Billy Bob began to bark, a low, deep-down growly bark that meant danger. Quincy's body went cold.

"Ceara?"

He wiped frantically at his eyes in an attempt to see. It didn't help. Blood clogged his vision. Disoriented, he headed for the sink. *Water.* He needed to wash his eyes. His boot struck something soft; he tripped and went down, managing at the very last second to catch his weight with his hands. Ceara lay under him. Quincy pushed up onto his knees, shoving both dogs out of the way, groping blindly to see what was wrong with her. Limp. Her entire body was limp. *Oh, sweet Christ. Holy Mother. God help me.* Quincy jerked the tails of his shirt loose from under his belt and swiped with savage urgency at his face. When he could finally see, it was through a red haze, but at least he could make out his prostrate wife and where he was in the kitchen. Bubba was whining and licking Ceara's white face.

Pressing his fingertips to Ceara's throat, he felt for a pulse. His own was pounding so hard he couldn't tell if Ceara had one. He bent low to put his face near hers and felt a shallow breath on his cheek as she exhaled. Alive, she was alive. He ran his hands over her. So much blood. Had she fallen on the knife? He rolled her this way and that, but he saw no wound. Thank God, she hadn't been cut. His blood, he decided. So what the hell was wrong with her? He was afraid he knew: She'd passed out from the effort of saving him.

At that instant her long lashes fluttered. Then she opened her eyes, looking as disoriented as he'd felt only seconds earlier. "Quincy?" she said faintly. "The bleeding. 'Tis stopped?" Billy Bob crowded between them. "Out!" Quincy yelled. "Out and stay out!" For once they got the message and hurried into the adjacent room, lingering at the door. Maybe they'd caught the terror in his voice.

Fear for his wife and child had wiped all thought of his own safety from his mind. He looked stupidly at his wrist, and all he saw on his skin were his wife's bloody fingerprints and thick smears of crimson. The slash—and Quincy knew it had to have been deep—was gone. Not even a shallow cut remained.

"Oh, my God, what did you do?" Quincy grabbed her up in his arms, shaking so badly that he could barely support her still-limp upper body. "You promised me you wouldn't use your gifts, Ceara. You gave me your word."

She turned her face against his crimson-soaked shirt

and started to weep. "But Quincy, ye"—she stopped and gasped—"were bleeding bad. 'Tis ... sorry ... I ... am. I ... dinna ... think. When I saw ... the blood spurting from yer arm ... I just reacted."

"But the baby. What about the baby?"

She placed a bloody hand over her belly. "She is fine, I think."

Quincy spared a thought to turn off the gas burner under the pot of curry. Then, weak at the knees though he was, he swept his wife up into his arms. Once in their suite, he laid her gently on the bed. She smiled faintly up at him, her pretty face smeared with his blood, tear tracks zigzagging paths through the scarlet.

"All went black," she murmured. She rested quivering fingertips on his left wrist. Her smile wavered and then deepened. " 'Tis gone," she whispered with quiet satisfaction. "The deep cut, 'tis gone. Me gift dinna fail me when I needed it. Ye could have died, Quincy."

Quincy couldn't argue the point. He went to the bathroom to wet several washcloths and returned a moment later. "Let me get you cleaned up."

When she made no protest and just lay there, letting him wash her face, arms, and hands, Quincy's stomach clenched with worry. "Are you sure you're okay? You and the baby, you're both okay?"

She sighed and closed her eyes. " 'Tis weak I am, just verra weak."

"You shouldn't have done that. We could have gotten the bleeding stopped some other way." The instant Quincy said that, he saw tears slip from beneath her thick auburn lashes. He felt like a jerk. "I'm sorry, honey. I wasn't blaming you. You saved my life. Don't think I don't know it. And I know it's pure instinct for you to use your gifts in a crisis, and that it's really hard for you not to use them right now because of the baby. I do understand how you would just react in a situation like that. Please, honey, don't think I was blaming you. I was just plain scared to death for you."

"Ye make me heart sing," she whispered. "I couldna watch ye bleed to death. And 'tis fine we are, both of us. 'Tis just the drain, ye ken. I'll be okay."

He made her heart sing. Quincy wanted to gather her close in his arms, but if he did, he'd get blood all over her again. So instead he wiped his hands clean and went to her walk-in closet. He found the flannel granny gown she'd worn in the early days of their marriage. In central Oregon, the evenings grew cool even in mid-September, when the afternoons were still summery warm. The gown would keep the chill away while he quickly showered and cleaned up. Then he'd join her in bed and keep her snug with his body heat.

Ceara allowed him to tug off her clothing and managed to sit up so he could help her into the nightgown. When she fell back against the pillow, he pulled the flannel down, lifting her hips for her so he could get her legs covered.

"'Tis sorry, I am. Ye're dressing me like I am a helpless babe."

"Don't worry about it." Quincy leaned over her. "How are you feeling now? Still only weak?"

She nodded.

"I can take you in to the hospital," he suggested. "I'm sure Stevenson would meet us at the ER to give you a quick check to make sure both you and the baby are okay."

She shook her head. "Just let me rest for a wee time. Then we shall see. Yes?"

"Okay, but if you're not feeling stronger by the time I get out of the shower, I'm taking you in."

She smiled. " 'Tis a deal, provided ye're in the shower long enough to get yerself wet."

Quincy was grinning on the way to the bathroom. She knew him pretty well, Ceara did. Okay, he'd humor her, but this was going to be one quick ablution. He turned on the water to make Ceara think it was longer, stripped off his blood-soaked clothes, threw them in the tub to deal with later, and forced himself to stand under the hot jets of water while he counted to sixty . . . fast. Wrapping a towel around his dripping body, he went into his closet to don a fresh set of clothes from the skin out, plus another pair of boots.

When he approached the bed, Ceara awakened, pushed up with her elbows to a reclining position against the pillow, and smiled at him. " 'Tis better I am."

"Are you positive? I'm ready for town. I can bundle you up and carry you to the truck. Going to the ER is no big deal."

She grinned. "I'm verra hungry. I think ye bled into our supper pot, sad to say, so we've naught to eat."

Quincy remembered the mess downstairs, which he needed to clean up, but he didn't want to leave Ceara alone that long. "How does some soup and sandwiches sound? I can make that fast."

Her stomach snarled, and she laughed, placing a hand over her swollen belly. Just then the baby must have kicked, because she lifted her brows. "Our wee girl says she is verra hungry, too."

"Well, a man has to feed his ladies." Quincy leaned down to kiss his wife, and then he bent to kiss the back of her hand where it rested on her stomach. "Will you both be okay while I run down to make a quick meal? I'll turn on the intercom."

" 'Tis fine we shall be."

Before leaving the room, Quincy switched on the intercom. "If you need me, just holler out. I'll be here in two blinks."

Once downstairs, Quincy missed a step at the sight of the kitchen. Blood was everywhere: all over the counters, the cooktop, the oven fronts, and the floor. He stood for a moment to take it in and then looked incredulously at his wrist. It had taken a very deep slash and a severed artery to cover such a wide area with blood, but now no one would ever know that he'd been injured. It had never occurred to him that Ceara's gifts might include healing. Now he could only wonder why she'd never mentioned it. And he also wondered why in hell she hadn't used it on Loni.

After making sandwiches and heating two bowls of soup in the microwave, Quincy carried the tray upstairs and asked his wife those questions over their simple meal. She frowned before answering. "To be verra honest, I thought the gift was lost to me," she said softly. "Me other gifts—well, they are only a shadow of what they once were, ye ken, and the gift of healing takes a great deal of power. I didna believe I still had it in me. And while me gifts can also work on illness, Quincy, I've no power to break an illness coming from a curse. 'Tis a different thing entirely. I couldna help Loni in that way, only by marrying with ye."

Quincy took a bite of his sandwich and handed her a paper napkin to dab mayonnaise from the corner of her mouth. "So, because you believed you no longer had the power to heal, you saw no point in mentioning it." He didn't state that as a question. "In a way, I understand how you must have felt." He spooned some chicken noodle soup into his mouth, took a moment to chew, and then swallowed. "Take me, for instance. In my twenties,

I reigned as king in rodeo cutting and roping competition all across the nation. I traveled the circuit for a while, and that was a lot of fun while it lasted." He smiled at the memories. "Winning big purses, hearing the roar of the crowd, and having my pick of the buckle bunnies after an event."

"Yer belt buckles all have horses or steers or the like. I've ne'er seen one with a rabbit."

Quincy winced. Then he shrugged. "In my misspent youth, I liked the ladies. Buckle bunnies are young women who flock to rodeos, hoping to catch the eye of some champion cowboy who just won a big purse."

"Ach!" She narrowed her gaze on him. " 'Tis unsure I am what a rodeo is, but ye'll be competing in them ne'er again."

Quincy leaned over the tray on her lap to gently nip her earlobe. "You're my one and only now. No more buckle bunnies for this fellow."

"Just so ye're remembering it. I'll na be happy if ye fancy another."

Quincy couldn't imagine any other woman catching his eye. Ceara outshone them all, in his estimation. "Anyway, back to my story. Nobody can remain the king forever. Some younger guy always comes along to steal your glory. Some men fight to the finish. Some stay on top for a decade, but I can't imagine the price their bodies and their relationships pay. I enjoyed myself for a while, and then I threw in my hat. I quit while I was ahead, while I was still a champion, and focused on my ranch. I'd done what I set out to do: earning some renown for the horses I raise and train."

"I do na see how yer story relates to me lost powers."

Quincy chuckled. "You haven't let me get to that yet." He chucked her under the chin. "Some guys can't turn loose of the glory, even after they're burned out, so they blow their own horns to anyone who'll listen about how great they used to be. Whenever I hear someone brag about how big a man he once was, I get a sour taste in my mouth, so I seldom tell anyone of my successes in rodeo competition. I once had a great run, but that's done and over."

She still looked perplexed.

He continued. "And your gifts, once so very powerful, are now diminished. You no longer believed you still had the power to heal, so you didn't mention it to me."

"Ah," she said, drawing out the word. Then she nodded. " 'Tis a wee bit the same, I ken. I believed I had lost the power; it made me sad to think of it, and I saw no reason to talk of it."

"Precisely." Quincy sighed. "I just thank God that what happened tonight didn't harm you or our little girl."

After Ceara finished both her sandwich and soup, Quincy set the tray on the table in the reading corner, laid and lit a fire, and then stripped down to his boxers to join his wife in bed. She turned into his arms, her belly bumping his just under his ribs. He felt their daughter give a hard kick and smiled as he burrowed his face into Ceara's beautiful hair.

"It must feel like you've got a kickboxer inside of you," he said.

"What is a kickboxer?"

Quincy explained, turning so she could rest her head in the hollow of his shoulder, and let his eyes fall closed.

"What of our romantic ending to me celebration?" she whispered.

He hugged her closer, pleased to feel his daughter move again. "I think we'll postpone that until tomorrow night. After what happened, I'll feel better if you just rest."

She yawned sleepily. Then she nodded. " 'Tis a good idea. I am verra tired."

"But other than that, you feel fine?"

"Fine as a frog's hair."

Quincy grinned. He had picked up some of her speech patterns, and she had learned some of his sayings. It was a good mix. He reached up and backward to turn off his bedside light. The amber flicker of the fire played over the walls, creating a nice blend of dance and shadow. Good mood for making love, but that wasn't happening. He took a deep breath, loving the smell of Ceara's hair and the wispy curls that tickled his cheek. His eyes drifted closed, and he turned loose of the day to join her in dreams.

"Quincy!"

Ceara's cry jerked Quincy from deep sleep. He bolted upright in bed. "What?" Not liking the fear he'd heard in her voice, he switched on the lamp. His wife was sitting up and her eyes mirrored terror. His stomach vised. "What it is, sweetheart?"

"Something . . . I am wet, and I swear to ye, I dinna pee."

Quincy's heart caught. He snapped back the covers and blanket. Ceara's gown had damp, slightly pink splotches at the hip, and as the sleep cleared from his eyes, he saw that the sheet beneath her bottom was soaked.

"Oh, my God." He leaped out of bed. "Your water broke. Are you having pains?"

She planted a trembling hand over her middle. "Nay, but I ache deep inside." Just then her face twisted, and she turned on her side, drawing up her knees. "God's . . . *teeth*! It hurts—Quincy, it *hurts*."

"Sweet Jesus, you're in labor." Quincy turned in a full circle twice, searching frantically for his pants. He no sooner got them in his hand than he dropped them to the floor again to grab his cell phone from the nightstand. After dialing 911, he hurried around the bed to put a hand on Ceara's shoulder. "Just lie still, honey. Don't try to get up, okay?" A dispatcher answered his call. "Yeah, this is Quincy Harrigan. My wife has gone into premature labor." He quickly explained how far he lived from town. "It'll take an ambulance close to thirty minutes to reach us. I don't think she can wait that long, so I'm taking her in. I'll need a police escort to clear the way for me once I reach the city limits. There'll be more traffic there, and I may have to run a few lights." He told the woman where the car should meet him. "I drive a big green Dodge with a bent cattle guard and a winch. Tell the officer to be watching for me and take the lead. I may not be able to stop for a powwow."

Quincy ended the call, threw on his clothes, pulled on his boots, and then bundled his wife up in the coverlet. As he carried her downstairs, he felt her body clench as another pain hit her. *Too soon.* She was what—twenty-five weeks along? The baby couldn't come right now. It just couldn't.

" 'Tis too soon," Ceara cried, echoing his own thoughts.

"It's fine," he lied. "I'll get you right in. On the way, I'll call Stevenson, and she'll meet us at the ER. They can give you a shot to stop the labor." They could do that, couldn't they? Quincy prayed to God that was normal procedure. "You'll be fine; our baby will be fine. No worries, okay?"

Quincy got Ceara comfortably settled on the rear seat, slipped back out of the cab, slammed the door, and checked to be sure he'd brought his cell phone before leaping in on the driver's side. Pawing the dash cup for his damned keys, he swore viciously when he didn't find them. They had to be here. He'd left them in the truck earlier that day. He was sure of it.

Just before the dome light blinked out, he caught a glimmer of metal from the corner of his eye. *Floorboard.* In the dark, he skimmed his hand over the rubber mat, finally found the keys, and shoved them into the ignition.

"Ah-hhh-h!" Ceara wailed behind him. " 'Tis bad, Quincy. 'Tis verra bad."

Quincy gunned the engine, jerked the shift into reverse, and backed away from the house at such a speed that clumps of grass and gravel struck the roof of the cab and rained down over the windshield. As he headed toward the main gate to his property, his first instinct was to crawl along the gravel road so as not to jar Ceara in the backseat. But then he remembered the afternoon Symphony had dropped her foal. At high speeds, his truck had sailed over the rough spots. Pedal to the floor mat.

Once he reached the asphalt two-lane road and turned toward town, Quincy called the ER, instructing the head nurse to prepare for Ceara's arrival and call Stevenson. When he'd done all he could, he focused on his driving, not caring when the speedometer bumped the hundred mark. He knew this road and could have taken the curves in his sleep. Unless an elk stepped out in front of the truck, Quincy would deliver Ceara safely to St. Matthew's ER in record time, faster than any damned ambulance would, anyway.

As he maneuvered the truck, Quincy could no longer hold the fear at bay. Twenty-five weeks. Could a baby survive when it came so early? He had no idea. Their little girl might die. Just the thought brought a burn to Quincy's eyes and a sharp ache to his chest. And, oh, God, what about Ceara? This had been brought on by her healing the deep cut on his wrist. He just knew it. Using her gifts, even for small things, made her woozy and sometimes weak at the knees. What kind of energy drain had it caused her and the baby to heal a bleeding, gaping wound?

He heard a muffled scream and jammed his foot harder against the pedal. Over the roar of the engine and the road noise he heard her sob, "Me babe. I've kilt her. How ye must hate me fer that."

Quincy's stomach lurched. "No! *No*, Ceara. Don't even think such a thing. I love you with all my heart, and I always will. This wasn't your fault, honey. It just happened, and you reacted. Knee-jerk response, we call it. You didn't have time to think. You just did what had to be done."

"And our wee girl is dying because I did. I've kilt her, Quincy. I know it."

"She's *not* going to die." He heard the rising note of hysteria in his own voice and somehow found the strength to clamp it down. "It's going to be okay! I promise you! Stevenson is the best OB in Crystal Falls. She'll be waiting for us. She'll know just what to do."

Ceara moaned as another pain struck. It seemed to Quincy that they were coming hard and fast. He hadn't thought to time them, damn it. How could he be such an idiot? He glanced at the dash clock. *Twelve twenty-two.* "Breathe, Ceara. Try not to tense up. Can you do that for me?"

He heard her trying to haul in a deep breath. Then she let out a keening wail. He wanted so badly to pull over and help her through this. But every second counted, and he didn't dare.

"Ach," she said faintly, " 'twas bad."

"Better now?"

"Yes, better. But it'll come again." She sighed shakily. "Quincy?"

"What, sweetheart?" Quincy braked, wrestled the truck around a tight turn, and floored it again.

"Yer words that ye say. 'I love you.' I ken that they mean much to ye. Tonight, right afore I bumped ye and ye cut yerself, ye looked sore disappointed because I dinna say them back."

Right then, the last thing Quincy cared about was hearing those words. Hell, if Ceara didn't have that depth of feeling for him, he loved her enough to make up for it. And he'd spend the rest of his life making her happy. *Please, God, let her live so I can do that, and please protect our baby. It'll break Ceara's heart if our little girl dies, and it'll break mine, too.*

" 'Tis na the way of it to home," she pushed out, her voice barely reaching him over the roar of the truck engine. "We say it with different words, ye ken."

Quincy thought of all the times he'd squirmed when she'd tried to tell him of her feelings for him, using her different words. *The sight of ye fills me heart with joy.* Or, *When ye enter a room, me heart warms.* She'd been describing her feelings all those times, now that he thought about it, and he'd been foolish enough to make light of that and want the pat phrase everyone in his time spouted: *I love you.* God help him, when he considered it, he knew that Ceara's way of expressing love was probably a lot more sincere. She never took the easy way out by saying three simple, overused words. Instead, she dug deep and tried to convey precisely how he made her feel. If there was a Ditz of the Year award, he deserved the crown, the unrivaled king of *dumb*. Suddenly the beam of his headlights blurred on the asphalt, and he could barely see the center line.

He felt rather than heard her tense up again. *Shit.* His gaze shot to the clock. Only four minutes had passed since the last pain.

"I . . . *love* . . . you!" she screamed at the peak of the agony. And then, on the downside wave, she repeated the words between pants. "I"—grunt, pant—"love"—pant, pant—"you."

Well, shit, now he couldn't see the frigging road for sure. He even felt his mouth jerk and spasm as he battled emotion to regain control. "No!" he yelled back. God, hearing her parrot the words half killed him. She never said *you.* She nearly always said *ye.* To her, it was like one of his crazy sayings. *Right as rain. Fine as a hair on a frog's back.* Nonsensical expressions to her that she'd picked up. She probably had no clue what they meant. She said them only in an attempt to fit into his world.

And now she was saying *I love you,* which clearly meant little in her time. Hell, Quincy bet that more than half his country's population said those words thought-lessly, and seventy-five percent of those probably didn't even mean them. He gulped, blinked to clear his vision, and said in a more normal voice, pitched just loud enough for her to hear, "Tell me your way, sweetheart. How I make your toes tingle. How I make your heart do a happy jig. How, when I walk into a room, you feel warm all the way through. My words—hell, they're kind of like fake crystal balls. When I say them, I mean them from the very bottom of my heart. Please, please believe that, but to you, they are just words. Right? And I'm sorry I've never dug deep, like you do, to tell you how much I love you in other ways."

Just then he saw cop lights flashing up ahead and real-ized the patrol car he'd requested was waiting beside the road. Sentiment had to be put on hold. He started flashing his headlights and pounding on his horn to alert the officer. "Thank Christ! There's our escort!" he called over his shoulder, flashing the lights again. To his immense relief, the state boy got the message. The police vehicle spun out on the graveled shoulder of the road, fishtailed when the tires caught hold on the asphalt, and then straightened in the lane. Quincy floored his accelerator to catch up and ride the trooper's back bumper. He clenched his teeth in frustration when his speedometer needle hovered around ninety. *Bastard.* That damned cop's wife wasn't in the backseat, having contractions every—

"Ach, God's *teeth*!"

Quincy glanced at the clock. Every *three* minutes. *Holy hell.* He'd never paid much attention to the hen chatter about Loni's labor pains, but for some reason ten minutes stuck in his brain. He saw city lights and sent up a disjointed prayer of thanks to his Maker. Was the baby coming now? Quincy didn't know. He'd delivered or helped deliver nearly a hundred foals, and he didn't frigging know *anything* about human birth. How did that equate?

The cop decreased speed to fifty in town, yet another frustration for Quincy. When, quicker than a blink, Ceara screamed again, Quincy said, "Son of a frigging *bitch*!" Then he shoved his foot down hard on the accelerator, swerved out into the oncoming lane to go past the police car, hit the flashers, pressed his hand to the horn, kept it there, and hit eighty, slowing to fifty only when he cut a sharp right onto the street that led to the hospital. At any other time, his mental calculator would have been going at warp speed, tallying the cost of the ticket he'd get, but moving violations be damned. He wouldn't let Ceara deliver on the backseat with her body cocooned in a thick comforter. Their little girl would never have a prayer of survival.

The cop turned on his siren and sped up to stay on Quincy's ass. "Well, asshole, if you think I'm pulling over, you've got another think coming," he said.

"Quincy!" Ceara cried shrilly. "Ach, Holy Mother, help me. I canna hold her back. She's coming!" With an elongated moan and then an equally dragged-out grunt, Ceara yelled, "'Tis done! Sweet Mother, help us. She's here, Quincy. I feel her between me legs."

Quincy darted his Ford into the ambulance lane, slammed on the brakes under the portico, shoved the damned rig into park, and literally spilled out of the truck, stumbling, scrambling at a foot-and-knee sprint around the front of the vehicle like a clumsy runner pushing off from the starting line, regaining his balance as he opened the rear door, and jerking the thick, smothering comforter off his wife. Sure as shit, she'd delivered on the bench seat. Only their bloody, mucus-smeared baby wasn't anywhere close to being as big as Quincy's hand, and she looked deader than a doornail, not moving, not crying, not *breathing*, for Christ's sake.

Black spots swam in front of him. Bursts of light went off, like dud fireworks in the gravel on the Fourth of July, little flashes and then a fizzle. Somebody shoved him out of the way, and he staggered, grabbing hold of his truck bed to keep from dropping to his knees. In a daze, he watched ER personnel grab the baby, slash the umbilical cord, and race back into the building, while two male attendants tied off the cord, and then shoved a thick plastic board inside the vehicle, one hopping inside, Quincy guessed to get the flat under Ceara. A moment later they pulled her out. He saw blood and other fluid all over her thighs and gown. The next thing he knew, his wife was being expertly transferred onto a waiting gurney and rushed back into the building.

Quincy staggered, forced some strength back into his noodlelike leg bones, and raced after his wife. Only problem was, he felt as if he were running against a headwind. Not going anywhere. Was there glue on the soles of his boots? The ER doors loomed in front of him, a barrier he had to get past. He turned a shoulder to push them open, but the damned things were automatic. He rammed into empty air and entered the ER in a baseball slide for home, his cheek rub-a-dubbing on the tile until he came to a stop.

Shit. Now lighted sparklers were swirling madly in his brain, as if held by little kids who were wagging them wildly in the air and turning in dizzying circles to make trails of brightness in the dark. Quincy well remembered doing that, dancing around Sam, who still needed their dad to hold her hand and help twirl the stick.

"Mr. Harrigan?"

Quincy felt a feminine hand grasp his shoulder. He blinked, trying to see.

"Mr. Harrigan, are you injured? Are you all right?"

Hell, *no*, he wasn't all right. His baby girl had just been stillborn, and his wife might be dying.

Chapter Seventeen

Quincy staggered woozily to his feet. One side of his head hurt like a son of a bitch, and bright spots still danced before his eyes. Placing his feet wide apart, he shook like a dog shedding water in an attempt to regain his senses. He didn't know if he'd struck his temple and, bottom line, he didn't give a shit. He'd live through it. He couldn't say the same for Ceara.

He strode in a zigzagging line to a little admittance window to the right and leaned over the shoulder of an old, frail gentleman who was yelling, "I don't want medicine this time, damn you. I just want my fucking shoulder fixed! And I wanna see a *real* doctor, not some goddamned nurse practitioner!"

Dimly, Quincy registered the gist of what the oldster was saying and could have told him nurse practitioners were every bit as good as doctors in most instances, but he didn't have time to dole out advice. He focused on the plump lady inside the cubicle, a blonde dressed in a smock the color of merlot.

"Where'd they take my wife? My name's Quincy Harrigan, and I need to find her!"

The woman's green eyes snapped with irritation. "Sir, you are standing in the *privacy* zone. Please walk over to that little window at the other side of the hall, give them your information, and wait your turn to be called."

"Yeah," the old man shouted, crimping his wrinkled neck to glare up at Quincy. "I been here for hours, asshole. You can't just barge in and expect instant service."

Brains still joggled, Quincy blinked again, trying his damnedest to collect his thoughts and speak sanely. "Sorry, sir, but my baby girl just came in stillborn, and they've taken my wife somewhere. I need to find her, you know? She might be dying, too."

The old man—whom Quincy judged, even in a dazed state, to be a few fries short of a full order—stared up at Quincy for a long moment. He wore only his uppers, and his bottom lip sucked in over his toothless lower gums. He had faded blue eyes, a face with crisscrossing lines deep enough to pass for tire ruts at a monster-truck mud-slinging contest, and a huge sore on the side of his nose that was probably a stage-four melanoma.

"Your baby girl is dead?"

The question ran a knife straight through Quincy's heart. His throat convulsed. His already unclear vision blurred even more with tears. "Yep, pretty sure. My wife delivered premature on the backseat of my truck. I"—Quincy gulped—"couldn't get them here quick enough."

The old guy rounded on the admittance secretary. "Jesus help us all. You people run us through this joint like we're steers going to slaughter!"

"Now, Randall, let's not get excited," the woman said. "You need to stay here this time so we can help you."

"Yeah, right. Send me home with pain pills that make me so dizzy I fall again!" Randall brought his liver-spotted fist down on the admittance counter. "Did you hear what the man just *said*? What's *wrong* with you, telling him to step back out of the privacy zone? You can take that stupid tape line on the carpet and shove it where it'll never again see daylight."

Frantic as he was, Quincy noted that the woman's attitude suggested she'd heard all of this before, often. Her tone was patient, much like a kindergarten teacher's. "Randy."

"Don't you *Randy* me! I'm not a four-year-old. Find out where this poor sap's wife is, and do it right now, or I'm calling the cops."

Quincy had a bad feeling that wouldn't be necessary. He'd blown that state trooper's doors off, and he guessed he'd soon be facing charges of some kind.

"Please, ma'am," he said to the woman, relieved that his head was starting to clear. "I'm not here to get admitted. My wife is here somewhere. My name is Quincy Harrigan. All I want is to find her."

The woman passed a hand over her frizzy blond hair. "It's gotta be a full moon. Never gets this crazy otherwise." She punched a phone button—Quincy guessed it connected her to the ER over the headset she wore—and hummed the tune of the Beatles' famous hit "Yesterday," tapping her fingers on the desk as she waited to connect. Quincy wished with all his heart that it *were* yesterday so he could relive every moment up to the present with the knowledge he had now. "Yeah, I got a guy out here named Quincy Harrigan whose wife was just brought in. Says his baby girl was DOA, stillbirth." She listened a moment, then nodded. Glancing up at Quincy, she said, "Someone will be right out. Now will you *please* step behind the privacy line?"

Quincy put his boots into reverse, mission accomplished. Randall nodded and grinned at him. Then he doubled a fist and jabbed at the air. "You've got my prayers, boy. I'm real sorry about your baby girl, but if your wife is okay, you'll have others." His faded eyes went bright with tears. "Me and Gladys lost one. Just about killed us at the time, but in the end, we had eight. All healthy as goats in a rich man's garden and clamoring for more food. Three boys, five girls."

Quincy wondered where the hell all those kids were now. A burst of anger shot through him. "Randall, what's your last name? I wanna look you up after this all settles and take you out for a whiskey."

"Whitmeyer! And damned proud of it."

The old man turned back to continue his argumentative and loud exchange with the plump blonde with frizzy hair. Quincy dipped his chin and stared at the white tape on the carpet right in front of the toes of his boots. *Privacy line.* He kind of got Randall Whitmeyer's rage, because right then, nothing would have felt better to Quincy than shoving his fist through a wall.

Just then a tall blond guy emerged from the bowels of the ER treatment facility and walked toward Quincy. "Mr. Harrigan? If you'll follow me, you can be with your wife. Dr. Stevenson is here. She's with your baby. Mrs. Harrigan is receiving treatment right now, and she'll be moved to the maternity ward soon."

Quincy's heart did a squeeze, as if a huge fist had closed over an orange to drain it of juice. "Stevenson is with our baby?" He was afraid to believe their little girl was still alive. "Why? I mean, she looked dead, so *why*?"

"Your baby isn't dead. She's just . . ." The orderly took a deep breath and lifted his bony shoulders, making his blue scrub top shift over his torso. "It's not really my place to give you details about her condition, sir. But I can say she is alive."

Quincy put a hand against the wall. "Sorry, I need a second."

"Hey, man, I get it. You drove them in. Must have been one hell of a ride." The fellow clapped Quincy on the back. "But, hey, you did good. You got both of them here in the nick of time."

Quincy straightened and trailed behind the fellow to the ER doors, which opened only by a punch code. Then he was following the orderly—or was he a nurse?—down corridors with curtained cubicles, all of which branched off from the ER main desk, where doctors, nurses, and assistants bustled, checking charts, talking on phones, and rushing away. Randall had it all wrong, Quincy thought. These people here were doing the best job they could. He just prayed they had magic in their fingertips to save his wife and baby.

Ceara was in cubicle forty-six, and when Quincy pushed through the curtain, he found his wife lying on a bed with nurses working over her, hooking her up to an IV, putting sticky disks at strategic points on her torso to monitor her heart, and fastening an automatic blood pressure cuff around her arm. Ceara lay flat, her face nearly as pale as the white sheets. He saw that her eyes were squeezed closed and tears trailed from their corners into her wildly curly red hair.

One nurse, a thin brunette, glanced up. "Mr. Harrigan?"

Quincy nodded.

"We're moving your wife upstairs to the maternity ward in just a moment. Dr. Stevenson wants to oversee her care up there. You can take a seat just outside and follow us if you like."

"I'd like." A whole team of draft horses couldn't have kept Quincy away from his sweet Irish rose.

"Quincy?" Ceara's eyes flew open at the sound of his voice. When she saw him at the foot of the bed, she tried to reach for him, but the nurse trying to anchor an IV stent to her arm grabbed her wrist and held it down. "Our baby. She is dead, and 'tis all me fault!"

"She isn't dead. She's a fighter, just like her mother," Quincy said quickly. "Dr. Stevenson is with her right now."

Ceara's haunted gaze clung to his. "Truly? Ye wouldna lie?"

"Of course I wouldn't," Quincy assured her, "and what happened isn't your fault, sweetheart. Don't be thinking that way."

A nurse on the left, also a brunette but chunky of build, said, "You see? I told you the baby isn't dead. Dr. Stevenson is upstairs doing everything she can to save her. She's a great doctor, so your little girl is in the best of hands."

" 'Tis me fault," Ceara said again. "I used me healing power. I should ne'er ha done that."

A petite blonde kicked off the bed brakes, and nurses on both sides of the bed jerked up the rails and locked them into position. Quincy backed out of the cubicle, frightened by the attendants' urgency in getting Ceara moved. He stood helplessly out of the way as his wife was wheeled from the cubicle, one nurse pushing, two others keeping pace with the IV tripod and the monitor.

The little blonde, who carried only a chart and a tray of blood samples, gestured to Quincy. "You can go up with us in the elevator. It might be a squeeze, but we can all fit."

"Thanks." Quincy hurried to get abreast of her. "How is my wife?"

Speaking softly so as not to be overheard, the nurse said, "Well, her vital signs are jumping all over the chart right now, but that's probably due as much to her emotional state as it is to the physical trauma. Either way, Dr. Stevenson wants her moved upstairs for more specialized care." She flashed Quincy a reassuring smile. "It's very upsetting to a woman when she delivers prematurely, and your wife is understandably frantic with worry about the baby." She winked conspiratorially. "She's said some pretty weird things. The doctor will most likely give her a sedative to calm her down. That's about all I've got for you. Sorry. Dr. Stevenson has ordered several blood workups." She nodded toward the tray filled with vials. "And once we're upstairs, the PA will do a full exam and perform any after-delivery procedures necessary, and Dr. Stevenson will update you as soon as she has a moment to talk."

"Do you have any information on our daughter?"

The blonde shook her head. "Sorry. They whisked her straight upstairs to the NICU."

"What's that?"

"Natal intensive-care unit. It's where they take preemies or any babies in need of special care. Sometimes our preemies don't require it immediately, and they go in later, when problems start to crop up. But your little gal—well, she's a twenty-five-weeker, and some of her vital organs may not be quite ready to rock and roll without some help."

Quincy missed a step. His stomach burned as if he'd just swallowed ground glass. "I know you don't have any solid facts, but you must know, general rule of thumb, what her chances are."

The blonde jutted her chin at the elevator. "Hurry. Don't want to miss our ride."

Quincy allowed the nurse to squeeze into the car first. He found himself standing to the left of Ceara's bed, toward the foot. The only comforting gesture he could offer his wife as the doors closed and the elevator slipped into gear was to gently squeeze her toes. Ceara's swimming blue eyes sought out his face; then her gaze clung to his.

"It's going to be okay," Quincy said, injecting confidence into his voice that he was far from feeling. "You'll see, honey. They have a special place up there for babies who come early, with all kinds of fabulous equipment and medicines. It's called NICU, which stands for natal intensive-care unit."

The petite blonde grinned at Ceara. "And, hey, private rooms for each baby, and specially trained nurses assigned to them. As hospital care goes, it's the Ritz."

"What is the Ritz?" Ceara asked tremulously.

The nurse laughed. "You've never heard of the *Ritz*?"

Quincy squeezed Ceara's foot again. "In truth, there isn't only one Ritz-Carlton." To Ceara, he added, "They're luxury hotels. Someday soon we'll stay in one."

The elevator stopped, Quincy exited first to get out of the way, and before he could even think about getting close to his wife to reassure her further, hospital staff in green scrubs moved in, taking Ceara up the hall and through two big swinging doors.

Ever since learning that Ceara was pregnant, Quincy had pictured himself being a totally hands-on dad during the last months, attending Lamaze classes, being with Ceara as her coach during delivery, and then staying with her in the birthing suite with their baby by her bed and his family coming in to visit. He'd been envisioning his child's arrival much like it had been when Aliza was born, he guessed. The hospital had fabulous quarters for new mothers, with pullout beds for fathers, lots of comfortable furniture for visitors, and a family-friendly atmosphere.

Instead Quincy went to a small nurses' station and was directed to a waiting room. He sat on a bench-back sofa that was about as inviting as cement, braced his forearms on his spread knees, and stared blankly at the mottled floor. He consoled himself with the thought that Ceara was receiving the best of care. That meant she'd be okay, right? Someone would surely come out soon to update him on her condition.

The minutes ticked by, and no one came to tell him anything. Not knowing . . . well, to him that was almost worse than hearing bad news. At least then he'd be able to face it—and somehow deal with it. He thought about contacting his family, but decided against it. Might as well wait until dawn. There was nothing they could do.

"Mr. Harrigan?"

At the sound of a female voice, Quincy jumped so violently that he nearly parted company with his boots. Dr. Stevenson walked into the room, her expression solemn, her blue eyes rimmed with red, probably from lack of sleep. Quincy shot to his feet.

"My wife—how's she doing?"

"Holding her own, but she's very weak. We're keeping a close eye on her."

"And our little girl—did she . . . Is she still alive?"

She patted his arm. "Let's sit, shall we?"

Quincy didn't want to sit, damn it. He wanted to hear about his baby and then more about his wife, and he took bad news better on his feet. But he obediently sat again. Stevenson rubbed her slender hands together.

"Your baby is hanging on—for now."

"For now?"

The doctor nodded. "At twenty-five weeks, she's very premature, Mr. Harrigan, so she's extremely tiny. She weighs only one-point-four pounds, which is only slightly below the average weight for a fetus at that stage, not at all abnormal if she were still in the mother's womb, but that's very low for a birth weight."

Quincy had seen his daughter and already knew how tiny she was. "Give it to me straight, Doc. Don't beat around the bush."

She sighed. "All right. For starters, she has retinopathy, which is believed to be caused by disorganized growth of the retinal blood vessels. In her case, I suspect it's mild and may resolve itself, but her low birth weight may cause complications."

"You mean she'll be blind."

Stevenson inclined her head. "Possibly. She also has respiratory distress syndrome, the most common single cause of death in preemies. I'm treating her little lungs with a medication called a surfactant, a substance normally present, but absent in her case. She also has pulmonary hypoplasia, which essentially means her lungs haven't properly developed yet. She's incubated and also intubated to assist her in breathing, but when you go in to see her, Mr. Harrigan, you will notice retractions of her chest wall, grunting when she tries to exhale, and cyanosis, which is a blue or purple tint to the mucous membranes and sometimes to the extremities, especially fingers and toes. The nail beds often turn bright blue or purple."

Quincy felt as if a steel clamp had closed around his chest. "So, in short, she's dying."

Stevenson stared at her palms. When she met Quincy's gaze again, her eyes had a haunted look. "She may make it, but it would be cruel of me to offer you too much hope. Her chances of survival are very slim, and if she does live, she may have both physical and mental abnormalities. There's little point in my listing all those possibilities for you now. I think I've hit you with enough for the moment."

Quincy nodded.

"If she makes it through these first twenty-four hours, we'll have a longer talk then. All right?" Stevenson smiled faintly. "For now, I can assure you that everything that can possibly be done to save her is being done. She has been assigned her own nurse, so she'll be closely monitored in case she grows worse. If that happens, you'll be told immediately."

Quincy felt himself nod again. His throat had closed off, and he didn't think he could speak.

Stevenson stood up. "Because she's at such a precarious stage, I'll be remaining here in the hospital, hopefully able to sleep a little in a room not far from hers. The nurse will wake me immediately if I'm needed."

She started for the hallway.

"Wait!" Quincy said. "Before you take off, can you tell me anything more about my wife?"

The doctor turned back. "As I said earlier, Ceara is very weak, but for the moment, she's stable. Preliminary examination revealed no internal damage, so she should be able to have other children." Leaning a shoulder against the doorjamb, she searched Quincy's gaze. "What happened, Mr. Harrigan? When I examined Ceara and the baby a little over a week ago, the pregnancy was progressing normally. I saw nothing in the ultrasound to alarm me. Do you know what brought this on?"

Quincy had to swallow hard twice to use his voice. "I do know, but it's a story you would never believe, so there's not much point in telling you."

Dr. Stevenson arched an eyebrow. "Try me."

Quincy was too damned exhausted and mentally drained to think up a good lie, so he blurted out the truth. Stevenson returned to the sofa and sank onto one of the hard cushions as if her legs would no longer hold her up.

"Oh, my God." Quincy expected her to call him a bald-faced liar. Instead, a thoughtful frown pleated her forehead. "That's the most incredible story I've ever heard, but now that you've told me, so many things make more sense."

"You believe me?" Quincy blinked owlishly at her. Maybe he was still halfway out of it, but he'd expected her to summon the guys who wrestled people into straitjackets.

She rubbed her hands over her face and blinked. "I'm not sure, but . . . well, I've come to know Ceara during exams, and"—she fluttered a hand—"now all the little strange things she said and did . . . Oh, my *God.*" She laughed, but there was no real humor in the sound. "A druid from the sixteenth century. I feel like I've wandered into the middle of a time-travel book."

"It's not fiction," Quincy replied. "Believe me or don't, that's your choice, but in a way, maybe it's good I told you. Ceara's weak because she expended so much energy to heal the deep cut on my wrist. I wish now that I'd brought her straight here, but after she came around, she swore she felt fine. She ate well when I brought her dinner. She mostly just seemed tired, so I thought she'd feel better after a good night's sleep." Quincy's voice went thick. "The energy drain did something—made the baby come early. If I'd brought Ceara in, you may have been able to prevent the premature labor."

Stevenson clasped Quincy's arm. "Maybe, maybe not. Right now, even knowing what you just told me about Ceara, I can't think of what I can do to restore her strength. She needs no blood. Her vitals are normal. There's nothing I can put my finger on that might be causing her weakness. And babies are born prematurely every day, Mr. Harrigan. Most mothers rush straight in when they begin to feel contractions, and sometimes doctors can do something, but just as often they can't." Her fingers tightened on his sleeve. "You made decisions that almost anyone would have made. In your shoes, I think I would have made the same call."

"Really? Don't bullshit me, Doc, just to make me feel better."

"Really," Stevenson said firmly. "I would have encouraged her to rest." Her gaze held Quincy's. "The problem tonight wasn't caused by bad decisions, Mr. Harrigan. If what you've told me is true, we're dealing with—what?—something paranormal, supernatural? Definitely way out of normal range." Her eyes grew distant with thought for a second. "Healing powers. You cut your wrist so badly it severed a main artery. Along the wrist arteries lie tendons and nerves that control the movements of the hands and fingers. Yet your cut is healed, and your hand is working perfectly fine. It's incredible."

Quincy flexed his fingers. "You saying that deep slash could have crippled my hand?"

"A surgeon may have been able to fix it," she replied, "but severed nerves can be buggers. Sometimes they can be reattached and will heal over time, but just as often, the nerves never really mend. Chances are good that you wouldn't ever have had full use of your hand again. Sometimes the fingers won't work just right. Other times the fingers are fine, but the side-to-side movement of the hand at the wrist is gone."

"Damn." Quincy stared down at his upturned palm. He wished with all his heart that he were in surgery right now, even if it meant having impaired use of the damned thing for the rest of his life. "I don't feel real good about the fact that my baby is dying because of me."

Stevenson pushed to her feet again. "I'd like to discuss this further, but if I'm going to be any use at all to your daughter, I need to grab a few winks."

Quincy forced a smile. "I hear ya, Doc. The more rested you are, the better for her."

Stevenson once again paused at the doorway and turned. "You've shared an amazing story with me, Mr. Harrigan, and I know that when you did, you didn't expect me to believe a word of it."

"And yet I have the feeling you went for it."

She lifted her thin shoulders in a shrug. "I'm a doctor. When I first started practicing I was an agnostic. I believed there *might* be a greater power, but I didn't believe in God, or in the power of prayer, or in miracles."

"And now?"

"I've seen prayers turn things around when I knew, as a physician, that a baby didn't have a chance in hell. I've seen preemies whom I knew beyond any shadow of doubt were brain-damaged grow into normal, healthy, active, *bright* children. In short, I've seen miracles happen. I mean *real* miracles." Her mouth curved in a slight smile. "But it isn't always about miracles. Sometimes it's only about failures and still finding a reason to go on. There's an e-mail that circulates now and again about a cardiac surgeon about to operate on a young boy's heart, and the boy repeatedly tells the doctor that when he cuts into his heart, he'll find Jesus there."

Quincy had seen that e-mail. "And after the surgery, the surgeon knows the boy is going to die, but when he's asked what he found when he opened the heart, he says, 'I found Jesus.'"

Her bloodshot eyes went bright with tears. "Some doctors have deep faith as they begin to practice and then lose it. I had none when I started out, but somewhere along the way, I found it. Not because I never lose

my babies, because sometimes I do, and not because I've
seen what appeared to be miracles, although that's certainly part of it. It's more about the amazing perfection
of a newborn—how complicated their little bodies are,
how one system depends upon another system, everything so intricately designed that high-tech computers
begin to look like child's play. I couldn't continue in my
profession without starting to believe that there's someone up there a whole lot smarter than I am. Once you
take that leap, you're a goner, because faith in someone
all-knowing is right around the corner."

Quincy nodded. "I hear ya. Thanks, Doc. And while
you get some rest, I've got some praying to do, myself."

"I'll pray for your baby as I drift off for a catnap." She
gave him a thumbs-up. "Let's not give up on her just
yet."

"Have you told Ceara about our baby's condition?"

Stevenson shook her head. "I've only said the baby is
in NICU and putting up a good fight, and, of course, that
we're doing all we can. I don't think Ceara is strong
enough just yet to deal with anything more."

"Can I see our baby?"

Stevenson jabbed her thumb toward the ceiling again.
"Just go to the nurses' station. They'll help you. It'll be
scary when you see her. Be prepared for that."

Quincy was allowed five minutes with Ceara. She was
tearful and guilt-ridden, insisting that their baby's plight
was all her fault. Quincy hoped he said all the right words.
Being careful of the gadgets attached to her, he bent over
the bed to hold her gently in his arms. She sobbed. He
fought to be calm and strong for her. And he sent up
prayers that God would help both of them get through
what was to come. Dr. Stevenson hadn't come right out

and said their baby would die, but Quincy knew their little girl was on a slick, downward slope and her chances were almost zilch.

When he went to the nurses' station to ask about seeing his daughter, he encountered a tall, hefty, broad-shouldered nurse he immediately thought of as Sarge, though her nameplate read NANCY. She was a no-nonsense, stingy-with-smiles woman who handed him over to another gal who was equally solemn and authoritative. She led him into a room where he was ordered to scrub his hands and arms to the elbow with disinfectant soap. Then he had to don sterile scrubs over his street clothes and pull disposable blue slippers over his boots. After all that, he still had to pump disinfectant into his cupped palms outside the NICU room before he went in to see his baby girl.

A big heavyset nurse in pink scrub pants and a loose top patterned with bright balloons blocked his view of the incubator. She was such a massive woman that, bent over the unit, she covered it like a thick canopy of clouds. When she sensed Quincy's presence, she turned and smiled. Quincy instantly liked her. She had kind eyes and a sincere smile.

"You must be Papa."

Quincy nodded.

She beckoned him over. "Don't panic. It's always hard for parents to see their baby with all the tubes and IVs and life support. Just remember that all of it is needed to help her win this battle."

She inched aside, and Quincy got his second look at his daughter. His knees almost gave out, and for an awful second he feared he might faint. She was even tinier than he'd thought, the span of her shoulders and chest about a third the breadth of his palm. She was perfectly formed, but so small she couldn't be real.

The nurse explained what this tube and that tube did, but Quincy barely registered the words. *My baby girl*. Seeing her so tiny and helpless, battling with her whole body to survive, was one of his most horrible moments. The nurse clapped a strong hand on his shoulder, gave it a hard squeeze.

"I'll give you ten minutes alone with her. Then it'll be time for me to check on her again." She pointed to an opening in the side of the incubator dome. "It's highly recommended that parents reach in and touch their babies, Mr. Harrigan. Just open the cover if you wish to do so. The human contact, especially contact with Mama or Daddy, is so very important. Your little girl needs to feel your love. And hearing your voice is important, too." She smiled broadly. "She's been hearing it all along while inside her mama's womb. You are a familiar person in her little world. She'll know it's you, and that will comfort her."

Quincy could barely see through a blur of tears. He didn't try to hide them. His dad said any man who was afraid to cry sometimes wasn't a real man.

The nurse pushed a nice recliner closer to the incubator. Quincy sat on the chair, no longer able to feel his legs, his gaze stuck on his impossibly tiny baby girl inside the incubator. Would she ever be strong enough for him to hold her against his chest? *Oh, God.* For that opportunity, he would gladly sacrifice his arm.

She wasn't going to make it. He knew it, felt it in his bones. Modern medicine was a fabulous thing, but it had its limits, and his little girl needed much more than what it offered.

She needed a miracle, and Dr. Stevenson didn't have one to pull out of her pocket.

Chapter Eighteen

Because Ceara was still far too weak to come see their baby, Quincy started to take pictures of their daughter with his cell phone, but before he flashed the device, his arm fell limply to his side. He sighed and stuck the phone back in its case. Snapshots of this would scare Ceara half to death. Tubes and wires seemed to cover their baby girl's body. Quincy knew all the probes and needles and machines that blinked were necessary to save her life, but they would be foreign to Ceara. Hell, they were foreign to him, too.

He stood two feet from the incubator, staring at his daughter until his eyes grew dry and sticky. No bullshitting himself: He was afraid to reach through that hole and touch her. He'd feel the warmth of her bluish skin, the beat of her heart, the softness of her wispy black hair, and then she'd be real. *Safer here, two feet away*. If he didn't touch her—if he just left without letting her seem real—he'd be able to handle it better when she died. *Walk away. Go to Ceara. Make her your main focus. She's going to need you to be strong for her before this is over*.

Quincy almost got his feet unstuck from the floor to leave the room, but just then the baby—*his* baby—grunted to discharge a breath, grunted again, and tensed, pushing frantically with her incredibly thin arms and legs. Quincy knew instantly that she was in trouble, and before he could formulate another thought, he'd jerked open the door and thrust his hand through the incubator hole. Lightly, he curled his fingers over her narrow chest, felt the furious chug of her little heart and the spasm of her underdeveloped lungs. *Love.* It didn't always come softly and sneak into a man's heart. Sometimes it went off inside of him with no warning, like a sunburst.

"Hey, hey, hey," he whispered, carefully massaging her chest with his fingertips. "It's okay, little one. Daddy's here. I'm here. You remember me?"

Her body jerked, and then her lungs turned loose of the captured breath. Her chest retracted and then expanded again. Quincy could no more have withdrawn his hand than he could have made his own heart stop beating. He sank onto the recliner, keeping his fingers on her chest. After a moment, he gathered the courage to let his palm lower. Skin against skin. His daughter relaxed under his touch, expelling this time without any visible difficulty. She seemed comforted by his touch, reassured. Quincy thought of all the times he'd held his hand over her mama's tummy, feeling the baby's feet kick and elbows thump. The nurse had it right: This tiny little person knew the sound of her daddy's voice and his touch.

"Seeing you fills my heart with joy," he told her. "I feel it all the way into my bones. You're so gorgeous, Daddy's precious little girl."

In that moment, Quincy completely and irrevocably lost his heart to this child. He hadn't believed himself capable of loving anyone more than he had come to love Ceara, but this was a totally different kind of love. No getting-to-know-you period required. It had hit him between one breath and the next, and in a blink of time, Quincy knew he would lay down his life for this child.

Beautiful, so beautiful. Her hair was sparse, and it was every bit as dark as his, but even in the dim light it gleamed with red as well. She was a miraculous blend of Quincy and Ceara.

Then it struck Quincy that it might not matter. His baby girl struggled to breathe. Beneath his palm he could feel her fighting for life, and he knew it was a battle she might not win.

His shoulders jerked with sobs. He yearned to grab his daughter from the incubator and hold her close against him to infuse her with his strength. Only he couldn't share this struggle with her. She had to fight this battle alone.

How can this happen, God? Please let me die in her place. As he prayed, Quincy remembered a country song, the recurring refrain being "Please don't take the girl." Before Ceara's appearance in his world, Quincy had never really felt the meaning of that song. He did now, and he knew, finally, how his father must have felt when Quincy's mother died giving birth to Sam: devastated by one loss yet feeling blessed by the arrival of a daughter. Quincy didn't know how his father had lived through it and kept putting one boot in front of the other to care for five kids.

When the nurse returned, Quincy didn't worry about his face being red and swollen from crying. If ever he'd had a good reason to blubber, this was it, and he wasn't ashamed of the emotions that threatened to take him to his knees. This was *his* baby girl, a miraculous creation that he and Ceara had made together. And now, before she ever got to experience life, she was going to die. Quincy couldn't remember all the things wrong with his baby. He just knew the name of each condition was a lot bigger than she was, and her chances of survival were almost nonexistent.

"I think my being here soothes her," he told the nurse.

She nodded. "She knows who you are. From her first moment of consciousness, she has heard your voice." The nurse sent Quincy a kindly smile. "I need a few minutes with her. You can come back in ten and spend more time with her. It may make all the difference."

Quincy stepped away, but then he couldn't make his feet move. He stared long and hard at his girl. Then he lowered his gaze to his healed wrist. Oh, how he wished Ceara had resisted the urge to reach out and grab his arm. If only she'd just let him bleed out, then their daughter wouldn't have been born too soon. She would have remained snug and safe in her mother's womb. Quincy would have gladly traded his life for this child's. No hesitation, no thinking about it: He would step in front of a bullet for her.

Quincy expected to find Ceara sleeping when he returned to her room. Instead, she was wide awake, her eyes dark with panic. When he came up beside her bed, she grabbed hold of his hand, her gaze fixed on his.

"I heard them talking in the hall. About our baby. 'Tis dying she is, and they say there is no hope."

Quincy wanted to race back out into the hall and ask those stupid nurses where their brains were at, because they definitely weren't between their ears. No mother should hear that kind of news from the whispers of strangers. He met Ceara's gaze and knew he couldn't paint this pretty for her. She deserved honesty from him, and though it half killed him to give her that, he had to man up.

"It's not good, sweetheart. She came way too early, and she didn't have enough time to grow big enough. Her lungs aren't developed. She's having a hard time breathing. That puts a lot of stress on her little heart. Her chances aren't good."

"Ye must help me, Quincy. I must go to her."

Quincy shook his head. "There'll be time enough for that tomorrow. Right now, you need to rest and regain your strength."

"I canna lie here!" she cried. "Do ye na ken that I can heal her?"

Quincy's heart jerked. "No way. Ceara, think of what healing me did to you. No way, not when you're already so weak. Sweetheart, *think*. It could kill you."

She sat up in bed, and before Quincy could react to stop her, she jerked the IV from just below the bend of her elbow. After tossing it aside, she pulled off the O_2 finger stall, ripped off the blood pressure cuff, and then shoved an arm inside her gown to pull away the disks that electronically monitored her heart.

"Jesus," he whispered, "what the *hell* are you doing?"

The heart monitor went off, clamoring urgently. Quincy heard the squeak of rubber-soled shoes in the hallway, the chirps growing louder as staff raced toward the room.

"'Tis going to me baby I am." Ceara swung her legs over the edge of the bed and sat completely straight. Never had she looked more beautiful to Quincy than she did in that instant. It was one of those cameo moments—Quincy had heard his dad speak of them about his mother—a snapshot of time that engraved itself on a man's heart, something he'd never forget and would never want to forget. "Me life be *damned*!" she cried. "If 'tis the price God asks me to pay, I will pay it. Do ye understand?"

Only moments ago, Quincy had touched his daughter

and thought how much he wished he could trade places with her, giving his life to save hers. He knew—deep down where reason held no sway—that Ceara did have enough power still left within her to heal their baby girl. Only problem was, in the doing, Ceara could very well kill herself. He remembered Stevenson saying she didn't know how to help Ceara, that there were no medical indicators to tell her what was needed. If Ceara healed their baby, she'd drain herself dry, like a power cell bled to death by too many current taps.

Everything within Quincy rebelled at the thought. He couldn't let his wife offer her life in exchange for their daughter's. He just *couldn't*. His instincts compelled him to protect Ceara *and* his baby, but he was powerless to help either of them.

Hold on. Back up. In the NICU, he'd been feeling just as Ceara was now, ready to happily die to save their child. Throw himself under a bus. Put a gun to his head and pull the trigger. But, *damn*, God didn't do bargains. If Quincy did put a gun to his head, his precious baby girl, who'd recognized his voice and had relaxed and been able to breathe when he touched her, would still die. Quincy had nothing within him to save her.

But Ceara did.

Acutely aware of the footsteps coming toward them, which became louder with his every breath, Quincy looked Ceara dead in the eye and said again, "If you heal our daughter, it may kill you."

Ceara, her eyes bright with defiant tears, said, "Then let me be in heaven three minutes before the devil knows I am dead."

Quincy wanted to tell the nurses who flooded into the room to give his wife a shot and knock her out. He could say she was still in shock, hysterical, out of control. In short, if he lied through his teeth, he could save Ceara's life. But he saw in her eyes how love for their baby burned within her. He'd felt it—*still* felt it: that inexplicable kind of love that exploded inside of you. And in that NICU room, he'd wished and prayed he could die in his daughter's place.

Was he a male chauvinist who would do it himself, but never allow his wife to do the same? Visions flashed through his head of himself standing over Ceara's open coffin. A wave of imagined grief nearly knocked him off his feet. But then the pictures changed, and he saw Ceara standing by his coffin, Ceara left behind to live with the pain of losing him.

Who was the bravest: the one who sacrificed his life, or the one who stayed behind to do the mourning? And taking it a step further, who was the strongest? For the first time in his life, Quincy questioned things he'd never questioned. Behind him, he sensed recruits moving in to overpower his crazed wife. All he had to do was turn and ask them to help. Coward that he was, he almost did exactly that.

Ceara grabbed his forearm, her nails digging into his skin. "They are here." Her voice twanged like a loose guitar string. "Will ye fight fer me, Quincy, or will ye fight against me? 'Tis our baby girl's life at stake. I have it within me to save her. Will ye deny me that? *Will* ye?"

And when she asked Quincy that question, he took his stand. Never replying to her question, he scooped his wife up into his arms and turned to face a half dozen hospital attendants, good people, trained and hired to do a job, and he was about to ruin their whole day—maybe their whole year. They instantly screeched to a halt and formed a front line. Four were men—tall, but not muscular—and three were women, two of them plump, one toothpick thin. Quincy measured his opponents. He could almost hear his dad's voice: *Shee-ut, son, this'll be like stompin' grapes.* It hit Quincy then that despite the late hour—well into the wee hours of morning—he should have called his dad. If he had, instead of thinking he should wait until dawn to wake everyone, the whole Harrigan clan would be with him now. He wouldn't be standing alone; that was for sure.

"My wife needs to see our baby," he said, trying to inject calmness into his voice. "Please don't get in my way. You can bring all this equipment to her in the NICU, get her back on the IV and monitors. But you have to understand that she *needs* to see our baby, and she needs to see her *now*."

Choice made. At the back of his mind, Quincy knew he'd just signed the death warrant of his precious Irish rose. He didn't remember when he'd come to think of her as that. Maybe it was because her hair was such a deep, dark red. Maybe it was because of the rose water she so often wore—or because she was so delicate and beautiful, like the fragile blossoms of that flower, reminding him of the song *My Wild Irish Rose*. Quincy only knew that he loved her as he'd never loved anybody. Well, correction. There was another little Irish rose just down the hall, so tiny and delicate she didn't seem real, but Quincy loved her enough to give her a place in his heart as big as a mountain.

He loved her enough, in fact, to let the woman in his arms try to heal her and in the process possibly die. Quincy was brand-new to this dad stuff, but it didn't take much thinking to figure out that once a kid popped into your life, both parents went all or nothing. Quincy would have liked to be the one making the sacrifice, but he wasn't being given that choice. He and Ceara were a team, the game was about to end, and one of them had to throw a Hail Mary pass. Quincy didn't have a prayer of doing that, but Ceara did.

The biggest guy, tall, gangly, and rawboned, spread his feet. "We can't let this happen, Mr. Harrigan. Your wife needs to be put back in the bed. When she's stronger, she can go see the baby."

Quincy took the man's measure. He was no long-stemmed tulip to be taken out with one hard bump, and Quincy held precious cargo. "Look, I just need to take my wife down the hall to see our daughter. Then I'll bring her back and you can hook her back up to everything."

"Not happening," the tall nontulip replied. "Against all procedure. You can't just rip everything off a woman in her condition and go waltzing down the hall. She's had heart irregularities, man. *Think*."

Quincy hadn't been told that Ceara's heart had been acting up. For just a second, he questioned his own sanity, but then he felt her press her face to the side of his neck, trusting in him. And suddenly it all came clear to Quincy. It wasn't only men who were allowed to be heroes. He wouldn't deny Ceara the same privilege that he would have taken for granted himself. He'd move through that front line, holding her in his arms, and he'd take those four men out. Quincy wasn't a tall man and was of lean build, but hard work had turned his muscles to steel, he was quick and agile enough to turn on a dime, and not one of the gents standing against him was as challenging as a thirteen-hundred-pound stallion in a rampage.

Quincy guessed the nontulip fellow to be in his middle twenties. "Son," he said, "you'd best step aside. If you get in my way and make me drop my wife, I'll kick your ass nine ways to Sunday."

"*What* is going on in here?"

Quincy cut his gaze past the front line to the doorway of the room. Dr. Stevenson stood in the opening, her usually tidy braid mussed with tendrils of hair frizzing out around her head, her eyes droopy, the whites red, but the pointedness of her gaze signaled full cognizance. Quincy locked on, and the physician didn't look away.

"My wife needs to see our baby. She believes that she can heal her. These folks are trying to stop me from taking her to NICU."

The physician pushed forward, waving her hands. "Get back to your stations, *now*!"

"But she's all unhooked!" the tallest guy protested. "Without doctor's orders. This is unprecedented."

Stevenson turned. For some reason, Quincy had always believed her to be taller than she actually was, possibly because she had an imposing presence. But in reality, she wasn't all that big a woman. Didn't matter. She faced down the nontulip with a searing look. "Who the hell do you think is the doctor in charge? Did I or did I not tell you to return to your stations?"

The seven fled, the women going first, the men trailing behind, the nontulip last. He stopped at the door. "I don't get it."

Stevenson said, "Well, when you become a doctor, maybe you will. Right now, you're working under me, and if you question my orders, kiss your job good-bye."

Quincy, still cradling Ceara in his arms, decided that Dr. Stevenson was one hell of a lady.

She folded her arms at her waist, scrunching her scrub smock into pleats under her breasts. Meeting Quincy's gaze, she said, "I have two patients. I'd really like both of them to survive. Good for the résumé. In the ordinary course of my days, I don't have to make a choice between one or another. Do you get that?"

Quincy nodded. Ceara lifted her head from his shoulder and cried, "Me babe is dying. I need to hold her in me arms. Do ye get *that*?"

"I do." Stevenson directed her gaze to Quincy. She had blue eyes that could cut straight through a man. "I just need to know that you understand, Mr. Harrigan. If you take her in there, I have no magical medicines to offset the result. Are we clear on that? This is beyond what I learned in med school. It's beyond *everything* in this world, as we know it."

Quincy tightened his hold on his wife. "So you do believe what I told you?"

Stevenson nodded. "Life never ceases to amaze me. I do believe what you told me. Now believe me." She shifted her gaze to Ceara. "Your vital signs have been irregular for the last hour and a half, Ceara. Low blood pressure, irregular heartbeat, and a couple of times we nearly had to put you on supplemental oxygen. I know about your gift and that you used it to heal your husband's wrist. That somehow drained you in a way that my medicine can't treat. If you go to the NICU and try to heal your baby, same goes. I will have nothing in my arsenal to help you, and if you grow worse, with your blood pressure diving as it has been and your heart patterns bouncing all over the place, there will be no way for me to fix you."

"I ken what ye're saying," Ceara replied. "Do ye have any wee ones of yer own, Dr. Stevenson?"

"It's Marie, and no, I don't. Not yet."

"Well, when ye hold yer firstborn in yer arms, ye'll understand how I feel right now. 'Tis na a choice fer me. 'Tis what I *must* do, ye ken?"

Marie Stevenson nodded. "I ken." She looked at Quincy. "Don't just stand there. Take your wife to the NICU. I'll have staff standing by to help me afterward. We'll be on the ready right outside." Tears filled her eyes. "So now it's your turn to say a prayer for me, Mr. Harrigan. Ask God to slip a couple of miracles up my sleeve."

Quincy hurried from the room and angled left up the corridor. He paused for a second outside their daughter's unit. If he walked in there, he'd be putting his wife's life on the line. His pulse slammed in his temples, and for just a second he almost lost his nerve. Then, acutely aware that someone might rush up to stop him at any moment, he said, "To hell with it," and bent to open the door. The big nurse in the colorful balloon top whirled from the incubator to gape at him and Ceara.

"You need to leave," Quincy told her.

"No, sir, you're the ones who need to leave. I'm still checking on your baby girl."

Quincy took two steps into the room. "I've cleared this with Dr. Stevenson, and you need to go." He didn't want this wonderful nurse to be held responsible for anything that was about to happen. "Please, at least go out and check with the doctor. If she doesn't back me up, you can always rush right back in here."

The nurse glanced at Ceara, taking long measure of her pallor. "She should be in her room, not here." Despite the protest, the woman slumped her shoulders and cut a circle around Quincy to reach the door. "I hope you know what you're doing. Your wife is sick, you know."

Quincy wasn't sure anymore if he knew what he was doing—or sure about much of anything, as far as that went. From the moment he'd found Ceara in Beethoven's stall, his whole world had been turned topsy-turvy, and things he once wouldn't have believed now made total sense to him.

He gently deposited his wife in the recliner. She smiled weakly up at him. "I love ye, Quincy Harrigan. I need ye to ken that now, fer I may ne'er be able to tell ye again."

Quincy's heart felt as if razor-blade chips were being pumped through his valves. He cupped her pale face in his hands. "I'd like to hear you tell me your way, Ceara."

Her eyes went bright with tears. "Looking at yer dear face makes me heart dance with joy."

Quincy swallowed hard to make his voice work. "You've brought color into my life. Before you dropped into my arena, my life was painted in different shades of gray. Now it's painted in bright hues and sunshine, even on rainy days."

Her tears spilled over her lower lashes to trail down her pale cheeks. For what seemed an endless moment, their gazes locked, and messages that couldn't be expressed with words passed between them.

"Ye'll be a good da," she whispered. "I ken that ye will always be there fer her. And ye'll tell her every single day how much her mum loves her? With me words, not yers. Ye'll tell her in me own way?"

Quincy nodded. "And I'll make sure your mum sees her, and that our little girl sees your mum—all of them, all of your family, in the crystal ball. Loni will do that for us."

Ceara nodded and smiled again. " 'Twill be good fer her to know me family." Just then, the baby grunted, trying to discharge a breath, and Ceara glanced over at their tiny daughter in the incubator. " 'Tis time, Quincy. Give her to me."

Quincy turned to do that, but the baby had so many

wires and tubes hooked up to her that he didn't know how to pluck her minuscule body out of there.

"Take all of it off," Ceara told him. "She shall have no need of it once she's in me arms. 'Tis me word ye have on it."

Quincy's hands shook as if he had palsy, but he started removing lifesaving tubes, leaving the breathing tube for last. His baby girl was so tiny that he was able to lift her out through the hole, using only one hand, with his other cupped against the dome just in case, so he wouldn't accidentally drop her. The love he felt when he actually held his daughter nearly overwhelmed him.

"Hurry," Ceara whispered. "I canna bring her back if she dies. I can only heal her."

Quincy carefully placed their baby in his wife's slender, fine-boned hands.

"Ach," Ceara said. A radiant smile spread over her pale face as she tucked her daughter close against her neck, just under her chin. "Me precious wee one." With one last look at Quincy, she whispered, "Ye make me heart sing happy songs," and then she closed her eyes and began whispering prayers in Gaelic. Even as Quincy watched, Ceara's face turned whiter—so white that the faint tint of pink to her lips went chalky.

Never in his life had he felt so helpless. Seeing Ceara do this . . . Oh, God, allowing it was the hardest thing he'd ever done. He dropped to his knees beside the chair, afraid to touch mother or child for fear he would somehow put more drain on his wife's body. He rested his head against the cushiony recliner back, his cheek against Ceara's burnished curls as he gazed down at their daughter and the rhythmic movement of his wife's chest. One of the baby's itty-bitty hands was splayed over Ceara's collarbone. Quincy watched those fingers, barely wider than a strand of uncooked spaghetti, go from purple to a healthy pink.

" 'Tis done," Ceara murmured. "Ye must take her now. Swiftly."

Quincy carefully lifted their baby into his hands. He was startled half out of his wits when the infant jerked and started to cry, her wails as tiny as she was, but even so, Quincy knew his little girl now had functioning lungs. One glance at Ceara almost made his knees fold. She had gone limp and slumped sideways on the chair, her head resting on one of its arms. Her skin looked waxen. The only colorful bit of her left was her beautiful hair. And—oh, God—Quincy no longer saw her chest rising and falling.

"Help!" he yelled. "Now, Marie! Hurry!"

The door burst open. Quincy tucked his daughter against his neck, as he'd seen Ceara do, and stepped back so hospital staff could try to care for his wife. Bedlam. Cursing. So many people in the tiny room that Quincy backed into a corner, both hands cupped over his daughter, which was overkill. He could have protected her on all sides with only one palm. A gurney was brought in. Men worked in tandem to gently but quickly lift Ceara from the recliner and put her on the mattress. Before Quincy could blink, his wife was wheeled from the NICU.

The big nurse in the balloon smock entered the room as soon as the doorway cleared. When she saw the empty incubator, her gaze shot to Quincy's cupped hands just under his chin. "Oh, my God, what have you done?"

Quincy felt his daughter's tiny arms and legs moving, and in one part of his brain, he wanted to shout, *I've saved my baby!* but the other half of his brain was yelling, *I just let my wife commit suicide.* He leaned into the corner, no longer trusting his legs, and as Ceara had done only seconds earlier, he told the nurse, "Take her. Swiftly. I think I might pass out."

The nurse muttered curses as she took the baby from him. She didn't waste time on any more words as she rushed to the incubator to get the infant hooked back up to life support. Quincy watched it all in a daze, unable to push away from the walls that pressed against his body like an embrace to keep him on his feet. Other nurses rushed in, both male and female. In the dizzying kaleidoscope of his reality, all of them were a blur. Words bounced into his brain and then ricocheted around, like echoes inside a canyon. *It's a miracle. Look at her, breathing on her own. Have you ever seen anything like this? My God, sweetie, what a little fighter you are. Brett, she doesn't need to be intubated now. Let it go.*

Slowly, Quincy's senses righted enough for him to gather the strength to stand on his own. He got to the door, and then found himself in the hall. His mind felt as if it were stuck in neutral. But he had to get down that corridor to Ceara's cubicle.

Ceara, his precious Irish rose, was dying. He had to be with her, let her know again that he understood, that he would be all she wanted him to be for their beautiful daughter. Even unconscious, she'd sense, somehow, that he was with her.

Chapter Nineteen

Prevented from entering Ceara's room, Quincy found himself on a corridor bench, staring stupidly at the floor. Shock? He didn't know. *This isn't happening,* he thought. It was crazy beyond belief, totally off the reality chart. But as Father Mike had said the night of his and Ceara's marriage, there were mysteries in the universe that mere humans could not grasp.

So all of this *was* happening. His wife had just put her life on the line to save their baby. Their little girl was now doing well on her own. And Quincy had allowed all of it to happen. His guts churned and clenched. *Ceara.* Dear God, how could he have let her do it?

Even as Quincy asked himself the question, he knew he'd done the right thing. He couldn't have denied Ceara the opportunity to do what he would have done himself if only he'd had the ability. Not if he believed in equal rights. And he did, damn it. It just sucked that in this instance, standing up for what he believed in might cost him so dearly. Knowing you'd done the right thing didn't make it easy.

Quincy felt disconnected from everything around him, yet the pain in his chest was so intense it made breathing difficult. He had to concentrate on it. In. Out.

Again. Suddenly Quincy remembered that he hadn't called his family. He knew they couldn't help, but when the going got tough the Harrigans hung together. He had enough problems right now without all of them screaming at him for not contacting them. Pawing blindly at his belt, he located his phone. He decided to text Clint, because his dad, not being of the cell phone generation, often missed calls and messages. *Need u at hosp. Urgent. Get Father Mike over here, pronto.*

As Quincy stuffed his phone back into its case, he realized he had no clear recollection of where he was in the hospital. He guessed maybe that was because his entire being yearned to be elsewhere—with Ceara, a woman so sweet and dear that she had filled up his whole world with her light. His chest ached so much he wondered whether it would kill him. But that would be too easy, a quick end and a fast escape. Life never played out that way. He could lose Ceara, his fiery-haired, beautiful, impossibly precious wife. And somehow he had to live through it to raise their child, just as he had promised her he would. Quincy knew his father had somehow managed to keep going after losing his wife, solely for the sake of his kids, but Quincy didn't know if he had it in him.

Suddenly Stevenson sat beside him. He had no idea where she had come from. It seemed to him she'd shot up out of the floor tiles. She seemed to sense the agony he felt, for she touched his hand.

"You made the right choice," she said softly.

"Did I?"

Her fingers squeezed his. "It was the *only* choice. Ceara wanted it, and if either of us had tried to stop her, she never would have forgiven us. Where there's still life, there's still hope. Let's not give up just yet."

Quincy felt as if his thoughts floated in thick syrup, and bringing one to the surface so he could focus on it took gargantuan effort. "Hope? I thought the baby was doing great."

Stevenson chuckled. "Oh, yes. I've never seen anything like it. She's a preemie in every way, but all the symptoms that usually present such risk with a preterm birth have vanished. She's perfectly okay now except for being so incredibly tiny, and over time, she'll grow." She sighed. "I only wish Ceara were doing as well. I've tried everything I know, but I can't get her to stabilize."

Quincy straightened. "You mean she's still alive?"

"Oh, God." Concern wrinkled Stevenson's usually un-lined countenance. "No one came out to update you? I told one of the nurses to find you."

Quincy barely heard her. Somehow he found himself standing up. "Where is she? Can I be with her? Please don't say I can't. Hearing my voice, knowing I'm there — well, maybe it'll give her strength to fight the weakness."

Stevenson stood. "I agree, but I'll go you one better. The baby is still incubated, but now only because, with her body mass being so slight, I think the stable temperatures inside the incubator are better for her. If we swaddle her in blankets, I think it would be safe to take her in to see her mommy. Ceara is too weak to hold her, but if she's at all aware of what's being said to her, knowing her baby is near and doing well might help her make a turnaround."

In a daze, Quincy followed the doctor to the NICU. His daughter protested when she was removed from the incubator. Her tiny fists and feet pumped, her face went bright red, and she let out a small, enraged shriek. Somehow it reminded him unbearably of Ceara. Stevenson laid her on a dressing table and began to efficiently wrap the little girl in prewarmed receiving blankets. Quincy, standing with his back to the window, was startled when wind gusted against the glass, followed by rain that struck like a spray of bullets.

"My goodness," the doctor cried as she hurried to swaddle the infant. "What a storm! That sounds like really high wind."

Quincy frowned and stepped over to peek out past the blinds. Below, he saw people struggling to walk across the parking lot, their bodies bent to press forward against the gale-force gusts. Beyond the asphalt area where full-grown pines peppered the hospital grounds, the evergreen canopies whipped to and fro like feather dusters. Water had already pooled in the parking lot, so deep it reached above people's ankles.

Unusual, he registered. There had been no sign of a storm when he'd driven Ceara to the hospital. Behind him, he heard the doctor making cooing sounds as she surrounded the child with the warm blankets, and the baby suddenly stopped crying. A chill pebbled Quincy's skin when the storm abated in tandem with his daughter's change of temperament. He remembered Ceara's story of her birth, how she'd called up a terrible gale when she left the warmth of her mother's womb.

Coincidence?

Quincy turned to study his baby girl, now tightly wrapped in the soft, oven-warmed blankets and happy again. *Shit, she's a druid.* She'd clearly inherited her mother's gifts—at least some of them, anyway. Raising her without Ceara's guidance would be challenging, Quincy knew, but he was too overwhelmed right then to think about it.

The doctor carried the baby to Ceara's room with Quincy nearly treading on her heels. A wave of sadness hit him when he saw that his wife was in a maternity suite now, only it had been transformed into a temporary ICU. There was a bassinet near her bed, seating for family, and a sofa that could be pulled out for a father to stay overnight. This should have been such a happy moment. Instead Ceara was hooked up to machines and so pale that for a panicked instant he wondered whether she'd died while Stevenson had stepped out. But no, that machine was still bleeping.

Quincy took his daughter, cautiously getting her swaddled shape cradled safely in one arm, and then he stepped close to Ceara's side. "It's Quincy, honey. I'm here with a very special visitor: our baby girl. You saved her, Ceara. It was the most incredible thing I've ever witnessed. You healed her completely! She can breathe just fine on her own now. Her skin tone is a healthy pink. Doc Stevenson says except for her size, she's perfect now."

Ceara didn't so much as wiggle an eyelash. Quincy studied the heart monitor. The beats came intermittently, and in between he saw flutters. He didn't like her blood pressure numbers, either. When he glanced at Stevenson with an arched brow, the doctor touched a finger to her lips, signaling him not to ask questions. Quincy agreed with the woman's call. If Ceara could hear—if she was aware on any level—discussing her condition in her presence wouldn't be wise.

Quincy cuddled his daughter closer. She felt so insubstantial, and yet when he looked down she had poked her tiny fist in her mouth and was sucking on it to beat the band. "She's sucking her fist, Ceara. You know what that means, don't you? She's wanting her mum so she can nurse."

Still no response. Stevenson was studying Ceara's

chart with a frown and not really paying attention, so
Quincy decided to just keep talking. "She's so beautiful,
Ceara. Absolutely gorgeous. And you'll never guess
what! When Dr. Stevenson took her out of the incubator
to bring her here, she got mad as blazes when she felt the
cool air, just like you did when you were born." Quincy
forced a laugh, even though he was far from feeling any
trace of amusement. "And you guessed it: The little
stinker called up one hell of a storm. I've never seen
anything like it, wind strong enough to nearly uproot
full-grown trees, and rain falling so hard and fast it would
have caused flooding if the doctor hadn't gotten her
wrapped and warm as fast as she did to end the temper
tantrum."

Just then a tap came at the door. Quincy turned to see
his dad poke his head into the room. Water dripped off
the brim of Frank's Stetson, and the shoulder of his shirt
was drenched. "Family's all here," he said. "We'll wait
outside."

Stevenson approached Quincy to take the baby. "I
think we've visited long enough. You can bring her back
later. I'll have a nurse return her to NICU, and then I'll
talk with your family out in the hall. I'm sure all of them
have questions."

Quincy watched the physician leave and then returned to his wife's bedside for a private moment with
her. He scooted a visitor chair close and sat down, curling his hand over one of Ceara's. Her flesh felt cold as
death. Beneath his fingertips, he felt the weak flutter of
her pulse. Tears nearly blinded him, for he knew he was
going to lose her. How cruel could life get, damn it?
Deep in his heart, he'd believed her to be already dead
when he'd been sitting in a daze on that hallway bench.
Then he'd learned differently and allowed himself to

hope, only to face the fact now that she was going to die on him anyway.

"You make my heart sing, Ceara." Quincy groped for other words—special words to describe how she made him feel. "You're my sunshine, honey. My only sunshine. Please fight to live. With every smidgen of strength you've got left, fight to stay here with me and our little girl. Without you, I'll have no light in my life. You understand?"

Quincy thought he felt her hand twitch under his, but the movement was so slight he might have imagined it. He stood and bent low to kiss her white cheek. "I love you so much, Ceara. Try with everything you've got to come back to me."

Wiping his cheeks, Quincy crossed the room and exited into the hallway. Just a few feet away at the opposite side of the corridor, he saw his family gathered with the doctor in a waiting area. On feet he could no longer feel, Quincy moved toward them. Everyone jumped up to hug him and whisper words that didn't register in his brain. When the hellos were finished, Quincy sat down next to his father, maybe because, even at forty, a guy needed to be close to his dad at a time like this.

Stevenson gave the family a quick but thorough recap of events, telling how Quincy had slashed his wrist and Ceara had healed him. "Ceara's use of her powers apparently brought on premature labor."

Quincy heard soft gasps when the physician went on to tell his relatives about Ceara's decision to heal her baby.

Palms pressed together, the doctor sat forward on the sofa to brace her arms on her knees. "Ceara knew she was putting her own life at risk to save the child," she said softly. She glanced toward Quincy. "And her husband gave her his unswaying support, backing her decision all the way. I gave it to Ceara straight. She was already very weak, and nothing I had tried seemed to help. If she weakened herself even more by trying to heal the baby, I knew I might be helpless to save her. Ceara understood the consequences, but she still insisted on being taken to her daughter."

Frank cleared his throat. He'd removed his hat, and now he turned the Stetson in his hands. "So what are we lookin' at now, Doc? Is Ceara gonna pull through?"

Stevenson shook her head. Tears shimmered in her eyes when she met Quincy's gaze. "I'm so sorry. I won't overwhelm all of you with medical terms or lists of medications I've tried. It's enough to say that Ceara is barely clinging to life, and nothing I've done has had any effect at all." She lifted her hands in a helpless gesture. "There's nothing more I can do. From here on out, it's up to God."

Standing, the physician crossed over to place a hand on Quincy's shoulder. "Power of prayer, remember? I have seen miracles happen."

Quincy nodded. He couldn't, for the life of him, push out a word. After the doctor left the waiting room, silence descended over his family. Quincy hunched his shoulders, shrinking into himself.

Then, with a ragged sob, he whispered, "I don't think I can do it, Dad. I can't lose her and go on living. I don't think I've got it in me."

Frank whacked Quincy on the back. "You've got what it takes," he said firmly. "You may not know it right now, but if Ceara dies, you'll have plenty of time to face it and figure your way through it."

Quincy wasn't so sure about that. With a dull gaze, he looked around the sitting area. All his brothers had shown up with their wives, and Tucker had come with

Sam. That was the Harrigan clan in a nutshell: When one member of the family needed help, they circled the wagons. Dimly, Quincy realized Dee Dee was missing. He guessed that she'd stayed behind with the kids.

Just then Father Mike burst into the waiting area. "Dear God, what happened?"

Frank gave the priest a hurried recap; then he turned to Quincy. "Come on, son. The rest of us shouldn't go in, but you should be with your wife when she receives the Anointing of the Sick."

Still in a fog, Quincy followed Father Mike. Once in Ceara's room, Quincy held her hand, somehow reciting prayers when called for and giving responses on cue. It was a beautiful sacrament. What stuck in Quincy's brain was that Father Mike called upon all the departed, and all the angels and saints, to become Ceara's escorts to heaven. Quincy didn't want her to go, but even so, it comforted him to know that she wouldn't be alone.

After the ritual was over, Father Mike led Quincy back to the waiting area, where he once again sat beside his dad. People started shoving a sandwich and a drink into Quincy's hand. He couldn't even see what he was holding. *Ceara*. She had been such a bright light in his life, and now she was blinking out like a candle flame.

A nurse came to tell Quincy that he could see his wife again, but he had to go in alone and could stay only ten minutes. When Quincy entered the maternity suite, he saw nurses working frantically over Ceara, checking her vitals, giving her IV injections. Quincy knew nothing they did would help.

Because his time with Ceara was limited, Quincy moved in close to her side as soon as the nurses backed away. Precious seconds. He used every one of them to stroke Ceara's hair, kiss her dear face, and whisper to her how much he loved her. He could only hope that something he said might call her back to him, but she remained white, waxen, and unresponsive.

When he was ushered from the room by one of the nurses, he left a huge chunk of his aching heart behind. Would Ceara last long enough for another visit? Would he ever see her alive again? Only God had the answers to those questions.

Once back in the waiting room, Quincy headed for his dad again. After sinking onto the cushion, he told everyone, "No change. Well, that's not true. I'm no expert, but judging by the frenzy the nurses were in, I think she's losing ground fast."

Mandy choked on a sob and pressed her face against Zach's shoulder. Loni bent her head and leaned closer to Clint. White-faced, Sam just stared blindly at the floor. Quincy tried to think of something else to say. They were nearly as upset as he was and needed him to be strong. He just found it difficult right now. He suddenly noticed that there wasn't a person among them who wasn't wearing damp clothes, including Father Mike.

Voice hollow, he said, "Looks to me like all you guys got caught in my daughter's storm."

"Your daughter's storm?" Clint looked bewildered. "What do you mean?"

Quincy told them how his baby girl had protested when she was removed from the warm incubator. "The instant she started throwing a temper fit, a storm struck. I've never seen the like unless it was on the news."

"Your baby girl caused that storm?" Zach arched both eyebrows. "The wind damned near took my truck off the road."

Everyone started talking at once, describing their own close calls during their drives into town. Father

Mike had been caught as he walked from the rectory over to the church.

Suddenly Loni held up her hand, calling for silence. "Whoa, whoa, whoa," she cried. "Can you repeat that for me, Quincy?"

"Repeat what?"

"Did you or did you not just say your daughter caused that horrible storm?"

Quincy shrugged. "She's her mother's daughter. Ceara told me the same thing happened after she was born, that—"

Loni cut him off. "I'm aware of the story, Quincy. Ceara told me about it, too. Don't you get what this *means*? Your baby is a druid. She has *gifts*."

"Nothing strange about that, I don't guess," Quincy replied. "Her mama's a druid, and according to Ceara, I've got druid blood, too, watered down though it is. The baby had every chance to be born with some of her mother's powers."

Still comforting his wife, Zach spoke up, clearly aiming for a jovial remark to lighten things up. "I think we should nickname the little sprite Stormy. It's a cute name, and if she brought that gully-washer on, it suits her to a T."

Loni sent her youngest brother-in-law an exasperated look. "Zach, for once—just this once, mind you—can you keep your lip zipped?"

Mandy's head came up. "That isn't very nice, Lonikins. He didn't say anything wrong. I think Stormy is an adorable nickname for the baby."

Loni rolled her eyes. "Hello? Earth to the Harrigans. Can everyone please try to focus? The baby has *powers*." She sent Quincy a pleading look. "*Think*. What if she has the gift of healing?"

Quincy knew Loni was trying to make a point, but he didn't get what it was. "I'm sure she probably does—or there's a good chance of it, anyway. All I can think about right now is my wife. Sorry, but I'll worry about how I'm going to cope with the child-rearing problems later."

"Child-rearing problems?" Zach echoed. "If tonight's any example, if the kid gets in a serious snit, she might level your house in a high wind."

Loni waved a hand again. "God, you people are so *dense* sometimes. If the baby has the gift of healing, she may be able to heal her mother. Why is nobody else tuning in to my channel here?"

Quincy's heart jerked with a warm surge of hope. He quickly squelched it. "You haven't seen my daughter." He tried to show her size, but his hands were so big he couldn't possibly convey the image to Loni. He fell back on stating the facts. "She weighs one-point-four pounds. She's so tiny she doesn't look real. So what if she has powers? She's way too little right now to focus on using them. She can't even really see yet."

"It doesn't matter!" Loni shot to her feet. When Clint tried to grasp her arm, she shook free, apparently as frustrated with him as she was with everyone else. "Gifts like these are *instinctive*. Do you think I *ever* in my entire life *invited* a vision? No, they came at me from nowhere from the time I was little, really little. My whole damned life until I met Clint was like a series of train wrecks, because I had no control, absolutely *none*, over my gift. My having no control doesn't mean my gift wasn't just as powerful, though."

Quincy was still trying to keep a lid on the hope trying to blossom inside him. "When I cut myself, Ceara consciously decided to grab my wrist. She *consciously* called upon her gift to heal me. Stormy is way too tiny to consciously do anything. Don't you get that, Loni?"

"See?" Zach said. "It stuck. I claim dibs on naming her. Even her dad is calling her Stormy."

Loni rounded on her brother-in-law. "Credit for that can come later. Right now, Ceara may be dying, and we're running out of time." She shook off her husband's hand again. "*Please*. You guys have to listen to me. I'm the only person here who can come close to understanding any of this. You have to trust me and do what I say."

Frank stood up. "We got us a wrinkle here, honey, because it ain't real clear to any of us what you're sayin'."

Loni moved two steps toward Quincy. "Then let me be clear. Quincy, go get your daughter."

"She's in intensive care. I can't just go get her without an okay from Stevenson."

"Then *get* an okay," Loni persisted. "That baby needs to be in her mother's arms." She closed the remaining distance to clutch Quincy's shoulder. "Don't think; just *do* it. Trust me, Quincy. I think it may save Ceara's life."

Quincy didn't know if he could get Stevenson on board for another paranormal venture or not, and deep down, he doubted he could plead the case very convincingly, because he honestly didn't believe his tiny baby girl could do much of anything right now besides find her mouth with her fist. He roused the OB from a nap. She emerged from the closet, where she'd been passed out on a cot, to blink up at him, her dishwater blond hair poking out from her French braid as if she'd stuck her finger in a live light socket.

"Is it Ceara?" She glanced at her watch. "I was with her only fifteen minutes ago."

Quincy quickly related to the doctor his sister-in-law's theory that his daughter had the power to heal her mother.

Stevenson gaped at him. "That baby was waltzing with death not long ago. This healing business clearly drains the body. I'm sorry, Quincy, but sometimes a doctor goes with the odds and other times she sticks with the sure thing. The baby is going to be fine. I'm *sure* of that. I can't possibly put her at risk again. Ceara *chose* to do it, so that was different. The baby can't make choices for herself yet. I can't make a call like this, and I won't allow you to, either."

Loni appeared at Quincy's side. "Dr. Stevenson, I'm Quincy's sister-in-law, and a clairvoyant."

The doctor passed a hand over her bloodshot eyes. "Oh, great. A family full of druids and clairvoyants." She shook her head. "Nothing you say is going to change my mind. A baby cannot make life-or-death decisions for herself, and I sure as hell won't make them for her—end of conversation."

Loni rushed to insert, "It isn't a life-or-death decision for Stormy."

"Stormy?" Dr. Stevenson cocked an eyebrow.

"Our temporary nickname for the baby," Loni explained. "As tiny as she is, we've good reason to believe she caused that awful storm earlier." Loni waved a hand. "Anyway, the baby—"

"Whoa!" Dr. Stevenson held up a hand. "That baby caused the storm? What on earth makes you think that? A nurse told me it took down trees all over town, and weather forecasters are scratching their heads because it wasn't predicted, came on suddenly, and then just ... stopped."

"It stopped the instant you got Stormy swaddled in

the warm blankets," Quincy said. "She was happy again." He related the story of Ceara's birth to the doctor. "It's clear that my daughter has inherited her mother's gifts, possibly even the ability to heal, and using her gifts won't harm her in any way, shape, or form."

"She was born in this century," Loni inserted, "and her powers are completely undiminished. Before Ceara came forward through time, she was told that the trials of the journey would either take away all her gifts or greatly weaken them. But for Stormy, that isn't the case. Using her powers is as natural to her as breathing and won't hurt her at all."

Quincy pinched the bridge of his nose. "My only worry is that Stormy is too little to focus. How can she heal her mother if she can't zero in on what's wrong with her and consciously—" Quincy broke off. "Hell, I don't know the name for what Ceara did when she healed my wrist and then the baby. To me, it felt like I got zapped with a high-voltage electrical current."

Loni reached out and grabbed the doctor's hand. "Please don't let us down. Ceara is dying. All we want to do is tuck the baby into her arms to see what happens."

"I could lose my license for allowing that."

Loni laughed, albeit humorlessly. "Yeah, right, for letting a dying mother hold her newborn? I would think that's a pretty common thing for doctors to allow."

"But this is no ordinary newborn," Stevenson pointed out.

"No," Loni agreed, "but if you attempt to tell anyone that, you probably *will* lose your license, at least temporarily, because people will think you're crazier than a loon."

Stevenson smiled faintly. "At this moment, I'm wondering if they wouldn't be right." She searched Quincy's gaze. "Are you sure—beyond any shadow of a doubt— that doing this will put your daughter in absolutely no danger?"

Quincy nodded. "I'm absolutely positive."

"And are you willing to release me from any legal responsibility? I'll take your word, Mr. Harrigan."

Quincy glanced at Loni. She nodded.

"Yes," he said. "I am."

Quincy's only uncertainty was that Loni might be wishing on rainbows.

Chapter Twenty

Stevenson hugged her waist, bent her head to stare at the floor, and began tapping the toe of her Dansko Professional, sending out a solid thumping sound. When she finally glanced up, she sighed.

"Okay, here's the thing." She glanced at her watch again. "In twenty-eight minutes, give or take a few either way, two other doctors are coming on board, one to take over Ceara's care, the other to take over Stormy's. I'm an OB, and Ceara's condition has moved clear out of my orbit. And Stormy is a preemie. It's common practice with preemies for a pediatrician to take over. I've only been in charge of both of them this long because they were brought in during the middle of the night, and the storm caused so much damage that both specialists have had trouble reaching the hospital. Trees down over roads, no power in some areas. It's a mess out there."

Loni interjected. "So in a very short while, you'll have no say in what happens."

"Correct," Stevenson replied, "and until you woke me, I was glad of it. I put in a full day yesterday, and I've been up all night. To say I'm exhausted is an understatement. I was looking forward to getting some relief so I could sleep."

"And now?" Loni pressed.

Stevenson frowned, and then her mouth curved into a ghost of a smile. "Now I'm thinking I have a very small window of time to authorize a short mother-daughter visit." She directed her gaze to Loni. "You're right. It isn't uncommon for a dying mother to be allowed to hold her baby toward the end. Supervised, of course, so no harm comes to the infant."

"So you'll do it?" Loni grinned at Quincy. "She'll do it."

"I will," Stevenson conceded, "but time is of the essence. Once those other doctors arrive, this little experiment probably won't happen. We need to get Stormy out of NICU, ASAP, and get her into Ceara's arms."

She spun away. Over her shoulder, she fired at Quincy, "Well, don't just stand there! Get your family gathered outside Ceara's room. I'll take care of getting the baby there and clearing the birthing suite of nurses." She turned to walk backward for a second. "I want no medical professionals in there, period. If a healing occurs, it will be the second unexplained miracle of the day, and we usually only get a couple a year. I definitely don't want witnesses. You understand? My whole career is hanging in the balance."

Loni left Quincy leaning against the wall outside Ceara's room and went to the waiting area to gather the Harrigan troops. Quincy took advantage of the opportunity to close his eyes and just rest his brain for a couple of minutes. Soon he felt feminine hands rubbing his arms, and then big, hard ones, lightly grasping his shoulders. Family. Quincy thanked God for each and every person who'd stepped close to show love for him, but he didn't have any remaining energy to respond to the gestures.

Thoughts of Ceara circled in his mind, kind of like a

movie chopped into bits, tossed in a bag, given a good shake, and then played willy-nilly on a television screen. Ceara grasping his hand and leading him toward the bed on their wedding night, insisting that they do their duty. Ceara terrified the next morning when her hair got sucked into the outtake valve of his Jacuzzi tub. Ceara in Beethoven's stall, wearing the old-fashioned gown and what looked like an oil filter on her head. Ceara standing at his stove, waiting to knock his eyes out with her new haircut, makeup, and seduction outfit. The memories brought tears to Quincy's eyes and made him smile both at once. How could it be that he hadn't known a little more than six months ago that she even existed, and now he couldn't begin to imagine life without her?

Beside him, Quincy felt Loni press close. She whispered, "If Stormy has healing powers, there is no closer bond than that between a baby and its mother. Maybe just the baby's touch will heal Ceara. Your little girl needs her mama. On some level, isn't it possible that she might sense that her mother is ill and about to die?"

Quincy didn't know, and he was afraid to place too much hope on a possibility. At this point, he needed to dig deep for strength and brace himself for the worst. If he ended up getting a miracle and Ceara lived, he'd be on his knees thanking God at least once every day for the rest of his life. But it was a big *if*, and he couldn't count on it.

Stevenson arrived with Stormy carefully swaddled in her arms. She stood off to one side of the door as nurses filed out. One, a redhead who looked a bit older than the other two, paused to express her disagreement with the decision. "The patient is extremely unstable, Dr. Stevenson. It strikes me as very odd that you're pulling off the nurses. I understand that the family would like a few minutes to say their good-byes, but it seems to me that they could do that while medical staff is present."

Stevenson nodded. "I understand, Sharon, and I'll call all of you back in shortly. The family just wishes for this to be a special moment. And that's all it will be, a moment. You won't be out of here for long."

Quincy felt himself being guided through the open doorway by gentle hands. Once he saw Ceara, he could see nothing else. She'd lost ground since his last visit. He knew it with one glance. In his estimation, she could die at any moment, between one heartbeat and the next.

Stevenson handed the baby over to Loni. "This is your show."

Quincy was glad it was somebody's show, because he felt too numb and his thoughts were too disjointed for him to be in charge. Loni cuddled the baby close and moved quickly toward Ceara's bed, approaching on the side where no tubes or cuffs were attached to her arm. Shifting the infant into the bend of one elbow, Loni drew the sheet away from Ceara's chest. Then she beckoned to Mandy.

"Help me get her gown open. I want them to be skin-to-skin so Stormy recognizes who's holding her."

Quincy recalled how the baby had recognized his voice and touch. The memory jerked him out of his stupor. He watched Mandy bare Ceara's right shoulder and breast. When he glanced at his brothers, he saw that they had the good manners to look away. Tucker, too. Only Quincy watched as Loni unwrapped Stormy's minuscule body and placed her against her mother's breast. The baby wailed at the feel of cold air against her, but then, as if instinct took over, the infant went still and nuzzled the side of Ceara's breast, making tiny mewling sounds. Loni laughed softly.

"Yes, dear heart, it's your mama." Loni leaned over the bed, blocking Quincy's view. Then she laughed lightly again. "There you have it, tiny one. Suckle all you like. Recognize the bond, that this is your mother and all is not well."

Stevenson surged forward. "You *can't* let her nurse. We've got Ceara pumped full of so many drugs it's—"

Loni turned to face the doctor, her left hand curled over the baby, now covered with the sheet, so there would be no danger of her falling off the bed. "It's only colostrum, already in Loni's ducts before any drugs. Can it really be that dangerous? She'll only suckle for a couple of seconds. This should happen quickly if it's going to happen at all."

Stevenson threw up her hands. "I honestly don't know if the drugs have tainted the colostrum."

Loni held up a forefinger. "Only for a few seconds. Let Stormy come to understand who is holding her. It's only a getting-acquainted time. The baby is new at nursing. She probably won't get much of anything, and this is important."

Stormy had not yet perfected the art of suckling while practicing so briefly on her fist, so the sounds of missed draws reached Quincy's ears. If Ceara died with the baby at her breast, what would he one day tell Stormy? A lie, he guessed, because hearing the real story . . . well, no little girl needed to be burdened with something so awful.

And yet, watching through a blur of tears, Quincy also realized just how beautiful it was: his beloved wife and his precious baby girl, bonding for perhaps the first and last time.

"Look!" Loni cried. She beamed an excited smile over her shoulder. "Ceara's heartbeat. *Look*. I can see it on the monitor."

Stevenson raced around to the left side of the bed. "I'll be damned. Nothing I've done has worked, and now . . . holy God."

Quincy was afraid to hope. Ceara's breathing had been so shallow and slow. For all he knew, she might already be in the company of the angelic escorts who would guide her to heaven.

Loni sighed. Quincy saw Ceara's previously lifeless arm tighten slightly around her daughter. Loni turned to Quincy with tears in her eyes. "It's not just Ceara's heartbeat that has changed, Quincy. So has her breathing. It's working! She's rallying."

Quincy finally found the presence of mind to make his feet move to go toward the bed. Loni laughed and hugged his waist. "You gotta eat crow, bro."

Quincy gaped at the heart monitor. As he watched, he saw Ceara's blood pressure coming back up toward normal. Slowly. Fractionally. But steadily. He was afraid to believe his eyes, and yet he couldn't deny the evidence. He glanced at Stevenson. She wore a smile so radiant that it had erased the lines of exhaustion from her face.

"Trust in it," she said softly. "These machines don't lie."

Quincy suddenly felt as if his bones had melted. He jerked his gaze to Ceara's face and saw that color was returning to her lips and cheeks. "Oh, my God. It *worked*."

Behind him he heard laughter, both deep and light, the music of his family when something incredibly wonderful had happened. Quincy gently elbowed Loni out of the way to bend over the bed and embrace his wife and baby girl, almost afraid to credit what all his senses were telling him. Just as quickly as Ceara had healed their daughter, now their daughter was healing her mama.

Stevenson approached again and reached to check

the baby's breathing and pulse. Then she nodded, clearly satisfied that Stormy had suffered no ill effects.

Quincy saw Ceara's lashes flutter. Then he was looking into her beautiful blue eyes, the most gorgeous he'd ever seen. Ceara smiled drowsily. Loni pushed in to kiss her sister-in-law on the forehead. Then to Quincy she said, "This is a time for you to be alone with your little family. We can all come back to visit later. Out, Harrigans. Right now."

Like a drill instructor, she got every Harrigan into marching mode and herded them from the room. At the door, Stevenson swung back to say, "Get that baby *off* the breast *now*."

Quincy heard that sucking sound again and glanced down to see his daughter going after her mother's breast like it offered Thanksgiving dinner with all the trimmings. Ceara smiled and cupped a trembling hand over the baby's dark head.

"Sorry," Quincy said. "You've been pumped full of drugs. It isn't safe for her to nurse any longer."

He plucked Ceara's nipple from Stormy's eager little mouth. The baby instantly stiffened and started to cry. Almost simultaneously, wind hit the windows of the suite, and rain quickly followed, striking the glass like lead from a scattergun.

"Shit!"

Quincy offered his daughter his knuckle. It looked like he was trying to shove a torpedo into a flower stamen. The baby screwed her face into a frown and geared up for another screech. Ceara saved the day by offering her own knuckle, which was smaller and softer. Stormy seemed to find that more satisfying. The gale beyond the window immediately began to lessen and then abruptly stopped.

Quincy, still embracing Ceara with one arm, actually

felt strength returning to her body. "She healed you, Ceara. You were dying, and our baby girl healed you with her touch. I didn't think she could do it, her being so tiny and all, but Loni swore up and down she could, and she was right."

Ceara nodded. "'Tis as it happens with the gifts. From the instant we're born we have them. 'Tis good that we got her quieted quickly. 'Twould na be good if she got in a temper and called up a horrible storm."

Recalling Stormy's first tantrum, Quincy laughed, and oh, how good it felt to laugh, really laugh, with all the pain gone from his chest. He quickly disabused his wife of the notion that their daughter hadn't already wreaked havoc on Crystal Falls. Ceara, still weak but growing better by the second, smiled and nodded.

"Ach, 'tis a job we have afore us, Quincy. We canna allow her to make trees fall down every time she feels unhappy."

Quincy just thanked God there was a *we* in that sentence. Ceara didn't seem to realize how miraculous it was that she was alive. "You came so close to dying. Do you understand that?"

She cuddled their baby closer and closed her eyes, still smiling. "I dreamed of ye. Ye called to me and said lovely things, asking me to come back to ye."

"It wasn't a dream." Quincy's throat went tight. "Well, more like a nightmare, the worst of my life."

Ceara yawned sleepily. "'Tis time to name our daughter."

"I'm thinking of naming her after a famous hurricane." Quincy perched on the side of the bed, content to watch his wife drift in and out of sleep. "Zach nicknamed her Stormy. That's probably better. It's cute and sort of suits her."

Ceara nodded drowsily. "Fer now, 'twill do. Later,

when I can stay awake, we shall think of a better name fer her."

Quincy leaned over again to hold his wife and daughter carefully close. He felt as if he were holding two beams of sunlight in his arms. While mother and baby dozed, he sent up a fervent prayer to thank God for saving both of them.

They were right where they belonged, alive, well, and held snugly against his heart.

A nurse burst into the room. Quincy recognized the redhead who'd protested so firmly about having to leave earlier. She advanced on the bed, her manner all business. "I must see to my patient. For now, you'll hold the baby, please. Either that, or take her back to the NICU."

Quincy had no intention of taking Stormy that far away from her mother, so instead he lifted the infant from the curve of Ceara's body. Stormy immediately started to shriek, and Quincy wasn't surprised when, an instant later, high wind and torrential rain slammed against the windows again.

"Hey, baby girl, you've got quite a temper."

Quincy guessed the child came by it naturally. The Harrigan clan had a corner on mad sometimes. Hoping that Crystal Falls and the surrounding area could survive another of her temper tantrums, Quincy gently bounced her on his shoulder.

"It's time for you to get better acquainted with your da," he told her. "I'm not going to allow you to pitch fits, you know." Quincy considered his options and wasn't exactly sure how he meant to exert his will over someone so tiny and helpless who didn't understand a word he said anyhow. "You can't unleash your fury like this and cause trouble for people. Somehow you have to learn how to control it."

Mouth open to scream, Stormy turned her head and got an accidental taste of Quincy's neck. Apparently she liked the saltiness, because she began to suckle. Quincy lifted the blind and watched the violent weather subside. When the sun peeked through the clouds again, he knew that his baby daughter was once again content. *Smart girl.* Her mama had found her way into his arms, and now Stormy recognized safe haven there as well.

Quincy exchanged a long, silent look with his wife, who'd been awakened by the nurse. Ceara smiled at him. Given the fact that she had saved his life last night, he couldn't say that her radiant grin was the most extraordinary gift he'd ever received, but it was definitely the sweetest.

Epilogue

Quincy couldn't believe a whole year had passed since his daughter's debut into the world, but today they were celebrating her first birthday. Though the name Stormy had started out as a temporary handle, it had stuck and become official—for very good reason. Every time the child grew displeased and started to cry, the heavens opened up, weeping and wreaking havoc with gale-force winds. Zach loved the fact that he had named his niece, and Quincy figured it would take at least fifty years or so before his youngest brother stopped bragging about it. No matter that her middle name was Daireann, after Ceara's mother. She went by Stormy.

After a brief and sporadic crystal-ball reunion with Ceara's family so they, too, could be present for part of the child's name-day party, the whole Harrigan clan had gathered to celebrate, along with all their furry friends that weighed less than three hundred pounds. Mojo, Nana, Rosie, Billy Bob—well, hell, with them milling around, Quincy couldn't do an accurate head count. Frosting and cake bits drew the animals like yellow jackets to raw meat. Quincy and Ceara's kitchen looked . . . well, Quincy didn't have words to accurately describe the room. It was a people-animal zoo, and he seriously needed a larger area to hold everyone. In this family, all they did was celebrate something: birthdays, anniversaries, and God only knew what else. Last weekend it had been Trevor's soccer game win.

True to his word, Quincy had looked up Randall Whitmeyer in the phonebook and taken him out for a whiskey. Before Quincy could pay the tab, he'd known that he couldn't let the old fart continue his lonely existence. Though he had eight kids, not a single one of them called regularly, and only two sent Christmas cards. Randall sat with Father Mike at the safe end of the table, beyond the reach of the birthday mess. Stormy, elbow deep into her own special cake, had frosting everywhere. In her dark auburn hair. All over her face. Globbed on her small fingers. And, well, hell, that wasn't to mention any surface of the kitchen within ten feet of her high chair. All sane adults sat well beyond her throwing distance.

Quincy had come to believe that his daughter might grow up to be a famous pitcher, and maybe a great batter, too. She had a swinging arm that was impressive for someone so little. Last week, when Ceara had given the child a wooden spoon and a pot to play with, the whole house had resounded with metallic thumps.

Quincy, who prided himself on being a hands-on dad, decided to give Ceara a break by cleaning their daughter up. Problem: The moment he disengaged Stormy's highchair tray and lifted her from the seat, she puckered up and stiffened her body to shriek. Quincy knew what was coming, and he was right. Still warm in mid-September, it had been a fabulous, sunny day, so they'd left the kitchen door open. Rain suddenly slammed against the screen door in sheets. The solidly built house trembled in the high wind. Quincy had good reason to wonder how his pastured horses were faring.

"How in the *hell* are parents supposed to deal with temper tantrums of this caliber?" he asked no one in particular.

Ceara, now able to drink wine again, had been enjoying herself at the long kitchen table with her sisters-in-law, the indomitable hens. Sam, early in a much-yearned-for pregnancy, sipped sparkling cider, and Tucker, ever the supportive husband, was matching her glass for glass because he'd sworn off alcohol. *They* were finally pregnant again.

Quincy, holding his sticky child well away from his shirt, stared at Stormy's contorted face and wondered what he was supposed to do with her. Frank said Stormy was a pistol, and Quincy had no better word to describe her. *Holy Mother*. He could control a huge stallion with clicks of his tongue, but he had no impact at all on Stormy, who was still very tiny for her age. Quincy figured she'd always be little, a mixture of prematurity and sixteenth-century stature playing against her. If as an adult she topped five feet, he'd be surprised, but he'd still take his hat off to any man who came along in the distant future who thought he could handle her.

Someone rushed to close the kitchen door, and Ceara jumped up from her chair, plucked the child from Quincy's arms, and firmly said, "*Nay!*"

Quincy decided to make himself one of his dad's Jack and Cokes. Two Irish roses, beautiful and dear as they were, truly could, on occasion, drive a man to drink. As he measured booze into his glass, he heard Ceara speaking to their daughter behind him.

"'Tis na the way we follow. Do ye ken? Ye be *druid*, little one. Ye canna unleash yer powers and hurt people and animals. I shall na have it. Ye'll straighten up or I'll box yer ears."

Quincy had never yet seen that disciplinary tactic occur. Ceara threatened the child with it all the time, but he'd never seen her so much as grab one of the baby's earlobes. For some reason, Stormy got it, though. Maybe it was an Irish thing, and if so, he should start making the same threat. God knew he needed some way to handle his daughter. She was feisty and willful and bullheaded, challenging him at every turn. Even worse, she had her mum's big blue eyes, and damn it, when they filled with tears, all Quincy could think about was how to keep her from crying, partly because he loved her so much, but also because Stormy's tears equated to possible property damage.

The stern tone of her mother's voice had Stormy gulping and swallowing her yells. Quincy just didn't get it. He was starting to think of himself as Good-time Da. He was in charge during baths. He pointed to the pictures in storybooks. He played on the floor, carefully tumbling his daughter around, always cautious not to hurt her. But when it came to discipline, he could talk himself blue, and Stormy continued to pitch a fit. He guessed it was something to do with the druid bond. When Ceara spoke, the little girl snapped to attention.

He glanced over his shoulder to see mother and daughter sharing a long look, and just like that, the storm subsided. Ceara cleaned the baby up at the kitchen sink and then sat at the table to hold Stormy on her lap. Quincy leaned against the counter to sip his J and C. What was he going to do if his daughter threw a tantrum when her mother was out shopping with the hens, enjoying a well-deserved break?

His dad had told him stories of the old days, when parents had dipped what they then called sugar tits into whiskey and let a baby suck on them. Instant sleepiness and calm.

Was he *really* considering *alcohol* as a parenting tool? Quincy gave himself a hard mental shake. Of course he wasn't. He just needed to find a way to console his baby girl when she was unhappy. He glanced over his shoulder at his dad, who had aged with his granddaughter and was another year older, yet still more fit than most men twenty years younger. Time for a talk with him in the woodshed, Quincy decided. Quincy had to be missing something as a father, or doing something wrong. Frank had raised Sam alone, and yeah, there'd been a few times when Quincy had found her weeping inconsolably, usually as a teen, when Frank hadn't understood makeup and girly issues, but mostly Quincy applauded his father's fine parenting. Sam hadn't been an unhappy girl as she grew up. Far from it, in fact.

Quincy sat beside Ceara at the table. After kissing his wife's curly hair, he stroked his daughter's dimpled cheek. With the cessation of the storm, the adults had begun talking and laughing again. Quincy knew all members of his family worried about how he and Ceara were going to deal with Stormy. Some parents had to handle hyperactivity, ADHD, or severe learning disabilities. But, hello, houses and barns losing their roofs were on a whole different level, redefining the term *child-rearing challenges*. Repetitions tended to make insurance companies suspicious, and telling an agent the roof blew off because your druid baby daughter had a tantrum wasn't an option Quincy had ever seriously entertained.

Quincy bent close to nuzzle his wife's ear. "We'll get through this somehow," he whispered. False bravado. He didn't know how the hell they'd get through it. He had a bad feeling one section of roof had blown off the holding shed again, and as soon as Stormy blew out her candle on the *adult* cake, with the aid of a few puffs from her mother and aunts, he'd wander out to check while dessert was being served. "It won't always be this way when she grows angry, will it?"

Ceara grinned and tipped her head back to nip him on the chin, her way of promising him a great night later, complete with a mind-blowing seduction outfit and the purr of Mr. Midas. "Self-control comes with experience. Bouts of bad weather may lie ahead, but between the gales, we shall eventually teach Stormy that giving way to her temper is na the way."

Quincy muttered a curse under his breath and thanked God he had enough money to do frequent roof repairs. Then he chuckled. Looking deep into his Jack and Coke, which he probably wouldn't finish, he remembered where he'd been a year ago. If his daughter threw a fit and flattened the whole house, he'd still count himself the luckiest man alive.

He had the woman of his dreams in his life, and his baby girl was so damned beautiful that looking at her made his throat go tight. He could get through a few storms, because, for the most part, their lives together would be sunny, happy, and filled with contentment.

Ceara whispered to Quincy that she loved him so much she couldna describe it with words. Quincy knew from experience that she was the queen of describing her feelings with words, so the emotions he elicited within her had to run mighty deep.

He leaned in to kiss her, not caring if everyone in his family saw, because, damn it, he knew she loved him with every fiber of her being, and he felt precisely the same way about her.